HOT FLASH DIVAS

by

Shirley B. Garrett

Positive Directions LLC
Huntsville, Alabama

This is a work of fiction. All of the characters, organizations, and events portrayed in this novel are either products of the author's imagination or are used fictitiously.

HOT FLASH DIVAS

ISBN: 978-1-943065-06-6

Published by Positive Directions LLC, Huntsville, AL.

Cover illustration and design by the author

Also by Shirley B. Garrett,

Charlie Stone Crime Thriller Series

Brianna Kelly Paranormal Mystery Series

DEDICATION

To all the women of a certain age, who have combustible moments.

ACKNOWLEDGMENTS

Many people helped this book on its journey to being published. I'd like to thank the Huntsville Literary Association, Coffee and Critique, and the Coffee Tree Writers groups who made numerous suggestions to improve my work and were kind enough to laugh at all the right places.

Edi Peterson, my beta reader, always offers encouragement while keeping me on the right path.

My editor, Lisa Prince, has the gift of making my work into something better, every single time.

The support of my family and friends was vital during all the ups and downs of writing this book. Thanks for loving me and cheering me forward.

My largest debt of gratitude is to my husband Bob, who enabled me to chase one of my dreams.

Table of Contents

Table of Contents, continued

Table of Contents, continued

Chapter 1: Knifed in the Psyche

With six small words, "I — think — I — want — a — divorce," Todd O'Leary shocked the last fertile egg from my ovaries and divorced me straight into menopause. I know that sounds incredible, but it's the truth. Along with casting me into a new phase of existence, he tore out my heart during a vulnerable period. Now I must pull out my emotional super glue and paste together a new single life from the shards of what's left.

After Todd declared his intention to end our twenty-year marriage, my friends, the Divas, came to my aid, the way close friends always do in a time of crisis.

The "Diva" saga began twenty-one years ago after we performed "Respect" by Aretha Franklin at a local Karaoke bar.

Latishia Snide sang the lead vocal. At five feet tall, she was and is still built like a basketball with braids strutting on three-inch heels. Latishia sang in her church choir and had some serious pipes.

Gina Bongiorno, my best friend since parochial school, sang soprano. She's all Italian curves and curls.

Kat Wang sang a powerful alto, despite her petite stature. A Chinese-American beauty, she'd just completed her masters in nursing at the University of Alabama, and this was the reason for the celebration.

I was working on my doctorate in psychology at the time. I figured if I performed cool dance moves, and whipped around my long ginger hair, that the audience wouldn't notice that staying on key wasn't my best attribute.

When we finished, the crowd whooped, and we received a standing ovation. As we hugged on stage, Latishia whispered, "If anyone asks, we're the Divas."

We've been the Divas ever since.

We left the bar and drove to El Palacio. We were seated around a table, sharing a platter-sized Nachos Supreme, when I told the Divas I had a date with a funeral director.

"A mortician!" My friends screeched the words in unison, scrunching their noses.

Latishia looked like she'd just smelled embalming fluid. "Yuck, are you going to let that Undertaker touch you after he handled dead people? Phoenix, he could have corpse cooties."

I chuckled a bit. "I'm pretty sure he washes his hands before he leaves work."

"Does he look like a vampire, all pale and gaunt?" asked Kat.

"He's cute, y'all. Tall and slim. His name's Todd O'Leary."

Kat pushed her glasses up. "You know, Phoenix, funeral directors, have a higher than normal rate of cancer due to exposure to hazardous fluids."

"I don't plan to marry him, y'all." I waved my hand in dismissal. "It's just dinner and a movie."

I reached for my margarita and sipped it with care, to avoid spilling it on my new dress.

"If it were me, I wouldn't let him in my house." Gina plopped down her glass of Bordeaux, sloshing a little onto the table. "If he gives you any strange diseases, I'll sue him for all he's worth."

I nudged her with my elbow. "You're only a first-year law student. You can't sue anyone."

"Heck, lawsuits take too long. Anyway, by then it'll be too late." Latishia grimaced and aimed a chip dripping salsa in my direction. "Girl, I'd Lysol him from one end to the other."

* * * *

Despite the Divas' disapproval, I kept the date. Todd arrived in a navy 1985 Cadillac Eldorado. He opened the door for me, and I scooted into the car. The seat was so slippery I landed on the floor. It was *not* one of my more graceful moments.

Struggling to suppress a grin, Todd reached in to help me up. "Um, sorry about that. I just cleaned the seats with leather polish, so they're a bit slick. You may want to fasten your seatbelt, so you don't slide to the floor again when I brake."

I took his advice and buckled up.

When we arrived at Steak and Ale, Todd rushed over to open my door. I tottered toward the restaurant on heels much higher than my norm. The moment we entered, the aroma of grilled steaks surrounded me, making my mouth water. I'm a lady who likes red meat. The cozy seating arrangements and the beautiful stained glass windows combined to create an ambiance of intimacy.

Over prime rib and candlelight, Todd told me how his mother raised him and his brother after his alcoholic, philandering father abandoned them.

"I contacted him when I turned eighteen," Todd said. "Guess I'm still looking for the dad I never had. It's not much of a relationship, but we keep in touch."

He explained the off and on pattern of their interaction based on whether he was on a bender or not. We lingered so long over the meal that we missed the movie.

* * * *

Todd's work with the deceased didn't keep me from marrying him, almost a year after our first date. I'm not the least bit squeamish. It wasn't unusual for me to munch on a sandwich after dissecting a human brain in my neuro-psych class.

What did bother me about Todd's profession was the way it controlled our lives. Our first argument was because we had to live within a certain proximity to the funeral home in Decatur, or else he'd have to sleep at the facility when he was on-call.

"This means a forty-five-minute commute to Huntsville for me and only a ten-minute drive for you," I complained.

Todd shrugged. "We can live in Huntsville, but don't bitch at me if I'm gone three or four nights a week because I live further than fifteen minutes from the funeral home."

Another major disadvantage of our chosen professions was we were both on-call during the wee hours of the night. Every couple of months, I'd receive a call from a patient who had plummeted into suicidal despair while watching late night infomercials. This was why I couldn't roll over and ignore the phone when it jangled at all hours, and it jangled a lot.

Todd averaged five death calls a week. After our first date, he warned me, "People don't wait until office hours to die." He winked. "They can be inconsiderate that way."

The phone would jar us awake. Todd would groan as he fumbled for the receiver. "Uh-huh, yeah, fax the information to me at the funeral home." He'd flip back the covers, allowing frigid air to invade my warm cocoon. "It's mine, Phoenix, go back to sleep."

I'd rewrap myself in my electric blanket and gradually relax again. The slit of light knifing under the door seemed bright as I listened to him fumbling to dress in the bathroom. He'd always kiss me good-bye before he left.

I'd lay wide-awake, tossing and turning. It always seemed that the moment sweet slumber came; Todd would slip into bed beside me and chase it away by fanning the covers. After turning this way and that like a restless dog, he'd sigh and put his cold feet on me. Brrr!

Todd worked days, nights and weekends. Not once during our marriage did I have a full major holiday with my husband, another source of discord.

"Surely you can have one full Christmas or Thanksgiving at home with your family," I said.

"I don't have control over this." Todd would shrug. "Such is the life of a funeral director."

Despite all the rigors of our careers, I thought Todd and I were a team. We made it through his father and grandmother's deaths. We survived two changes of ownership at the funeral home where Todd worked. These caused bouts of gut-wrenching indecision for him — stay or seek new employment. Then my mom died of a stroke. Yes, there were those rough spots, but we also had many years that were as creamy as yogurt.

Chapter 2: "When It Rains It Pours"

I believe the demise of my twenty-year marriage began with my father's illness. My dad's lung cancer, self-inflicted by smoking, stole the life-sustaining breath from his body. As I struggled to care for Dad while maintaining my private practice and marriage, I felt I was dog-paddling my way through waves of crisis without a lifeline in sight. It was a real Morton Salt year: "When it rains it pours."

My only sibling, Kevin, lived a thousand miles away. He told me at the beginning that he had no intention of offering assistance. I wasn't surprised. Based on his past behaviors, Kevin's abandonment in my time of need wasn't new.

Todd's on-again, off-again support was a complete surprise to me and rather confusing.

* * * *

"Todd, I have an important meeting on Wednesday with social services about a child on my caseload. It's your day off, could you take Dad to his radiation treatment that morning?"

"Don't want to spend my off day hauling your Dad around. Can't you find someone else to do it, or just reschedule your meeting?" He was leaning against the kitchen counter, ankles crossed, drinking coffee.

“It’s only a couple of hours.” I hated the pleading tone in my voice. “I don’t have control of the meeting time.”

“Sorry, I’ve got plans.” Todd turned his back on me, poured the dregs of his coffee down the sink, and pushed past me to leave.

What plans? No kiss? Tears welled in my eyes.

I knew the Divas would help me if they could, but that week none of them were available. Gina had a full week in court. Divorce, it appeared, was a profitable legal career. Latishia’s job as a loan officer kept her at a harried pace at present, with Huntsville and Decatur in the midst of a building boom. Kat checked on Dad whenever she could, but her hours working with Dr. Howard were structured from seven to five.

Weary down to my molecular structure, I tried to focus on the next thing to do. My shoulders slumped as I phoned the caseworker at social services to report I couldn’t attend the meeting and gave her my recommendations.

* * * *

Months later, it became apparent that the radiation treatments didn’t have the desired results. Reality crashed my delusions of a cure when the doctor suggested I call Hospice. When I returned home that night, I poured a glass of Chardonnay with trembling hands and told Todd.

“Hate to hear that, Phoenix. I know you had high hopes the treatments would work.”

I crawled into Todd’s lap like a little girl and cried. He was warm, and I felt comfort in his arms, as I had for so many years.

Chapter 3: The Heavy Truth

Dad dropped the truth in my lap mere days before his death. It landed heavy, like my grandmother's cast iron skillet.

We were in his room at the assisted living facility. I sat in the chair beside his bed and squeezed his hand. I'd scheduled an extended lunch, so I could see him before I started my back-to-back appointments that began at two. Evelyn, the sitter on duty that day, was in the bathroom.

"I worry about you, Phoenix." He patted my hand as his green eyes looked deep into mine.

"Why, Dad?" I shifted in my seat. I didn't want him to worry about anything.

I felt his hand tense underneath mine. "I'm not sure Todd will take care of you when I'm gone."

I reared back in the chair. "Why'd you say that?"

"Well, I've never told you before, but time is…." He looked down and cleared his throat. "Todd's always been about Todd. You could never see it, but I did. I'm not saying that boy hasn't loved you in his own way. I'm just not sure that when life gets rough, he'll be by your side to help you. He's the center of his universe."

I felt my back stiffen. My hand slid out from under dad's. "How much tougher could life get than this? Todd's not perfect, but I do believe he loves me."

"I'm sorry, Pumpkin, I shouldn't have said anything. I didn't mean to upset you." He picked at the blanket with his knobby fingers, the blue veins prominent on the back of his hands. "It's just…you're my little girl, and I worry."

"Don't worry, Dad, you named me Phoenix for a reason." I placed my hand atop his, rubbing my thumb across the top of his arthritic knuckles.

Dad chuckled, then winced. He slowed his breathing; a trick the nurse had taught him to ease his pain.

Evelyn exited the bathroom, walked over, and pulled the covers at the foot of the bed. "They always make his bed so tight it hurts his toes."

I nodded and looked back at Dad.

He sighed and closed his eyes. "Have you heard from your brother?"

"No, but I'll call him." *Again.*

From Dad's desperate tone, I surmised he was holding on to life until Kevin arrived. I could feel my insides knot as I pondered what I would say to Kevin. I rubbed circles on my stomach trying to ease the cramping, while I walked down the long carpeted hall to the lobby to make the call.

"I can't come right now. I'm sick with a cold." Kevin didn't sound congested.

I plopped my free hand on my hip, ready for battle. "What does that have to do with you coming to Huntsville? Dad's near the end. There's no need to worry about infecting him."

So much for my stab at logic.

"You're not working right now, so that's not an issue."

Okay, that was a low blow.

"You know you can stay at my house. I've even offered to pay for the plane ticket." I tried to rein back the irritation in my tone. My face felt hot. I suspected I looked like a teakettle ready to blow apart.

There was a long pause. I surmised he was regrouping since I'd just removed his top four excuses.

"My doctor said not to fly when I have a cold."

"Kevin, *this is it.* Hospice says that Dad only has a day or two left on this Earth. This is your last chance to see him. He keeps asking me when you're coming?" I blew a stray hair out of my face.

"I'm not good in these situations, Phoenix. I'm not you."

More silence. I took a deep breath and wondered, *What does that mean?*

"If you won't come for Dad, come for me. I need you." The minute I spoke the words, I knew they were true.

"I can't. Call me when it's time to come for the funeral." He hung up.

The dial tone buzzed in my ear like an angry hornet.

I felt a scream punching my innards, fighting to escape. I leaned against the wall, closed my eyes, and took deep breaths until I could face my father without falling apart.

Trudging down the hall, I cursed my brother for being a coward. I squared my shoulders and steeled myself before I entered Dad's room. Once inside, I locked gazes with Evelyn, who was still standing at the foot of Dad's bed. She cocked her head to one side and raised a brow.

I shook my head.

The corners of her mouth turned down. She patted my Dad's foot and then turned to straighten a stack of magazines on a nearby table

"Evelyn, why don't you take a break and eat lunch while you can? I have to leave in an hour. I've set the alarm on my phone to alert me."

"Sure." She nodded, pasting a noncommittal expression on her face, and left the room. After eleven years of caring for the sick and the dying, she undoubtedly knew what I was about to tell my father.

I crawled into Dad's bed and cuddled against him, hugging the bundle of bones beneath his blue striped pajamas.

"He's not coming, is he?" I could feel the vibration of his voice against my cheek.

While I was growing up, Dad smelled like cigarettes, coffee, and Old Spice. Now the essence of the approaching grave clung to him.

"No. Kevin has a cold. He said his doctor told him not to fly."

Dad's eyes closed. A tear traced his weathered cheek, dropping to the clean, white cotton pillowcase, where it was absorbed.

"He's still resentful because your mom and I didn't accept Beatrice when they first married. You know what a hard woman Agnes could be."

I nodded my agreement. “Mom was a force.” *More like a cocked pistol.*

“My only concern about the marriage was that he would quit college. Thank God he didn’t. There’s not a day goes by that I haven’t regretted letting your mother bully me into that situation. I should’ve stood my ground.”

I could feel hot blue flames of anger scorching my innards. “Maybe. Who knows what’s going on with Kevin?”

I placed my hand over my stomach, willing the anger to abate. We both knew from years of experience that Kevin’s way of dealing with tough emotions was avoidance.

I snuggled closer, offering comfort to Dad and needing it from him. Exhausted, I fell asleep beside him.

Chapter 4: Cancer 1 — Dad 0

The next day I walked into Dad’s room and knew his guardian angel was on standby.

To be truthful, I was ready for both of our sufferings to end. Tired and beaten down by Dad’s cancer, I felt like a cookie, baked too long, burnt on the edges and ready to crumble. At first, I felt guilty about those feelings. It took some time for me to accept that clinging to my father while he endured intense chronic pain was selfish.

I crawled into his bed and held the man who rode me on his shoulders and taught me to ride a bike as he took his last shuddering breath.

“I love you, Daddy. It’s okay for you to leave if you’re ready. No need for you to continue to suffer.” Despite these words, I clung to him just as I had when I was a little girl.

Dad’s spirit left his body as if someone had cut the cord to his humanity.

Now I was orphaned.

It sounds strange that a professional woman who is forty-five should think of herself as orphaned, but that's the way I felt. I knew the last person on this Earth who loved me unconditionally was my daddy, and now he was gone. Gone forever.

I crawled out of bed and called Todd. "Daddy just, just…." I couldn't say it.

"I'm at a funeral. It's about over. Jackson and I will be there with the hearse as soon as we can."

I sat in the chair next to Daddy's bed as Evelyn, and the Hospice nurse prepared him for transport.

Thirty minutes later, Todd and his boss arrived and placed my Daddy in the back of the hearse. After a quick hug, Todd climbed behind the wheel, and they drove away. I watched him leave, tears welling in my eyes, feeling abandoned and alone.

I tried to pull myself together, but my hand trembled as I scribbled out a check to clear the bill for Dad's sitting services. Evelyn, tall and cushy, pulled me into a hug after I handed it to her. She sat with Dad more often than any of the other ladies in her agency. I suspect he was one of her favorites. I was grateful she was there with me at the end, or I would've faced this loss alone.

"You stand tall, ya hear?" she told me. "Your daddy was proud of you and appreciated all you did for him. Do you need me to drive you home?"

Swiping at the tears coursing down my cheeks, I said, "No, I'll be fine. Thank you. I couldn't have done it without you and the other ladies."

She hugged me again. Dabbing at a tear with a tissue, she paused to look at the unoccupied bed. "I'll miss your daddy's jokes." She wiped her eyes again and left.

I called Marie, who was in charge of my answering service, and told her about Dad. "I'll need you to cancel my appointments for the rest of the week, please."

"Don't you worry, Doc, we'll take care of everything." She paused a moment and said, "You know all the ladies here have been praying for y'all."

"I do, and those prayers were most appreciated." I yanked a tissue from the box on Dad's bedside table. The stubborn tissue came, but the box flew across the room. I shook my head as I bent to retrieve it. *Nothing's going right today.*

"I'll call Todd later to get the arrangements," said Marie, before she disconnected. The funeral home where Todd worked used the same answering service I did. She and her staff of Christian ladies were the culprits who woke us in the middle of the night with emergency and death calls.

Still holding the tissue box, I grabbed my purse and stood to scan the room. My gaze froze on the bed, empty and rumpled. I remembered napping there with Dad the day before.

Fresh tears welled in my eyes. I stood tall, took a snotty inhalation, locked the door and closed it.

The hallway to the administration office of the assisted-living facility seemed like it was miles long. I stopped out of sight of the open doorway of the administrator's office to regain control of my emotions. Then I took the final step and knocked on the doorframe.

Katherine Mays was a bird-like woman in her forties. She looked up with a sharp expression at the sound of my knock. Katherine's expression softened when she saw me. I noticed her shoulders drooped before she rose and walked around her neat desk.

"I'm so sorry. I planned to come see you, but I wanted to give you a few moments to…, you know." She shrugged her shoulders and gave me a brief hug.

I clutched the tissue box to my bosom as I made arrangements to clean out Dad's room in a few days. Staff members entered Ms. May's office and waited their turn to hug me. Each one told me their favorite story about Dad. One of the aides, Kathleen, said, "He loved bingo. You'd think those little prizes were gold."

Still holding the box of tissues, I found I was seated in my car. I couldn't remember walking there.

I drove home in a bleary fog of grief. Once parked in my two-car garage, again, I couldn't recall the ten-minute drive home. *I'm losing my mind.*

Buffy, my blonde Cocker Spaniel, greeted me as I walked into the den. I dropped to my knees, cocooned her and bawled while she licked my tears.

Some time later, using the nearby couch for support, I stood on unsteady legs and walked across the room to the sliding glass door to heave it open. Buffy leaped past the two steps and landed on the concrete patio, where she broke into a silent run toward a squirrel under a pine tree in the back corner of the fenced back yard.

Left alone to deal with my loss, I paced the living room and wailed my anguish. After an hour of gut-wrenching sobs, I felt flayed of all emotion. Dehydrated. Empty.

I called Gina while I opened the sliding door.

Buffy burst into the room and bounded past me. I heard her nails on the kitchen floor. Lapping sounds soon followed.

"What's up? Is your dad all right?" Gina's voice rose an octave.

I couldn't get the words out.

"Phoenix!" She sounded panicked.

"He's...gone." I couldn't say the word *dead.* I leaned against Todd's recliner for support.

"Oh, God. Phe, I'm so sorry. Is Todd there?"

"He's at the funeral home." My voice sounded raspy, so I trudged toward the kitchen. My feet felt like anchors, my head like a balloon.

"He's not there with you!" Gina screeched the statement. The volume forced me to move the receiver from my ear. "Are you alone?"

"Yes." I reached into a cabinet and grasped my favorite double-walled tumbler. Shuffling to the fridge, I filled it with water and drank as I listened to Gina's rant, part English and part Italian.

"I'll be right there." She hung up.

Buffy whined and pranced in place at my feet, begging for food. I removed the top of the dog food container and dropped a scoop into her bowl.

Slogging into the den, I aimed my backside in the general direction of the sofa and plopped down. I sat there looking out the door at the sunny day, drained.

Within ten minutes, the manic jangle of the doorbell dragged me from my stupor. Buffy barked a furious counterpoint to the doorbell's chimes, her hackles raised.

Like a ghost hauling chains, I floated through the living room toward the door. My head trailed behind me like a helium balloon tethered to my neck, an apparent aftereffect of the crying.

I opened the door, cringing from the bright afternoon light.

Latishia stood on my doorstep with her hands fisted on her hips. "Sweet Baby Jesus! Look at you. I'm gonna kill that man. Leaving you alone at a time like this. What's wrong with him?" She wrapped me in her arms and squeezed until I couldn't breathe.

When she released me, she closed the door and led me like a child, back into the den to the sofa. Buffy raced around us, making the little sounds she made when she wanted to be petted. I sat and hugged a throw pillow, using it to ward off the need to cry.

"Hey there, sweetie pie." Latishia reached down and petted Buffy. "Gina called me first, 'cause she knew I was the closest. When did your Daddy pass?"

"Around two." My throat closed around the words.

"Was Todd at least with you then?"

I shook my head. The movement made me feel dizzy.

Latishia's brows drew together in a frown. "Bless your heart, were you alone?" I knew that look so well. Tee-totally pissed.

"Evelyn was with me. She's been such a big help. Oh, I forgot. I've got to call Kevin." I reached for the phone, but Latishia stayed my hand.

"There's no hurry. Let's get you a bit on track first." All the Divas knew the Kevin saga.

Gina was the next to arrive. She must have broken the land speed record from Huntsville to Decatur. Gina paced back and forth in front of me, her curls springing from her head in all directions, and her hands gesturing as she spoke. From my perspective on the couch, she looked like a fire-breathing Medusa in a business suit.

She stopped pacing and faced me, arms akimbo. She looked ready to drop-kick Todd to the next county. "That ano di maiale, I can't believe he abandoned you this way!"

"What does that mean?" asked Latishia.

"Pork butt. He probably thinks he's doing the right thing by taking care of Daddy for me."

I wasn't sure why I defended Todd. My thinking seemed muddled. To be honest, everything around me seemed to have dropped a few RPMs. I felt like I was quaking inside.

Gina's brown eyes blazed. "His place is with you!" Her Italian family pulled together during any crisis, so to her, Todd had deserted me in my time of need.

I knew from experience that in her current state, Gina would verbally eviscerate Todd in two languages if she encountered him.

Latishia would probably stomp on whatever Gina left of him.

The doorbell chimed again.

"That's Kat." Gina motioned for Latishia to keep her seat.

Kat entered the room and gave me an assessing look. She sat beside me to my left, squeezed my hand, and rested her cool forehead against mine. Sweeping my hair over my shoulder, she rubbed circles on my back. Calm washed over me. I felt as though I was being absorbed into the cushions of the couch.

Kat lifted the tote bag from her lap and laid it on the coffee table. "I brought a few things. Gina, please find a few glasses for brandy."

Gina disappeared and returned with four red wine glasses. "This is all she had. No brandy snifters." She lined them up on the table in front of me.

Kat nodded and began unloading items from the tote. A box of tissues, a small bottle of brandy, and a small brown prescription bottle with a white cap.

"Dr. Howard sends his condolences and these." She shook the bottle, and the pills rattled around inside. "They're benzodiazepines, only seven, but enough to help you sleep the first week."

I blinked, trying to clear the muck from my eyes. "Tell Doc thanks for me." My contact lenses seemed blurred. They felt pasted to my corneas.

Gina poured brandy into the glasses with a trembling hand.

"Just a sip for Phoenix, because she'll take one of these pills later," said Kat. Gina complied.

We all raised our glasses high.

"To Bill O'Heir, he was a good man and a good father," said Gina.

"To Bill," we all chorused and sipped the liquor.

Kat tilted her head as she adjusted her glasses further up her nose. "When do you expect Todd?"

I shrugged. It was the most I could manage.

The doorbell rang again.

"Who now?" I rubbed the area between my brows. A whopping sinus headache was forming storm clouds inside my skull, complete with rumbling thunder.

"Pizza." Gina raced toward the front door like a bundle of fuming energy.

"You can't help but love a friend who remembers to order the pizza." Latishia heaved herself from the sofa. "I'll get the napkins and plates."

Kat stood and moved the coffee table to the side. Planting herself in front of me, she took my hands and hefted me to my feet.

She looked me in the eye. "Phoenix, I know you're probably not hungry, but I need for you to eat something before you take one of these pills."

I nodded, causing my head to throb in response.

She took me by the elbow and walked me through the kitchen to the dining area, where she pulled out the chair at the head of the table. I practically fell into it.

Latishia placed plates and napkins on the table and sat to my right. Kat and Gina claimed chairs to my left. Between bites of pizza, they all cast worried glances in my direction. From the expressions on their faces, I imagined I looked like hell, served sunny side up.

At first, the pizza tasted like cardboard, but after a few bites, something took over, and I realized I was famished *No wonder I've been feeling so faint. I haven't had a full meal since last night.*

After three slices, my internal quivering had slowed, and I felt ready to deal with the Kevin situation. I explained to the Divas what I needed to do.

Latishia lumbered to her feet and began clearing the table.

Gina sprinted to the den, returned with her laptop, and fired it up. She tapped on the keys and found a deal on round-trip tickets from Chicago to Huntsville.

Kat handed me the cordless phone, sat beside me at the dining room table and patted my hand. Latishia stood in the doorway leading to the kitchen.

"Kevin, Dad's…dead." There, I'd said it, the "D" word.

"Um, are you like…all right?"

"My friends are here. It's been hell."

There was a long pause.

"What's the plan?" His voice sounded strained.

"Can you leave from O'Hare at ten tomorrow?"

"Yeah." I could hear the ice dispenser in his fridge dropping cubes into a glass.

"Your ticket will be waiting for you at the American Airlines desk. I'll pick you up at the airport, just plan on staying with us." I nodded toward Gina, who clicked her mouse, finalizing the reservations.

"Thanks. I appreciate it. You know things are tight for me right now." His voice cracked.

"No problem. I need to go. I'll see you tomorrow." I hung up before I could spew my building anger over the airwaves. I knew if I started, Kevin would catch the fury I felt toward him, Todd, cancer, and even God, for taking my daddy.

My cell phone rang just as I disconnected the call on the house phone.

"I'll get it," said Latishia.

She returned holding the phone out to me. "It's Todd's mama."

"Hi Joyce, did Todd tell you?" I asked.

"Tell me what? Is Bill…."

"He died at two this afternoon."

"Good Lord, I'm going to kill that boy, he never called me. If I'd known, I would've dropped everything and come right over."

"The Divas are here, and Dr. Howard sent some pills to make me sleep. I'm about to take one and go to bed."

"Have you eaten, Sweetie?"

"Yeah, Gina ordered in a pizza." I glanced up at Gina. She was leaning against the doorframe with her arms crossed.

"You sure you don't want me to spend the night?"

"I think I'll be fine, but thanks." I was drooping fast.

"Put Todd on the phone." I could hear her dog barking in the background.

"Um, I can't. Todd's not here." I looked at Gina again. Her dark eyes turned flinty when I mentioned his name.

"Where in the world is he, at a time like this?" Joyce sounded agitated.

"I haven't seen him since he picked Daddy up at the assisted-living facility."

She sighed. "I'm real sorry about your dad. He was a fine man. You go to bed. I'll call Todd on his cell phone. That son of mine is gonna get a piece of my mind for leaving you alone."

Kat left, and reappeared by my side. She handed me a pill along with a glass of water. "We'll start calling folks to give them the news, and make a list, so you'll know who we contacted. You need to get some sleep because there's a lot to handle tomorrow."

While the Divas tidied my house and let Buffy out, I changed into my warmest pajamas. It was only September, but a cold front had just moved into the area, and I despised cold weather. Kat turned my heating blanket on low and tucked me into bed.

The Divas were there for me when Todd wasn't. Their love brought tears to my eyes. The last thing I saw before I fell into a comatose sleep, was the Divas standing in a semi-circle around my bed.

Chapter 5: The Trio

The next day, Todd jumped into overdrive and handled all the funeral arrangements. This surprised me since he'd never bothered to drive my father to a doctor's appointment or even visit him when he was sick.

Despite all his years as a funeral director, he didn't know how to deal with his grieving wife. He offered no emotional or physical comfort unless I sought it.

As a Catholic, Dad had requested a visitation, rosary, and funeral mass. Kevin used the ticket I bought for him and flew in from Chicago for the trio of events.

That night, standing between Todd and Kevin, I greeted everyone who came through the receiving line during visitation. Joyce was aflutter, not quite sure what to do to help. She settled next to Todd, greeting folks and handing me an unending supply of tissues when needed.

All five of Dad's care sitters came to pay their respects. Each one hugged me and shared her favorite Mr. O'Heir story.

Evelyn held my hand. "Remember when Imogene came to your daddy's room and told him she'd cook him anything he wanted if he'd eat for her?"

I chuckled. Built like a refrigerator, Imogene presented a tough persona but was more like memory foam inside. "I sure do. He ordered crisp bacon. He *loved* bacon and coffee."

Evelyn grinned. "He sure did. I'll never forget it. Imogene planted her fists on her hips and said, 'Well, heck, that's not on your diet, but I'll cook you an entire pig if you'll eat.'"

My eyes misted as I laughed. "He ate every bite and asked for two more slices."

She released my hand, turned, and introduced her staff to Todd. "I'm Evelyn, the owner of Sitters for Comfort. This is my staff — Janie, Rosy, Debi and Sarah. Todd, I saw you the day Bill died, but you were so busy *rushing off*, we didn't have an opportunity to be introduced."

Todd's face flushed. He mumbled something and offered his hand.

Evelyn turned to my brother. "Are you Kevin, Bill's son?" she asked.

Kevin shuffled his feet. "Uh, yes, ma'am."

"Your daddy talked about how much he loved you. He was doing his level best to hold on until you could come to say goodbye. It's a *shame* you didn't make it here in time."

Now it was Kevin's turn to blush.

Evelyn's staff offered glares with their condolences as they shook hands with Todd and Kevin. I almost felt sorry for them. Almost.

Evelyn smiled at Joyce. "Miss Joyce, it's so good to see you again. Bill looked forward to every one of your visits. I know you'll take excellent care of Phoenix."

Joyce hugged Evelyn. "I gave him my word that I would."

Gina, Latishia, and Kat were next in line, offering hugs and support. Todd shifted from foot to foot and had trouble meeting their eyes when he greeted them. I never did find out what transpired between him and the Divas two nights earlier, during my drug-induced sleep.

Father Culotta walked to the lectern in the chapel and asked everyone to be seated so that the rosary could begin. I felt uncomfortable calling Marco, "Father," since we graduated high school together. He's Gina's cousin, and I'd had a crush on him during my sophomore year. It's strange how things turn out.

The rosary droned on and on with the repeated recitation of Our Father's and Hail Mary's, punctuated at regular intervals with Glory Be's. After what seemed like a millennium, it was time to go home to rest and prepare for the funeral the next day.

Todd and Kevin stood to one side as the Divas surrounded me for final group hugs.

Todd and I drove separate cars since he'd arrived early to arrange everything to his specifications. He stayed behind to handle any lingering details.

Joyce walked me to my car, with Kevin trailing behind.

"You call me if you need me," she said and squeezed my arm. "Take care, Kevin. I'll see y'all tomorrow for round two."

Kevin looked straight ahead as we traveled the ten-minute trip home.

His voice broke as he said, "You're lucky to have such good friends."

I shot a glance at him. "Yes, I am. They've been lifesavers."

"I'm sorry I didn't come sooner. I didn't think I could take seeing another person die after Bea." He sniffled and wiped at his eyes with his fingers.

I pulled into a lighted church parking lot and handed him a tissue. Killing the engine, I unbuckled my seatbelt and shifted in my seat to face him in the dimly lit car.

Beatrice had died two years earlier of multi-organ failure after her colon ruptured. It was apparent to me, as a mental health professional, that Kevin hadn't dealt with his grief over his late wife's death. His habit of avoiding emotional pain hurt him, because now he had double the grief, one piled on top of the other.

"Dad thought you didn't come because you hadn't forgiven him for his and Mom's initial rejection of Bea when you first married. He wanted to say goodbye to you. He loved you until the end."

Kevin shook his head. "Hell, I got over that years ago." He raised his brows as if surprised. "Is that really what he thought?"

"Yes, he told me that the day before he died, when I called and asked you to come. The day you said you had a cold." My words were harsher than I intended, but the boiling anger in my stomach leaked out through my tone.

Dropping his head into his hands, he sobbed. I slumped exhausted as I patted his shoulder and handed him more tissues. When Kevin recovered, he honked and swiped at his leaking eyes.

"Feel better?"

"Yeah. Wish I could've done that when Bea died. I was trying so hard to hold it together for the girls. They were both barely in their teens, and Susie was such a drama queen."

I nodded. *She still is.*

He shook his head as if to clear it. "Melinda was so quiet and self-contained, she just shut down and stayed in her room."

Just like her father.

"By the time I could cry, it was like I couldn't do it."

I told him, "I call that emotional constipation."

He barked a laugh and honked again into the tissues.

"It's just the two of us now, Kevin. We need each other." I reached over and started the engine.

"I know I shouldn't ask this. I-I don't have the right," he stammered, "but do you think you can forgive me? I mean for leaving you with all of Dad's care?"

I stared out the windshield for a moment. "I'm working on it, okay? Give me some time. It wasn't just about me, you know. Dad needed you, and you weren't there for him." I thought about all the things Dad did during the years to take care of us. *Kevin just chickened out and deserted him.*

I took a deep breath and shoved the gearshift into drive. "What's more important, Kevin, is can you forgive yourself?"

* * * *

The next morning, I stood sandwiched between Todd on my right and Kevin on my left in the front pew at the Annunciation of the Lord Catholic Church. Joyce stood beside Kevin. From time to time, she glanced over at me with a worried look, as if I might faint or go berserk.

The flag-draped coffin occupied most of the center aisle making the entrance into the front pews near impossible. Candles glowed on the altar, casting flickering light on the image of the crucified Christ hanging on the apse wall. Statues of Mary and Joseph looked at the congregation with serene smiles from niches on each side of the chancel. The stained glass windows cast pools of colored light across the pews.

As a recovering Catholic, I found the scene familiar and comforting. I responded by rote in all the right places during the funeral mass.

Mid-sermon, I felt the pew begin to vibrate. Todd's left leg was bouncing, so I patted his knee to still it. He smiled in apology and put his arm around me. I leaned against him, grateful for the gesture.

I peeked at Kevin, concerned about how he was handling his guilt. The majority of the mourners the last two days had bombarded him with their disapproval, through actions and snide comments like, "Phoenix, you were such a comfort to your dad during his illness. At least *you* were there when he needed you."

Kevin was sitting stoic, with his jaw clenched.

Father Culotta called me to the ambo to give the eulogy.

My heart pounded in my ears. My legs felt like cooked linguini. Clutching my notes, I gave my complete concentration to walking up the stairs. I flattened the paper over the open Bible and grasped the sides for support as I looked at the silent crowd.

"As many of you know, Bill O'Heir was a decorated veteran. He piloted a C-69 Constellation during the Korean War. When he returned home, he met my mother and began his family. There are things about Dad that many of you know first-hand. He was a man of honor, and his word was titanium."

I paused to cinch in my emotions. Joyce leaned forward in the pew, listening, but Todd sat back with his arms crossed. Kevin pulled his handkerchief from his pocket to wipe his eyes.

"A man's actions speak volumes. My Dad believed in returning things in better shape than when he borrowed them. When I was a kid, he once borrowed my grandmother's Oldsmobile while our Chevy was in the shop. When we picked up her car, the gas tank was half-full. When we returned it days later, that car had a full tank and was freshly washed."

I took a deep breath, trying not to cry. My eyes strayed to the Divas in the third row. Latishia and Gina were mopping their eyes with tissues. Kat sat rigid, struggling to control the tears welling in hers. My dad was a second father to each of them. Kat nodded for me to continue.

"My father was there for his family for the small things as well as the large ones — the easy and the hard. When that special embarrassing time came for me as a girl, he asked me every month if I needed quarters for the machine." My voice cracked.

"Daddy loved NASCAR and was a die-hard Alabama football fan. Bless his heart; he was a redneck, from the top of his funny ball caps down to his white socks. That didn't matter to anyone, in any walk of life, because he was a quality person."

People were smiling and nodding their heads.

"The thing most of us will remember about Bill O'Heir was his sense of humor and his practical jokes. I'm sure many of you shared a laugh with him over some of his jokes. How many of you tried to pick up the quarter he glued down on the sidewalk outside of the Piggly Wiggly?"

Chuckles filled the church. Many people nodded or with sheepish expressions raised their hands.

"Daddy loved to plant a little laughter in people's lives and then watch it grow and spread to others. This is the way I'm sure he would want you to remember him. Continue to spread the joy."

Latishia boomed, "Amen!"

I returned to my seat and pulled my dress over my knees. Kevin reached over, took my hand and squeezed it.

After the mass, Father Culotta led the procession from the church. "I'm sorry for your loss, Phoenix. Again, I regret that I won't be able to perform the funeral service in Huntsville."

"That's no problem. Dad would be pleased that Father O'Brian is officiating. Did you know he was the pastor at Dad's church when he lived in Huntsville?"

"Yes, Father O'Brian told me that when we discussed the arrangements."

"Thank you for everything, Marco; I mean Father." I felt my cheeks burn.

He smiled. "You're most welcome. I'd like to see you in church on Sunday morning."

I stepped back a few paces. "Thanks for the invitation. Perhaps I'll see you at the reunion next year."

"I'll be there."

Todd drove the funeral home's Cadillac Town Car. Joyce and Kevin piled in the back seat while I rode shotgun. The funeral directors loaded Dad into the hearse for his final ride.

The police officers hired to provide an escort took their positions, and the slow motorcade crept along the streets of Decatur at 25 mph. All the cars turned on their lights to signal their inclusion in the funeral procession. In true Southern tradition, all the traffic in both directions stopped and pulled over out of respect for the deceased. When we hit Interstate 565, the police escort dropped away.

The forty-minute drive to Maple Hill Cemetery in Huntsville was quiet. We were all deep in our own thoughts. I gazed at the 363-foot-tall Saturn V moon rocket as we drove by the U.S. Space and Rocket Center. They were installing the lights that would turn it into a giant Christmas tree in a few weeks.

The idea of Christmas without Dad brought tears to my eyes. I swiped at them with one of the tissues I'd tucked away in my purse.

When I stepped out of the car at Maple Hill, I spotted only one cloud in the cerulean sky. The recent cold snap had turned the maple trees into a blaze of reds and oranges. The cemetery, founded in 1882, was dotted with a bounty of old gravestones and mausoleums.

A dark green funeral tent marked the spot of my Dad's final resting place. A rug of green plastic grass covered the red Alabama clay. Metal folding chairs offered two rows of seating.

Kevin took my arm as we walked together to the spot. I was grateful for his support. I sat on the front row, Kevin to my left, Todd and Joyce to my right. The Divas sat in the chairs behind me. I felt a twinge of pain in my chest and tried not to hyperventilate. As the tears began to trickle, I dug in my purse for a tissue, but Kat reached over my shoulder and handed me two, and Joyce reached across with another.

Father O'Brian opened his Bible, and with an Irish brogue said, "Dear God —"

Upon this pronouncement, the sky opened and poured a deluge of rain. I looked around and saw everyone pressing closer together with hunched shoulders. The pounding downpour drowned out his shouted eulogy. A mist traveled on a tender breeze that kissed my face.

"Amen," Father O'Brian bellowed, closing his Bible with a snap. The rain stopped, as though someone had turned off the spigot.

Wiping her eyes, Latishia said, "Even the sky cried for your daddy."

Chapter 6: Clues

After Dad's funeral, I tried to focus on two things: overcoming my grief and reconstructing my life. It was time to pull out the emotional super glue. It wasn't easy since many things I saw on a daily basis brought memories of my father.

My dungeon moment occurred when I cleaned out my dad's bathroom at the assisted living facility. I picked up his denture holder and found myself sitting on the cold tile floor, blubbering, as I recalled the nights I'd filled it with water and dropped in the tablets that fizzed away the stains. A blue plastic denture holder took me to my knees.

The next morning, for some reason foreign to me, I woke resplendent with hope. I called my landlord and agreed to sign a lease to expand my office space. I'd been considering the expansion for a year, but the time had never seemed right. With my private practice finally showing a profit and my care-taking responsibilities gone, things appeared to be stabilizing.

There were clues, scattered like breadcrumbs over the past year that Todd was headed at full tilt toward a midlife crisis. If I hadn't been in a tizzy, running from crisis to crisis while blanketed with grief, I might have noticed.

Todd had turned forty that March, before my dad's death in September. One day I caught him examining the top of his head with my hand mirror. I backed out of the bathroom, not wanting to embarrass him while he contorted his six-foot frame for a better view.

I'll never forget the night he came home worried that his company would transfer him to Tennessee.

I shrugged. "Hey, I'm okay if we move. I'm licensed in Tennessee."

"I'd have to take the Tennessee licensing exam. You know I'm phobic about standardized tests." Todd flopped into his recliner and grabbed the remote.

He was wound into a tizzy, convinced that he wouldn't pass. I tried to ease his stress with a little lovemaking, which had worked well in the past. The fear plagued his mind to the point where he couldn't obtain an erection. It took weeks before I could coax him into a sexual situation again.

Todd's work caused him angst in other ways, too. A workaholic, he reached the point in his career where he knew he should be in management but wasn't. He so wanted to be in charge of *everything.*

After years of overworking him, the funeral home finally hired enough staff for him to have normal work hours. This change occurred as I revved into overdrive to care for my dad while struggling to keep my psychology practice in the black. The timing was lousy.

To Todd, it was okay for me to be home, alone, all those nights and weekends for nineteen years, because his job required it. He considered my absence during my year of transition and crisis to be neglect.

A particular incident comes to mind.

* * * *

Buffy greeted me at the door, tail whipping, smiling her doggy grin.

"Hi, Buffy, Mom's happy to see you, too." I bent and rubbed her from stem to stern. I looked up to find Todd scowling at me.

"*Where* have you been? It's nine o'clock, for chrissake."

I stood and stretched my back. "Picking up Dad's prescriptions. I told you I needed to do that this morning."

His mouth formed a tight line, a sure sign of disapproval. "Couldn't you do that earlier?"

"I tried, Todd. I took Dad to his radiation treatment this morning. There's a forty-five-minute commute both ways. I had to shift all my patient appointments to this afternoon and tonight." I lowered myself to the sofa, feeling stiff. Buffy hopped up beside me. "This is the first chance I've had to pick up his pain medications and deliver them to him. He'll run out tomorrow morning."

"What about me? I've been sitting here, *alone*, all night. Don't I matter?" He pushed out of his recliner and stomped down the hall to the bedroom.

* * * *

Shoving these past incidents behind me, I was determined to look forward. Visualizing blue skies in my future, I let down my guard. *The bad times were over — right?*

Chapter 7: What's Going On?

The Christmas holidays — my first without Dad — were wretched. I slogged my way through the days, flooded with memories.

One Tuesday, Latishia had business at her bank's location in Huntsville, so the Divas grabbed the opportunity to meet for lunch. We tried a new place rumored to specialize in every combination of chicken salad conceived by a woman. We nabbed a table near the window that overlooked the parking lot of the busy strip mall located on Airport Road.

Latishia looked out the window and frowned, ignoring the menu in her hand. "I don't get it. Why do they call this Airport Road when the Huntsville International Airport is located halfway between Huntsville and Decatur on Interstate 565?"

"There was once an old airport here years ago," explained Gina, never looking up from her menu.

A flustered waitress arrived and confused our orders several times before she departed, clutching her order pad. Gina did the sign of the cross.

Kat grinned. "What's that for?"

Gina raised her eyebrows. "A silent prayer that we get what we ordered."

The waitress returned with our drink orders and sped off. I placed my menu to the side. When I looked up, I found myself under scrutiny. Gina opened her mouth to speak, but Latishia's voice came out.

"Just look at you!" She gave me a squinty-eyed look, the one I've come to know so well. Usually, she reserved it for women who performed a fashion faux pas, like wearing hot pink panties under white pants. Latishia didn't tolerate tacky.

"What?" I looked at the front of my beige shirt for stains.

"Where is your Christmas sweater? I know you own nineteen Christmas sweaters —"

"Twenty," said Gina, dumping a yellow packet of sweetener into her iced tea.

"I stand corrected, twenty." Latishia nodded to Gina and glared at me again. "Why aren't you wearing one?"

"I'm in mourning — remember?"

"I don't see any black. Do any of you ladies see any black?" Latishia punctuated her statement by crossing her arms.

"I'm not feeling it this year." I sipped my tea and grimaced. "This is *not* sweet."

"Oops, sorry." Our passing waitress snatched the glass and disappeared.

Gina tasted her tea and smiled. "You're the Christmas Elf incarnate. Have you put up any decorations at all?"

"Um, no. I don't think it's appropriate under the circumstances."

"Appropriate! Your dad loved Christmas. He's in Heaven right now, frowning that you aren't celebrating his favorite holiday. Remember his Christmas caps?" Gina had her arms crossed.

I looked at Kat to save me.

Kat's serious expression told me she'd aligned herself with the rest of the Divas. "Phoenix, your paradoxical reaction to Christmas this year worries us. We're concerned that you may become depressed during the holiday."

Our waitress loomed into view, carting a large tray. After delivering our food, she turned to leave.

"Excuse me, but I need my sweet tea." I smiled and pointed at the spot where it should reside.

"Oh!"

She returned with my tea after I'd almost finished my lunch. Thank goodness I had a glass of water.

We all agreed to three things during that lunch. First, we wouldn't return to that restaurant, as both the chicken salad and the service were mediocre at best. Second, our price limit for the gift exchange this year was twenty-five bucks. Third, I would decorate for Christmas in honor of my father.

I knew the Divas were right. Dad would want me to put up a tree and a few decorations. I didn't have enough spirit to provide a full-out festive experience, but a few baubles might cheer me a bit.

"Thanks, ladies. Being there for each other is what the Divas are all about as friends," I said as I swiped at a tear.

"Don't forget the food," Latishia said.

* * * *

When Saturday arrived, I asked Todd, "Would you get some of the decoration boxes down from the attic?"

"I'll get them down later." He never looked up from his phone.

From experience, I knew what "later" meant to Todd — never — at least until I nagged him five or ten more times. I didn't have the energy to treat him like a rebellious, passive-aggressive teenager this morning.

"Please, do it for me, now. I won't have time to put them up later. I'd really appreciate it."

Todd rolled his eyes to the ceiling and exhaled like a bull ready to charge. "I don't know why in the hell we have to get those damn decorations out of the attic every year."

The footrest on the recliner clanged back into place. Mumbling under his breath, Todd heaved himself from the chair.

"Why are you being Mr. Christmas Cranky Pants?" I followed him to the garage, wondering what had come over him. True, he would grumble a bit, but he'd never protested this much in the past.

He pulled down the creaking attic steps and climbed, cursing under his breath. All I could see of him was from the waist down. Pulling down a large blue plastic bin, he shifted and looked at me. He was scowling.

"Here." Before I could step forward to take the bin, he flung it at me.

It rammed into me, knocking me into my car. My side-view mirror jabbed me in the back.

"Ow!" I glared at Todd, my stomach aching where the plastic bin hit me. "What the hell! Stop throwing them at me, that hurt."

Todd's face contorted with fury. For a moment I thought he would throw something else, but then his expression shifted into a smirk.

"Get your damn decorations yourself. I have better things to do."

He pounded down the attic stairs. Opening the door to his silver truck, he slid in and slammed it. The garage door cranked open as he started his truck and revved his engine. With tires squealing, he backed out of the garage and raced down the driveway.

I stood holding the bin, wondering, *What the hell just happened?* Cold air blew through the open door adding a creepy chill to the experience.

Chapter 8: The Ring

The ring was the symbol of both the beginning and end of my marriage. It was also the clue that caught my attention.

The next day I noticed Todd's wedding band lying on the chest-of-drawers. On occasion, I've run out the door and forgotten my jewelry. No big deal.

When Todd failed to wear it several days in a row, I felt a wrench in my gut. Fingering it, I thought, *Don't panic. You need more information.*

The next night I remarked, "I noticed your wedding ring is sitting on the chest-of-drawers. Is there something wrong with it?" I forked a bite of roast and placed it in my mouth. Folding my hands in my lap, I chewed and waited.

Todd looked up and reached for his glass of iced tea. "It's too tight."

"Does it need sizing?"

Gulping his tea, he looked down at his piled-high plate and shoved around the carrots and potatoes with his fork. "I've already had it sized two times. The jeweler told me he couldn't stretch it anymore."

Unbidden, my gaze dropped from his eyes to his waistline. Once a thirty-three, he had exploded to a forty-inch waist. It seemed his gut wasn't the only thing that had expanded.

"Oh, I see."

* * * *

The next morning I called Joyce.

"Todd's wedding ring is too tight and can't be stretched anymore. You want to help me shop for a larger size?" I wedged the receiver between my ear and shoulder to free my hands. Buffy assumed her "you may pet me" position at my feet.

"Sure. That boy needs to lighten up on the eating, or he's gonna have a heart attack like his father. When do you wanna go?"

"While Todd's attending a meeting in Birmingham on Saturday. I plan to surprise him with the ring on Christmas."

With our adventure planned, I hung up.

Buffy whined and pranced, giving me one of her "I'm starving" looks. I walked to the kitchen while she ran circles around me. At six months, she was a gangly adolescent with two speeds: run and crash.

Buffy's adoption was my idea. Childless, I needed somewhere to focus my maternal affection. Todd voiced no opposition to owning a dog — as long as he didn't have to do any of the work. Perhaps he acquiesced since *he* was the reason we couldn't have children, not that he wanted any. He had anti-sperm antibodies, which are immune system cells that mistakenly identify sperm as harmful invaders.

I unscrewed the top to the plastic dog food container and bent to fill her bowl. Food pellets bounced out of the bowl, scattering onto the floor. Buffy jumped across me to reach the pellets and knocked me flat on my back. I lay there sprawled like a starfish. The chill of the floor seeped through my nightshirt while I listened to the slurping and crunching sounds within inches of my left ear.

"I need coffee," I moaned.

"What the hell!" Todd stood in the doorway, scowling down at me.

"Buffy and I got tangled up."

"You're such a klutz!" He threw up his hands and rolled his eyes.

I lifted my hand toward him so he could assist me to my feet.

Instead, he shook his head, turned and left.

Grasping the kitchen counter, I hoisted myself to my feet and rubbed my bruised hip. "What hornet buzzed up your backside?" I muttered at the empty doorway. *He's never been this ornery before.*

I screwed the top back on the container and glanced at the clock.

"Crap, I've got to get moving. I'll be late for my hair appointment."

I limped to the bedroom to get dressed.

Chapter 9: The Great Ring Quest

On Saturday afternoon, Joyce and I met at the new mall in Huntsville to shop for Todd's ring. When I made my request and showed Todd's ring to the clerk in the first store, he shook his head and walked away to help another shopper.

"Can you believe that?" asked Joyce. "That was rude."

In the second store, a plump, motherly type took the ring and looked at it.

"We don't carry anything like that, hon. Narrow rings are in style right now."

We thanked her and trudged to the next store, on the far side of the mall. We told a perky young lady at the counter what we wanted.

She frowned. "I haven't seen anything like that in our inventory. Sorry."

I was beginning to lose hope.

At the last store, the clerk took pity on us and retrieved a catalog from under the counter. He flipped through the pages until he found the correct section.

He pointed at a ring, tapping the paper. “Is this the ring?”

I squinted to see the photo on the glossy paper. “No, it’s wider.”

He flipped to the next page. “Is this it?” He cocked a brow.

“That’s the one!” I grinned and nudged Joyce.

“I can special order it, and it’ll arrive the week before Christmas,” he said, as he typed on the store’s computer.

“Order it,” I said. “That’ll work because it’s a Christmas present.”

Joyce nodded her agreement and checked her watch. “I’m getting hungry.”

The clerk looked up from typing. “Do you know what size he needs?”

I dug through my purse and handed him the gold ring Todd had inherited from his dad. “Use this for sizing.”

High on success, Joyce and I traipsed out of the store.

We decided to celebrate by eating dinner at a restaurant located in the mall. Scooting into the booth across from me, Joyce asked, “How are things going, Phoenix?”

“To be truthful, I’m struggling.” I unrolled my flatware and placed the napkin in my lap.

Joyce’s brows drew together. “What’s wrong, Sweetie?”

“I’m having trouble sleeping. I guess the lack of sleep has me on edge.”

“That would put anyone on their last nerve. I hate it when I have insomnia. I get downright cranky.”

The waitress appeared, took our drink orders, and vanished from sight.

I propped my elbows on the edge of the table and rubbed my temples. “It’s more than that.”

“What do you mean?” asked Joyce.

“Everywhere I go, something reminds me of Dad. Sometimes it makes me smile, other times I’m melting into tears at the most inopportune times. Just yesterday, I stood in line at Wally World, tearing up because I bought pork chops."

Joyce nodded. "Your daddy did make the best-barbecued pork chops. Remember how he buttered the corn, wrapped it in aluminum foil and grilled it?"

I nodded and grinned. I could almost taste that corn. Then it hit me like a baseball bat. "I'll never have my Daddy's special pork chops ever again," I wailed.

Joyce left her side of the booth and slid in beside me. She draped her arm around my shoulder. "It'll be all right," she comforted me. "Now don't cry or your mascara will run, and then you'll look like a depressed raccoon."

That made me laugh. Snuffling, I dabbed under my eyes with my napkin and continued, "Todd's been so grumpy for some reason. I can't seem to do anything right."

Joyce gave me a squeeze. "You know how men are. His daddy got that way with me before he vamoosed. He's probably going through a stage. I spoiled that boy too much after his daddy left us."

Our waitress approached, stopped, and looked unsure what to do.

"It's all right. She's just having a bad day." Joyce motioned for her to set down our drinks.

We both ordered lasagna. Looking ill at ease, the poor girl skedaddled toward the kitchen with our orders.

Joyce moved back to her side of the booth. Steepling her fingers, she studied me.

"Phoenix, I know both of your parents are gone, and you feel all alone, but you know I've always thought of you as my daughter."

"Thanks, Joyce, you've been like a mom to me, and I appreciate it."

"Don't worry so much about Todd, he was needy as a baby and never got over it. I'll talk to him."

Chapter 10: Horrid Christmas

Early on Christmas morning, Todd and I took our steaming mugs of coffee into the living room to open presents. I set mine on the table that separated our beige recliners.

Todd had to report to work at the funeral home by eight. At noon, he would be relieved of duty, and we would drive to Joyce's house for lunch and more gifts.

We tore into several of our smaller items. Boxes and paper littered the carpet around our feet.

Buffy scooted from one package to another, poking her nose inside and sniffing. Like many human children at Christmas, she wanted to play with the packaging, instead of her new rawhide bone.

Life was good. The coffee went down smooth. Buffy was providing the morning's entertainment, and so far, I loved my presents.

Todd got my attention and pointed at Buffy. "Look at her."

Buffy had managed to fit her entire head inside the end of a long box. When she backed up, it came with her. She raised her head and the container tilted toward the ceiling. Todd and I laughed as Buffy shimmied, trying to dislodge her cardboard prison.

"Come here, sweetie. Momma will get that mean box off your head."

Buffy turned her cardboard-shrouded head in my direction. I rose from the chair and dropped to my knees to free her.

"That's so funny," said Todd, chuckling.

It was nice to see him in such a good mood. Encouraged by his soaring spirits, I hefted the large wrapped carton that camouflaged his ring and placed it on his lap.

"Open this one next." I sat down on my chair, hands on my knees, waiting for his reaction. Joyce had left strict orders that she wanted a play-by-play of the scene.

After ripping away the paper, Todd pulled a knife out of his pocket and slit the packing tape holding the box shut. A grin spread across his face as he dug in like a kid. Styrofoam peanuts rustled and boiled over the edges of the box onto the carpet as he searched for his prize.

I felt the zing of excitement I received anytime I watched someone open the perfect present. My smile widened. I couldn't wait until Todd saw the ring.

"There's a brick in the bottom of this box." He looked at me and laughed. "I've been wondering for weeks what was so heavy in here. Ah, I found it!"

Todd pulled out the small wrapped box and held it aloft. After he yanked the paper away, he lifted the lid and stiffened. He squinted at the ring. The smile melted from his face.

"It looks like my first one." He placed the petite box with the ring inside on the table between our chairs.

I squirmed in my seat, waiting. "Do you like it?"

"It's nice." He didn't sound enthused. Silence stretched time like a rubber band.

"Your mom and I shopped at every jewelry store in the mall. None of them carry a ring that wide anymore. We special-ordered it. I took one of your rings that I knew fit for the sizing," I prattled. At last, I compressed my lips to stop the flow of words.

Todd furrowed his brow as he examined the ring. "Mom went with you?"

"Yeah, we spent *hours* looking for that ring. Does it fit?"

Reaching for the box, he removed the ring and held it in his palm as if weighing it.

"Did I get the wrong one? Do you want something different? We can exchange it if you want?" I was babbling again. The mood in the room felt frigid, despite the fire blazing in the fireplace.

"The ring is fine." Tossing it in the air, Todd caught it. "I just don't want to wear it." He placed it back in the box on the table.

The breath left my body, as though someone had piled concrete blocks on my chest. I reminded myself to breathe.

"I don't understand?"

"Phoenix..." He paused and screwed his face into the look he reserved for unpleasant tasks.

I nodded for him to continue.

"I'm not happy." He looked up, hands clenched. "I think I want a divorce." He rested his elbows on his knees and leaned forward.

Those were the six words, and he couldn't even say them with conviction.

It didn't register in my mind at that moment that I'd just hit the first stage of grief regarding the death of my marriage — shock. It took some time for my thoughts to form into words.

With an incredulous tone, I said, "You *think* you want a divorce? Don't you know? This is a joke, right? You're messing with me." Stage two — denial.

Todd looked at his feet. A flush started at his neck and worked its way up to his bald spot.

Tears sprang to my eyes. "What did I do wrong?" My heart felt like he'd ground it into the pavement.

"You're gone all the time, Phoenix. I'm not your priority anymore. I need to be someone's priority."

"Someone's priority?" I clenched the throw pillow to my chest to shield me.

"Listen, we're not getting into this right now. I waited to tell you until after your dad died. I planned to wait until the holidays were over, but then you gave me that." He gestured toward the ring.

"Todd, we celebrated our twenty-year anniversary six months ago, and you want to throw it away because I had one lousy year filled with crisis after crisis? I was there for you when your father died." I counted my points off on my fingers. "I was there for you when your grandmother died. And I was there for you — twice — when your company changed ownership."

He crossed his arms and jutted his chin forward. "I'm not happy. I want out."

I took a deep breath into my constricted chest and felt it loosen a bit. *Use logic,* I thought. "Have you talked to anyone about this? Have you sought any advice? Does your mom know?"

He looked up, alarm widening his eyes. "No."

Of course, Joyce didn't know, she would've told me.

"Would you go to see someone — a counselor? Your insurance will pay for it."

"I'll think about it." His dismissive tone said otherwise.

My stomach burned like an arctic winter. *Something more is going on here.*

"Who is she?" I sat straighter. "How long has this been going on?" My voice rose an octave. Tears cascaded down my cheeks.

He shook his head and glared at me. "Don't go there, Phoenix. Just drop it." His tone held a threat, but his face flushed as he looked back down at his feet.

I felt the urge to snatch his chin and force him to look at me. Instead, I curled my hands into fists, sheathing my claws. *Doesn't he know what's at stake here? This is our future, the rest of our lives.*

"This is a major decision, a life-altering decision. I suggest we give it a month. We'll both talk to a counselor. I'll agree to see any therapist you choose for marital therapy. I love you, Todd. We can work through this mess."

Can we if he was unfaithful? My stomach tumbled. *That's a deal breaker for me, and he knows it.*

Todd shrugged, shook his head, and reared back in his recliner to bring up the footrest. "I want a divorce. If you need a little time and therapy to let that sink in, fine." He picked up a remote and turned on the C.D. player.

Instead of cheery Christmas music, I heard Elvis sing, "You Were Always on My Mind." The words wound around my emotions and squeezed like a boa constrictor.

Chapter 11: On the Defensive

I fled from the living room and locked myself in the master bath with Buffy. I slid to the cold floor and leaned against the garden tub as convulsive sobs racked my body. I wondered how my life had managed to crumble to bits. Still reeling from the death of my father, I now was losing my marriage.

Buffy licked my salty tears and climbed into my lap. I buried my face in her honey-colored fur and sobbed. My innards felt like they'd melted and pooled on the floor around me.

Todd knocked on the door.

Startled, I jumped.

"I'll tell Mom you aren't feeling well and couldn't come today."

"Asshole," I muttered.

* * * *

I did what any woman would do in a time of crisis. I called my best friend, Gina.

"Hey, girl, what's up? Was Santa good to you?" Gina sounded full of holiday cheer. I could hear Bing Crosby crooning "White Christmas" in the background.

I was fortunate she hadn't left to spend Christmas with her large family, which included one sister, three brothers, and a bevy of nieces and nephews. The black sheep of her family, Gina had failed to marry a nice, Italian, Catholic guy and produce a house full of bambinos.

By this point, I was so stuffy from crying I sounded like I was infected with snot monsters. "Todd *thinks* he wants a divorce."

Silence.

"What?"

"Yep, he told me after he opened his replacement wedding band." I stood up. My legs felt shaky.

"Has he lost his damn mind? What happened?" Bing's voice stopped after "white" when Gina switched off the music. I could imagine her pacing off her anger.

"He said he needed to be someone's 'utmost priority.' " I snatched a tissue and wiped my eyes.

"Doesn't he know what he's got? How many people would put up with his career demands all these years?"

"Apparently not." I pulled my long, ginger hair back into a scrunchy.

"Phe, what're you going to do?"

"I asked him to see a counselor and told him I'd go to marriage counseling with him." I stood, peered at my reflection in the mirror, and winced. I looked hideous, all puffy-eyed and red-nosed. "Shit!"

"What?" Gina sounded alarmed.

I put my hand to my forehead. A drum solo was pounding away in my sinuses. "I look like a Zombie version of Rudolph. I'm exhausted. I'm going to blow my nose and go back to bed."

"Phe. It's eight in the morning." Gina said, in her pragmatic lawyer tone.

I lowered the lid on the toilet at the end of the counter and plopped down, knees together. "Well, this explains all the hostility since Dad's funeral."

Her voice lowered to a growl. "Has Todd hit you?"

I told her about his refusals to help while Dad was ill, his temper tantrums, and the Christmas decoration incident.

"Don't forget how he abandoned you the day your dad died. Are you safe?"

I shrugged. "Todd wants to divorce me, not kill me."

"Are you sure? People do things during divorces that are out of character. You can stay with me."

"I'm not abandoning my home." I could feel my anger mounting. "Besides, Buffy would chase your two cats."

"True, but I'd feel better if you at least locked your bedroom door tonight. Are there guns in the house?"

"No, at least I don't have that to worry about." I started blubbering again. "How can he do this to me, Gina? He promised for better or worse."

"Now you know why I've avoided marriage. Give me your word you'll make an appointment with Ron Jacobs for counseling. I refer some of my divorce clients to him. He's great."

"I've heard of him, but I don't know him. I'll call him Monday." Buffy was sitting at my feet. I boosted her onto my lap and held tight, as if she was a flotation device in rough seas.

"Good. I hate to ask, but do you think there's another woman?"

"I believe so. I asked him. He wouldn't talk about it, but I know Todd's guilty face, and he wore it today. I could be wrong."

"Testa di cazzo! Do you want me to represent you in this divorce?"

"I don't want a divorce. Although, I'm not sure I can forgive Todd or trust him again if he's screwed around on me. As crazy as it sounds, I still love him. We've had some good years." I felt like I was having an internal earthquake.

"You may not have a choice. If he files, do you want me to represent you?"

"Yes, I know you'll have my back. If it comes to that, how much of a retainer do you need?"

"No charge. This is personal — real damn personal. I haven't forgotten how you came to my aid when my Nonna died."

Tears flooded my eyes, causing my vision to blur. "That was nothing. Are you sure?"

"You saved me, Phe. Yeah, I'm sure. Here's what I need you to do. Make copies or download files onto a thumb drive of all y'all's financial statements, just in case you have to leave or he files for divorce. Get any important documents out of the house, like your birth certificate and passport."

"I'd love to ask you if this is necessary, but my Daddy's favorite quote was 'Better safe than sorry.' " My mind flashed back to all the women I'd counseled in the past. The ones who'd ignored my warnings to be prepared for the worst, had all regretted it.

"Good. Where's the king of the undertakers? Is he there now?"

I put Buffy down and walked out of the bathroom into the bedroom. "He's at work — of course."

"Good. Get started now. Let's meet for lunch tomorrow. We'll have comfort food. Better yet, I'll call the Divas tomorrow morning, and we'll all go. I'm sure you need some time alone today to wrap your head around this."

Gina was right. I did need time alone.

After we had disconnected, I trudged around the bed into the walk-in closet and grabbed what Todd would need for work tomorrow. I walked across the hall to the guest bedroom and with great restraint laid it on the bed. My pissed-off inner child wanted to set his clothes on fire and throw the flaming garments out the back door, but I did the adult thing.

Todd had told me that when Joyce caught his dad cheating, she cut the bottom off all his ties. I thought that was rather extreme at the time, but I could relate now. Memories of the horror stories I'd heard in my office from women in abusive relationships flooded my mind.

I started tapping my foot and felt a twinge of pain in my back. The angry sneer on Todd's face when he'd hurled that heavy plastic bin of Christmas decorations zoomed across my mind. I walked to the dresser mirror and lifted my sleep shirt. The large bruise on my back had faded to a disgusting combination of yellow and green.

I dropped my shirt and entered our walk-in closet, where I grabbed armfuls of his clothes and moved them, load by load, to the guest bedroom closet. The dry-cleaning bags rippled as I carried them to their temporary new home. Next, I transported his heavy, size-eleven shoes. I left the dresser drawers till last.

I exhaled with relief after his belongings were out of the master bedroom.

On a mission, I tromped through the living room toward the kitchen on the other side of the house. Clawing through the junk drawer, I discovered the mace canister hidden at the back. While clasping it, I remembered my knuckle stun gun. I scooted through the den and opened the door that led to the two-car garage. A tenderfoot, I walked with care down the stairs in my bare feet. The cold concrete helped to center me in the moment. A spot of oil pooled on the floor in the empty left bay.

Shivering, I dug through the center console compartment of my car until I found the device and its charger. On the way back in, I snatched my purse and keys off the kitchen counter. If I needed to flee to shelter, I'd need to have them close to me. I'd heard many a tale over the years of women trapped because a rampaging guy got between them and their keys.

I dumped my stash on the dresser. On a roll, I invaded our office located to the right of the guest bedroom, and like a marauding army, I began the task Gina had assigned me.

Hours later, I hid a thumb drive, extra cash, and my jewelry under the spare tire compartment. Replacing the cover, I lifted my luggage and toiletries case into the trunk. After loading in Buffy's travel kit that had an extra harness, leash, and bowls, I heaved a bag of dog food in next to it. If Todd threw a hissy fit because I threw him out of the bedroom, I was ready to flee if necessary.

I glanced at my watch and frowned. I didn't have time to drive to my office today, but I would store the emergency supplies there tomorrow. *Just in case.*

I wove my way through the house. Back in the master bedroom, I closed the door with a satisfying slam and locked it. Dragging the chair from in front of the bedroom desk to the door, I wedged it under the knob.

Tomorrow, I'll call a locksmith to install a new lock on this door and change the one on the door to the patio. Buffy can scoot out that way to do her doggie business.

I wanted her in the bedroom with me, in case he tried to punish me by abusing her. Just last week, a patient had recounted how her husband kicked her Yorkie across the kitchen while they were arguing. I wouldn't let that happen to Buffy.

The patio door was also an escape route for both of us.

Todd returned at seven that night. I'd already eaten, so I was holed up in my mini-fortress, reading a book on the bed.

Bang, bang, bang!

I jumped, my hand flying to my chest to hold in my gallivanting heart. Buffy barked, hackles up, and planted herself in front of the door.

"Phoenix, open up!"

"What do you want?" I eased closer to the door and reached down to soothe Buffy. She stopped barking and licked my hand.

"I told mom you have a cold. She gave me your Christmas presents. They're here by the door. Um…, would you tell her we're getting a divorce later? I didn't want to ruin her Christmas."

My face burned with anger. "Let me get this straight. First, *you* want a divorce, not me. Second, it's okay to ruin *my* holiday, but not hers? And third, she's *your* mother. It's not my place to tell her something like that." I was pacing back and forth in front of the door.

"All right, I'll tell her, but give me some time, maybe a week or two."

"Grow up, Todd."

He banged on the door again. "I need to get in there to get ready for bed."

Buffy growled.

"Your clothes are in the guest bedroom. Oh, and your toiletries are in the guest bath," I yelled.

"You're throwing me out of our bedroom?" He kicked the door. "Let me in. This is my damn house, too." He banged on the door again.

I jumped back. Buffy started barking again.

"Are you having an affair?" I countered. The thought of him touching me after he had an affair sickened me.

"Don't ask questions if you don't want to hear the answers." His tone was menacing.

I laid my palm against the door to steady myself. Touching it reminded me that we'd had solid doors installed inside the house for sound control. I was happy about that decision now. "You made a vow. I have a right to know," I said, my voice cracking.

He sighed. "Yeah, I've screwed a few women, no biggie. They were just a quick piece of ass."

Who is this man? "A few! How many is that? Three or more?" I staggered, grasping the edge of the dresser.

My head started pounding again. Sliding down the wall, I pulled my knees to my chest. Buffy rushed forward, her stump of a tail wagging. I straightened my legs, and she crawled into my lap and tried to lick my face.

"Just three. Those women were flings, okay? No big deal. Are you happy now?" he screamed.

My shoulders slumped. I felt drained. "Todd, do you love me at all?"

There was silence. "I care about you, Phoenix, but I don't love you like a wife anymore. Now open the damn door!" He kicked it again.

I yelled, "If you kick that door again I'll call the police and have your mortician ass hauled off to jail."

I heard him muttering as he stomped away.

I slumped into a chair. *Good grief, I'm beginning to sound like Latishia.*

Chapter 12: Divas to the Rescue

After Todd had left for work the next morning, I checked the bedroom door for damage. There were scuff marks and a slight dent.

After I had downed a leftover muffin and coffee, I called the psychologist Gina had recommended and made an appointment. With that task checked off my survival list, I drove to Huntsville.

My office building's parking lot was empty due to the holidays, so I pulled into a spot right by the front door. I hauled all the supplies I'd hidden in my trunk up the two flights of stairs to my office and stored them in the chart room. With all this emotional turmoil, I was grateful I'd closed my practice until the second day of January.

While I was there, I checked the automatic feeder on my aquarium. My red-eared slider paddled over to see me.

"Hi, Betty Jo. Are you lonely here all by yourself?"

The word *lonely* hit me like an ache. I slumped into one of the reception chairs and cried, again. After I had saturated half a box of tissues, I regained control of the water works.

Angry, I stomped down the stairs to my car.

"Get a grip, Phoenix." For a few moments, I clutched the steering wheel, unable to move. After several deep breaths, I started the car.

I drove to the bank that housed my business account and marched inside. My mission was to open a personal checking account and acquire a safety deposit box. Thirty minutes later, I walked out and opened my trunk to retrieve my treasures that I'd hidden in the spare tire compartment. Feeling like a secret agent on an assignment, I placed all my valuables inside my new safety deposit box and left to drive to the restaurant.

I wasn't hungry, but I'd already agreed to meet the Divas at one of our favorite Mexican joints. I only hoped the food I swallowed would stay in my stomach since my tummy felt as though I'd been gulping shards of glass.

I spotted Gina's, Latishia's and Kat's vehicles in the parking lot of El Palacio. Leaving the bright sunny outdoors, I walked inside the darker restaurant and blinked. The Divas were waiting for me, lined up in front of the register across from the door.

I straightened my shoulders, lifted my chin, and smiled. I could see by their expressions that I didn't fool them one little bit.

Gina grabbed me first for a hug.

Latishia asked, "You want me to kick his ass?" That vision made me laugh because she was a foot shorter than Todd. She wrapped me in a hug and smashed me against her voluptuousness, rocking me from side to side. The comforting gesture squeezed the tears right out of me.

Then it was Kat's turn. She stepped forward, hugged me, and stepped away. Her dark eyes looked flinty. "What Todd's doing to you isn't right."

Gina had chosen the restaurant. A stress eater, she carried twenty extra pounds on her cushy frame, which only served to make her look sexy. She waved her hand toward the bright, gaudy decorations. "It's hard as hell to stay sad in a place with this much color and comfort food."

I wasn't sure I agreed with Gina's statement, but I was willing to try.

The hostess led us to our favorite round table in the empty dining room on the right. The rest of the patrons dined in the larger room to the left.

Our favorite waitress, Sue, took our order and brought our drinks. We sat and stuffed our faces with chips without saying much.

I wasn't ready to talk yet. I could tell the Divas were dying to ask questions but seemed to be waiting for me to start the conversation.

A man showed up with plates of food lining both arms, and our waitress unloaded our lunches. A Chile Relleno later, I had to admit that at least my tummy was happier than before.

I sat back, rubbed my stomach, and said, "Okay, I think I can talk about it now."

Gina furrowed her brow, looking concerned. "Have you called Ron yet?"

I ran my fingers up and down the side of my sweating plastic glass. "Ron had a cancellation, so I can see him tomorrow."

"Good. Promise me that you'll follow his guidelines. I'm worried about you."

I nodded. "I'm worried about me, too."

She scooped salsa on a chip. "Did you lock your door last night?" She popped it into her mouth, leaning over her plate to avoid spills.

Latishia, who sat to my left looked up, her taco halfway to her mouth. She put it down and wiped her hands on the napkin in her lap. "What's going on here? Spill."

I described Todd's recent aggressive behavior, including the door-banging and kicking incident the night before.

"Todd's trying to make you leave him, so he doesn't have to be the bad guy and file for the divorce," said Kat, who was seated to my right. She scooped rice onto her fork, as calmly as though she hadn't just dropped a major verbal bomb.

The tea I was swallowing went the wrong way. I had to grab my napkin and cough into it.

Gina dropped her chip. Latishia sat slack-jawed.

Gina was the first to recover. "Why didn't I think of that? Tell them the rest, Phoenix."

"Last night he admitted to having three extramarital affairs." Tears sprang to my eyes. "And…I can't stop c-crying." I reached for a fresh napkin in the center of the table.

Kat patted my shoulder.

"Were they dead?" Latishia tilted her head, her eyes wide.

Kat whipped her head in Latishia's direction. "Was who dead?"

"Those women Todd was screwing. Were they dead, you know, was he doing that necra whatever."

Mouth ajar, I asked, "Do you mean necrophilia?" I shivered at the thought.

"Gross!" We all chimed in unison.

"I can't believe this is happening." I stabbed a chip into the salsa. It shattered into fragments, just like my life.

"Male menopause." Kat looked around the table and pushed her glasses back in place on her nose.

"What?" I looked up and scowled. "That's so cliché." In a deep news announcer's voice, I declared, "Man turns forty, has an affair, and divorces his wife. Details at ten."

Gina giggled, but then she assumed a serious look. "Who are these women?"

I paused and thought. "I don't know. The only woman working at the funeral home is twenty years his senior and outweighs him by twenty pounds. You know what a snob he is about weight on women. He complains if I gain an ounce."

"Which I find ironic since he bulked up in all the wrong places," said Gina, frowning.

Glowering her disapproval, Latishia crossed her arms over her ample bosom. "What's wrong with that man? Why can't he appreciate a woman who has a little extra love attached to her bootie?"

"Yeah, well, we both know how that goes." I took a swallow of my tea. "The double standard."

"Don't get me started on that," said Gina, brushing crumbs off the front of her suit.

"To change the subject, Latishia, I think I need a loan."

Latishia had arranged the financing for our building loan two years before.

"Girl, you're talking to the right woman. What kinda loan you need?"

"I may need to buy a house. If things escalate, I'll want to buy a house. I hate living in apartments, and Buffy needs a fenced yard."

Silence ruled the table while she let that digest.

Latishia would knock the moon out of orbit for me. Several years ago her son, Dante, had had problems in school. I suspected he had dyslexia. Latishia was a recently widowed mother who was beginning a new career. She couldn't afford to pay for the specialized testing, and her insurance was giving her the runaround. I referred her to an organization that did the testing for free. As a result, Dante qualified for a special program that helped him to read better.

"You sure you don't want me to kick him in his undertaker nuts?" Latishia rubbed her hands together like she was ready to complete the task.

"Tempting, but no, just a loan. The way things are going; I'm losing hope that we'll work this out. I'll need to expedite the process if it doesn't."

"Girl, you take the fun outa everything. I'm even wearing my pointy-toed shoes. I can do some damage with these. Can you come in this afternoon?"

"I can be there at two."

Latishia pulled out her phone and checked her calendar. "That'll work." She listed off on her fingers what I needed to bring to help her start the process. "Tell me, is the coffin-tosser moving out?"

I'd been feeling pretty glum that morning, but Latishia's description of Todd knocked a guffaw right out of me. Everyone else laughed, too.

"He'll probably buy me out, and I plan to use my part of the equity as a down payment." I reached into my purse and pulled out a tissue to dab under my eyes — only these tears were a product of laughter.

Latishia handed me a business card. "Call this guy and get your house appraised. Tell him I referred you and that I need the paperwork sooner than later."

"Will do," I said, placing the card in my purse.

We all focused on our lunches for a while. I was doing a mental rundown of the list Latishia had given me, when Kat said, "You need to come in for testing. Call me at the office this afternoon, and I'll make sure you get in right away."

Startled, I jerked my attention back to the present. The Divas were all looking at me.

"Testing for what? I just had my blood work done...." My voice trailed off. "Oh!"

Everyone but Kat became interested in the food on their plates.

A chill crawled over me like giant spider legs. I shivered. "If that asshole gave me something I'm going to cut off his wanger."

To borrow one of Latishia's words, I felt "cootiefied." I wanted to go straight home and shower.

Kat tilted her head. "Did he use condoms?" Leave it to her to get straight to the important things.

"How the hell would I know? I wasn't there." I ran my hands through my hair and tugged. "Besides, even if I asked him, he'd probably lie about it."

"Let's not panic." Kat reached over and squeezed my forearm. "The tests will rule out any problems, and then you can stop worrying." Her tone of voice was soothing.

"What about HIV? Won't I have to wait six months and take a second test?" I felt bile inching up my esophagus. I swallowed, pushing the burning mess down.

"Yes." Kat reached over and patted my arm. "Don't worry about things that might never happen. Remember, we've got your back. I haven't forgotten how you got me on at Dr. Howard's office when Jack got in trouble. I shudder to think what might have happened if I was still working the late shift at the hospital."

Sniffling, I wiped my eyes and looked at my friends. "Thanks, ladies. y'all are the best!"

Latishia stiffened. We all looked her way. Her face darkened as she clawed off her sweater.

"Let me out!" she bellowed, her face glistening.

Gina rushed to scoot her chair over.

Latishia leaped up and raced toward the door. In her headlong flight, she cut off a wide-eyed waiter who was carrying two plates of steaming food. She disappeared out the door into the frigid air, sleeveless.

"Hot flash," said Gina. She dipped a chip into the salsa.

Kat glanced toward the door. "They've hit her hard since her hysterectomy three months ago. The doctors haven't stabilized her hormones yet."

Chapter 13: The Shrink

The next day I settled into Ron Jacob's comfortable swivel rocker. I crossed my right leg over my left and straightened my shoulders. I was ready to discuss all the issues we needed to cover. Determined, I planned to use logic and reason to create a plan of action. I glanced at Ron's trophy wall and found I was impressed with his credentials.

Ron closed the door and sat in a chair opposite me, smiling.

I began rocking at a slow steady rate.

"Hi, Phoenix. I understand you're a psychologist too. I've heard good things about you. What brings you in to see me?" Ron's hazel eyes looked so concerned. A lock of salt and pepper hair rested on his forehead.

Resolute to maintain control, I opened my mouth to speak.

"I, I…" Instead of answering, I blubbered for the next fifteen minutes and emptied his box of tissues. I'm surprised I didn't wear out the rocking mechanism on the chair. The safety of that room released my lassoed emotions and allowed them to gallop free. At last, dry of tears, I told him the trauma-by-trauma account of the most recent year of my life.

"Wow!" Ron sat back in his chair. "You've had a year that would put most people in a psychiatric ward. You're a definite Steel Camellia."

"I don't feel strong," I told him. "I feel lost. I'm not sure I can make it through this emotional minefield. Every time I make a decision or move, something else blows up in my face. Dealing with Dad's death is hard. The Todd thing is a mixed bag of negative emotions. I feel so stupid for not seeing all the clues."

"Why would you? Your focus was where it needed to be, on the crisis at hand, not on something that might happen."

"That's true, I had my hands full, with *no* help from Kevin or Todd." I blew my nose once more and tossed the tissue into the now-full waste paper basket. "I'm feeling very angry and resentful about that, too. After the rosary for my dad, I wanted to blast Kevin into the next county with my feelings, but he started crying. You know what I did instead?"

Ron leaned forward. "What?"

"I comforted him. I'm sitting there boiling with anger, and I'm handing him tissues and patting his shoulder." I threw up my hands in frustration. "What's wrong with me?"

"You're a good person."

I didn't acknowledge the statement. "I don't know what I'd have done if it hadn't been for the Divas."

Ron cocked his head to the right. "The Divas?"

"Gina, Latishia, and Kat. When we all started hanging out in college, Latishia named us the Divas."

He rested his forearms on his knees and clasped his hands. "So you've known Gina since college?"

I shook my head. "Longer. Gina and I have been best friends since the first grade. We attended parochial school together."

Ron nodded his understanding. "Our time is almost up." He reached for his notes and summed up our session, doing a brief recount of what I had told him.

"I'm glad you stopped counseling grief clients," he remarked. "I suggest you do the same with divorce cases. You can't be objective about them right now. Until the two of you can see someone together, if he will, my best advice is don't pick fights or give Todd any reason to aggress on you. Treat him the way you'd like him to treat you. Journal your frustrations onto paper. Don't act them out. If you feel you need to leave, do you have anywhere to go?"

I nodded and handed him a check. He waved it away.

"Consider this as a professional courtesy."

"Thank you," I said, rising from the chair.

"Reschedule with my receptionist in a week. As you know, these situations can get dicey fast."

I ducked into the ladies' room on my way out and confronted my visage in the mirror. I was puffy-eyed, and my face appeared blotched, like I had a skin condition. Embarrassed by my appearance, I hung my head and skulked from Ron's building.

* * * *

Later that night I came out of the bedroom to broach the topic of marital counseling.

I found Todd in the kitchen.

"I'm seeing someone about our marriage," I told him. I reached for my favorite mug that had "Survive until you bloom" printed across the front and poured some coffee. “Have you picked anyone that we can see together? Do you need any suggestions?”

Todd was leaning against the counter several feet away, holding his cup of black coffee. He shook his head. “Nope, and I don’t plan to, either.” He straightened and headed toward the living room. A moment later, I heard the television blare a car dealership commercial.

I wanted to stomp in there, turn off the blasted TV, sit on Todd’s chest, and demand that he talk to me. I remembered Ron’s advice, added cream and stevia to my coffee, and stirred. I carried the mug across the living room to the bedroom. Todd never looked away from the TV screen. I closed and secured the door, placed my mug on a coaster and flipped open the new journal I’d purchased after my session.

How can I work on our marriage by myself! I agree with Ron that overworking was killing my marriage. Hell, it was killing me. My private practice is sound now. I can limit my night appointments. I’ll honor the ones scheduled, but won’t accept any new appointments past five.

Can I ever trust Todd again? Do I want to stay married to a cheater?

With my confused emotions twisting my gut, I closed the journal. I’d had enough therapeutic interventions for one day.

Chapter 14: Denial Be Gone

Two weeks passed. It was a Sunday night when I walked into the living room, took the remote from the table and turned off the television.

“We need to talk.” The dreaded four words for most people.

Todd rolled his eyes and sighed as he crossed his arms.

"I've had four therapy sessions with Ron. He's helped me to understand that you felt abandoned. My work and Dad's illness took a great deal of my time this past year."

Todd nodded. "That's true. You've left me here alone night after night, while you worked." He glared at me with narrowed eyes. I could feel his hostility ramming against me in waves of negative energy.

My mouth flew open. I was ready to tell Todd that he'd finally got a taste of what *my* world was like for most of our married life. I shut it and clenched my teeth to hold the words inside. I could tell by the set of his jaw that saying them wouldn't do any good.

"I hope you've noticed that I stopped accepting appointments past five and that I'm home earlier." I sat across from him.

"How long will that last?" His sarcastic tone matched the sneer that slid onto his face.

"It's a permanent change. It wasn't fun for me to work all those long hours. You, of all people, should know with all the overtime *you* worked for nineteen years." That taunt slipped right past my lips. Inhaling, I tried to get back on track. "Have you seen anyone for counseling yet?"

Todd shook his head. "I told you I wouldn't go to counseling. I'm done. Are you deaf?"

I held my hands out, palms up. "What do you want me to do?" My heart felt as though he was squeezing it like a sponge.

Todd glared at me. "Phoenix, I don't need you to do anything." He leaned forward and placed his hands on his knees. "I don't love you anymore. I don't want to work on it. I don't want to stay married. I don't know how to make it any plainer."

I pushed myself from the chair, intending to retreat. My stomach rolled and gurgled. I couldn't breathe.

Clutching my chest, I thought, *Dear God, am I having a heart attack?* Heat boiled from my core and rose like a volcanic explosion, sending my face into flames. Sweat beaded on my forehead and upper lip. *Hot flash? Food poisoning?*

My stomach clenched and revolted. The Chinese food I'd bolted down for dinner spewed across Todd's starched white shirt. His mouth gaped as he looked down at his splattered shirt. With bulging eyes, he watched my stomach contents drip onto his suit pants.

"Fuck!" He looked up at me, fire sparking in his eyes.

I turned and fled to my room, slamming the door and locking it. I ran straight to the toilet, dropped to my knees and heaved any hope of saving my marriage into the toilet.

After I cleaned up and cried a little, I took out my journal. With Buffy settling down beside me, I flipped to a clean page.

No more denial. No more bargaining. It's over. Now I need to pick up the pieces. I only wish Dad were here to hold me and tell me everything will be okay. He's not, so it's up to me. Dear God, please help me through this mess.

I never had another menstrual cycle. I'm convinced Todd's cruel words catapulted me into menopause at the vital age of forty-five. It's such an interesting word, men-o-pause. It certainly put a pause on men for me.

Chapter 15: Woman on a Mission

The next day I grabbed my journal to gather my thoughts before I even sought a cup of java.

To survive this, I need my own space, ASAP. I need to update the Divas and call Ron to move up my next therapy appointment. I'm so pissed; I could bite nails in two. I've officially entered the anger stage of my grief. I best get things done before the depression stage hits. I have a feeling it's going to be a doozy. Dear God, please keep me from kicking that cheater's balls into Mississippi.

After I had arrived at my office, I placed a call to a realtor friend, Jeremy Haddad. I paced in my lobby, gulping water, while I waited for him to answer.

Betty Jo turtle-paddled her way to the top of the aquarium and gulped the floating pellets dropped by the feeder. At least her appetite was hearty. I hadn't eaten since I upchucked on Todd's shirt.

"Jeremy, how's it going?" I remembered that he got married last year.

"Good, and you?" His tone was upbeat as usual.

"Todd asked for a divorce. I need to buy a house. Think you can find me one?"

There was a pause. "Has Todd lost his damn mind?"

"Why does everyone keep asking me that question?" I sighed. "Before you ask, no, I don't want you to kick his ass. Just help me find a house. I've already met with Latishia Snide to start the loan application."

"If anyone can get you approved, she can." His tone became serious. "You sure you don't want to try an apartment first, to see if this settles out?"

"Jeremy, the man told me he doesn't love me, and I discovered he's been having multiple affairs." I could feel my anger zinging through my veins.

"Oh, I see. I'm kinda booked up the next couple of days? All those people coming to work at the Arsenal are looking for houses."

"I'm not off until Wednesday, but I'm meeting Latishia that morning. She hopes to have me approved by then."

"Wednesday's good for me. Tell me your price range and what you're looking for in a home. Meet me at my office, around two."

With those details settled, I felt a sudden pang of hunger.

Chapter 16: The Hunt Begins

On Wednesday at ten, I tapped on Latishia's doorframe and poked my head inside her glass cubicle.

"Phoenix! Girl, get yourself in here and give me a hug."

I leaned down and let her smash me in an embrace. Latishia hugged from the heart.

My heart hammered in my chest as I eased into the chair across from her desk. *What if I don't qualify on my salary alone? I don't want to move into an apartment again.*

Memories of my last apartment-dwelling experience flooded my mind. The computer whiz next door who left for Christmas and turned his heat down so low that his pipes burst and flooded both of our apartments. I'd never forget the engineer who lived above me that walked like Bigfoot. I could hear him urinate, and when he flushed, the sound of rushing water in the pipes swooshed behind my bathroom wall.

Latishia spoke up, distracting me from my memories. "I've been working like a crazy woman since Monday. Your excellent credit rating made my job easier. You've hit the rates at a great time too."

I sighed with relief and blinked back the tears that sprang to my eyes. "I'm so relieved to hear that good news."

She whirled the paperwork around on the desk to face me and smiled, revealing the slight gap between her front teeth. "This is the amount that we can lend you."

My mouth dropped open. I closed it before returning the smile. "I won't be spending that much, but it's good to know I can."

"Don't you go letting a real-estate agent try to upgrade you into something you don't need. Who're you using?"

"Jeremy Haddad. He goes to Gina's church. Do you know him?" Stupid question, since she knew *everybody* in the real estate and loan business in the area.

She nodded. "Jeremy's a good guy, he'll do you right." With a flinty grin, she added, "If he doesn't, you let me know and I'll —"

"Kick his ass? Thanks for all your hard work."

Latishia lumbered from behind her desk. Balanced on her three-inch leopard-skin heels, she wrapped me in another mama-bear hug.

I hugged her back. "Thanks for everything, Latishia."

I walked to my car, feeling pleased that all those frugal years of money management and timely bill payments had paid off. From my estimate, the house payment would be more than manageable. This was important since I was losing the security of a second income. That thought made my stomach somersault.

* * * *

As planned, I met Jeremy at his office at two o'clock, ready to search for my new home. He looked up and flashed his bright whites at me. Lebanese with a wiry build, he looked ready to spring into action on my behalf.

"Let me grab my binder, and we'll head out." He zipped into a back room and reappeared, with a binder in one hand and a smart phone in the other. Jeremy always reminded me of a squirrel. He talked and moved fast.

He anchored his phone into a dash mount. After a few taps, his map app appeared along with the first address on a list. He touched "start," and we were on our way. Jeremy rammed his foot on the accelerator, sending my head back against the headrest. The G-force pinned me to the seat.

"This app works much better than paper maps for me because to be truthful, I can get lost in a small walk-in closet." Jeremy glanced my way. His wide smile produced dimples.

Was that admission supposed to instill confidence in him?

We were en route to Madison, a community midway between my art class in Decatur and my private practice office in Huntsville. I spent most of the journey pounding the nonexistent brake pedal on my side of the car, as Jeremy weaved in and out of traffic.

I nearly bounced out of the seat from surprise, when his phone blasted a love song over the car speakers. Jeremy looked over his shoulder, pulled off onto a side street and turned off the engine. He dislodged the phone from the mount and plastered it to his ear.

"Hi, baby. Working. Showing houses. Phoenix O'Leary." Jeremy looked at me and held up his hands in a "what're you gonna do" gesture. "Gotta go. Love you. Yeah, I'll call you later."

He appeared embarrassed. "My wife."

"Sorry, I've forgotten her name." My memory of her from a chance meeting at the mall was vague. She was a thin, pale blonde, with an ethereal quality about her.

"Sheryl. She's a little...um..."

"Emotionally dependent?" I regretted that clinical choice of words and wished I'd said, "insecure" instead.

"Her therapist described her as a Borderline Personality Disorder." His complexion deepened to a darker hue. Jeremy knew I understood the ramifications.

I raised a brow.

"I know, I know." He held up his hands to ward off further comments. "Don't be surprised if she calls several more times."

I looked straight ahead and calculated in my head how many more calls would come from Sheryl, while we toured the six houses on our schedule in Madison. For a person with that personality disorder, I estimated a total of six more calls. I was off by one — it was seven.

None of the houses suited my needs. Each had an irresolvable flaw. The house with the beautiful landscaping and koi pond that I thought was *the one* wasn't. The builder had hacked the floor plan into minuscule rooms, and it reeked of cigarette smoke.

The house that met my interior requirements had a railroad track that ran parallel to the back fence, forty yards from the house. I could imagine a train barreling by at midnight with its horn blaring — vibrating me out of bed.

When we arrived back at Jeremy's office, we made arrangements to meet Saturday morning.

"Jeremy, I think we need to focus our search on Huntsville. My practice is there, and I'm tired of commuting."

He brushed his dark hair out of his eyes. "Can't blame you there. Where's your office located?"

"Two blocks from the hospital. I'd like to find a home no more than fifteen minutes from work."

He nodded. "I'll coordinate with our Huntsville office and check out their listings."

I heard Jeremy's phone sing the tune assigned to his wife as he pulled open the door to his building.

I rolled up my window, glad to be back in my Prius. On the drive home I was feeling drained and frustrated. *How hard can it be to find a house?*

Fifteen minutes later, I walked into my home. Todd hung up the phone and turned to face me. Perspiration dotted his upper lip and his hair stuck up in random patterns on his head.

I was surprised by Todd's current state and wondered, *What's going on?* I didn't tell him where I'd been, and he didn't ask.

In a raspy voice, he said, "I told Mom that I asked you for a divorce. She knows!"

Chapter 17: Mom Knows

Two minutes after Todd's announcement, my cell phone rang.

Todd's eyes were wide with alarm. "It's Mom, I know it's her. She had me on the phone for an hour chewing my ass up one side and down the other."

That brought a smile to my face as I accepted the call. "Hello, Joyce."

"I don't care if that idiot son of mine is divorcing you, I'm not. You're still my daughter." I could tell by her tone that Joyce was pissed. "Grandmother O'Leary feels the same way. You're still invited to the family reunion in August."

"Tell Grandmother O'Leary that I appreciate the invitation to the family reunion this year."

My grin widened when Todd looked at the ceiling and shook his head. He propped his backside against the counter with his arms and ankles crossed, prepared to eavesdrop.

"What're you going to do about this?" Joyce's voice rang with indignation.

I wonder how much she knows? I glanced over at Todd. His eyes were round with panic. *I bet she knows nothing about the affairs.*

"Not much I can do about it, Joyce. He doesn't love me and doesn't want to stay married." I glanced at Todd again. His mouth took on a grim expression.

"I can't believe this," she said, sounding exasperated.

"Me neither. If you hear about any houses for sale in the fifteen hundred square-foot range in the Huntsville area, let me know. I don't want anything too big. Oh, and it needs a fenced yard for Buffy."

Todd looked up. Now that I had his attention, I thought I'd go for a smidgen more shock value.

"I'm approved for a loan and looked at houses in the Madison area this afternoon, but didn't see anything I liked."

Todd stared at me, mouth unhinged. I hate to admit that his shock felt good.

"I'll help you find a house, don't you worry about that. Maybe you can move closer to me, that way I can watch out for you. Mom's beeping in on the other line. Gotta go. Bye."

I disconnected and glanced at my battery indicator. I reminded myself to plug my phone into the charger in the bedroom. *I might need it if Todd blows a gasket.*

"Did I hear you right? You've got a loan and went looking at houses today?" Todd pushed away from the counter.

"Yep." I walked to the carafe and poured a steaming cup of java. Doctoring it with liberal amounts of stevia and fat-free half and half, I stirred it with deliberation. I took a sip and glared up at him. The sweet concoction slid over my tongue and trailed a warm path down my esophagus. It was the nicest thing that had happened to me all day.

He took a step closer. "Who's helping you with all that?" His tone was like razor blades.

I started toward my room, coffee in hand. "You told me that you didn't love me and you wanted a divorce, so this is no longer any of your concern." I stopped and turned back. "By the way, after you pay me my half of the equity, you can have the house. I suggest you get a loan, *soon*."

Todd took another step toward me. "I thought we could use one attorney and split the fee."

"Why should I split the fee? So you can achieve the divorce *you* desire? To free you to screw around?" I placed a hand on my hip. I could feel my face burning from the heat of my anger.

"It'll save us a ton of money, that's why." Todd crossed his arms.

"Gina is representing me at no charge." I threw that fact out there, like a slap in the face.

He took another step forward and held out one hand. "Do you think Gina would write it up for both of us?"

I rolled my eyes, feeling disgusted. "You're not listening, Todd. If you want a divorce, you'll have to hire an attorney. Gina will look over the papers and negotiate any changes on *my* behalf. What this means is that the more you try to screw with me, the more it will cost you. Capisce?"

His cup flew past my head. I ducked and stumbled to the left, my heart hammering in my chest. It smashed against the wall behind me.

I turned to see coffee running down around a dent in the wall. The mug lay shattered on the floor.

My instincts screamed, run!

My mind said, *back him down*.

Fury ripped though my body. I gripped my cup so hard; I'm surprised it didn't explode in my grasp. I pointed at the wall. "I'm not cleaning up that mess. Furthermore, if you try to harm me, I'll phone the police and have you arrested for domestic violence." I took several steps toward him. I don't know what my face looked like, but he backpedaled. My tone held a menacing quality. "Then, I'll call your mother and tell her *everything* you've done." I turned to walk away. The flush of anger left as fast as it came, leaving my knees feeling like cooked linguini.

"Fine. You should get the divorce papers at your office this week."

I slowed. Todd's words felt like a blow between my shoulder blades.

Looking over my shoulder, I said, "It looks like we'll both be busy." I stomped into the bedroom with Buffy trotting at my heels. Slamming the door hard enough to cause a vibration, I locked it and leaned against it.

I haven't slammed this many doors since I was fifteen.

I would've cried, but my tear ducts were dry. Instead, I crawled under the covers with the mace and the stun gun and prayed while I trembled from the aftereffects of the adrenaline.

Chapter 18: The Search Continues

Saturday I met Jeremy at his office and demanded that I drive. He paired his phone to my Bluetooth, brought up his map app, and we were on our way.

"How are things going?" asked Jeremy as he flipped through his blue binder.

"It's going. We had a bit of an incident last night." I kept my eyes on the road.

"What happened?"

I sighed. "Todd wanted to know who was involved in helping me find a house. I told him it wasn't his concern. I didn't want him hassling anyone." I glanced over at Jeremy, who watched me with rapt attention. "When I told Todd he had to hire an attorney and that I wasn't willing to share the costs, he threw a coffee cup at me."

"Did he hit you?" Jeremy's voice dropped several octaves.

"No, thank God."

"Do you think it's safe to stay there?"

"I think I'll be okay. I told Todd I'd call the police and tell his mom about his affairs if he tried anything again." I looked over at Jeremy.

He shook his head. "I don't know. You don't know what he may do. We need to find you a house in a hurry."

Ten houses and twelve phone calls from Sheryl later, I still hadn't found the right one. The last two-story we toured I considered a possibility. The yard was level, and the landscaping was pleasing to the eye. The spacious interior was workable. The only drawback was a bedroom that blinded me with pink and purple painted stripes.

Jeremy winced when he entered the room. He plastered on his real estate smile and said, "It's just paint and paint's cheap."

"That's the first thing they teach you to say in real estate school, isn't it?"

He had the decency to blush. I eyed the walls and calculated what it would take to obliterate a little girl's former dream.

"It'll take a coat of Kilz and two coats of regular paint, and about two to three days of work due to drying time." I tapped my index finger against my lips as I pondered the situation. "Okay, let's discuss a contract."

Jeremy's face creased into a broad smile. We drove to the Huntsville office of the real estate company. He wrote up the contract, I signed it, and we faxed it to the other agent.

I paced the floor with excitement zinging up and down my body. "Do you think my offer was too low?" I turned and walked closer to Jeremy who sat at a nearby desk. "Too high?"

Jeremy's fingers drummed on the marred surface. "I think we hit it just right. Stop worrying."

Just when I felt I would self-combust from frustration, the fax came in. Jeremy stood and walked with deliberation to the machine. He picked up the paper, read a few sentences and frowned.

"I'm sorry, Phoenix, someone placed it under contract an hour ago."

I slid into a chair and exhaled. "Maybe the financing won't go through." My tone was full of hope.

Jeremy shook his head. "The agent says that an older couple made a cash offer."

I deflated like a punctured hot air balloon. After I had made a quick trip to the ladies' room, we piled back into my Prius and started the journey back to Decatur. To make things worse, I had two five-minute episodes of feeling like a blast furnace on our forty-minute drive home. Jeremy looked at me bug-eyed when I pulled up my sleeve, powered down my window and stuck my arm out.

"Phoenix, it's thirty-eight degrees out there."

Being a cold-natured person who wore sweaters on occasion during the summer, I couldn't believe that I was roasting on the spot. "Would you prefer I turn on the air conditioner? When your wife gets older, she'll have hot flashes too."

If you stay married that long, I thought.

I felt a sense of relief when Jeremy exited my car. I might retch if I had to endure one more phone call from Sheryl followed by Jeremy's reassurances of undying love. How he managed, was beyond my comprehension.

Bless his little heart. I knew he was stuck. If he tried to divorce Sheryl, there would be hell to pay. Borderlines don't handle perceived abandonment well, and the Catholic Church frowns on divorce.

I pulled into my garage just as my phone jangled the tune assigned to Joyce.

"Phoenix, what're you doing tomorrow afternoon?"

"Nothing much, why?"

"I have a few houses for you to see near where I live. I think you're going to like them."

I paused. *How could a fun exploration for a new home shift into such an energy-draining disappointment?* Nothing I'd seen so far seemed like home. Even the house I lost wasn't quite it. "I can meet you at two o'clock at your house."

That settled, I trudged into my bedroom with Buffy prancing at my feet, wedged the chair under the door, and took a nap. I needed the solace of sleep.

Chapter 19: House Hunting

Sunday after lunch, I rang Joyce's doorbell. I filled my lungs with frigid air while I shifted from one foot to the other. She opened the door and smiled when she saw me. After pulling me inside the warm house, she wrapped me in her arms.

"I don't know what's gotten into that boy of mine. Do you think he's inhaled too many fumes from that embalming fluid?"

I suppressed a smile and shrugged. "Joyce, I don't want to talk about this. He's made up his mind. I need to focus on finding a new home."

"Is he making you move out?"

"No, I'm tired of the long commute to work. It seems like every day the price of gas goes up."

She shook her head in agreement. "Ain't that the truth?"

Joyce, a petite spitfire, stood mere inches above five feet. It was difficult for me to believe she gave birth to such a tall son. Her manner of dress was as meticulous as her home.

The only thing that didn't fit was her bulldog, Rex. A brute of a canine, he snorted, slobbered, and farted in fits of exuberance.

I glanced around. "Where's Rex?" As if on cue, Rex rounded the corner and sped toward me. Before I could move behind Joyce, he latched onto my leg with his front paws and humped me. I struggled to stay upright.

Joyce pointed her finger at Rex. "No! I said NO!"

Rex's tongue lolled out of his mouth. She snatched his leash off a nearby shelf, hooked it to his harness and yanked.

Rex didn't release my leg. Jerked off balance, I pin-wheeled my arms trying to stay upright.

Joyce yanked again. This time she put her entire ninety-eight pounds into it.

Rex let go, and I fell on my ass.

"I'm so sorry. I don't know what's with him."

I stood up and brushed off my pants. "I think it's time for you to have Rex neutered. He's become an out-of-control sex-crazed dog."

"Perhaps you're right. I woke up this morning with Rex humping my thigh."

Joyce wrestled the dog into his crate. I tried to help, but the leash kept getting wrapped around my legs. That task completed, we both sighed and straightened our clothes.

I wanted to drive, but Joyce insisted that it would be easier if she did. Unlike my search with Jeremy, we had to call the realtor listed on the signs and wait until he or she arrived.

The first house would need all the carpet ripped out. Even then, it might need fumigating.

"I can't believe anyone lives this way," Joyce whispered to me.

"It looked normal from the outside," I whispered back. I was getting that sinking feeling again.

The second house was clean, but it was located across the street from a school, which would mean lots of traffic. My spirits dropped lower.

The third house was almost *the one*. I felt my excitement rise as I moved from room to room. The floor plan was ideal for my needs.

"Does it have a fenced back yard," I asked the realtor.

"Yes, let's go look."

I walked out onto a wooden deck that needed to be stained and spotted the Jacuzzi. I felt my shoulders slump. A friend of mine once owned a Jacuzzi. I knew about the upkeep and expensive chemicals, not counting the additional cost of electricity to run the pump. The owner had also priced the home in the upper range of what I was willing to pay.

We thanked the agent for her time and walked toward the car.

"Now that I know what floor plan I like, we just need to find another house in the area with the same floor plan," I said.

Joyce beeped open the car doors. "That does help narrow things down."

We both agreed to keep looking and to alert each other if we found a possibility.

* * * *

A week later I drove through a neighborhood I didn't know existed and turned onto a street named Morning Star. At the end of the street, a "For Sale" sign poked out of the yard of the last house on the left before the cul-de-sac. The exterior looked like the house I liked so much. I felt a clunk in my gut, like two pieces of a puzzle slipping into place. I called the agent listed on the sign, and she agreed to meet me the next day after work.

I phoned Joyce. "I may have found my new home. Can you meet me tomorrow after work to tour it with me?"

"Sure can." I could hear the smile in her voice.

* * * *

The next day, Joyce and I looked at each other like two kids about to enter a toy store. My stomach fluttered, and I reached down to rub it, but it didn't help. The agent handed me a sheet of paper with the floor plan. It was just what I wanted.

My stomach flittered as I walked inside. I stopped, and my gaze traveled up. The high cathedral ceiling in the living room made it feel expansive and open. The carpet was a neutral color and was clean. I ambled around checking the smooth ceilings for cracks.

The dining room joined the great room and was large enough for a full-sized dining table. The kitchen was perfect with lots of storage, counter space, and convenient placement of the appliances. Next to the kitchen was a breakfast nook with a bay window, perfect for a bistro set.

"I love the flow of the space," said Joyce, as she smoothed her hand along the granite counter top.

"The bedrooms are on the other side of the living room." The agent pointed the way.

Two decent-sized rooms were on the left. I knew one would be a guest room, the other an office. I placed the furniture in my mind. Between the guest rooms and the master bedroom was a bath with a tub/shower combination.

The master bedroom stopped me in my tracks. It was large, with a trey ceiling.

"I can paint the inside of the trey sky blue and sponge in clouds so that I can wake to blue skies every morning."

"That would be pretty," said Joyce, as she looked up.

The master bath had double sinks and a large tub with Jacuzzi jets for long hot baths, with a closet on each side.

"I can put my summer clothes in one closet and my winter things in the other."

We walked back into the living room.

Joyce's gaze roamed the area from this side of the house. "I love the open floor plan."

"Me, too. My cherry table and chairs I ordered will look great in the dining room. In this house, I can entertain with ease. All I'll need is a guest bed and a dinette table for that breakfast nook area."

"Don't worry about that. You can eat in the dining room until you find one."

Opening the back door, I walked onto a small covered porch. The backyard was fenced and large.

"This will be perfect for Buffy. She'll have plenty of room to run." I waved my arm in an arc to emphasize the space.

"The yard is flat, too. You can cut ninety-five percent of it with your riding lawnmower."

Best of all, the price was right.

When I got home, Buffy pranced around me in greeting. I poured a glass of iced tea and took it to my room. After I had placed the glass on the desk, I scratched behind her ears. She squeezed her eyes shut and stood still. When I stopped, she ran to the door and whined. Todd was at work, so it was safe to give her the run of the fenced yard. I opened the door, and she streaked out, barking.

Settling on the chair, I opened my journal. *I found my new home! I made an offer. For once something is going right.*

Chapter 20: Bump in the Road

My two o'clock patient canceled, claiming a bout of the flu. Not wishing to share her infection, I thanked her for calling. I'd just settled down at the desk in my business office to do charting when my mobile phone rang.

"Don't be mad." Todd's voice sounded tense.

I sighed and rolled my eyes. "What now?" I could already feel my shoulders tensing.

"My house loan was denied."

"What!" I stood so fast; the chair rolled back against the wall. "What do you mean, denied?" I paced from where I was down the hall to the lobby and back.

"They say I don't have enough income without a cosigner."

I raked my hair away from my face as I paced. I stopped and closed my eyes, trying my level best not to scream. *This doesn't make sense. Todd should've qualified based on his salary. I asked Latishia about this when I applied for my loan.*

"Don't panic." His voice had a desperate tone. "I'll talk to Mom. Maybe she can cosign with me."

"I don't care if you call Joyce, your Aunt Fanny or make a pact with your Uncle Lucifer — fix it. I'm using my part of the equity as my down payment and my loan is approved and waiting for you." Dad had left me a small inheritance and some insurance, but I wanted to put that away for my retirement.

"I'll call Mom after I hang up."

"Todd, I don't understand? Your truck is only two payments away from being free and clear. Our joint credit cards were paid in full every month. I made sure of that." I plopped back into the chair. Rolling it closer to the desk, I propped an elbow on the desk and rested my chin in my hand.

"Did you lose your job?" *Please, not that. He'll never get approved if he's unemployed.* I felt as tense as a string on a tuned guitar.

Silence — a long scary silence. I looked to see if I accidentally disconnected the call.

"Todd? Are you still there?"

"Um, you see, Phoenix." Another long pause. "I opened a few new credit cards in my name last year and —"

"What! How many is a few?" I was on my feet again, pacing.

"Three."

I stopped and put my free hand to my head, where tom-toms were beginning to pound. *Three women and three credit cards, what else didn't I know about this man?* Sweat beaded my upper lip.

"How much are you in the hole?"

"Around twenty-five thousand."

"Twenty-five thousand!" I sped back down the hall to the lobby and turned left into my therapy office. If I didn't get relief soon, I would explode like a Red, White, and Boom firework, and in my mind, it would be Todd's fault.

"Phoenix." He hesitated before continuing. "I'm sorry. I screwed up."

Yanking off my jacket, I reached up and pulled the chain to start the ceiling fan. The cool breeze swept across my heated face, providing minimal relief.

"No, you didn't screw up, your life is down the toilet, and your crap is flowing in my direction, again. It's not fair that Joyce has to clean up your mess, either." I wanted to rant some more. The only thing that kept me from a full-out verbal assault was my respect and love for Joyce.

"Fix it, Todd. You know my closing date. Get it done, ASAP." I thumbed off my phone, which somehow lacked the release of slamming a receiver into a cradle.

"Siri, call Latishia Snide, mobile."

After a few rings, she answered with her usual perky greeting.

"Hey girl, you caught me at a great time. What's up?"

"Do you know a good hit man?" I sighed.

Latishia laughed. "You need to ask Gina about that stuff, her being Italian and all." After a brief pause, she said, "What did the Casket King do this time?"

"He opened three new credit cards in his name and is twenty-five thousand dollars in debt."

"I don't see the problem. Your name isn't on any of the accounts, right?"

"No, thank goodness, but this caused his house loan to be denied. He can't pay me my equity. That means I don't have a down payment."

Chapter 21: Wiggly-Wobbly

I filled pages in my journal, scribbling my wrath about Todd's financial stupidity onto the clean white pages. It felt good to write out my emotions. I imagined the pen drained them from my body and inked them on the paper that absorbed them for safekeeping.

Todd called later that morning to report that Joyce had agreed to cosign the loan with him.

"How did you manage that, Todd?" I tapped my pen on the table, feeling my initial relief morph into anger.

"I had to confess about the credit cards and allow her to help me set up a budget."

I'd taken care of all the bills during our marriage because Todd didn't seem to understand money management.

Later that day, Joyce phoned me. "If I could put that boy over my knee and spank him, I would. Then I'd ground him for a year. I can't believe he did such a stupid thing."

You haven't heard the half of it. "Well, he did. Sorry, you got caught in the middle of this."

She sighed. "It's part and parcel of being a mom. Gotta go."

Todd shook his head every time he heard the latest updates about my new house. My plan, since the divorce wasn't final, was to do some painting and cleaning before I moved.

My threats, to phone the police and do an exposé to Joyce, doused Todd's temper tantrums. After the credit card fiasco, the last thing he wanted was for his mom to find out about the affairs. There hadn't been another tense moment since the coffee cup-throwing incident.

Despite this, I didn't lower my guard. The dent in the wall served as a healthy reminder.

The previous homeowner of my new house-to-be had moved to Tennessee, so he gave me a key and told me it was all right to clean and paint. Every weekend, I spent my time feathering my new nest. I dragged our carpet cleaner over and shampooed all the carpets.

The wall where the television and bookcases would reside was painted a dark burgundy and didn't go well with my furnishings. The overpriced house similar to the one I was purchasing had a sponged wall that looked like terra cotta marble, which would coordinate nicely with my furnishings. I decided to copy that wall.

I had the equipment and expertise to achieve the desired effect. The tool had two small patterned rollers on each side of a handle. The technique was simple. Pour two different colored paints in the special divided pan, load the rollers, and make V patterns on the wall to mingle the paints. The drawback was that the corners and edges had to be sponged in with care. The largest obstacle was that the wall was sixteen feet wide, and twenty-two feet tall at the apex. This project would require a ladder.

“Todd, I need a favor.” I hoped he’d do anything I asked at this point, to keep me from tattling to Joyce.

He stiffened as he reached for the cup of coffee he’d just poured. “Maybe. What do you need?”

“I need a ladder that will reach the apex of a tall wall.”

He cocked his head. “How tall?”

“Twenty feet.”

“That would take the extension ladder.” His mouth turned down.

My shoulders drooped. I hated the extension ladder. It had to lean against the wall and always felt unstable.

“Can you take it to my house Saturday morning?”

He stood straighter. He hadn’t seen my house yet and had asked questions about it. “Sure, I’ll carry it in my truck. What are you painting?”

“I’ll need the tall stand-up ladder too. I’m doing clouds on the ceiling in my bedroom and repainting one wall in the living room.”

Todd nodded. “I can arrange that.” He picked up his coffee and headed for his recliner.

* * * *

Saturday, I had the entire floor of my master bedroom covered with clear plastic that crinkled with every step. The roller pan was full of paint, tinted robin’s egg blue. I rolled the smooth ceiling inside the trey and turned it into a sky.

I smiled, pleased with the shade and that the ceiling wouldn’t need a second coat of paint. My plan was to let the ceiling dry while I painted the living room wall. I would come back when it was dry to sponge on the clouds.

Half of the living room was covered in plastic. The dreaded extension ladder sat propped against the wall, under the apex. I eyed it and shuddered. Unlike the stepladder, this ladder had no shelf to place items like paint trays. This task would be a battle — *woman vs. ladder.*

Sponging the edge next to the ceiling was the logical first step. Wearing my yellow rubber gloves, I dabbed a sea sponge into the terracotta paint. I slowly climbed the demon ladder. It wiggled from left to right as I took each step. I stopped to let the ladder settle before venturing to the next step. With my arm fully extended, I was able to reach the peak.

I could have moved up one more step, but the idea made my stomach do somersaults. I'm not scared of heights. I'm afraid of falling off of wobbly ladders.

After I had sponged in the area, I shimmied my way down and loaded the sponge with warm beige paint to blend into the mix. The burgundy base combined with the terracotta and beige to create the perfect marbled effect.

The edging process was tooth-grinding slow. By the time I finished hand-sponging the edges, my right shoulder was cramping, and my stomach was growling.

"Fried chicken. That's what I need. Spicy fried chicken."

I knew just the place. I pulled off my gloves and checked the bottom of my shoes for paint.

Fifteen minutes later I was back, sitting in a webbed lawn chair and bent over a dilapidated TV tray, stuffing my face with chicken and slurping a chocolate shake. Comfort food: A Hot Flash Diva's best and worst friend.

Fortified, I was ready to conquer that evil ladder. After what felt like fifteen thousand trips up and down later, I had completed the large wall. I stood back to admire my work and was feeling flushed with success when I saw one spot that needed a tad of blending. I wanted to ignore it, but I knew my eye would wander to the spot every time I entered the room. Of course, it was near the summit of the wall.

I quivered my way up the ladder, my legs feeling like silly string, and sponged the area. Two steps from the bottom, the fiendish ladder shifted. I stepped off in a panic, right into the paint tray.

"Crap!"

I counted my blessings that the pan was almost empty and it was latex paint. With one foot anchored in the paint pan, I circled with my free foot until I could reach the paper towels. I felt like the hands on a clock.

Twenty minutes and several descriptive phrases later, I managed to wash and towel the latex paint off the bottom of my shoe.

My malignant thoughts metastasized toward Todd and his hellish ladder. It was his mid-life crisis that had caused all these problems. If he could hear my heated thoughts, his ears would burn to a crisp.

At eleven that night, I finished the clouds on my bedroom ceiling. They looked fantastic.

Exhausted, with my calves hardened like concrete blocks, I drove home to Decatur. I trudged into the house around midnight. I wanted to crawl straight into bed, but I knew I needed to shower first.

Todd was in his recliner — as usual — watching a movie.

"You're late." He eyed me from top to paint-speckled bottom.

"It takes a lot of time to walk up and down an unsteady ladder twenty million times."

He nodded, and his lips thinned. "I thought about that ladder. When you weren't home by ten, I wondered if maybe you fell and knocked yourself out or broke something."

I held up my phone. In my most sarcastic tone, I said, "It was considerate of you to call and check on me to make sure I wasn't hurt."

I hobbled toward the bathroom.

Todd's actions — or rather, lack of action — spoke volumes.

Chapter 22: Moving Day

It was Valentine's Day. Instead of receiving a card and flowers from my husband, I was moving my belongings out of the house that he and I had built together. To my dismay, it appeared to be harder on Todd than on me. He sat in his recliner, feet propped up and watched the movers haul my furniture and boxes out our front door with a furrowed brow and clenched teeth.

I was too caught up in the process of directing the movers to let my emotions surface.

"Is that the last one?" I leaned over to see what I marked on top of the box.

"Yes, ma'am."

When the biggest guy wheeled it out the door, Todd dropped the footrest, placed his head in his hands and sobbed.

I felt my mouth drop open as I stumbled to a stop to stare at him.

The boss of the crew came to a halt inside the door, his gaze riveted on Todd's emotional meltdown. We exchanged incredulous glances. His two helpers piled in close behind him, trying to see what was happening.

After shifting from one foot to another, the head guy looked at me, shrugged, and jerked his head toward the door. Hands in their pockets, the men looked at their feet as they shuffled back outside.

I walked to Todd, patted his heaving shoulders and thought, *Shouldn't I be the one falling apart? I'm the one who's been cheated on and tossed aside.*

"Todd, you were the one who filed for divorce, not me. Why are you crying?"

"I just didn't think this day would come."

"I've been packing for weeks." I removed my hand from his shoulder, along with the comfort it offered.

"I know." He pulled a white handkerchief from his pocket and blew his nose. His mottled face looked pinched, and his eyes were red.

I walked around the house one last time to check for forgotten items. I swept my hand across the kitchen countertop that I chose to match the tile floor. Its smooth granite surface was cool.

When I entered the living room, my glance skidded across the fireplace and mantel that I helped to design. *At least I was able to decorate it for one Christmas.*

The master bedroom was empty. My mind flitted across memories of moving in the furniture, hot lovemaking, and the last two months that this room was my fortress.

I waved. "I'll see you tomorrow when you come to hang the paintings and drapes." *I don't want you in my house, but that's the least you can do.*

He pulled his handkerchief from his back pocket and wiped his eyes. "Mom wouldn't have it any other way."

Swallowing a sob, I slung my purse over my shoulder, hooked Buffy to a leash, and walked out the door. On the driveway, I stopped and looked back. I admired the red brick I had chose and worried that Todd wouldn't water the pansies I planted.

Head down, I plodded to my car and settled Buffy inside. I started the engine and backed out of my former life.

Chapter 23: Surprise!

Saturday morning Todd slunk into my house, carrying a ladder. His jaw dropped when he spied his mother cleaning the windows in my living room.

"Uh...hi, Mom. I didn't know you were going to be here?"

"I'm just helping Phoenix get settled." She smiled and turned back to scrub a window.

He left and returned with a toolbox. "Show me where to hang your paintings."

Thirty minutes later, Todd lay scrunched on the floor, red-faced and cursing as he tried to install a puppy gate. I was in the middle of unpacking dishes when someone knocked on the door leading to the garage.

I hollered, "Come in."

Todd's brother James, followed by his daughter Heather, walked into the house.

"Hi Phoenix, where do you want it?" asked James.

"Over there, in that little alcove of windows. Just move those boxes to the side." I resumed unloading my plates into the kitchen cabinets.

They nodded, turned, and left the house. Todd supported himself on his elbow and gave me a questioning look. I caught Joyce looking over her shoulder with a smug smile on her face.

"What are James and Heather doing here? What's going on?" Todd put down his screwdriver.

Before I could answer, they returned, hauling a small wooden breakfast table.

Todd struggled to his feet with a grunt. "That looks like Grandma O'Leary's table."

"Yep." James grinned. "Granny bought a new one, so she asked us to deliver her old one to Phoenix so that she can use it in her new house." He appeared to be enjoying his younger brother's discomfort.

Todd's eyes bulged. "You brought that all the way back from Indiana?"

James nodded. "We drove up yesterday to pick it up for Phoenix."

They walked back out and returned with the chairs.

"Thanks for bringing it down," I told him. "You have no idea how much I appreciate it."

James smiled. "You just let us know if you need anything else."

Heather came over and gave me a hug goodbye.

"Wait a minute, James." Todd paced the kitchen floor, running his hand through his thinning hair. "I didn't know anything about this."

I shrugged. "I didn't either, until this morning when your mom told me."

"You're *my* family, not hers." Todd's face flushed red as he walked over to his brother and poked him in the chest with his index finger. "You're supposed to be on *my* side."

James shoved away the offending finger and stepped closer. "Hey, brother, you're the one who asked for a divorce, not me," he said.

I stepped between the brothers, placing a hand on each of their chests.

James backed away. "Don't worry, Phoenix. I won't start a fight in your house. See y'all later. Bye, Mom."

He looped an arm around Heather's shoulders and turned to leave.

"I'll call Grandma O'Leary to thank her and let her know you arrived safely."

"You do that," James called over his shoulder.

I exchanged a concerned glace with Joyce before I picked up my phone and walked out onto the back porch to make the call. Buffy followed with her tail twitching.

When I returned, Todd and Joyce were arguing. Todd was looming over his petite mother, who looked up at him, her fists balled on her hips.

"Mom, *I'm* your flesh and blood, not Phoenix." He threw his screwdriver into his toolbox with a clatter, picked it up, and stormed out of the house.

Joyce and I stood staring at each other.

"Joyce, I didn't mean to cause an argument."

She ran a hand through her hair and blew out an exasperated breath. "You didn't cause the problem. That boy just needs to grow up." She picked up her bottle of window cleaner and walked toward one of the guest bedrooms.

After Joyce had left, I popped a frozen dinner into the microwave and zapped it. I dined on my newest acquisition, Grandmother O'Leary's table, while I compiled a mental to-do list.

* * * *

At nine that night, the doorbell chimed. Exasperated, I strode to the door. I'd waited all afternoon for the delivery of my formal dining room table and chairs. The store told me they would be delivered sometime after two, but this was ridiculous. I yanked open the door, ready to breathe fire and recriminations on whoever was there.

A twenty-something guy wearing drooping jeans, sneakers and a hoodie stood on my doorstep, squinting at paperwork on a clipboard.

"Are you Ms. O'Leary?" He looked up and took a step back. "I...I'm sorry for the late delivery, but one of our guys called in sick, so I had to deliver both trucks. Otherwise yours would have been delayed until tomorrow." If the look on his face was any indication, he'd already survived several rounds of verbal assaults. Gripping the clipboard, he glanced from side to side, like he was trying to decide which way to run.

Still grasping the doorknob, I inhaled a deep breath to steady myself. *Calm down, Phoenix, it's not his fault.* When I found my voice, I said, "Yes, I'm Phoenix O'Leary. Call me Phoenix. What's your name?"

"Seth?" He said it like he wasn't sure of his own name.

I held the door wide. "Well, Seth, you look like you've had a bad day. Come inside. It's getting colder by the minute out there."

His shoulders were hiked high like they were hinged from his earlobes. "Where do you want all the boxes?"

"Boxes?" I took several steps toward him.

He backpedaled until he stood on the sidewalk. "Yes ma'am, all the furniture from this store is delivered in boxes." He cringed a little.

"They never told me it would be in boxes! I expected the furniture to be delivered already assembled otherwise, I wouldn't have bought it." I stood glaring at Seth with both hands on my hips when the hot flash roared to life like an exploding volcano. Molten lava boiled in the area between my hips and neck, and inched its way up to my face. *This mess is Todd's fault. If he hadn't tripped over the testosterone edge, I wouldn't need to purchase new furniture.*

"Let's talk outside for a moment, please?" I was only wearing a long-sleeved tee shirt and jeans when I stepped outside into the delicious sensation of thirty-four degrees.

Seth backed up a bit to give me plenty of room. "Ma'am, I'm sorry. I'm new with this company and I've had this reaction all day. The salesmen didn't tell *anyone* that the furniture came unassembled." He was still clutching his clipboard. "That's the other reason why I'm running late."

Feeling my temperature drop back to normal, I walked back into my house, trailed by Seth.

"How many more deliveries do you have tonight?"

"You're my last one."

An idea blossomed in my mind. "Seth, have you eaten yet?"

"No ma'am." A gurgle from his stomach confirmed the information

"Do you have a date or something tonight?" It was, after all, Saturday — date night.

"No ma'am." He looked down, and his ears turned pink.

"I have a proposal for you."

His eyes widened in alarm.

"I'll pay you a hundred bucks if you'll help me assemble this furniture tonight. I'll even throw in a pizza. We can eat it while we work. Are you game?" I crossed my arms and smiled.

His face lit with a broad smile. "I like pepperoni on my pizza."

"Great! The table and chairs go in this room." I led the way. "Stack the boxes, so we'll have room to assemble. While you're unloading, I'll order the pizza and get some tools."

We had four chairs assembled by the time dinner arrived. We sat at my hand-me-down breakfast table and gobbled pizza. I nibbled on my second slice of the large pie, while Seth fortified himself with the rest. After an explosive burp that shot pepperoni fumes across the table, he apologized and sprang to his feet, ready for action. I threw the cardboard box into the recycling bin in my garage and joined him.

We worked until midnight. We both groaned as we hefted the heavy, solid cherry wood table from its side to rest on its two pedestaled feet. Seth slid underneath to unlock the top so we could slide it apart to install the two leaves. Once the additions were in place, he crawled back under to lock the pieces together, while I wrote him a check. He was worth every penny.

"Thanks." He looked at the check and smiled.

"Not a great way to spend a Saturday night."

He shrugged. "It turned out better than I thought it would when you first opened the door."

We both laughed.

I sat at my new dining table and opened my journal. I was tired, but I could feel something bubbling up inside, and I knew I needed to write it down. Pen in hand, I waited. My journal wasn't there for me to account for every event of each day. I sat in quiet repose until the words surfaced without effort.

Why is everything always so damn hard?

One sentence, but it was a complete summation of the past two years of my life.

Chapter 24: Discovery

The Friday after I moved into my new home, I shut down my practice mid-day, for three hours. Todd insisted he couldn't do this any other day due to scheduled funerals.

I drove to Decatur to close our joint accounts at the bank, and to remove my few remaining papers from the shared safety deposit box. I had no concerns that Todd would abscond with my goodies because I possessed both keys. I envisioned him combing the house, looking for that second key. The thought made me smile.

I was still firmly entrenched in the anger phase. While I was furious with Todd, I was also pissed at myself. I'd had time to think through our years of marriage.

Two nights before, I'd found a box that contained the entire collection of cards, notes, and little trinkets that he'd given me through the years. The contents confirmed that we once had a vital marriage and that he did, indeed, love me.

When I woke the next day, it was as if someone had injected me with a giant syringe of emotional Novocain. I felt numb, except for breakthroughs of rancid, hot anger. To be truthful, this scared the bejeezus out of me. I knew I loved Buffy, but I couldn't feel it.

I opened my journal and wrote, *Will I remain a shell empty of emotion, except for anger, for the rest of my life? If not, will it disappear in a flash, or wear off in a gradual way?*

When I strode through the doors of the bank, my eyes slid over to Latishia in her glass cubicle. Her plump red lips were flat-lined as she directed a baleful glare across the bank. I tracked her gaze to Todd, who sat at a desk occupied by a blonde beauty. Laughing, they leaned toward each other across the desk.

I walked up to them, and the laughter died.

"Oh, um..., Phoenix, we were just waiting for you." Todd ran his finger inside the collar of his starched shirt.

"Hi, I'm Brandi, with an i." She stood and extended her well-manicured hand. She had a squeaky little girl voice, but the rest was a beautiful, sexy woman.

I shook her hand and gave her my *he isn't divorced yet* look, as I sat in the chair next to Todd.

Fifteen minutes later, our joint finances were separated, and I held a cashier's check. I slid the check into my purse and pulled out the safety deposit box keys.

Todd's eyes widened with recognition. "I've been looking for those everywhere!" His shoulders slumped with relief.

"Really?" I tilted my head and tried to look innocent.

We both signed in, and Brandi escorted us into the vault. After she had left, we were alone in a small room with a counter and two chairs. Todd and I pulled out all the items. After inspecting all the envelopes, we divided them into his and her piles. Mine went into a nylon bag that I took from my purse. He tucked his back inside the box.

The minute we opened the door of the tiny room, a rush of cool air blew past us, and Brandi appeared, all smiles. She replaced the box and secured it.

Todd looked at his watch and shifted his weight. "Gotta go, my lunch hour is almost over." He moved closer and lowered his voice. "My attorney told me that the papers are on the judge's desk, waiting to be signed."

He skulked out the door of the bank like a wraith.

Brandi looked at me and tilted her head to the side, like a bird. "It's so awesome that the two of you decided together that it's time to end your marriage and are working it out so amicably."

My hand tightened on the strap of my purse. "*We* didn't decide to get a divorce. I intended to honor my marriage vows for the rest of my life. Todd turned forty and asked for a divorce after he committed adultery with three other women. I'm trying my best to be Christian about the whole thing. If he lied to you about this, you might consider what else he's bent the truth about."

Her cupid mouth formed a perfect O.

I stalked across the bank into Latishia's office and plopped into her chair. She rose, tottered on red three-inch heels to the door of her office, and closed it. "What did Ms. Brandi say that twisted your thong into a wad?"

"I don't own a thong."

"Really? Well, you're single now; we'll have to do something about that. Now tell me the dirt about Brandi."

"Todd told her that we both decided to call it quits."

"That corpse-loving husband of yours comes in every day with the funeral home's deposit and spends fifteen minutes flirting with her at her desk. I think she's one of the three." Latishia tapped her pen on the shiny desktop and tossed a glare over her shoulder toward Brandi, who was watching us. Brandi's eyes widened, then she bent over a paper on her desk and began writing.

"It won't be my problem much longer," I replied. "Todd told me the papers are on Judge Givan's desk."

Latishia glanced at her desk calendar and giggled. "He'll sign them Friday."

"How do you know?" I leaned forward.

"It's Friday the thirteenth." She tapped the date with her pen. "He's famous for holding divorce decrees so that he can sign them on that day."

I shook my head and glanced at my watch. "Gotta go. Keep me on your speed dial."

"Same to you."

She gave me a mushy hug. I left, feeling Brandi's gaze escorting me from the building.

Chapter 25: Depression

I thought things would go easier now that I was in my new home. My assumption was incorrect. Depression, the next to last stage of grief, caught me in its slimy hands and ran me down like road kill.

It was early March, and I was in full nesting mode. I spent my nights unpacking or on the phone with one Diva or another, as they kept tabs on my progress and tried to cheer me up. They offered to help me unpack, but I needed to do it myself.

I craved seclusion. It took everything I had to be there for my patients, so when it was time to go home, I felt spent. For weeks, the best I could manage was to collect food from a drive-thru window, eat, and unpack a box or two.

The boxes that once lined all the rooms were emptied, collapsed and stacked inside the two-car garage, one by one. It wasn't a fast process since I had the motivation and speed of a slug.

When I finished, I hauled them out to the curb along with my rolling green plastic garbage container that had "Property of Madison County" painted in white on the side. The next day the guy emptied the can but ignored the boxes.

When I arrived home, there they were, only the wind had blown them across several lawns. Tears of frustration streaked my cheeks while I chased down the boxes, restacked them and tied them into a bundle.

The next Monday, I left open the first two morning-appointment slots on my schedule and lay in wait to corral the garbage collector. After he pulled up and maneuvered the mechanical arm to pick up the container, I gave a sharp rap on his window.

He jumped. "What the hell?" The container fell off the mechanical arm.

I pointed at the stack of collapsed boxes. "Why aren't you picking up these boxes?"

He opened the door and climbed down. "You have to call for a special pickup. I don't have room for those." He realigned the container.

"Call who?"

He shrugged. He pulled himself back into the cab of his truck and said, "Madison County, I guess." He slammed the door, picked up the container, and dumped it.

I stomped back toward the house, blaming Todd for one more inconvenience in my life.

After another grinding day and a fast food dinner, Gina called. "I've been patient, Phoenix, but this has gone on long enough."

"What are you talking about?"

Gina sighed. "You've turned into a hermit. Have you seen Ron lately?"

I sat down in my recliner and elevated my feet. "It's been a month. Ron told me to call him if I needed him."

"You need him. Call."

Chapter 26: He What?

There were a few bumpy spots on my road to recovery, like the day the divorce papers came in the mail. The judge, as predicted by Latishia, signed them on Friday the thirteenth.

Part of me was relieved that the whole mess was over. The other part of me knew I might be legally divorced, but my heart was still padlocked to a wedding ring.

I sat at Grandma O'Leary's little table and cried until my throat burned. Buffy, always aware of my moods, pawed at my leg until I put her in my lap. There's nothing like a warm, fluffy Cocker Spaniel — and of course, chocolate ice cream — to make a lady feel better. Despite all my ice cream binges, I'd lost ten pounds since Todd's fateful words.

My next ass-kicker occurred on one of my Wednesdays off.

I drove to Decatur for my art lesson and decided to eat at one of my favorite restaurants, Hickory Stick BBQ. While sipping my sweet tea, I checked email on my phone.

The waitress came up and said, "I'm sorry to hear about your divorce."

A plump, silver-haired woman in her sixties, she'd waited on Todd and me many times during the years. I looked up and offered a weak smile. "Thank you."

"I just couldn't believe it. The two of you always seemed so happy." She shifted the round tray she carried to her other hip.

I shrugged. "I thought we were too."

Her brow creased. "Then why did you ask Todd for a divorce?"

I felt my shoulders stiffen. "What?" I put down my phone.

"Todd told me you asked him for a divorce."

"He what?" I almost yelled the words. I felt my face burn, and my scalp began to tingle.

She placed a palm on the table and leaned on it. "I'm confused."

I told her the brief version of the saga. "If you don't believe me, go to the courthouse. Divorces are part of the public record."

"That philandering rascal!" She plopped a fist on her plump hip. "Why did he lie to me?"

I thought a minute. "Funeral directors deal with ministers who don't approve of folks who divorce their wives without a biblical cause. They are also highly opposed to adultery. Do me a favor, pass on the truth."

"Oh, *I will*. Todd ought to be ashamed of himself, that scoundrel!"

I could tell by the jut of her jaw that she didn't appreciate Todd's lie or his extra-curricular jaunts. While walking to my car, I pondered what other lies Todd had been telling about our divorce.

People always want a bad guy in situations like this. Todd seemed determined for it to be me.

Chapter 27: Help, Help me Ron

I was in a rant and about to rock Ron's chair into orbit.

"People think that just because I'm a psychologist, I should breeze through hard times like a robot. I'm human, and I have to move through my stages of grief like everyone else."

Ron sat back with his fingers laced over his bump of a belly and his ankle resting on his knee. He nodded for me to continue.

"The only difference is I'm educated on the stages, so I can click them off my mental to-do list as I transition through them. It doesn't mean that I process my grief any faster, or with any less pain." I paused to take a breath. "I'm feeling rushed like everyone thinks I should be over it already. It's like they've forgotten that I'm double grieving. Well, I'm not over it, and Todd's part of the reason."

I stared at Ron, waiting for a response.

Taking a deep breath, he sat straight and placed both feet on the floor. "I agree with all that, Phoenix, but what's set you off today?"

I thought about that for a moment. "Several things. Since I've moved into my new house, I've become a hermit. I go to work where I give it my all and come home to unpack boxes and rearrange my stuff. I do still attend my art class, but it takes effort. Most folks don't understand what I'm doing, but Gina does. She knows I must have my home — my safe place — in order. I feel the same way about my office. Once that's achieved, I'm *usually* ready to take on the world." I slowed my rocking.

Ron cocked a brow. "But this time…."

"Gina called the other night and said I should come see you because I'm depressed."

"You know the symptoms of depression, which ones are you having?"

I paused and thought. "Low energy, trouble falling and staying asleep. I've spent many restless nights pondering what went wrong with my marriage. Now I'm wondering why Todd's sabotaging my life with lies."

Ron's eyes sparked with interest. "What's he lying about this time?"

"He's told two separate people a lie about our divorce." My rocking increased in speed. "I'm sure there's more."

"And this makes you feel?"

"I'm pissed off." I ran my hands through my hair. "I'm not the bad guy here! I didn't screw around with three women and ask for a divorce." I stopped and concentrated on my breathing. When calmer, I leaned forward. "To be truthful, I'm frustrated with myself for allowing him to trigger anger spurts that drop me into a funk for hours."

"What'd Todd say to these people?"

"He told a bank employee that we both decided to call it quits and a waitress we've known for years that I asked for the divorce." The chair began to squeak when I resumed rocking.

"What'd you do?"

"I set them straight." I stopped rocking. The squeak was grating on my raw nerves. "This fiasco is due to his idiocy, and it goes on and on. I keep wondering, how else does he plan to screw up my reputation and my life?"

"So you're concerned about your reputation. I can see that since you're a professional and have a practice. Is that all?"

I felt my lower lip pooch out a bit. "I want Todd to man up, tell the truth about the divorce, take responsibility and tell Joyce about the affairs. Joyce not knowing about the affairs is looming like a giant grand piano hanging out of a window, waiting to crash."

Ron chuckled. "You've known this man for how long?"

"Twenty-one years."

"Do you really think that's going to happen?"

I slumped in my chair. "I guess not. I'm pretty sure Todd's lying to protect his reputation and job."

"I agree. I don't think he's trying to mess up your life, Phoenix. You're just getting caught up in his deceptions, poor choices, and cover-ups. Instead of owning his mistakes, Todd's throwing you under the proverbial bus. You have a right to be angry, but is it getting you anywhere?"

"No, I guess not." I threw my hands in the air. "That doesn't make my situation any better. I understand now why some of my divorced clients have said that it would be easier if their husbands had died, instead of divorcing them."

Ron's eyes held a concerned look. "I have to ask, are you feeling suicidal or homicidal?"

Shocked, I held his gaze. "Good Lord, no! I like myself too much for that. Yes, I'm upset with Todd, but I've never thought of hurting him."

Ron sat back in his chair, looking relieved.

"Ron, what's bothering me the most is my energy level is so low. I'm an energetic person, but right now, a sloth is moving faster than I am. Do you think vitamins will help?"

He tapped his pen on the side of his chair. "Maybe. I work with a psychiatrist who would be willing to assess you for medication."

I raised my chin. "I don't need antidepressants. I'm experiencing normal grief."

"You're a stubborn woman."

"I've been told that from time to time."

We both laughed.

"At least you haven't lost your sense of humor. I'm recommending three things, all of which you already know and haven't been doing." He cocked a brow to emphasize his point. "Walk every morning. If necessary, use a crowbar to wedge yourself out of bed. Eat less junk food. Your neurons need brain food. Go somewhere with your friends every weekend, even if you don't want to go."

Surprised, I asked, "How did you know I was eating junk food?"

"Sloths don't cook. I think you need a safe place to vent, so I want to see you again in a week."

Chapter 28: The Puzzle Comes Together

I followed Ron's prescription and started taking a multivitamin. Struggling through my depression wasn't easy, but I began to feel a bit better.

One piece at a time, the pieces of the puzzle regarding my marriage inched into place. Working with Ron helped me to understand many of the problems.

One Wednesday morning I sat in Ron's office, berating myself for not seeing Todd's betrayal. "After all, I'm a psychologist. I should have noticed that Todd was having affairs."

He looked at me over the top of his reading glasses. "Phoenix, give yourself a break. The whole situation was too close for you to see clearly at the time. It's like reading a book with the page pressed against your nose."

Ron was right. His objective viewpoint offered the distance I couldn't achieve alone.

Ron placed his glasses on the desk. "The first truth you need to accept is that you married a workaholic guy who linked his identity to his job."

I nodded. "That's pretty sad since Todd wasn't very successful."

Ron leaned forward and rested his forearms on his knees and looked me in the eye. "Todd was married to his job. You were always number two in his world."

Ouch! That's true. The fact that I closed my eyes to that reality poked my pride.

* * * *

During our next session a week later, the second truth came to light.

Ron lowered his voice, the way he did when he wanted to make a point. "Todd loved you conditionally. Everything had to go *his way*."

It was true. I'd tried to overlook it; the way married couples ignore an annoying habit. Even simple things like grocery shopping had to come under Todd's control. I'd choose a tomato and put it in the shopping cart and move on to the corn. Todd would put the tomato back and choose a different one. If I placed a can of green beans in the front of the basket, he'd move it to the rear. I was too embarrassed to share this, even with Ron.

I clutched the arms of the chair. "I'll admit that I allowed Todd to wear me down through his demands. He would pout and throw minor temper tantrums to get his way." I looked down, feeling ashamed that I'd allowed that form of manipulation. "See that pattern makes me feel like a bad parent, rather than a wife."

Ron, who was jotting a note, pushed his reading glasses down and peered over them. "I suspect that you and Joyce are alike in many ways."

* * * *

The following week, Ron peeled the rosy glasses off my face and made me face another annoying fact. I'd pulled one of Todd's hurtful tricks and put my practice before my marriage.

Ron handed me a tissue and said, "You gave Todd a dose of his favorite relationship poison. Neglect. Lucky for you, his tolerance level wasn't as high as yours, or you'd still be putting up with his manipulations."

That thought disturbed me. "I feel no regrets for the time I spent caring for my father. It was an act of love as well as duty, and requires no apology to anyone."

Ron pulled off his glasses and held them in his left hand. "I agree about your dad. Do you admit that even before your dad's illness that you went a little overboard with your practice?"

"It took so much to get my business going," I explained. "I was scared knowing that someone wasn't going to hand me a paycheck every two weeks. No paid insurance, holidays, or vacation. It was all pretty daunting."

Ron waved his hand around the room. "Believe me, I understand. Was there a time when you could have slowed down and didn't?"

"Yeah, I felt that strong pull to be successful. I guess success is *not* worth any price."

* * * *

During our last session, Ron and I discussed the final ingredient in the ruin of my marriage. The fastballs life hurled at Todd and me weren't just the large tragedies, but little things like broken appliances and car repairs. All this combined to create a pressure cooker of stress.

I shook my head. "It's amazing I survived all that in one piece."

Ron shoved his reading glasses on top of his head. "I think you're good to go. If you hit a roadblock, come back to see me."

I nodded. "Thanks for everything." I rubbed the arms of the rocker before I stood. "I'm going to miss this chair."

Ron laughed. "I thought you were going to wear it out. I've had to oil it twice!"

Chapter 29: The Other Women

Todd's lovers were the last pieces of the puzzle to fall into place. Who were they and how did they get together with Todd? I needed to know. I couldn't seem to move on with my recovery until I did.

Divorce is an interesting phenomenon. While you're married, no one wants to tell you that your husband is a lying, cheating piece of cemetery dirt. Let a divorce occur, and all the gossip surfaces.

Latishia phoned with the first report. I was charting patient notes in my office when she called. "Phoenix, are you sitting down?"

"Yep. Why?"

I heard her take a deep breath. "I've confirmed through employees here at the bank that Brandi with an 'i' was one of Todd's little playmates while he was married. Our suspicions were correct. No one would tell me before today, because they know we're friends."

I closed the chart in front of me. "I suspected that from the way they were behaving at the bank, the day we closed our joint account."

"Interesting that you mentioned that day." Latishia laughed. "Later in the week, she came traipsing into my office for girl talk. She pretended to be all concerned about you and wondered what the corpse handler had done — you know — the inside story."

My chest felt tight. "What did you tell Brandi?"

"Oh, I just revealed a few of the highlights, like Todd throwing that coffee cup at you. When she heard about the other women, she turned so white; you'd have thought Todd embalmed her. When I insinuated that he might be infected with slut cooties, she couldn't wait to get her skinny ass out of my office. The scuttlebutt is that Brandi broke it off that same day and was overheard making a doctor's appointment to get tested for STDs. Brandi forgot that banks have ears."

"Latishia, what fries me is she has known me for years and knew he was married."

Latishia snorted. "That girl has the morals of a polecat."

* * * *

The next revelation occurred a week later, at a convenience store near the funeral home. After my art lesson, I pulled in and topped off my gas tank. I'd never ventured inside before, but the receipt dispenser ran out of tape. Once inside, I had a hankering for a chocolate bar.

A young, blonde woman in her late teens stood sniffling while she restocked the candy bars. I cast a sideways glance in her direction while I pondered my options.

"I'm sorry," she said. "I can't stop crying." She swiped at her nose with the sleeve of her smock.

"Guy trouble?" I asked as I read the label on a candy bar.

She wiped her eyes with her fingers. "Oh yeah. I can really pick 'em."

I reached into my purse and handed her a fresh tissue. I knew I would hear the whole story before I left. My dad always told me I had a flashing sign on my forehead that screamed "TELL ME YOUR PROBLEMS."

"Don't be so hard on yourself. Sometimes it's hard to tell the good guys from the bad ones." I put down the Snickers and picked up a Midnight Milky Way.

"Ain't that the truth? This guy seemed so nice. He always wore a suit with these starched white shirts. I remember the day we met. He came in for a soda and was wearing this blue tie with dancing red chili peppers on it."

I stiffened as the candy bar dropped from my grasp. *I gave a tie like that to Todd for his last birthday.* My hand shook as I bent to retrieve the candy.

"We dated for six months. I thought he loved me." Tears coursed down her cheeks. "I'm so stupid to believe all his bullshit."

"What happened?" I returned the candy to its proper place and turned to look at her.

"Last night, we had finished…you know." She looked down. "I asked him when we would get engaged. He shot out of my bed and told me he had to go to work. He got dressed and sped out the door like his flaming boxer shorts were on fire."

I wanted to believe that maybe it wasn't Todd, but I'd given him those boxers on our last Valentine's Day together.

The clerk sniffled. "I haven't seen him since, and he won't return my calls."

"Sounds like you're lucky to get out before you wasted more of your time." *Like me,* I thought.

"That's not the worst part. When I took the deposit to the bank today, I found out that until recently, he was married!" She dropped her face into her hands and sobbed. "I committed adultery and didn't even know it. His wife probably hates me."

I took a step back. *Shouldn't I want to slap this girl and call her names?*

After the shock had faded, I felt deep empathy for her. Todd victimized her, just as he did me. This girl was barely out of her teens. Todd was old enough to be her father. W*hat was he thinking*?

Then I remembered what part of Todd's body was in control, and it wasn't his conscience.

I patted her shoulder. "Was his name Todd?"

The girl looked up and froze. She turned to face me, her mouth slack with shock. I could feel a hot flash begin to roar in my chest. I pulled my jacket off before I exploded.

She blew her nose and said, "H-how did you know?"

"I'm his ex-wife, and no, I don't hate you. We both got screwed." I turned on my heels and marched out the store, my body on full broil. I thought, *Two down, one to go.*

* * * *

The next Wednesday, Todd texted me while I was in my art class.

You left your dad's photo album in the bookcase. Will leave between the doors.

After my art class, I drove to my former home. My palms felt sweaty on the steering wheel as I pulled onto my street. The grass looked perfect, but the bushes needed trimming, and the flowers hovered near death. *I knew he wouldn't water the pansies.*

I strode up the walk to the porch and pulled open the glass storm door. As I bent to pick up the album, I heard a voice behind me.

"I wondered if I'd ever have a chance to talk to you again."

I jumped back, ramming my funny bone against the door handle on the way. I whirled, rubbing my elbow. It was the next-door neighbor.

"Uh..., Hi, Ruth. You startled me." I reached down, grabbed the album, and grasped it to my chest like a shield. My heart ran laps inside my chest.

This lady made the hairs on the back of my neck stand up and salute. Fanatics always do.

"I want to apologize to you," she said.

"Oh? For what?" I took a step back.

One of the reasons why Ruth made me feel uncomfortable was she only wanted to discuss politics and religion. Ultra-conservative, she belonged to a small church that handled snakes and spoke in tongues. It wasn't just the snakes; she had a crazed look in her eyes.

"I knew your husband was fornicating. While you were gone at night, he had Deloris over at your house. I saw them through the window."

I felt my jaw drop. My gaze slid over to the beige brick house across the street. Deloris lived there with her husband, who traveled a good bit with his job.

"Fornicators, they're both fornicators." Ruth's eyes blazed as she pointed at Deloris' home.

"Why didn't you tell me before?"

"Luke told me not to interfere with matters between a husband and wife, but you're not married now."

"Thanks for telling me. This will help me to achieve some closure. You need to know, as a wife, I had the right to know my husband was sinning against me. Your husband was wrong to tell you otherwise. Wouldn't you want to know?"

Ruth crossed her arms and tilted her head as if considering the validity of my words.

"What do you plan to do about *her*?" She jerked her head toward the house across the street.

"Nothing. Justice is in God's hands, not mine. Goodbye, Ruth."

I wove my way through the shrubbery and across the grass, so I wouldn't have to walk past her. I suspected that something was off in Ruth's mind and I didn't want to excite her.

On the way home, I stopped by a mattress store, bought one of those dial-a-number airbeds, and arranged for delivery the next day.

Once home, I stripped the sheets off the bed and added bleach to the washer. Tears spilling down my cheeks, I heaved the mattress out of the house, dumped it curbside, and went back for the box spring.

I called a meeting of the Divas. We met at Starbucks and crowded around a table in the corner.

"Your across-the-street neighbor! In your bed!" Latishia shivered.

"Yep, the mattress and box springs are sitting by the curb." I swallowed some of my caramel macchiato. Desperate times called for special coffee.

Kat nodded as she warmed her hands on the mug holding her chai tea. Unlike the rest of the Divas, she never drank coffee. "That's interesting. Todd was an opportunistic cheater."

Gina shook her head. "A bank teller, a convenience store clerk, and a neighbor." She leaned forward, her gaze intense. "Do they all know?"

"Brandi with an 'i' knows, because she works at my bank and I told her. She doesn't know who the other two are, yet." Latishia blew on her hot chocolate. "She broke it off with Todd that very day."

I set down my cup and reached for a napkin. "Todd broke up with the girl at the convenience store last week, the night before I met her. She asked when they would get engaged. She knows I was his wife because I told her. She didn't know he was married until after the divorce. She doesn't know anything about the other two women."

"What about the neighbor?" Gina eyed a good-looking guy that passed the table.

I pulled the scrunchy out of my hair and shook it free. "She's cheating on her husband, too. The only thing Deloris doesn't know is that she was sharing Todd with two other women."

Latishia grinned. "So her husband doesn't know, yet?"

"I guess not, but when he finds out —" I shrugged.

"The proverbial shit will hit the fan," said Kat.

Chapter 30: What Did You Do?

I was watching the movie, "The Other Woman," when the phone rang. The display showed it was Todd. Curious, I wondered if I'd left something else at his house.

"YOU BITCH, WHAT DID YOU DO?" Todd screamed.

I held the phone away from my ear. "Why are you —?"

"WHAT DID YOU TELL HIM?"

"Who?" I shot to my feet, reached for the remote and paused the movie. "What are you talking about?"

"FRANK CAME TO THE HOUSE TONIGHT WITH A GUN AND TRIED TO KILL ME! I HAVE BULLET HOLES IN MY DOOR AND INSIDE THE HOUSE."

"Stop screaming at me, or I'll hang up." I strode to the kitchen and opened the fridge. I could hear sirens over the phone.

"WHAT DID YOU TELL HIM, YOU —?"

Click. *I'm not putting up with that kind of abuse from you, turkey.*

When the information settled into my brain, my hand flew to my mouth. *If Frank came over and tried to shoot Todd, he must know that Todd and Deloris are having an affair. But how did he find out? Hire an investigator?*

Reaching for the pitcher of sweet tea, I poured some into the glass I'd left on the counter after dinner. As I pondered the situation, I remembered my words to Ruth. "You need to know, as a wife, I had the right to know my husband was sinning against me." *I bet Ruth ratted on Todd.*

I could see Ruth in my mind's eye, telling Frank that Todd and Deloris were fornicators while pointing at Todd's door.

Kat would appreciate the karma of the situation.

Chapter 31: Moving On

On April first, I opened my eyes and told myself it was time to stop being a fool and move into the world. I'll admit, the thought of stepping out of my home and into the dating scene made me want to climb into my clothes hamper and lower the lid.

I contemplated the situation and decided to take dance lessons. Dancing is in my genes, so I felt frustrated because my family couldn't afford lessons when I was younger, and Todd refused to keep his promise to learn to dance. As a child, I was the kid who bounced to the music and whirled my way around a room.

A nearby dance studio, located in an ugly brown building, offered free introductory West Coast Swing lessons. An eager student, I'd go to a lesson ready to train my body to obey me. To my complete surprise, it often didn't.

The instructor, Shane, was a middle-aged guy shaped like an apple on two Popsicle sticks. His baby face, combined with a full head of dark hair, helped to belie his age. When he could tear himself away from his laptop, he would give a dance lesson. The class was a mixture of ages and sexes, with the youngest being teenagers.

A pattern soon established itself during the Wednesday night lessons. Guys would be on one side, gals on the other, facing each other. Shane would stand in the middle and demonstrate the pattern to the men and have them practice numerous times. Next, the ladies were given their steps and allowed to practice a few times.

I asked the lady next to me, "Does Shane think we're smarter, or does he feel we're unimportant because we aren't leading?"

She shrugged.

When Shane felt satisfied that the men were ready, he would have the students choose a partner. He always picked a perky teen.

We lined up facing our partners. Mine was an acne-speckled sixteen-year-old who tugged at his oversized jeans between the patterns.

After several tries to execute the pattern, Shane would yell, "Rotate."

I walked to my right to greet my next partner. When Shane paired with young girls, he smiled, exuding attentive charm as he crooned compliments and encouragement. When paired with a lady his age, he assumed a bored expression and sighed before he barked critical directives. This negative behavior is what he did with me. "Sigh. You need to wait until I lead you to come!"

If you offered a discernible lead, I might be able to follow, I thought.

"No, no, your steps are too long."

After two attempts at the pattern with him, my face felt hot from humiliation, and I wanted to introduce his manhood to my dance shoes.

After the lesson, I joined a group of Shane's rejectees over in the corner. While removing my shoes, I discussed my frustration with the other middle-aged ladies.

"Do y'all feel like Shane treats us different than the younger girls?" I asked as I struggled with the "easy release" buckle on my left shoe.

Susan rolled her eyes. "It's not your imagination. If he was any more rude to me, I might run over him with my minivan."

A titter rolled through the group. We all glanced at Shane, who was smiling down at a teen barely past statutory rape age. I wondered if at that very moment, my cohorts were imagining him laid out in the parking lot, with tire tracks on his white golf shirt.

Ginger shook her head. "I'm not interested in him, but he could at least act professionally."

Natalee eased her shoe off and rubbed her foot. "I heard he's dating a woman in her twenties with kids. I wonder if she knows he's down here flirting with anyone under the age of twenty-five?"

Susan shoved her Capezios into a shoe bag. "Probably not. It won't last. She'll figure it out, someday. For her sake, I hope it's sooner than later. What do you think, Doc?"

Natalee stood and stretched her arms over her head. "Yeah, what's your diagnosis?"

I rose and clasped my hands in front of me. Assuming the haughty pose of a snotty academic, I cleared my throat with authority and tried not to grin. "Ladies, you're observing the behavior of an insecure male who needs the constant attention of young women to reassure him that he's still attractive and not an old fart. That's the long version."

Laughter exploded out of Ginger. Everyone across the room turned to look, then returned to their conversations.

"What's the short version?" Ginger asked, still giggling.

"He's a cad." I picked up my dance bag and turned to look at my companions. "Anyone interested in food? Dancing makes me hungry."

Everyone had a husband or kids waiting for her at home, everyone but me.

Chapter 32: My Neighborhood

Many nights, I returned home from work and practiced my footwork while cooking, cleaning, and going about other tasks in my life. If someone bugged my home during that period, the microphone would pick up many "1-2-3 and 4, 5-6-7 and 8" or "slow-slow-quick-

quick-slow" conversations. Buffy had no idea what I was doing, but she pranced around, joining in the fun. Sometimes she would lie nearby and cock her head from side to side.

Once while I was dancing around, I spied my neighbor, Mike, gawking at me through the breakfast nook windows. He shook his head and continued to mow his grass. From the expression screwed on his face, I believed he thought I was even stranger than he suspected.

I resided in a nice peaceful subdivision populated by families with well-kept lawns and frolicking children. I was the only single lady there. As a childless divorcee with a dog, I kept receiving vibes that the neighborhood women viewed me as a threat. They would smile and wave, but that was the extent of our interactions.

I tried starting conversations with several of the ladies at chance encounters near the mailbox. After a few brief words, they would excuse themselves and leave.

I baked cookies and took them to my closest neighbors. Each of the wives smiled and thanked me for the treats, but none of them invited me into their homes to share a cookie over a cup of coffee.

One Friday night, the Divas and I discussed my neighborhood on our first girl's night out in ages. We were seated in a circular booth in the bar section of a chain restaurant.

Sipping a glass of pinot noir, Kat asked, "Have your neighbors warmed up to you yet?"

I pulled a basket of popcorn closer. "I think my female neighbors see me as a sex-crazed divorcee. Maybe they think I want to lure their husbands away from them while I mow my lawn." I tossed some popcorn into my mouth and chewed.

They all tittered.

It was May. The deluges of rain combined with unseasonably warm temperatures had served to coax my grass and weeds out of hibernation.

Kat cocked her head. "Are you mowing your lawn wearing a bikini?"

I giggled at the thought. "More like baggy, grungy work clothes with a sun hat."

"You have to watch those sun hats. They drive men wild with desire." Latishia pantomimed Betty Boop for a few beats before she reached over and stuffed her mouth with some pretzels.

Gina was swirling her glass of merlot. "It can't be that bad," she said.

"In reality, the ladies should all send me thank you notes. If I start my mower, I only make two passes across the front lawn before I hear garage doors rising. My male neighbors crank up their green and yellow John Deere lawn tractors and roar out of their garages. Rhumm, rhumm."

Latishia laughed so hard; I thought she would spill her margarita. I, on the other hand, sipped mine with the utmost care.

Licking the salt from my lips, I continued. "I'm not sure if I shame them into cutting the grass, or if they feel the need to show off the superiority of their lawn equipment, compared to my hand-me-down mower."

Chuckling, Gina asked, "Isn't that your dad's old mower?"

"Yep. I just putt-putt along, while these guys zoom back and forth, creating complicated angled patterns on their lawns."

"Come to my house," said Latishia. "My next door neighbor lets his grass get knee high before he cuts it. Maybe you'll shame him into action." Disapproval clouded her face.

"I will say this, I feel safe in my neighborhood. A Huntsville police officer who works the day shift is across the street, and a Madison County sheriff's deputy who works the night shift lives in the cul-de-sac."

"That's around-the-clock coverage," said Kat, as she watched a tall, blond guy walk past.

Latishia smacked her lips. "My, he's got a *fine* ass." She leaned over for a better view.

Kat blushed and looked down, fiddling with her cocktail napkin.

Latishia pinned Kat with her gaze. "Don't tell me you weren't checking him out."

"Guilty." Kat's blush bloomed from pink to red.

We all turned to watch as the guy pulled out a stool at the bar and climbed aboard, next to an equally attractive man.

"Ride 'em, cowboy." Gina acted like she was twirling a lasso.

Latishia wiped the salt off her nose and said, "Not my type. However, that luscious hunk of man next to him is my type."

We all turned to check out her choice. By now, Kat's complexion had advanced from red to puce.

"All right, ladies. Let's reel it in, or Kat will be too embarrassed to join us again." I nudged Gina.

"Just so you know," Gina emptied her wine glass, "I would never attempt to hogtie that man on one wine." She caught the bartender's attention and motioned for another. "Two is entirely another matter."

Latishia put down her glass. "I hate to change the subject, but I need some advice. I've got to have the 'birds and the bees' conversation with Dante. These brazen little girls from school are calling him at home. Can you believe it? My baby's only twelve!" Her brow furrowed with disapproval.

"I have some excellent pamphlets that you can use." Kat pulled her phone from her purse to check a text. "I let Jack read them before we talked."

Latishia nodded and reached for the pretzels. "That's good. Maybe if he reads those, I won't have to answer as many questions."

Gina's eyes never strayed from the guy on the barstool. "Sex talks. I knew there was some reason I avoided having kids." She grabbed the card that listed the wines and fanned at a frantic rate. "Is it hot in here?" Her face bloomed pink like a carnation.

We exchanged glances. Latishia helped her out of her suit jacket while I moved so she could escape to the ladies' room.

"Damn things sneak attack out of nowhere. Why don't men have hot flashes?" Frowning, Latishia continued to sip her drink.

The two guys seated at the bar were now laughing. All our gazes turned in their direction. Gina returned and gestured for us to let her back in the booth.

Once settled, Gina held her glass up for a toast. "To the Hot Flash Divas, may we set the world on fire with our charm and sex appeal."

"And hot flashes!" I added.

"I'll drink to that," said Kat.

"If we don't self-combust first," said Gina, as she continued to fan herself. "Why don't you go talk to that guy, Phoenix?"

Surprised, I said, "You're the one who wants to hogtie him."

Gina nudged me. "Go ahead, let's see how a psychologist does it. Impress us with your Freudian roping technique."

Latishia raised her glass to me. "Go on, girl. Show us what you've got."

Kat reached across the table and put her hand on mine, shooting a glare at the others. "Give her a break. She hasn't even had a date yet."

Fueled by tequila courage, I slid my hand from Kat's. "I'll go talk to them. It's no big deal. Maybe they have some more friends."

I wiggled out of the booth and straightened my clothes. I took four steps and paused. *What am I doing*?

I looked back at the Divas.

Kat looked concerned. Gina was grinning as she pantomimed twirling a lasso. Latishia made shooing motions with her hands.

I thrust my breasts forward and walked over to the two guys. Feeling a little dizzy, I sat down on a stool next to the blond Adonis. I slid a sideways glance his way. *What now?*

I was about to introduce myself when the two gorgeous hunks we'd drooled over left their stools. They draped their arms around each other in an intimate way and strolled past the Divas.

I wanted to hide under my barstool. I glanced around to see who noticed. The bartender was busy at the other end of the bar, and the other patrons were involved in conversation.

I popped off that stool like bread from a toaster and scooted back to the booth.

Gina's brown eyes were wide with surprise. "My mistake, Phe. You won't be riding that bull."

Chapter 33: Swinging Into My New Life

During my next West Coast Swing lesson, Susan asked, "Are you going to the East Coast Swing dance this Saturday?"

"What's East Coast Swing?" I stopped practicing in front of the studio's wall-sized mirror and looked at her.

"It's easier than West Coast Swing. You should go." Her plump roundness jiggled as she wiggled her hips at the end of a Sugar-Push. "I'll go if you'll go. Mark, my ex, has the kids this weekend."

"I don't know. I don't have anything to wear. Todd was boring. His idea of entertainment was watching television."

"Yuck! Couch potato?"

"No, he was a recliner slug." I laughed.

Everyone was gathering for the lesson to begin. Shane behaved as expected, honey and molasses with the young girls and battery acid toward the rest. After receiving my dose of criticism, I thought, *That's it! There has to be another dance studio somewhere in Huntsville.*

After the lesson, Susan sat next to me while we changed shoes. Bright-eyed and excited, she said, "We should go to this dance. Have you seen James Pattern, the lead singer of the band?"

"Never heard of him."

"I'd love to lick him all over like a lollipop. If I could lure him out to my minivan, I'd teach him how to play rock and roll." She grinned as she tugged off a dance shoe.

I tried to visualize her red minivan rocking in a parking lot. That van was a child transport vehicle, full of toys, athletic equipment, and the remains of too many dinners unwrapped and consumed en route to the next lesson or sporting event.

I glanced over at Susan and shook my head. "I've seen the inside if your van, Susan. It's hard to imagine it as the scene of a love fest."

Susan stopped fiddling with the strap of her other shoe and cocked her head as if considering my statement.

"Who's putting on this dance?" I asked.

Puffing from her exertions, Susan said, "Huntsville Swing."

"I'll think about it."

"Good, I'll see you there."

Back at home, I checked out their website. A Single-Step Swing lesson was on the schedule for Saturday afternoon and a group Triple-Step Swing class before the dance that same night. The band advertised to play was James Pattern's band, out of Nashville, Tennessee.

I wanted to attend, and I didn't. I had nothing to wear for such an occasion.

The only solution was to go shopping. After all, I am a female.

* * * *

Entering a clothing store at the mall, I fine-tuned my "outstanding bargain" radar. Bing......,bing..., bing.., bing, bing, bing! A clearance rack hidden in the back came into view. The word *clearance* makes my heart leap with excitement. I do *love* a bargain. My maternal grandmother was Scottish, so thriftiness runs in my DNA.

I found a cute swirly-skirted black dress for ten dollars that was an eye-catcher. It was on clearance because the tag said it was an eight when it was a four.

I called all the Divas, but each had plans for the night. I decided to go anyway. I marshaled my courage and marched into the Knights of Columbus Hall for my first Huntsville Swing event. I've come to think of this as my "coming out" party.

I pulled open the door and looked for Susan, thinking it would be easier to walk in with someone. She was nowhere in sight.

"Late, as usual, that woman will be late for her own cremation," I mumbled.

I paid the admittance fee and stepped through the doorway into my new life. The large rectangular room had a beige linoleum floor, beige wallpaper, and a drop ceiling. The band was busy setting up in the far corner. After spotting the guy I guessed was James Pattern, I could see why Susan had wicked thoughts about rock and roll in her minivan. Hot though he was, I had made it a rule to avoid musicians — too many groupies. I also avoided lawyers and physicians as possible romantic interests.

Gina had asked me just a week earlier, "What do you have against doctors and attorneys? I find men in those professions to be both intelligent and accomplished."

"I find those professions to be all-consuming occupations, littered with workaholics who are prone to loose zippers." I'd crossed my arms and glared at her. "Since my divorce, I've added morticians to my list."

I eased into the room and looked up. A large mirror ball hung from the center of the ceiling. Just then, the lights dimmed, and the colored can lights created pools of color on the neutral floor. The mirror ball twirled, spilling moving diamonds of light over every surface of the room.

I was hooked. I had mirror ball fever. For me, it may be incurable.

I sat and continued to watch the band set up for the gig while I waited for Susan. She arrived a few minutes later, hauling a purse big enough for a weekend stay at a resort.

Susan stepped through the doorway and stopped. Her gaze riveted on the bandleader as he leaned over to plug in an amp. His ass, encased in tight jeans, acted like a tractor beam pulling her in his direction.

Susan's tongue circled her lips.

I held my breath. I was sure that any second she would lean over and bite him, leaving her mark.

Susan's hand reached out as if it had a mind of its own.

He stood and whirled around.

Whipping her hand back, she smiled.

"Hi, Susan. Glad you could make it tonight." James reached out and pumped her hand.

"Well, you know I'm your number one fan." Susan's face flushed pink.

"The guys and I appreciate the loyalty of our fans. If you'll excuse me, we need to do a sound check."

"Oh, yes, of course." She backed away grinning.

I shook my head. *This guy's a pro. She'll never play rock and roll in the back of her van with him.*

Susan plopped into the chair next to me. "Isn't he luscious?" She reached inside her giant purse and pulled out her dance shoes and a folding fan. Her encounter appeared to have triggered a hot flash.

"I thought you were going to bite his butt." I leaned back to see her reaction.

Her head jerked in my direction. "Was I that obvious?"

"You were drooling."

"He heats me up every time I lay eyes on him." She fanned herself with gusto. "I'm about to self-combust!"

The band started playing and people filled the tables. I had to admit the musicians were good.

The number of single men who asked me to dance surprised me. I'm not a club person, so I'd wondered where I could meet some nice men. I relaxed and had fun.

I danced almost every dance and decided the only way to get a break was to relieve my bloated bladder. I wasn't sure it could withstand one more whirl around the floor.

My current dance partner, Brent Powers, steered me toward my table. He was an attractive man and a good dancer. I thanked him, sped out of the room into the hallway, and ducked into the ladies' room.

Hold on, hold on. I coaxed my bladder to wait until I could peel down my pantyhose. Lately, it seemed that my bladder had a mind of its own. The minute I spotted a toilet, it wanted to release.

The door to the stall next to me opened and closed.

"What are you doing?" Susan's voice drifted from the next stall in that peculiar echo typical of bathrooms.

"What do you mean?" *Surely she doesn't expect a pee or poop report? I'm not one of her children.*

"What are you doing that's making these men salivate over you?"

"No one's salivating over me. I'm just dancing."

"They aren't asking me to dance that much!" Her tone sounded indignant.

I didn't answer at first. I was busy wrestling my pantyhose over my hips. I tried to construct a reply that wouldn't offend my new friend, but none came to mind.

In truth, Susan was thirty pounds overweight. Fat formed rolling hills on the landscape of her midsection. Her tight, clingy clothes only amplified the problem. If Latishia saw Susan, she would take her under wing and drag her to a clothing store.

I flushed, left the stall, and was slathering soap on my hands when Susan came out of her stall and tromped toward the sink.

"So what's your secret, Phoenix?"

"Fresh meat."

"What?" Susan's eyes widened as she turned to look at me.

"I'm fresh meat, someone new. It's like when a new mall opens. Everyone wants to be the first to shop there."

She frowned as she rinsed her hands under the flow of water. Snatching a towel, she dried them as she eyed me from stem to stern.

"Maybe. It doesn't hurt that you're so damned pretty and skinny. I was that skinny once, before I had three kids and menopause tackled me."

I winced. I have a hard time thinking of myself as pretty. I feel more comfortable with the designation, "cute."

"I'm sure there are guys out there that think I'm too skinny." I reached for a towel and dried my hands.

Susan guffawed. "If you find them, send them my way."

I tossed my towel in the trash. "I don't think we should define ourselves by men's opinions of our bodies since they only think with their dicks most of the time."

“Testosterone-driven fools,” said Susan, grinning. The smile melted from her face. “I’m never going to get James Pattern into the back of my van, am I?”

“Why would you want to risk getting a sexually transmitted disease from a musician? Do you think you’re the only one after him? The man’s a groupie magnet.”

She tossed her paper towel in the trash. “I hadn’t thought of that.”

“I do think you could dress to better enhance your assets.”

Susan shot me a menacing look. “What do you mean?”

“For example, that color doesn’t suit your complexion. It makes you look pale.”

Susan walked back to the mirror and examined her visage.

She raised her chin, trying to make the second one disappear. “What do you suggest?”

“I have a friend who’s fabulous with clothes and knows how to ferret out sales.”

She plopped a hand on her hip and gave me a level look. “Is she skinny?”

“Latishia is a full-figured, beautiful woman who has panache.”

She tried to smooth the material over her bulges. “I admit, I do need some help.”

“I’ve got your number. I’ll have her give you a call.”

We returned to the dance. Pleased, I watched as a gentleman led Susan to the dance floor.

During the break, John, an engineer I’d danced with earlier, pulled out a chair and sat across from me. “I wondered if perhaps you’d like to go have a dessert and coffee after the dance? There’s a restaurant close by with a great dessert menu.”

“That would be great.” *Woohoo, my first date!*

The band sprang into a loud peppy tune, foiling any further attempts to converse. I turned when a gentleman named Nathan tapped me on the shoulder and asked me to dance.

After two hours of dancing, my swollen feet didn’t want to squeeze back into my dress shoes. John showed up as I was placing my dance shoes into my shoe bag.

We strolled into the parking lot discussing whether to go in one car or two. Nathan tagged my shoulder and stopped me.

"I thought you might like to dance some more at Hoppers. They have a groovin' band playing there tonight."

"Thanks, but I've had enough dancing for one night. My feet are tired." I smiled and turned to leave.

"You can slip your shoes off under the table, and I'll give you a little foot rub. You'll be back on your feet in a flash." Nathan offered a radiant smile.

While he seemed like an interesting guy, his shaved head was a turn off for me. I like to run my hands through a man's hair, not slide them over a shaved head.

"This gentleman," I gestured toward John, "has already asked me to join him for dessert."

Nathan frowned, his brows forming a V. "Can I have your number?"

"Sure." I dug in my purse and handed him one of my business cards.

I turned to John. "I prefer that we take two vehicles. I'll meet you there."

John's mouth turned down with an expression of disapproval. His gaze flitted between Nathan and me. Shrugging, he turned and walked toward his car.

Nathan cocked a brow. "You sure you don't want to change your mind?" He took a step closer.

"If I agree to do something, I do it. If the situation was reversed, Nathan, would you want me to take off with someone else?"

I saw pink flood his face. "Well, no."

I turned and strode toward my car.

The scowl on John's face disappeared when I walked through the door of the restaurant.

I gave him a knowing smile. "You thought I wasn't coming."

"Well, errr...he was kinda pushy." John's ears glowed red, highlighted from behind by the track lighting.

After we had settled into a booth situated in a corner next to a window, we ordered desserts. Mine was key lime pie. John expounded on his lifestyle for the next ten minutes.

"Since I was single and able to save so much money, I decided to retire at age fifty-five, while I could still enjoy my life." John forked a bite of carrot cake into his mouth.

"Sounds like fun. Aren't you afraid of running out of money?"

"I own my home, my car is paid off, and I have few expenses."

Placing a bite of pie in my mouth, I closed my eyes and felt the explosion of tart sweetness. I chewed enjoying the texture difference between the crunchy graham cracker crust and the silky smooth filling. Smiling, I thought, *Oral orgasm!*

"Is it good?"

I opened my eyes to find John watching me.

"Mmm. Very. Have you traveled much?" I took a sip of decaf coffee to clear my palate.

"Not really. I try to stay on budget."

I gawked at him. Disbelief flowed over me. "I'd prefer to work longer to travel the world than retire early to sit in my house." I waited for his retort.

John didn't respond to my remark.

The rest of the conversation centered on John's discussion of Argentine Tango, a dance he learned when he lived in New York. I'd never heard of the dance, so the nuances of the discussion didn't impress me.

The waitress placed the bill in front of John.

He picked it up and frowned. "Let's see, with a tip it'll be twenty dollars and twenty-five cents. That would be about ten dollars apiece."

Aghast, I turned and scowled at him. *You invited me for dessert, and you want me to split the bill!*

John looked over at me with an expectant smile. Silence fell between us with a thud as the smile slid off his face. "Of course, I asked you out. I'll cover the bill."

"Thank you." I smiled, but I'm sure it didn't reach my eyes.

I'd given him my business card earlier and now regretted it. The damage wasn't too bad. It was my office number. My answering service would filter his call.

John walked me to my car and with amazing speed moved in to kiss me and grab what he could. Feeling miffed, I turned my head, so his sloppy smooch landed on my cheek as I blocked his attempt to grab my breast with my elbow. I stepped away and thanked him for dessert. He was lucky I didn't hurt him.

Given his frugal mindset, I didn't plan to take any chances on what he thought his just due might be for ten dollars' worth of dessert and coffee if I stayed longer. With speed comparable to a Formula One driver, I slid inside my car, locked my doors, and squealed out of the parking lot.

So much for my first date in twenty plus years. I prayed the rest would be better as I wiped my wet cheek with a tissue.

I sat at a red light checking my rearview mirror to make sure I wasn't followed. My phone lying on the seat honked. Gina texted, *Call when you get home.*

Once settled in my PJs, I called Gina to give my report.

"Good, you're home. Did you have fun?"

I laughed. "Yes, Mama Gina, I had a great time dancing. I feel like my feet are twice their normal size and ready to split open."

"I've had nights like that. Take some vitamin I."

"What's that?" I rubbed my left foot and flexed my toes.

"Ibuprofen. Meet any nice men?"

I lay down and fluffed the pillow behind my head. "I'm surprised to say, quite a few. A guy named Nathan tried to get me to meet him at another club to dance. He promised to rub my feet."

Gina laughed. "A man who can do a good foot rub is worth his weight in platinum."

"I didn't go because a retired engineer named John asked me out for dessert."

"Did you go?"

"Yeah, but he tried to stick me with half the bill."

Buffy jumped on the bed, circled a few times, and collapsed against my thigh with a sigh.

Gina scoffed. “I hope you’re dropping that uomo frugale!”

I reached to pet Buffy. “What?”

“Cheapskate.”

“He’s history. Not my type. Is dating always this weird?” I asked.

“Sometimes it’s weirder.”

Chapter 34: Ouch!

During the Saturday night swing dance, Fred Tanner told me about The Dancer’s Club. This ballroom group danced on Thursday nights at a local skate center. Fred assured me there would be a complimentary lesson before the dance.

Revved with excitement, I attended the next Thursday night event. Since it was a mid-week event, all the Divas passed. Once in the door, the very sight of what seemed like miles of hardwood floor was daunting. *What am I doing here?* I scanned the gaudy carpet and florescent skates that that lined the walls. *Yep, it’s a skate center.* I was looking for a familiar face when I glanced up, and my jaw dropped. I spotted the largest mirror ball I’d ever seen — I knew I was home.

The lesson was the waltz. Everyone who didn’t know what they were doing, like me, lined up on one end of the floor. The more experienced dancers moved to the far side of the floor.

My partner for the lesson introduced himself. “I’m Harry. I should warn you,” he said with a rueful grin, “I don’t know what I’m doing. It’s my first time here.” He was built like a potbellied stove and sported a goatee.

“Mine too. We’ll learn together,” I said.

Every time Harry led me to turn, I collided with his belly. Despite this, I picked up the basics lickety-split and was excited to dance.

Once the music started, I was pleased to see the experienced dancers were gracious about asking newcomers to dance. I felt pretty jaunty about the whole thing since I knew a little swing and basic waltz. I was ready to go, right?

Pride falls fast and hard. It was a toe-crushing, crash course in dance variety. All my male dance partners were patient and kind. They led, or sometimes dragged or pushed me, through the basics of the Waltz, Foxtrot, Mambo, Rumba, Tango, Samba, Cha Cha and of course, Swing.

Nathan Rome, who I'd met at the swing dance, swept me into his arms for a waltz. "So, how was your date for dessert?"

"The key lime pie was delicious," I said, smiling. "Ouch!"

"Sorry. We need to get together for dinner or something."

He whirled me around, scooted between two couples, and then slowed back to a basic step. I held on for dear life, expecting a collision at any moment.

"Sorry about that, traffic jam. Newcomers think a dance floor operates like the interstate, but it doesn't."

"What do you mean?" The waltz beat of *one, two, three* ran through my head.

"In dance, the fast lane is the right, outside lane and the slow lane is the inside lane." Nathan held his left hand up, the signal for me to turn, so I did.

"I didn't know that. What's the middle? Ow!"

Turn completed, he scooped me back into his arms and took off.

"A place for spot dancing or for people who are turtling their way around. That's what drives most of the experienced dancers crazy."

I shrugged. "What do you mean?"

"Sometimes older couples get in the fast lane and move like a snail, causing dangerous dance situations."

"Oh, I see."

"About dinner —"

"You have my number, call me, and we'll discuss it."

The song stopped, and Brent Powers walked up. "May I have this next dance?"

"Certainly." I remembered him from Saturday's swing dance. With thick dark hair and dancing mischievous eyes, the man had my attention.

The two men glared at each other. Nathan's features hardened as I left his arms to dance with Brent.

Brent tried to engage me in witty conversation, which led to a number of mishaps. As a psychologist, I've been trained to listen with intensity. All the guys walked forward and steered. I had to intuit what the guy planned to do, walk backward and do lots of turns.

"So, are you from this area?" asked Brent.

"Ow!"

"So sorry," he said, as he looked down at my foot.

"No, I'm from Birmingham."

"Me too, the Center Point area. Where did you go to High School?"

"Ouch!"

"Oops. Maybe we shouldn't talk. You did much better when we just danced," said Brent, giving me a lopsided grin.

"I can't dance, talk, and listen at the same time, at least not yet. There's also the fact that I'm a complete klutz. If there's a corner on a piece of furniture, my thighs will find it."

Brent chuckled as he raised his hand to signal me to turn. "I understand. When I was learning, I needed to give dancing my full attention, or I'd run a lady into a wall."

When the dance ended, Nathan strode in my direction, but an older gentleman took my hand and led me to the center of the floor. Due to my inexperience, the best I could manage was to smile and ask, "What type of dance is done to this song?"

The white-haired man replied, "Rumba."

My various partners seemed to know, by magic, which dance went with what music.

After the Rumba, I thanked my partner. In my peripheral vision, I saw Nathan and Brent on a collision course, headed in my direction.

I escaped to the ladies' room.

While waiting for a stall, I told the woman next to me, "I've tried my level best tonight to keep my feet from being pulverized to bone fragments."

She eyed me with disdain. Her dress looked to be of professional quality, and her shoes glittered on her feet. "In the dance world, if a man steps on your foot, it's *your* fault, because *you* didn't move it. If a lady follows the man's lead, her foot won't be there to squash flatter than a fritter."

An older woman left a stall and gave the snooty woman a disparaging look. "Another common phrase in ballroom dancing is, 'Women are always right,' because we start with the right foot." She rinsed her hands. "Don't worry, dear. You'll get the hang of it. Buy some closed-toe shoes to wear until you do."

Despite my swollen feet, dancing addiction had a strong hold on me. The endorphins flooded my brain, giving me a dancer's high. All those years of my repressed dance urge surfaced and ran amok.

While Nathan and Brent were dancing with other partners, I limped out the door to go home and soak my feet.

Chapter 35: Survival of the Smartest

I hadn't dated in twenty years! Now dancing brought men into my life that wanted to escort me to all these fun events. I needed some survival strategies.

I called on the Divas. We met for dinner at Vickies to discuss my "dating plan."

Once we had our food, I said, "Okay, ladies, tell me how this dating stuff works." I took a bite of the tasty Normandy Chicken and nearly swooned.

Latishia pointed her fork at me. "Only meet your dates at your office or the location of the date. You don't want the guy to know where you live."

"That's good advice." I nodded.

Kat and Gina murmured their agreement.

I buttered my yeast roll and took a bite.

"Me next," said Gina. "Don't park in dark areas and always drive in separate cars. If the date falls apart or gets weird, you can escape. Oh, and make sure you aren't being followed home afterward."

The waitress stopped by the table offering refills on our drinks, which we declined.

"I already keep an eye out to make sure I'm not followed, because some of my patients are dangerous." I picked up my knife and sliced up a few large bites of chicken.

Kat leaned closer, so she could be heard over the din of competing conversations. "Men aren't allowed access to your home until deemed safe. This requires at least three dates unless you've known him for a long time. Keep your phone handy in case you need to dial 911."

She lowered her voice more, forcing me to lean closer to her. "Don't invite a man to your home for a date, unless you're willing to sleep with him."

I stopped chewing. My gaze circled, looking at each of the Divas who nodded their agreement. I resumed chewing and swallowed.

"So you're saying if I invite a guy to dinner at my house, he expects sex?" I reached for my sweet tea and gulped some.

"Yep, and don't forget the three date rule," said Latishia, as she reached for a roll.

A group of women filed past our table. After they had passed, I leaned closer and asked, "What's the three date rule?"

"For some crazy reason, guys think it's a guaranteed bootie call on the third date," said Latishia.

I sat back in my seat. *This dating thing is much more complicated than I thought.*

Gina twirled her pasta like a pro. "Phe, face it, most men want you to put out on the first date. Heck, some want sex if they've just met you in a bar."

That sent a shiver down my spine. I might consider a dinner date with a guy, but that didn't mean I wanted to see him naked, for chrissake. I felt like I was sixteen. I wondered what happened to first, second, and third base. *Are there only home runs?*

"What if I don't want to have sex?"

Latishia sat back and eyed me. "Girl, don't you like sex?"

I glanced around. Latishia's voice tended to carry, and several people at surrounding tables were now looking at me.

I leaned over and hissed, "Yes, I like sex, but I don't want to announce it to the entire restaurant."

Latishia looked down at her plate. "My bad."

"Geez, I'm not sure I'm ready for this yet. I've been with the same guy for the last twenty years." I looked down at my body. I looked good for a middle-aged woman, and people often thought I looked ten years younger than my age. I didn't look twenty-something either.

"Maybe I should work out in a gym for two or three years before I get naked in front of a strange guy. You know, to tone up a bit."

The Divas laughed. Gina held her tea glass above her head, and our waitress appeared like magic with a refill.

Kat presented another complication. All she said was "Condoms."

"Condoms?" I parroted.

"Always carry condoms. Have both female and male condoms with you, just in case he refuses to wear one." Kat looked at me over her cup of tea. "Oh, and make sure they're latex, none of that animal skin crap."

"What's wrong with animal skin?" I asked.

She took a sip and placed the dainty cup on the saucer with a clink. "Research shows they don't offer a complete barrier like latex."

"Check. Latex condoms." I said as I reached for my glass.

"Don't forget to check the expiration date," said Kat.

"They expire?" I said, before forking glazed carrots into my mouth.

Kat nodded. "Latex doesn't last forever."

No wonder people stay miserably married until they die.

Latishia reached for another roll. "Especially when the poor thing has been imprisoned in a guy's wallet and sat on for who knows how long?"

I nodded, remembering when I had to demonstrate how to place a condom on a banana for a classroom of teenagers during a sex education class back in the dark ages. I whispered, "I haven't put a condom on a dick since college."

Latishia waved her hand, "It's like riding a bike; it'll come back to you."

Maybe I need to buy a box of condoms and a banana to practice. I enjoyed the rest of my meal and digested all the information I'd just learned.

After taking her last bite, Gina pushed away her plate. "My advice, Phe, is to remain single for the rest of your life."

Todd had certainly tinted my view of men and matrimony a sooty gray, so I was in agreement with her on that point. Yes, I wanted to go out and have fun, but that was it. At the moment, commitment phobia had saddled me and was riding me hard.

"I need to put a dating plan into action," I said.

Gina raised her water glass to signal for a refill. "I have Plan A and Plan B." The waitress nodded and changed direction.

"How do you do that?" I asked. "I have to tackle a waitress to get a refill."

Gina shrugged and scooted her glass closer to the edge of the table, as the waitress approached.

"Girl, you've got two plans?" Latishia laughed. "I can't wait to hear this." She shoved her water glass over closer to the waitress.

"Plan A: Avoid the commitment monster by dating more than one man. Exclusive dating can lead to matrimony, or at least an attempt to move into your home." Gina paused and pulled her glass back in front of her.

After the waitress left, Gina continued. "Plan B: Someday find a suitable match and do the adult version of 'going steady.' "

I knew several couples in the ballroom dance world that didn't cohabitate or desire matrimony, but they provided companionship and support for each other.

Latishia gave a woman who passed our table a quick up and down and frowned. I followed her gaze. The woman's receding form revealed hot pink panties peeping over the top of low-slung jeans.

Latishia wiped her hands on her cloth napkin. "Not me, I'm looking for Mr. Wonderful, who will be a good father to Dante."

"Latishia, you're different than Gina. You're like me. You have a child to consider." Kat pushed her glasses up the bridge of her nose. "Every man has to pass both the good husband and good father tests."

I noticed the woman with the peek-a-boo pink panties was returning. Her skin looked fried to a dark shade of tanning-bed brown. She appeared to be in her sixties, dressed as if she was twenty.

I shook my head and picked up my fork. "Kids. That's another topic. At my age, I'm not sure I want to raise someone else's, children." I jabbed a bite of chicken, stuffed it into my mouth and chewed. I was getting full, but that smattering of food on my plate called to me. My parents indoctrinated me into the "clean plate club" at an early age. Then the nuns at school guilted all the kids into eating every bite of food by telling us about the starving children in China.

Gina nodded. "Kids are an important issue. Even grown kids can be an issue. Some of the guys I dated were still paying for their kid's rehab. Even worse, they move back home with grandkids in tow."

We all stopped and looked at the older couple at the next table who were smiling at a toddler seated in a highchair.

"Some of the folks in my neighborhood are raising grandchildren because the parents lost custody." Latishia sliced her carrots in bite-sized portions with neat precision.

"Ladies, you've given me a good deal to consider, but I need a quick pit stop." I started to rise.

Kat looked up at me and pointed to my seat. "You can't leave yet. We haven't talked about where you can get free condoms."

Good grief, I can't handle another condom conversation with a cranky bladder threatening rebellion.

"Later, I've gotta go!"

Chapter 36: Plan A

I set Gina's Plan A into effect with a Friday night date with Nathan Rome.

The day of our date, I was subpoenaed to testify as an expert witness regarding a custody case. I had to leave from work to be on time. Nathan and I met at TGI Fridays, located on University Drive. Dressed in a dark suit with low heels, I looked crisp and professional.

Nathan's attire strayed more toward dressy casual. I wasn't concerned since women often out-dress men on dates. Once seated at a table by the window, I perused the menu and frowned.

Nathan cocked a brow, looking concerned. "Didn't you find anything to your liking?"

"Oh, yes. It's just that all the portions here are so large and I'm not a big eater."

"What were you considering?"

I pointed at each entree as I gave my verbal list.

"Those were the ones I was looking at, too."

I sat straighter. "Would you consider sharing a meal?"

Nathan grinned. "Excellent idea."

Our dinner conversation fleshed out Nathan as a person. He was a military brat with three siblings who'd been drug around the world by the Army. I was fascinated by his mind. Nathan was a bona fide genius. While I was in Mensa range, he had at least ten IQ points on me.

Although I found his mind to be wicked sexy, his appearance didn't trigger my sexual juices. Every time I looked at him, "Cue Ball Head" popped up in my mind. I feared it would slip past my tongue one day. *Perhaps all that high-level brain activity singed the roots of his hair. My college friend Carolyn would go crazy for Nathan. She loves shaved heads. Too bad she's overseas, or I'd hook them up.*

Don't get me wrong, I liked Nathan and found him fascinating. For me, sexual attraction is there or it isn't. Nathan and I could become great friends; except I could tell by the way he was looking at me he wanted more than friendship.

After dinner, he took me to his company and introduced me to his staff. His business partner, an attractive redhead, checked me out from stem to stern. The corners of her mouth turned down before she pasted on a smile that didn't reach her eyes. She seemed almost possessive toward Nathan. At one point, she walked over and placed her hand on his shoulder. Her body language screamed, *mine.* I wondered if she had a thing for him — maybe an unrequited love.

Afterward, we took a walk in the area near Oakwood College. There were long stretches of sidewalks, and it was a lovely afternoon — not too hot or humid.

"Are you sure you're all right walking in those heels?" Nathan glanced down at my low-heeled pumps.

"Sure. I don't buy shoes I can't walk in and be comfortable."

Nathan shrugged. "Beautiful, intelligent, and practical — every man's dream."

"Really? I find that I scare the bejeezus out of most men after I open my mouth. I noticed that your partner was giving me a critical eye."

"I should probably explain."

He paused so long I wondered what he would say.

"She's my ex-wife."

I stopped. Nathan walked several paces past me before he realized I'd stopped. A little yellow flag fluttered in my mind. About that time a swarm of gnats surrounded me.

He held out his arms, palms up. "I know it's strange. We started the business together and just kept running it together. She's remarried now."

"Who asked for the divorce?" I crossed my arms and widened my stance.

"She did." He shrugged as he shifted his weight.

"Why?" I swatted the pesky critters away from my face.

Nathan stared at the pavement. "She fell in love with another guy."

"The guy she married?" I was practically cross-eyed from the gnats swarming my head.

"Yeah." He ran his hand over his bare pate, which was gnat-free.

I took off walking at a brisk pace, trying to outrun the gnats. The pesky buggers continued to surround me, undaunted by my flailing arms.

The waving yellow flag in my mind upgraded to red. I didn't get this arrangement. I didn't even want to look at Todd at this point in my post-divorce recovery, let alone run a company with him every day. I'd sensed an undercurrent of anger below the surface of Nathan's calm, kind exterior during our dinner. This emotion could be one of the causes.

We made it back to the cars. I unlocked my door. "I need to go. These gnats are unrelenting."

Despite my waving arms, one gnat flew into my mouth. *Yuck!*

"Please, open the door for me when I get back to this point. I'm going to try to outrun these gnats."

I raced around the car waving my arms like a crazy person and slid behind my steering wheel. Slamming the door, I inhaled and sighed. Running my hands through my hair, I found a few gnats and squashed them. The swarm was whirling with frantic intensity outside my window. I wondered if they would pace my car as I drove home.

I yelled through the closed window of my car. "Thanks for dinner."

"I'll call you," he bellowed back.

I waved and ground my engine to a start. The swarm moved to observe me through the windshield. I revved my engine and rammed the gas pedal to the floor, determined to leave the pesky creatures behind.

Chapter 37: Zydeco Babe

Latishia and Kat had their sons to chauffeur about and Gina's a bit of a workaholic. It was unfair for me to expect the Divas to entertain me, so I settled into a pattern of swing and ballroom dancing. To my delight, another dance opportunity presented itself. The Zydeco Stompers, a group who sponsors local dances, had their annual July Shrimp Boil at one of the member's home. It was an open invitation event, and all dancers were welcome.

Nathan phoned before the event. "Are you going to the Shrimp Boil? If so, would you like to be my date?" Nathan, who's a supreme strategist, tried to be the first at most things.

"Thank you kindly, but I'm going alone to this event."

"Oh, okay. I guess I'll see you there." I could hear the disappointment in his voice.

"I'll save you a dance. Gotta go." I was trying to keep commitment at bay by using Gina's Plan A.

The day of the Shrimp Boil, I arrived at the small farm and parked in a field of tall grass. There were already ten vehicles there. Thinking about snakes, I eased around to the back of my car and opened the trunk to retrieve my chair and cooler. I hopped my way out of the tall grass to a path that led past a chicken house. I followed the well-trodden path and discovered a pen that housed a potbellied pig. I waved away the smell as the little round guy grunted at me. *He's just a baby.*

Still keeping an eye peeled for poisonous reptiles, I was startled when two small barking dogs charged and surrounded me.

"Hi there. Aren't you two the cutest little guys in the world," I said, using my singsong tone reserved for infants and pets. They stopped barking and eased forward. I put down the cooler, dropped to one knee and let them sniff my hand. Soon their tails wagged as I petted their wiggling furry bodies. They were adorable, despite their eclectic pedigree. They escorted me the rest of the way. I spotted a horse in an open field to my right and wondered what other animals I would encounter.

By the time I reached the house, the dogs and I were best buddies. A portable wood dance floor was in place under the trees in Natasha's backyard. Lights were strung in the trees for when it got dark. Everyone in sight brought a cooler, a chair and a dish to share. I'd brought my special potato salad. I planned to keep it on ice until the last minute.

The brochure about the event stated the Zydeco Stompers would provide the boiled shrimp, potatoes, corn, and sausage, which would be cooked on site. A huge stainless steel pot stood on a large burner behind an empty table. A guy wearing shorts and a tee shirt leaned over, inspecting its steaming contents. Cajun waltz music filled my ears as the wafting aromas of boiling shrimp and chocolate cake filled the air. I was almost drunk on the smell of the chocolate cake. It's one of my weaknesses.

I found a level spot near the dance floor and set up my lawn chair. I squinted at the arrangement. *That ought to do it.* I meandered over to the second table that already held some side items. I eyed the fresh veggies with ranch dip and a variety of chips and dips.

A redhead splattered with freckles stood behind the table. "Hi, I'm Jillian. What do you have?"

"Potato salad. It needs to stay on ice until the last minute."

"Place it right here…"

"Phoenix," I said, smiling.

"I'll take good care of it, Phoenix." She reached over, took my cooler and placed it on top of another cooler behind the table.

Thanking Jillian, I wandered past to the next table, which held desserts. Only a pecan pie and a chocolate cake were present so far — two of my favorites. I leaned over and inhaled the aroma of the homemade chocolate icing. I could even smell the vanilla in the cake. I nearly swooned on the spot. I thought *if chocoholic Gina were here, it'd be hard to hold her back.*

I'd tried to get the Divas to come, but they all had family events. I returned to my chair and plopped down, feeling the plastic webbing tear a tad. *One more thing to add to my repair list,* I thought.

This was my first Cajun/Zydeco dance. I'm willing to try most things, and God blessed me with the ability to learn. The floor was down, and the music was blasting a peppy Zydeco tune about someone stealing a chicken. It would be thirty minutes before the food was served, and no one was dancing. A few people trickled in, but the music was going to waste.

Then it happened, Brent Powers asked me to dance. He stopped in front of my chair and flashed a smile.

"Would you like to dance, so we can get things started?"

In my seated position my eyes naturally started with his muscled legs and worked up his body. Lingering on the bulge in his pants, my gaze slid over his flat belly, up his blue tee shirt, all the way to his merry green eyes. *My, my.*

"Sure."

He bent down, offered me his hand and levered me out of my rickety lawn chair. I noticed his nails were clean.

As we threaded our way between chairs to the dance floor, I confessed, "I don't know what I'm doing here, you'll have to teach me."

Brent's mouth formed a perfect O. He stopped, took my hand, and squeezed it. "I'll show you what to do. It's easy."

We were alone on the floor, all eyes on us. Brent demonstrated the basic step, which I mimicked. I picked Zydeco up within minutes, and we danced up a storm. Cliché I know, but we can say that in Alabama because we live in Tornado Alley.

"Come and get it," echoed across the yard as the sound waves punched their way through the humid air.

It was a long time since I'd seen this much food in one place. A table was covered with shrimp, potatoes, corn, and sausage that was poured onto clean paper and covered with netting. The aroma was intoxicating. The electric fans forced the competing scents to bombard us with alternating hints of sweet and spicy. I could feel the salivation glands in my mouth crank into overdrive. I feared I would foam at the mouth like Pavlov's dogs from sheer anticipation.

People lined up and mounded their plates high with food. I made my way with deliberation down the first table, scooping a tad of this and a dash of that onto my plate. By the time I finished, there was little space left. I carried my plate to the second table that held the salads and side items, a colorful display of hot and cold delicacies. While I dipped into bowls on the second table, my thoughts focused on the third table that held all the desserts. Just the sight of that table could strike a diabetic into a coma.

Balancing my plate, I shot over to the dessert table and nabbed a slice of the homemade chocolate cake, whose decadent aroma had tortured me for the last hour.

I returned to my chair and set my plate on it. After I had covered it with a napkin, I stood in line at the drink table to claim a sweating plastic glass of iced lemonade. When I returned, Brent had pulled his chair over to sit next to me.

"It seems every time I try to ask you for a dance at ballroom events; someone whisks you away." He balanced his plate on his knees while placing his drink on top of the cooler between us.

"Everyone has been kind about teaching me new steps."

"You seem to be a natural and a quick learner."

"Thanks." My priority was to taste my potato salad, to make sure it was still cold. I spooned some into my mouth and chewed. It was perfect. I was happy with the outcome.

"So, what are you?" Bent began peeling a plump shrimp.

I looked over at him and grinned. "An alien female from the plant Eutopia located in the fifth-star system."

The shrimp paused inches from his mouth. He turned to look at me and chuckled. I was doing my best to not burst into laughter, but it was costing me.

"Funny, I meant what do you do for a living?"

"A psychologist." I popped some corn pudding in my mouth. While I chewed, I grabbed a shrimp, examined it, and started undressing it.

"Hmmm, good to know you're not an alien astronaut, long distance relationships can be a pain," said Brent.

This time I laughed. I covered my mouth to assure that I didn't spew corn pudding. I was surprised Brent didn't ask if I was analyzing him, most people did.

I glanced his way. "What occupation keeps you fed, besides showing up at events where they feed you?" I gulped lemonade to wash down the corn pudding.

"I'm working on my master's degree in software engineering. I'm also an assistant at the University."

"What was your undergrad degree in?" I grabbed my napkin and wiped my hands, which now smelled like shrimp.

"Physics and I went back to acquire an additional degree in electrical engineering."

The man was attractive, had brains, and hair. I felt a definite stirring in the Heart of Dixie.

"You have any kids?" I asked.

"Nope, never married."

My fork paused. *Interesting.*

"You?" He glanced at me, and then shifted his gaze to my chocolate cake with more than casual interest.

I shifted my dessert plate more to my side of the cooler to increase the distance between him and my dessert. "I've been divorced three months and was married twenty years."

"That's a long time. My parents just celebrated their fiftieth anniversary."

"That's great." I was impressed. "My parents had a long-term marriage, too. I wouldn't call it happy."

"What happened, I mean to your marriage?" Brent sat back, extended his long legs and crossed them at the ankles.

I shrugged and contemplated how much to reveal. "Several things. Todd, my ex, turned forty."

"Uh, oh."

"I neglected our marriage for a year because I was caring for my dying father while I tried to keep my practice open."

"Sounds like it was a tough year." Brent nodded for me to continue.

I looked down at my plate and fiddled with some baked beans with my plastic fork. "Then I discovered Todd had affairs with three different women." My gut knotted at the memory.

"Doesn't sound like he was worthy of you if he couldn't keep his pants zipped while you were taking care of your dad. Did you divorce him?"

"Nope, he told me he wanted a divorce on Christmas morning. I didn't find out about the affairs until after he asked for the divorce."

Brent stared at me and shook his head. "Did he lose his damn mind?"

I swatted at a fly buzzing near my cake. "Everybody keeps asking me that."

It was time. I placed the cake with reverence on my lap. Making sure I achieved the perfect balance of cake to frosting ratio, I took a bite, closed my eyes, and chewed.

It was moist. It was chocolaty. It was a slice of heaven.

After we had tossed our empty plates in the trash, Brent took me in his arms for a waltz. An assortment of large industrial and smaller box fans surrounded the dance floor. Alternating gentle breezes and hurricane force winds buffeted us as we circled the floor.

I spotted Nathan as he arrived, toting a lawn chair. Taking a breather, I sprawled in my lawn chair, bloated and content. Nathan rushed over and placed his chair on the other side of mine. "Hi, I'll be back after I get some food."

"Don't forget to try my potato salad."

Brent sat down next to me. "Are you on a date?"

"Nope."

"Good, let's dance."

This outdoor event occurred at the end of July. It was a tad warm, which was a diplomatic understatement.

I told Brent, "My dad would say, 'It's hotter than blue blazes,' today."

Brent nodded. "He'd be right."

"My mom always told me that in the genteel South, we don't sweat."

He laughed. "So what are we doing right now?"

"Horses sweat, gentlemen perspire, and ladies glow or glisten." I was beyond glowing and glistening. I sparkled like July 4th fireworks. A hot flash only served to escalate my discomfort. I stood, arms akimbo, in front of a five-foot industrial fan. I closed my eyes so my contacts wouldn't blow out and smiled as the gale blew me dry.

Since I knew I was going to be overheating like a jalopy short on coolant, I wore a short skirt with built in shorts, a cute Tee shirt and flashing tennis shoes. I have small feet, so I can wear children's shoes. Hence, I'm one of few adults who own tennis shoes that flash with every step. I'm also one of few adults *willing* to wear them.

Brent, Nathan and other members of the group asked me to dance and showed me new steps. I was well fed, sassy, and basking in the attention of Southern gentlemen. Things were going well until testosterone started flying like bottle rockets.

Nathan and Brent seemed to be in a glaring contest. Every time one of them escorted me to the dance floor, dirty looks were arrowed back and forth.

Dusk crept across the sky, and the temperature inched down the thermometer as the D.J. called for a line dance. I knew the dance from my college days, so I extracted myself from my wobbly chair to join the dancers on the floor. Both men parked themselves on the sidelines and watched me. Perhaps I bedazzled them into a hypnotic state with my flashing shoes. Nathan parried a few dirty looks with Brent before he joined the dancers.

After the line dance, Brent asked me to dance again. While we were on the dance floor, he asked, "Would you like to go out sometime?"

I answered, "Sure, that would be fun."

He whipped a piece of paper and a small pen from his pocket and wrote down my number.

Chapter 38: Crisis

I shot awake at one o'clock on a Saturday morning to the William Tell Overture blasting from my cell phone. In the dark, I ran toward the drop down desk where my phone was charging and fell over Buffy.

Yip!

"Ooomph!" Rubbing my right knee, I limped to the phone charger. The display showed the call was from Gina.

"Gina?"

I heard sobbing.

"Gina, are you hurt?" My heart ran laps inside my chest cavity. "Gina, can you talk?"

"He-he tried to —" She broke into uncontrollable sobs again.

"Do I need to call the paramedics?"

"No."

"Is he still there?" *Oh my God, what happened?*

"No." More sobs.

"Are you at home?"

"Y-yes."

"I'm on my way."

I texted Kat and Latisha: *Someone hurt Gina. Meet me at her house.*

I sprinted into my walk-in closet and threw on the clothes I'd set out earlier. I ran out the door, locked it, and froze. I rushed back inside, gave Buffy food and fresh water, and slid the panel out of the dog door. I wasn't sure when I'd return.

Once in the car, I revved the engine on my Prius and drove like I was competing in NASCAR. I screeched to a stop in the driveway of

Gina's townhome. When I reached the porch, I began ringing the doorbell like I was manic on energy drinks.

Gina opened the door, puffy-eyed and dripping snot and blood from her nose. She was shaking as if she had a fever. Her right eye was swelling shut and her blouse, half torn, hung from her torso.

"Oh, Gina! Who did this?" I wrapped her in my arms. Pushing her wayward curls from her face, I walked her to the sofa and eased her down.

"I'll be right back." I found an afghan on the foot of her bed and snatched it along with a box of tissues. I wrapped her up and had just handed her the tissues when the doorbell rang.

Kat stood at the door. Her brown eyes, hard as marbles, stood out in her pale face.

"Where is she? What happened?"

"I'm not sure yet, I just got here."

I sat next to Gina and put my arm around her. She was rocking, not a good sign. Kat knelt in front of her and began examining her.

"You did the right thing to keep her warm. She's in shock." Kat rose, rushed into the bathroom, and returned with two washcloths before disappearing into the kitchen. Gina was crying so hard; she couldn't form complete sentences.

"He-he…tried…to — to rape…me." She wailed. I held her tight and rubbed circles on her back.

Kat returned and wiped Gina's face clean. Then she placed a baggie full of ice wrapped in a cloth on her eye. "Hold that on your eye, Gina."

Gina nodded and held the makeshift ice pack in place.

Kat took off to the kitchen again and returned with a glass of water.

The doorbell chimed.

"That's Latishia," I told Gina.

Kat looked at her watch. "She made good time."

Kat opened the door and stepped aside. I looked up and saw thunderclouds form on Latishia's face.

"What in sweet Jesus happened here?" Latishia tromped to Gina's side with a force that vibrated the floor. She plopped on the couch and encircled her like a taco.

By now, Gina had gained some measure of control. She handed me her makeshift ice pack and proceeded to blot her tears and blow her nose.

Kat felt along Gina's nose, causing her to wince. "Your nose isn't broken, but that eye is going to be a doozy."

Latishia patted Gina's thigh. "You tell the Divas what happened, and we'll take care of that asshole." She looked ready to pound on someone.

Kat looked like a teakettle ready to boil over. Her son Jack was the outcome of a gang rape during a fraternity party. I knew this was hitting close to home.

I was pretty pissed myself. You mess with one Diva; you messed with us all.

"I had a d-date tonight with M-Mark Bird, a divorce attorney in M-Morgan County. We've known each other professionally for-for years."

She paused to catch her breath. Her voice sounded nasal and congested.

"He took me to dinner and brought me home." She looked at me, tears filling her eyes. "He's always been such a gentleman in my dealings with him at the courthouse."

Gina started to sob again. We waited, giving her time to regain control. She blew her nose. Reaching for another tissue, she dabbed at her eyes, flinching when wiping the swollen one. Taking a few deep breaths in through her mouth, she accepted the water from Kat and drank half of it. Kat took the glass, placed it on the table, and handed her the makeshift icepack.

"When I opened the door, he pushed me inside and had his hands all over me, like-like he thought we were going to have some passionate clothes-ripping sex." She placed the ice on her swollen eye and shuddered.

"I'll rip that asshole's clothes off him and shove them up his ass," growled Latishia.

"Keep the ice on your eye," said Kat, patting her knee.

"I pushed him off me and told him to stop. That's when he ripped my shirt. I tried to run, but he grabbed my arm, whirled me around and started pawing my breasts. I managed to slap him and pushed him away. That's when he punched me."

Kat, Latishia, and I exchanged looks. Anger rolled in my gut, seeking release.

"How did you get him out of here?" I handed her the glass, and she took another sip.

"When he punched me, he knocked me into the wall. When he saw the blood, I think it scared him, so he turned and ran."

Kat stood and felt the back of Gina's head.

"Does that hurt anywhere?"

"No, I didn't hit the wall very hard, I lost my footing and slid down it."

"Does she need to go to the ER?" I asked Kat.

"No, I think she's fine, at least physically, but I'm taking pictures." She pulled her phone from her pocket and snapped photos of Gina's face from several angles. Then she backed away taking pictures of her torn clothes.

"Are you ready to make a police report? Can we can call the police now?" asked Latishia.

Gina looked down, twisting the tissue in her hands.

"What?" Latishia leaned away and examined Gina's face.

Gina looked at each of us with a pleading expression. "The legal profession is still a 'good ole boys club.' If I press charges, it would only be a misdemeanor assault. He'd get a slap on the wrist, and I'd be the bitch that got a fellow attorney in trouble. It would hurt my career."

"What about the attempted rape?" I asked.

"It's still a misdemeanor." She looked down at her trembling hands.

Latishia's face darkened. "So he gets away with this!"

"Lower your voice. You're upsetting her." Kat paced back and forth in front of us. "Not necessarily."

I leaned forward and tracked her pacing. "What do you mean?"

"Well, there's legal justice, and there's Diva justice." Kat gave us a malicious grin.

Chapter 39: Diva Justice

I wouldn't want to be Mark Bird. Gina's mama saw her black eye and told her brothers. Sicilians can be loyal friends or dire enemies. The Bongiorno brothers were on the lookout for Bird to deliver a little Sicilian justice.

We, on the other hand, were out to deliver Diva justice.

We'd been taking turns following Bird to determine his after-hours habits. Bird liked to drive to Huntsville on Saturday nights to visit the Pink Lady Gentleman's Club on the north side of town.

It had been over a month since the attack on Gina. Bird maintained his habit of parking his baby, a 2013 red, Jaguar, F-Type convertible behind the club. We suspected that he used this dark area that was out of sight, to protect his reputation.

I'd smeared mud over my license plate before we left the house. After we parked at the back of the club, I glanced at Latishia, before I looked over my shoulder at Gina and Kat in the back seat. "Put your ski masks on to hide your faces and hair." I shoved my ponytail inside the back of my cap.

"Mama always told me, if you want to wallop a man hard, go for his car or his wallet," said Latishia, grinning.

"Ladies, we're going for both." Gina handed each of us a commercial-sized bottle of cooking oil. Her black eye was gone. She'd taken a week off, declaring she had the flu to hide the evidence of her attack.

Gina did the sign of the cross. “I’ll have to go to confession tomorrow, so that I can receive communion.”

“Maybe I need to convert,” said Latishia. “This confession you talk about so much sounds like a get-out-of-Hell-free intervention.”

“It’s a bit more complicated than that,” I told Latishia.

Kat unscrewed the top on her bottle. “Let me get this straight. First we pour the oil over the car.”

“Yep, cover every inch that you can, especially the windows and that nice vinyl top,” directed Gina.

“Everybody, make sure you don’t touch anything and put all the bottles and tops back in the bag. Leave no evidence. And don’t get that oil in my car,” I said.

I disabled the interior lights so they wouldn’t come on when we opened the doors.

Dressed in black, we stole out of my car into the dark like Diva Ninjas. We poured oil across every window, soaked the convertible top, covered the hood and trunk, and even saved some for the door handles and tires. The car was a slimy, dripping mess.

“Phase two,” whispered Gina.

We opened the bags of birdseed and covered the car. If it were daylight, the birds would flock to this car for breakfast.

We gathered all the evidence, shoved it in the grocery bags and took it with us as we drove away. Giggling, we pulled off our ski masks. We saw no witnesses.

“I wonder how long it will take him to get the oil off of his windshield wipers?” Kat asked, from the backseat.

“A long time. I soaked that area. I wish I could see Bird’s reaction when he comes out of that club.” Gina turned around and high-fived Kat and Latishia in the back.

“We can’t do that. That’s how you get caught. We also can’t talk about this, even to our families. That’s how word gets out. This is a ‘to the death’ Diva secret.” I looked in the rearview mirror. “Not even your mama, Latishia.”

“Why can Gina tell her priest, but I can’t tell my mama?”

"Your mother isn't sworn to secrecy by the church," said Gina. "I'm not telling my mom either."

"Okay." The protruding lower lip I spotted in the rearview mirror indicated Latishia wasn't happy about it, but I knew she wouldn't tell.

"We let him off easy, we didn't cut his vinyl top or puncture his tires," said Kat.

"You're right, and his male genitalia is still intact." I agreed. "He'll have to tow that Jag. There's no way he can see to drive back to Decatur."

"I'm satisfied. I think Mark Bird will suffer enough." Gina crossed her arms and grinned. "Besides, my brothers haven't taken care of him yet."

"Your brothers aren't going to give him cement shoes and drop him in the Tennessee River, are they?" asked Latishia.

Latishia's eyes looked round when I glanced in the rearview mirror.

"Naw, they're not the Mafia. They may give him a black eye, or two,...or maybe break his nose. Nothing too serious."

"I didn't hear any of that," said Latishia, shaking her head, hands over her ears, her braids flying.

We were silent for a few miles, each deep in our thoughts.

"The birdseed was a nice touch." I giggled, which sparked laughter that waned and flamed, again and again.

Chapter 40: Ken

Once I began to have fun, my life shifted into overdrive while I attempted to outrun my injured ego. My red "married" light turned green, and to my delight, eligible men wanted to feed me, take me sailing, dance with me and hold hands during movies. They also wanted to Salsa their way into my undies, but I wasn't ready for that yet. Gina's near-rape experience spooked me.

I ventured out every night to dance, go to a movie, or even sit in a coffee shop. Anything to outrun loneliness.

I've had many patients over the years complain of loneliness. I assumed they were just bored. I have a much deeper understanding of their plight now.

Once home, I crawled tired into bed hoping for six hours of sleep. In truth, I exhausted myself every night to remove the sting of an empty bed. A king-sized bed stood ready for me to claim; yet, I still slept on one side, while the ghost of my marriage claimed the other.

My current interest was Huntsville's free concerts in the park on Monday evenings. One of my clients mentioned them, so I researched them online. Determined to go, I contacted the Divas.

"Dante has ball practice. I would love to go, but ball season will go for awhile," said Latishia.

Kat was out of town for training, according to her mom. She'd mentioned the training last week, but it slid out of my memory bank. Menopause fog was creeping around my neurons and synapses. That left Gina.

"Come on, Gina, you know you want to go. There are two good bands." I wedged my phone between my shoulder and ear while I glanced in my purse to make sure I had my sunglasses. "You can work later."

I packed my lawn chair in my trunk and scooted back into the house to grab a bottle of water from the fridge.

Gina grumbled to herself in Italian. "Okay, but you better bring me a bottle of water. I'm not going to wilt in this humidity without some cold water."

"Deal! Don't forget to bring a chair." Gina disconnected the call, so I retraced my steps to the fridge and nabbed several more bottles of water and shoved them into the ice of a small cooler.

Once at the downtown park, I was stupefied by the diversity and sheer size of the gathering. Holding my chair in one hand and the small cooler in the other, I scanned the multitudes wondering how I would locate Gina when she tapped me on the shoulder.

"Glad I found you before you ventured into that swarm of people."

"Can you believe this crowd?" A lady walked past me with a black and white Great Dane. "Whoa!" I stepped to the side.

"She could saddle and ride him," said Gina, fanning her face with a hand fan that advertised a local mayoral candidate.

We both watched the dog walk away. His large, dangling testicles swayed with each step.

"Wow, that dog could be a porn star." Gina fanned harder.

"Gina!" I looked at her with my mouth agape. "What would your mother say?"

"Don't tell me you didn't think that dog had the biggest set of—"

"Shhh!" I felt my internal heater kick into overdrive. "Give me that fan. You shocked me into a hot flash."

Gina laughed while I waved the fan like my life depended on it.

We found a spot under the shade of a tree in front of a sidewalk. The stage was at the rear of the Museum of Art, which backed up to the park. I wasn't clear if the bands or the parade of people with dogs were more entertaining. There were big dogs, tiny dogs, fat dogs and just as much variety in their owners.

The highlight occurred when a white foo-foo standard Poodle came snout to snout with the Great Dane. Tales wagged. They circled, entangling their masters with the leashes. Bootie sniffing commenced, and the brute mounted the poodle. The owners yelled and yanked on the leashes. A titter spread from group to group like a virus. The Great Dane continued to thrust long after he was pulled off his uptown girl. The size of his equipment put Todd to shame.

"I told you he could be a porn star," whispered Gina.

I jabbed Gina with my elbow, and we both giggled.

"I was thinking about bringing Buffy, but I'm not sure now. Some giant dog might assault her."

Gina became quiet. A pensive look settled on her face.

"I'm sorry. I wasn't thinking. You all right?"

"Yeah, you just never know with people, Phe."

Five minutes later a guy walked up, pointed at the space next to me and asked," Is this spot taken?"

"No, it's available." I looked up and smiled.

My eyes went straight to his thick, sandy blond hair while he set up his chair and settled in. *I wonder how it would feel to run my hands through it.*

"I'm Kent Lands." He held out his hand.

"Phoenix." I shook it. He held it a little longer than necessary. I fought the urge to squirm in my chair.

"I'm Gina." She leaned over to offer a smile.

"Did I miss much?" He opened a cooler and extracted a Red Bull.

Gina and I looked at each other and burst out laughing.

A grungy guy seated to Kent's right looked over. "Yeah man, you missed a Great Dane with balls the size of Texas that mounted a Poodle. It was a sight. I wish I had a dick that long."

My hand flew to my face. I covered my eyes and looked down, shaking my head. My cheeks felt like they were on slow roast.

"I meant the band. Did I miss much of the music?"

Gina leaned past me and yanked down my hand. "You missed the first band. The second one is due to start in five minutes."

"Thanks." He looked at me and appeared amused by my embarrassment. "Warn me if you see that dog coming this way. I don't need the competition."

That brought laughs from everyone around us.

The band was good, and I boogied in my seat. Several couples danced on the sidewalk, but Kent seemed content to sit and listen.

After the second band had finished, we packed our chairs to leave.

Kent asked, "Would you ladies like to go to a nearby restaurant and join me for a bite to eat?"

His gaze focused on me. Swarms of people were leaving, toting chairs, coolers on wheels, and pulling little red wagons. Geese and ducks waddled toward the safety of the lake.

"Not me, I have work to do. I've played hooky long enough," said Gina, giving me a slight push toward Kent.

He named a restaurant that was a few miles away.

"That sounds good to me. I'll meet you there after I walk Gina to her car. We have a few things to discuss." I grabbed my chair and cooler and walked beside Gina. The exiting mass of humanity soon swallowed us.

Gina's red Miata was a few spaces away from my blue Prius.

"Be safe, park near the door of the restaurant. Don't go anywhere else with him. You don't know this guy. Oh, and call me when you get home," said Gina, as she piled her chair into the trunk and slammed it shut.

"Yes, Mom." I grinned, but I saw the worry on her face.

We hugged goodbye.

* * * *

Kent leaned near the door of Walton's, waiting for my arrival. When he spotted me weaving between parked cars, he stood straight and smiled.

"You came. I thought your friend would talk you out of coming."

"No, she wanted to remind me of all the precautions I should take, just in case you're a serial killer." I winked and pulled open the door. Kent scrambled to hold it open for me.

"Do I look like a serial killer?" His azure eyes widened.

"What does a serial killer look like?" I flashed him a grin before I turned and held up two fingers to the hostess. She gathered menus in her arms and motioned for us to follow her.

"I guess that's a good point," said Kent, as he trailed behind me.

We settled in a booth. Kent steepled his fingers and looked at me in a way that made me feel X-rayed. I probably was examining him in a similar manner.

"What would you like to drink?" The waiter startled us. He had a familiar lilt to his voice.

"Jamaican?" I asked.

"Ya mon, that's my home." He grinned, exposing bright, white teeth.

"Sweet tea, for me," I said.

"Me too," echoed Kent.

"My name is Antoine. If you need anything, just yell." He disappeared like smoke.

"Have you been to Jamaica?" Kent unrolled the napkin swaddling his eating utensils and placed it in his lap.

"Went there on my honeymoon." I glanced around the inside of Walton's. The building was formerly occupied by a Ruby Tuesday's.

He cocked a brow. "Divorced?"

"Yep. You?"

"Married once. One kid. A son. No baggage, end of story."

The look on his face and clamped lips would serve to convince many that this was all he intended to say on the subject. I was curious and a miner of the deepest and darkest of secrets.

I tilted my head, "How long were you married?"

"Ten years. You?"

"Twenty. How long have you been divorced?" I clasped my hands in my lap to control my nervous tremble.

He placed his forearms on the table and leaned forward. "Four years. What about you?"

"Only six months."

"You'll get used to it. It takes time to adjust."

"That's what I tell my patients." I tucked my hair behind my ear and glanced around the place. The booths and the tables and chairs were the same, but everything else had changed, including the paint color.

"Are you a shrink?" He leaned back and hid his hands in his lap.

I tilted my head, aware of his retreat. "Psychologist. How do you earn a living?"

"Computer programmer. I'm a private consultant." He listed the programs on his fingers. "I write in C #, C++, Java, and a few other programming languages."

As a total computer spaz, I had no idea what any of that meant. I smiled and nodded. We settled down to peruse the menu.

Antoine appeared like magic and placed our tea in front of us. He took our orders and seemed to evaporate on the spot. I blinked and wondered if this guy was a supernatural. Shaking my head, I chided myself for my choice of reading material.

"I'm curious, what happened to your marriage?" I keep forgetting that I don't have a right to ask people personal questions outside of therapy sessions. For some inexplicable reason, people give me answers.

He fingered his fork. "We just grew apart and decided to call it quits."

I wondered if that was the truth since that is what Todd told Brandi. I noticed that his eyes remained glued to the fork he stroked. Not a sure-fire sign that he lied, but my gut told me his ex might be able to supplement the facts of his tale. I decided to push things a bit.

"My ex-husband turned forty, had a midlife crisis, and while I was dealing with my dying father, had an affair with three women, one young enough to be his daughter. After my dad's death, he announced on Christmas day that he wanted a divorce." I admit I spilled the information like battery acid.

Kent looked up as he shifted back in his seat. "That was harsh!"

"What I said or what he did?"

"Asking for a divorce on Christmas. What kind of asshole does something like that to another person?"

What kind of asshole indeed? Kent was beginning to grow on me.

Antoine continued his eerie act. He served our meals. Mine was trout. Kent's was fried chicken. Safe topics of conversation made sneak appearances between bites of dinner.

After our meal was complete and the dessert devoured, Kent asked me to a movie on Friday night.

I accepted. "Here's my card. Let's both check to see what's listed. Call me, and we can discuss our top three choices."

Kent took the card and nodded.

Antoine placed the bill on the table in a black leather folder. I held my breath, remembering frugal John. This bill-paying ceremony was turning into one of my dating tests.

Without hesitation, Kent grabbed the bill, frowned at it, pulled some bills from his wallet and placed them in the folder.

Handing it to Antoine, he said, "Keep the change."

"Thanks, mon."

I blinked, and Antoine seemed to vaporize from sight.

"Is it me, or is that guy a little spooky?" asked Kent, his gaze focused on the empty spot where our waiter once stood.

"He's certainly a mystery. Every time I blink he disappears." I flung my hands in the air. "Poof!"

I tapped *Movie with Kent Lands* onto my calendar for Friday night and saved it. Saturday night I had a date with Nathan. We planned to attend a local dance. This reminded me to declare my commitment phobic status.

"Before we progress, you need to understand, I'm not interested in a relationship and have no plans to date anyone exclusively at this time. If you have a problem with this, we'll cancel Friday night."

His mouth fell open, but he closed it promptly. "That's fine. You're newly divorced and a little gun-shy. I understand. I'll walk you to your car."

Kent leaned on my car, his hand planted on the roof. The look in his eyes and the tilt of his lips alerted me that he planned to kiss me. I don't know what came over me. I reached over and gave him a butt-out, minimal body contact hug around the neck, and opened my door.

"See you Friday." I slid inside, locked the door, and drove off.

I felt high on pheromones when I eased to a stop at a red light. Fidgeting with impatience, I glanced to the right. There was the local steak house where my father dined every Friday evening. I ate there with him so many times.

"I want that steak well done. Now, you tell the cook, when he smells it, it's cooking, when it's burnt, it's done."

He ordered the same thing, the same way, every time.

Tears dripped down my cheeks. A beep, beep behind me shifted me to the moment. I glanced at the rearview mirror that framed the red V.W. Bug with the squeaky horn. I pressed the gas, determined to move forward.

Chapter 41: New Furniture Warming Party

It was Thursday, and all the Divas planned to gather at my house after work for an all-night party, to celebrate the final unpacking and delivery of the last of my new furniture. In reality, it was an excuse to hang out and escape the mundane.

The delivery and assembly of the new guest bedroom set and the daybed for my office was complete. My friends told me not to purchase any bed linen items because they would be bringing gifts.

We all agreed to take a day of vacation on Friday, so we could move like snails and ooze into the next day. Latishia's son, Dante, stayed the night with his grandmother, who would drive him to school the next day. Kat lived with four generations in one household, so Jack was in good hands. Gina cleaned the litter box and put out extra cat food and water for her two four-legged kids.

Chili bubbled in the crockpot, infusing the air with its spicy scent. All of us Divas are addicted to spicy foods. Tiny corn muffins laced with jalapenos baked in the oven. Plastic-covered bowls of shredded cheddar cheese, Fritos, and crackers occupied the center of the dining table. Salsa and other dips sat at the ready. One kitchen counter contained glasses, a blender, margarita mix, tequila, a bottle of each lady's favorite wine, and of course, a large chilled pitcher of sweet tea.

For dessert, I had three different ice creams, along with all the fixings for sundaes and a sample pack of cheesecake slices. All diets were on suspension for forty-eight hours.

Buffy knew something exciting was about to happen. She raced about and pranced at my feet, as I rushed to get everything ready.

Kat was the first to arrive. This wasn't a surprise. Like me, she's always early.

Buffy bounced with delight. Kat dropped to one knee and crooned as she scratched behind her ears.

"It smells wonderful in here. I could almost eat the air. Where do you want my bag?" Kat asked, looking around. She was the only Diva who hadn't been to my new house yet. Her grandmother's recent bout with the flu and a week of training had kept her busy. Since her Nai Nai had made a full recovery, Kat could relax and enjoy the evening.

"Follow me. I thought I'd put you in here." I gestured toward the white wrought iron daybed. Kat was tiny and would fit best on the bed. "You also have access to the computer in here."

"The design is great." She walked over and ran her hands over the day bed's smooth surface. "I love it."

"Latishia will sleep in here." I motioned her into the room next door. "This is the bathroom you'll share with her. And Gina and I will sleep in my room."

Kat smiled as her eyes traveled up. "So this is the famous 'blue skies' ceiling."

I gave her a quick tour of the rest of the house. She excused herself and returned to her car for the rest of her things.

Latishia followed Kat in the door, pulling a wheeled overnighter. "Yum! Is that cornbread I smell?"

"Yep."

"I can't wait. Where am I sleeping?"

"I'll show you," said Kat, giving her a hug.

Latishia looked down at Buffy. "Well, hello, baby girl. Let me put this suitcase away, and I'll love you all over." Buffy made little whining sounds and pranced alongside.

The doorbell rang again. Buffy barked and raced back and forth between the guest rooms and the front door.

Poor dog, she doesn't know which way to go, I thought.

When I opened the door, there was Gina, a broad grin on her face. "I'm so ready for this. It's been the week from hell. Did you get the margarita mix?"

"Yes, it's in the kitchen. Come on. You're bunking with me."

Gina sang a tune about blue skies all the way to the bedroom. She plopped her case on a luggage rack I had set up in the corner.

"That chili smells so good." Gina rubbed her hands together with anticipation.

Latishia walked in, with Kat trailing behind. "You've got that right. I'm starving." Everyone hugged and then scattered, the others back to their cars for more things, me to check on the corn muffins.

I moved the salsa and chips to a convenient spot and returned to find Kat's head in the fridge.

"Can I help you find something?" I leaned against the counter, trying to remember if I'd put out the sour cream.

"Nope, hot flash. I'll be out in a minute."

I laughed. "I've done that very same thing. Only I use the freezer."

"Good idea." She extracted her head, closed the fridge side of my side by side, and opened the freezer. Five minutes later, she removed her head and closed the door.

Latishia walked into the kitchen and plopped her hands on her hips. "Kat, why are your glasses fogged up like that?"

Kat pulled them off and wiped them on the tail of her blouse. "Hot flash."

"What?" Latishia had her head-weaving thing going.

"I had my head in the freezer." Kat replaced her glasses.

"Oh, I get it. I wonder what women do when they have their freezers on the bottom?"

Gina walked in. "They do like me, get on their knees and say a few Hail Mary's while they're down there."

After we each had a margarita and some chips and salsa, we filled bowls with steaming chili and sat around the dining table.

"Pass those corn muffins, they're calling my name," said Latishia.

After ten minutes of eating, interrupted only by exclamations of oral ecstasy, Latishia asked, "What's going on with the formaldehyde sniffer?" She popped a mini corn muffin in her mouth and chewed.

"Strange you should ask. I just received a letter from Todd today."

All spoons paused as the ladies stared at me. The tick of the mantel clock seemed loud in the ensuing silence.

Gina pinned me with a "tell all" look. "And...."

I sprinkled more Fritos on my chili. "I don't know. I haven't had time to open it. I'll look at it after dinner, but before dessert."

"Good timing," said Gina. "I want to be sober enough to understand it." She shoved a spoonful of steaming chili in her mouth. Waving her hand in front of her face, she grabbed her iced tea and gulped.

Kat frowned as she pushed up her glasses. "Why is he writing you?"

"Who knows? But for now, I want to enjoy dinner and my company."

After the meal, the ladies made an efficient team as they cleaned up while I stored leftovers.

Latishia poured a glass of wine and leaned against the counter. "What's for dessert?"

"We just ate," said Kat. "I couldn't stuff another thing in my mouth at this moment."

"Ice-cream sundaes and cheesecake. Let's get what we want to drink and meet in the living room in five minutes," I suggested.

Once in the bedroom, I slipped Todd's letter out of a drawer, scooted into the bathroom and locked the door behind me. I tore open the envelope, leaving a jagged edge. Todd would hate that since he insisted on clean slits with a letter opener.

After a quick scan, I knew I needed feedback from the Divas.

I returned to the living room to find Kat and Gina sprawled on my sofa. Latishia had laid claim to the love seat, with Buffy snuggled next to her. I walked to the recliner, gripping the letter with both hands like it might explode. A bomb resided inside that envelope — an emotional one.

I sat, pulled up the footrest, and gulped some wine.

Latishia looked at me. Both of her eyebrows hiked toward her hairline. "Are you gonna read that letter or what?" Buffy nudged her head under Latishia's hand. She smiled at the dog and scratched her ears.

"She may not feel comfortable reading this letter to us. It may be too private," said Kat. She pulled her glasses off, rubbed her eyes with the heels of her hands, and replaced them.

With a slight tremble, I pulled the letter rattling from the envelope.

Gulping air, I began to read the letter aloud.

Dear Phoenix,

I'm sure you're probably shocked to be receiving a letter from me. Mom and I have talked a lot since the divorce. I appreciate you maintaining a relationship with her. You're the daughter she never had, and she loves you.

Also, thanks for talking her into getting that damn dog of hers neutered. She would never listen to me about that perverted mutt.

I'm not writing to you about the dog, but us. I know what I did was wrong. I'm sorry. I was just so angry about being left alone all the time. Mom's helped me to realize that I got a dose of what you endured for years. I don't know how you put up with it.

I miss you. It's so lonely in the house, and there's no one here for me to talk to about my day or to advise me. Mom does what she can.

I've been dating since the divorce, and it's become clear, no one can fill your place in my life.

I know we have some issues to resolve. If you can forgive me and you are willing to make the changes I need, I'm willing to go to counseling to see if we can mend our broken relationship. Please contact me and let me know your decision.

Todd

Everyone sucked in a breath. It felt like all the oxygen left the room.

"Think of it this way, ladies. Karma kicked his butt. Read it again," said Kat, as she shifted to sit lotus style.

After I had finished the second reading, Latishia said, "Sounds to me like he wants his private therapist back. I bet he hasn't told his mother about the affairs. That twit has balls the size of BBs."

"Bingo!" I pointed a finger in her direction. "I bet she doesn't know that Frank shot at Todd, either."

"You didn't tell her?" Gina looked shocked, judging by the way her mouth was hanging open. "I would've told her about the women and the assassination attempt."

"I'm not Sicilian, Gina. Besides, I didn't want to hurt Joyce. She hasn't done anything but love and support me. If she finds out it needs to come from elsewhere."

"That's true." She ran her hands through her unruly curls.

"What I don't like," said Kat, "was the part of the letter where he said 'make the changes that I need.' What does that mean?"

I shrugged.

Gina morphed into lawyer mode. "What's your plan? Are you going to go to counseling with him?"

"Please, give me a little credit for having a brain left in my head. It's August, and he's just now claiming to come to his senses?" I held up a finger. "First, he rationalized that his cheating was because he felt lonely and abandoned. In other words, he's blaming me. I was home alone for nineteen years, and I didn't screw around on him."

"Amen, sister," said Latishia, pumping her fist toward the ceiling.

I held up the letter. "He all but said he's writing, not because he loves me, but because the house is empty, and he misses having his personal live-in therapist. I noticed he signed the letter with 'Todd,' not 'love, Todd.'"

"You go girl!" said Latishia.

I was on a roll, out of my chair, pacing in front of them. "He has the audacity to write that I have to make all the concessions for him to be willing to take me back. Hell, I don't want him back."

"Hallelujah!" Latishia clapped.

"I've had more fun this last month, than I've had the last sixteen years of my marriage to that low-life, cheating, workaholic, philandering, recliner-sitting, television-addicted, womanizing, buffet-loving creep."

"Don't forget corpse-loving," added Latishia.

The Divas leaped to their feet, clapping and cheering.

I reached for my glass of wine and held it aloft. "Here's to freedom from assholes, and the Hot Flash Divas."

"The Hot Flash Divas!" we chorused and clinked glasses.

"May Todd catch the clap, and his antibiotic therapy give him thrush and diarrhea," toasted Kat.

Gina spewed her white wine and began choking.

Latishia shook her head. "Only a nurse would make a toast like that."

Kat grinned as she swirled her wine. "What would you toast?"

"May his car loan for the Corvette he's trying to buy fall through," toasted Latishia.

I put down my wine. "Todd is trying to buy a penis extension? What color?"

"Cherry red, I think." Latishia shook her head. "I don't handle car loans. Don't know what makes him think he can get a car loan when his mama had to cosign for his house."

We all laughed and drank more wine.

"I feel better. Time to celebrate with dessert," I announced.

"And presents," said Gina.

Latishia waved a DVD case. "After that, I brought a great movie."

* * * *

At ten the next morning, the smells of fresh-brewed coffee, homemade biscuits, and a frittata lured the hung-over Divas to the dining table.

Latishia rubbed her eyes as she stumbled into the room, decked out in shiny leopard pajamas. "Coffee, I need coffee." Her long braids were pinned up and spewed like a fountain from the top of her head.

Kat followed in her wake, wearing a long cotton gown covered with tiny roses. Unlike Latishia, her smooth, blue-black hair framed her face with perfect precision. She poured hot water into a mug and dunked a tea bag that she'd found. The steam fogged her lenses, which she removed and wiped with a napkin.

Gina was the last to emerge, yawning and stretching. "Kat, start a caffeine and aspirin IV. I'm hung over." Her lawyer-like gray and blue striped pajamas did little to undermine her hair, which was an explosion of curls.

I greeted them in pink fluffy house shoes and a knee-length sleep shirt with paw prints that started at the hem and meandered up and over one shoulder and down the back.

"Good morning!" I chirped.

Groans were the only response. By the time we sipped our second cup of java and tea, we were all in better spirits.

"I want to thank everyone for the sheets and comforter sets for my new beds," I said. "They were perfect gifts."

Latishia stifled a yawn. "Timely too, since we slept on them."

"I was thinking about that letter while I was cooking this morning."

"Yeah?" Latishia yawned again, as she checked her phone for messages.

"I think Joyce was responsible for that letter. She's trying to get Todd to reunite with me."

"I don't disagree. Joyce loves you," said Kat. "What's your plan of action?"

"I don't think the letter was a genuine effort at reconciliation, so I won't respond at all unless he calls to follow up."

I stood and grabbed the coffee pot. After I had topped off the cups, I returned to my seat.

"What if he calls?" asked Latishia.

"The answer is hell, no," I said. "Joyce will have to get over it."

"Since that's settled, what's everybody got going this weekend?" Gina eyed a strawberry and popped it in her mouth. She looked like a chipmunk chewing it.

"Dante has a ball game tonight and tomorrow morning. It seems like all I do is shuttle that child around to practice and games. The rest of my time, I try to get the mud and grass stains out of his uniform." Latishia shook her head, braids jiggling, as she reached for another biscuit. She slathered it with butter and jam. "Saturday afternoon, I'm getting my braids done."

I'd always been curious about her braids, but the subject had never come up, until now.

"How long does it take to get yours done?" I asked. The jelly jar looked low, so I scooted over to the pantry, nabbed a fresh jar of raspberry jam, and plopped it on the table in front of Latishia.

"For me, about six hours. The larger ones take less time, but I don't think they look as good."

"Six hours!" Gina stared open-mouthed across the table at Latishia's hair. "I'd be stir-crazy."

"It's tedious work, that's why it costs so much."

Kat tilted her head as she examined Latishia's hair, "How much?"

"Normally six hundred, but she's my cousin, so she only charges me four hundred."

"Four hundred dollars!" The rest of us chorused in unison.

"Well, it lasts a long time." Her tone became defensive. She reached for another biscuit and busied herself by scraping the sides of the near-empty jelly jar.

Gina placed her mug on the table and asked, "How long? Six months?"

"More like six weeks."

Kat's eyes narrowed to mere slits. She looked toward the ceiling. "That's eight times a year, let's see...that's over three thousand dollars a year!"

Latishia's lower lip pooched forward. "I'm doing good now. I'm established in my job and can afford it. It's the one thing I do for myself that I don't scrimp on."

Silence landed on the table with a thud. Latishia focused on the glass jar, clanging the knife inside.

The rest of us exchanged glances.

"They do look good on you," I admitted.

No response.

"We're just worried that you'd get yourself into a financial bind," said Gina.

No response.

Kat shrugged. "Well, tonight I'm taking Jack to see the new action flick he's been dying to see. My Nai Nai's flu meant I had to keep canceling our plans. On Saturday, I'm picking up an extra shift for a friend. Her daughter's getting married this weekend. Gina, what're you doing?"

"Nothing tonight, but I have a dinner date Saturday with a defense attorney." She grinned and picked up her coffee. "What about you, Phe?"

"Tonight I'm going to a movie with Kent Lands, that guy we met at Concerts in the Park. Saturday I'm going to a dance with Nathan."

All eyes focused on me. Latishia put down the jelly jar but still held the knife. It was so quiet I could hear Buffy snuffling under the table looking for crumbs.

Kat plopped down her tea mug. "You have *two* dates this weekend?"

"Yeah, is that unusual?" *How would I know? I've been married the last twenty years.*

"Men of Huntsville beware, Phoenix O'Leary has entered the dating scene." Gina shook her head and downed the remains of her coffee. "I need more caffeine."

Chapter 42: Movie Time

I rubbed my stomach and tried to will it to stop turning somersaults. I don't know why I was so anxious? After all, I'm a grown woman, not a gangly teen.

I turned into the parking lot and found a spot close to the front. I remembered my dad, who always ribbed me about finding the best parking slots. He called it my gift — my magic. I wondered what he would think about his forty-five-year-old daughter meeting a near stranger for a date. I suspected he wouldn't be surprised at the turn of events in my life. He tried to warn me about Todd.

My trembling hands released the steering wheel, and I fumbled the keys from the ignition. I dropped them in my bag and zipped it. Reaching for the door handle, I paused. I opened my purse again to reassure myself that my keys were there, tucked away. I could only imagine my humiliation if I locked myself out of my car.

After I had locked my vehicle, I walked on unsteady legs toward the building. Kent appeared, holding the door open for me. I felt better about my decision to dress down when I noticed we both wore jeans and polo shirts.

"Good, you made it." His grin widened, crinkling the corners of his eyes.

I flashed him a smile. "Hope you noticed I'm on time." I gripped the strap of my purse, trying to ground myself.

"A punctual woman is a true blessing. Believe me, my ex never made it anywhere on time. Drove me nuts. Do you like popcorn?"

"It's my favorite." *So, there was some baggage with the ex-wife.*

He bought a combo of large popcorn with two drinks that cost more than the movie tickets. I followed behind him in the darkened theater, clutching my drink and a fistful of napkins. I concentrated so hard on not tripping that I didn't notice when he stopped. I rammed into his broad back, which didn't seem to affect him.

"Sorry," I whispered.

Kent moved to the center of the row and sat. I settled in next to him with my purse in the seat beside me and placed the drink in the cup holder. Reaching over, I grabbed a handful of popcorn and tossed some into my mouth.

The buttery flavor with its tang of salt marinated my tongue. I crunched the fresh hot popcorn, closed my eyes, and moaned my pleasure.

"That's the type of sound I always hope to hear from a woman," said Kent.

My eyes flew open. I could feel my face flame and hoped Kent couldn't see it in the dim lighting of the theater. My phone honked, indicating I had a text message.

"Saved by the honk." Kent smiled at me.

The people sitting around me turned and directed barbed looks in my direction.

"Jeez," I mumbled, "I forgot, okay? It's just the previews." I dug my phone out of my purse and thumb-printed it open. Shifting in my seat, I turned so he couldn't see my screen.

How's it going? G.

I texted back; *This isn't high school. Turning off my phone until after the movie. P.*

Fine. Text when you get home. G.

K.

I turned the phone to silent mode and shoved it back into my purse.

When I looked up, Kent asked, "Is everything okay?"

I reached for some popcorn. "That was a friend. She wants me to text when I get home."

"I see. Do you still think I'm a serial killer?" He cocked a brow and snaked his arm over my shoulder.

"Haven't decided yet, so better safe than sorry."

Someone seated behind us shushed.

The latest Bond movie filled the screen. It was a little unsettling to watch images of near-naked women projected across a screen when I was sitting next to a guy I didn't know very well. Still, the movie didn't disappoint. It was full of action and intrigue.

When the lights came up, Kent took my hand and walked me out of the theater.

I said, "Those people in the movie were beating the crap out of each other, throwing each other through walls and glass windows, yet they got up and behaved like it was a mere slap across the face." I craned my neck trying to remember where I'd parked. I saw a smidgen of the back of my Prius peeking out past a giant black SUV.

"That's Hollywood for you. I'd love to recover that quickly when I overdo on the weekends. What's on your schedule tomorrow?"

"I'm attending an event at Lowe Mill."

"Oh, I see." An upset look flitted across his face. "Want to get a bite? I'm craving a barbecue sandwich." He quirked one side of his mouth in a half smile.

"I could do barbecue. I'll meet you at the joint over there." I pointed across the Parkway at Gibson's.

"I'll drive," offered Kent, as he pulled his keys from his pocket.

"Thanks, but no. You would have to round-robin on the access road to bring me back to my car." I took off at a brisk pace toward my car to end the debate.

We met at the front door, which Kent opened for me. *At least he's a gentleman.*

The place had a plethora of pig knick-knacks. There were little pigs, big ones, cute ones, ugly ones, and some with wings.

Kent caught me eyeing the winged pigs. "Those are the ones we're eating tonight, they've earned their wings." He cackled and eyed the menu.

I put mine down. "I think I'll just have sweet tea and a pork sandwich. The popcorn was filling."

He leered at me over the top of his laminated menu. "Filling or fulfilling? I thought you would have an orgasm while munching away in the dark."

I felt my back stiffen. I wasn't ready for sexual innuendos and felt the sudden urge to flee the building. *This is silly.* I chided myself, *I lost my virginity at age nineteen.* I like sex, yet hearing Kent talk about orgasms under these bright lights while surrounded by pigs sent an uneasy shiver slithering up my spine.

I didn't run screaming for my car, but instead escaped to the ladies' room with my purse. Once inside, I called Gina.

"Hi Phe, are you home?"

"No, I'm in the ladies' room at Gibson's."

"I thought you said this wasn't high school." The comment dripped with sarcasm.

I ran my hand through my hair while I paced back and forth in front of the sinks. "Very amusing. Give me a break, Gina. This guy is talking about orgasms just because I enjoyed my popcorn."

"Are you afraid of having your first post-divorce sex, or is this guy freaking you out for some other reason?"

"Probably both," I admitted, as I eyed some graffiti written on a beige stall door. *Susie loves Jason.*

"What's your gut say? You have the most reliable gut intuition I've ever encountered. Listen to it."

"Thanks, Gina. I'll text you when I get home."

My sandwich sat wrapped in paper, centered on a pale green plastic plate when I returned to our booth. I put rib sauce on it and ate like I was a starving refugee. I finished before Kent and slurped the iced tea like I'd spent a week in a desert.

I couldn't pinpoint what was bothering me, but red warning flags were flying. I felt panicky. *Danger, danger, danger,* clanged in my head.

He looked at my empty plate. "Wow, I thought you weren't hungry." He grinned as his glance slid to my breasts. "I hope you're as eager for other things."

I didn't reply, just squirmed in my seat feeling slimed.

"Would you like to take a drive or —"

I raised my hand in front of my chest like a stop sign and interrupted him. Judging by the lascivious look on his face, I had to halt him before he said something that might really piss me off. "I enjoyed the movie, Kent, but I need to leave."

He sat back in the booth and eyed me like a bug on a branch.

"Did I do or say something to offend you?" He raised both hands, as if to indicate, *what gives?*

"I don't feel we're a good match. I know you've been single awhile and probably want a relationship. I'm not interested in a relationship."

He cocked his head and folded his hands on top of the table. "I noticed you didn't ask about my son like most women do."

"I like kids. I work with children all the time. I'm not interested in raising another person's child at this late juncture in my life."

He nodded as his gaze lingered on my cleavage. "I suppose 'friends with benefits' is out of the question? You're such a lovely and intriguing woman, Phoenix, and the world's so interesting with you in it."

I shuddered, feeling like a Popsicle on a stick. The hairs on my arms rose like I'd encountered static electricity. That last sentence skated around the edges of my memory. I tried to recall where I'd heard it before. While my mind struggled to remember, my body wanted to shoot out of that booth like a Redstone rocket. The countdown began in my head. *Ten... nine... eight... seven —* .

The waitress, an older woman with wiry gray hair, dropped the bill between us. Spotting the total, I whisked money onto the table to cover the bill and tip. *Six... five... four —* . I didn't want to hear any "I paid for the movie, so you owe me," rhetoric. *Three... two... one —* .

"Would you pay the tab for me? I need to leave now, bye." *Blast off!* I was out of the seat and halfway to the exit before he could rise.

I drove home trembling. I felt foolish and wise at the same time. I couldn't believe that I'd scooted out of that restaurant like a scared bunny.

Once home, I texted Gina that I was safe. I gathered Buffy into my arms to help calm me and sat on the sofa. While I loved on her, I felt my pulse rate slow.

I stood and shuddered, feeling an inexplicable desire to shower. My shoulders relaxed as I stood under the steaming hot water. It was then I remembered. What Kent said to me was similar to what Hannibal Lecter said to Clarice Starling in "Silence of the Lambs." Icy fingers ran across my body, despite the piping hot water.

Chapter 43: Shall We Dance?

Nathan Rome arrived minutes after I did at Lowe Mill. Formerly a textile mill, it was renovated into artist lofts and interesting little stores. The place sat in the middle of a dicey neighborhood. I was pretty sure I saw a former patient dealing on the corner when I turned onto the road that led to the gravel parking lot.

We were lucky to be able to park next to each other because the lot was filling up. Nathan bounded out of his red Sebring convertible and opened my door. "Hi there."

Offering a hand, he assisted me from the car.

Delighted, I once again asked myself, *when was the last time Todd helped me out of a car?* I couldn't remember.

"Are you ready to burn the floor, as they said in the golden days?" Nathan did a little tap dance on the gravel.

I laughed as I watched his shoes kick up dust. "My dance shoes are sizzling hot."

At one end of the renovated mill was the Flying Monkey, a place where bands premiered, and dances sometimes occurred. Tonight a swing dance was in progress, and I was ready to boogie. Once in the building, we walked up metal stairs and pushed open a lime green metal door to the second floor. A glass blowing studio loomed straight ahead, and the artist was at work. We paused for several minutes to watch the muscled woman pull her rod laden with molten glass out, twirl it, and place it back in the fire several more times. We walked hand-in-hand down the main corridor, looking at the wild colors and displays of the studios and shops. It looked like a 1960's flower child fairy decorated it.

I sniffed the air like a coonhound and looked at Nathan. “Do you smell bread?”

He sniffed and pointed to a table to my left. A sign on it read:

“Fred’s Bread

Loaves $10.00

Place money in the jug.”

A gallon milk jug with the top cut off was stuffed with bills. A lady dropped a ten into it and picked up a loaf of bread.

“Must be the honor system.” I pulled Nathan over to the bread. The aroma was fantastic. I chose a loaf of jalapeno cheddar bread and dropped in a ten. Nathan fished out his wallet from his back pocket.

“I want the rosemary bread.” He dropped in a twenty and took out a ten.

I could hear the band start up down the hall. Holding our bread, we made our way to the ticket booth, where Nathan once again produced his wallet and paid our admittance

The front entrance of the Flying Monkey was a wall painted with a giant monkey face with wings. This wall forced us to walk left or right. After we had turned the corner, we faced a wooden stage. Wooden bleachers wedged the installed dance floor between them and the stage. Small tables with folding metal chairs dotted the open areas on each side of the dance floor. The whole set up was crude, yet quirky. The original wood floors were rough. Plumbing and air ducts were visible above.

“Let’s sit at a table.” Nathan chose one a few feet in front of us and pulled out my chair. I smiled, feeling like a princess.

“I hope this band is good.” He pulled out two bottles of water, one from each coat pocket, and placed them on the table.

“Me too.” I frowned as I struggled to buckle one of my dance shoes. “Drat, this thing always gets hung up.”

“Can I help with that?”

I swung my foot onto his leg. Now it was his turn to frown as he maneuvered the buckle.

“Women’s shoes are a lot more complicated than men’s. There, I got it.”

"Thanks." I pulled my foot off his knees because his hand had strayed from my ankle to my calf and was on a journey to private places.

He sighed and the moment passed.

The band began their set with a peppy tune, so we started dancing. Except for the break, we never sat down. Every time a guy walked in my direction, Nathan took me by the hand and led me to the dance floor. He guarded me like a terrier; only I didn't like feeling like someone's territory, especially after the creepy experience I'd had during last night's date.

The air-conditioning system's feeble attempts to push cool air around the room left me glowing like a 150-watt bulb ready to explode. Due to the crowded dance floor, several people had trod on my feet. A couple doing the Lindy Hop near us seemed to be unaware of dance floor etiquette. He wore a red tee shirt, and she wore a polka-dotted dress. Show Off elbowed me and seemed unperturbed by my glare as he whipped his date around, crashing her into me.

I took flight. Nathan caught me and managed to keep his feet by backing up several steps.

He lowered me to my feet and gave me a gentle, lingering kiss. He smiled, took my hand and led me to our table.

"Are you injured?"

I frowned and rubbed a foot. "Not from that incident, but my feet aren't happy from being stomped on by some of the other dancers. The floor is so crowded."

"That guy in the red tee shirt is dangerous. He's not looking to see where he's sending his dance partners," said Nathan. "His partner is the one who bumped you off of your feet."

I nodded. "He's a dance floor hog and a showoff to boot."

We watched as Show Off broke into the Charleston. His partner was doing a daintier version, but he swung his arms and legs wide. A couple I recognized from a ballroom class was doing a Triple-Step Swing nearby.

"Dan and Rita better watch out or Show Off may clock them," I said as I pointed in their direction.

On a back kick, the wild dancer's foot connected with Dan's crotch. Dan howled in pain, his face turning as red as Show Off's shirt. Dan's hands tried to cover his tools of the trade as he swayed this way and that. Then his face paled, and he hit the floor. Once there, he curled into a ball.

"Ouch!" Nathan cringed and looked away.

The music stopped.

"Time to go," I said, unbuckling my shoes. "It's dangerous out there."

Nathan bent over to untie his shoes. "The dance is nearly over anyway."

Show Off was on his knees beside Dan. "I'm sorry, man. I didn't mean to do it, honest."

Nathan and I retrieved our bread and shoes and scooted out the door of the Flying Monkey. Walking out hand-in-hand, we laughed about the look on Show Off's face when he realized that he'd creamed the guy behind him.

"Poor Dan, I just hope he's all right," I said.

I was feeling my way over the gravel in the dim light when Nathan took my arm to offer stability. I looked up and ground to a halt.

Kent Lands leaned against my car with his arms folded.

The sneer on his face was barely visible in the dim light of the parking lot. "I see you ditched me for another guy. A bald one at that."

I could hear the blood pounding in my ears. I felt scared.

"What're you doing here, Kent? Are you following me?" My fear was transforming to anger.

"I didn't like the way you jilted me last night. I'm the one who decides when a relationship is over." Kent took several steps toward me and reached out as if he planned to grab me.

I stepped back, and Nathan stepped in front of me. Several of the other dancers who were returning to their cars crowded around.

"The lady would like for you to leave." Nathan's voice was calm, but I could feel the waves of tension bouncing between the two men. Nathan's hand clenched and unclenched almost as though he welcomed the opportunity to release some aggression. My heart was racing fast. I felt like I might faint.

"I didn't hear *her* say a word." Kent rested his hands on his hips and jutted his chest forward, making himself appear larger.

I swallowed hard, trying to keep my voice steady. "Please leave. We only had two dates, Kent. It wasn't a relationship. I don't want to hear from you ever again."

Several of the men moved in, forming a line in front of me. A lady I didn't know grabbed my arm and pulled me off to the side.

"You heard the lady." Nathan took a step forward. From my new vantage point, I could see his jaw muscle flexing.

Kent eyed Nathan. Time seemed to flow like a glacier as the two took each other's measure.

Kent was the first to break eye contact. He looked at the line of men, six of them now. He took one step forward and spit on the ground in front of Nathan. The woman standing next to me gasped.

Kent looked over at me, his face hard with anger. "You can have her. She's an ice queen anyway."

He turned away and faded into the darkness. The people around us all began to talk at once.

I exhaled my relief. As the tension left my body, I felt like overcooked linguini. "Thanks, guys, I appreciate your help."

"Damn fool's crazy," a male voice declared.

Nathan held the door for me as I slid into my car. I rested my head on the steering wheel for a moment to let my heart rate slow.

He leaned down to look in at me. "I'm following you home to make sure that guy doesn't try anything." He looked around, trying to spot Kent.

I didn't want him to escort me home, but I was more afraid for him not to follow me.

I nodded. "Okay, but I'm going to make extra turns to ferret him out just in case."

That's how Nathan made it into my house.

Chapter 44: Bread and Butter

It was with exquisite relief that I pulled into my garage. I waved goodbye to Nathan and lowered the door. Shaking like a palm frond in a thunderstorm, I exited the car and tried to put the key in the deadbolt to enter my kitchen. My hand wasn't steady enough.

I could hear Buffy whining on the other side. I put down my loaf of bread, two-handed the key into the lock, and opened the door. Buffy performed her happy dance as I retrieved my bread and placed it on the kitchen table. I petted her while I walked over to open her dog door. She pushed out. I could hear her barking as the doorbell rang.

"Damn!" I didn't want to let Nathan in my house. I was still quivering from the adrenaline rush. *I've had enough of men for one night.*

I turned on the porch light, peeked to make sure it wasn't Kent and opened the door.

Nathan winked. "I thought you were going to leave me out here."

"Um, would you like a cup of Chamomile tea and to sample my bread?"

His eyes lit up. "Let me get mine out of the car, and we can try them both."

He left to retrieve his loaf. I plugged in the electric teakettle I'd bought for Kat's visits. Pulling a large cutting board from a bottom cabinet, I plunked it on the counter. I rummaged through a drawer, looking for a particular knife. Frustrated, I glanced up and saw it. I plucked the long bread knife from the wooden block and turned just as Nathan hustled into the kitchen, with the bread tucked under his arm like he was running for a touchdown.

"Woah!" His eyes were round as saucers as he backpedaled.

Confused, I followed the trajectory of his gaze. I was brandishing a lethal-looking knife. "Oops!" I placed the knife on the counter next to the board and backed away, my hands held palms up.

"Would you slice the bread, please? I can't cut a straight slice to save my life. I'd like a thin slice of both."

After I'd made sure the front door was locked, I pulled down two cups and placed tea bags in each one. The kettle whistled as Buffy bounded through the door into the room. Spotting Nathan as he cut the bread, she ran toward him barking and growling, her hackles up.

He stepped back. "Hello there. Good puppy."

Buffy continued to bark, placing herself between Nathan and me.

"Buffy!"

She ignored me. I picked her up and walked past Nathan. She tried to snap at him as I passed. *Buffy's never tried to bite anyone. What's with her? Or better yet, what's wrong with him?* I opened my bedroom and put her down and closed the door.

I returned to the kitchen. "Sorry about that. I don't know what got into her."

I filled the cups and placed them on the table in the breakfast alcove. I returned to the kitchen for the Stevia, butter and raspberry jam.

We sat opposite each other. I smeared butter on a slice and took a bite. "I love this bread. It's just the right amount of cheese and spice."

"Try this one." Nathan reached across the table, offering me a small buttered section of the rosemary bread.

"Yum. I may get that one next time."

Nathan cocked a brow. "What's the story on the guy in the parking lot?" He placed a bite of bread in his mouth and commenced chewing. His gaze never left my face.

I buttered more of my bread. "My friend Gina and I met him at the park. He invited me to dinner, so I agreed to meet him at Walton's. He seemed nice enough during the meal, so I met him for dinner and a movie."

I reached for the jam and couldn't get the top off. I handed it to Nathan, who twisted it off with ease.

"Kent started creeping me out with suggestions of being friends with benefits. I barely knew the guy. I threw a twenty on the table to cover both our meals and got the heck out of there."

"He doesn't take rejection well. It's a shame he didn't throw a punch. I would've liked to do some damage."

I reared back in the chair. *Is Nathan spouting male bravado or does he mean it?* I finished chewing and swallowed some tea.

"Why are you so angry?" It slid out of my mouth like shit through a goose. I had no conscious intention of asking that question.

He stiffened and glared at me. I didn't like the look in his eyes. He took a breath and tried to relax, but I could still sense his edginess.

"What makes you think I'm angry?"

I just looked at him. Seconds stretched into minutes. He glanced at his watch and shoved back his chair.

"It's getting late." He rose and walked to the counter to retrieve his bread.

I walked him to the door. "Thanks for rescuing me and following me home."

His face looked tight, and his jaw flexed. "You might keep an eye out, a fella like that doesn't always give up that easy." Grasping the doorknob, he pulled the door shut behind him.

After sliding the deadbolt into place, I waited until I felt he had driven away before I turned off the porch light.

I returned to the bedroom and released Buffy. She shot from the room and ran around sniffing the floor wherever Nathan had walked, her sides quivering with the effort.

"It's okay, Buffy, he's gone, probably for good."

I texted Gina. *Home safe.*

She texted back. *Good. Me too.*

I cleaned up the kitchen and wondered if I'd hear from Nathan again. He was a mystery, but my gut warned, *He might also be dangerous, and Buffy doesn't like him.*

Chapter 45: Todd's Bomb

It was Sunday afternoon, the day after I managed to alienate two men in two days. All the Divas gathered at my house after lunch with their families. We were lounging in my living room talking and drinking iced tea. I mentioned that I'd received another letter from Todd in yesterday's mail, but hadn't opened it yet.

"Open it, I want to hear what the twerp has to say this time," said Gina. She kicked off her heels and bent to rub her feet.

I reached for the letter, ripped it open and read.

"*Dear Phoenix,*

I hated writing this letter, but my doctor said I should. I have syphilis. I'm not sure when or where I got it, so I'm telling all my sex partners. You might want to get tested.

Please don't tell Mom!

Todd"

"That fucking asshole!" Kat exploded off the sofa and shot across the room like the space shuttle.

We all turned wide-eyed to track her movements. Our calm, rational, logical Kat circled the room like she was orbiting.

Kat never says the "F" word.

"You might have syphilis?" Gina popped to her feet like a jack-in-the-box. Arms gesturing, she declared, "Quel verme di un imprenditore di pompe funebri!"

It was never good when Gina lapsed into Italian.

"What did you say?" asked Latishia. She had her shoes off, feet curled under her on the loveseat.

"That worm of an undertaker," said Gina.

"I like the worm part. If that worm gave you slut cooties, it would call for Diva justice." Latishia started fanning with her hands and turned two shades darker. "I'm on fire. Where's the switch for that ceiling fan?"

I stood, flipped the switch and curled back into my chair. Instead of enraged, I felt numb. *What next? Will this man ever stop throwing curve balls at me?*

I took a deep breath and slowly exhaled. "Calm down," I said, raising both hands. "Kat made me get tested right after we had discovered Todd was unfaithful, remember? All my tests came back clean. I don't have syphilis."

"What about AIDS? Don't you have to be tested six months after your first test?" Gina sat down, pulled a pillow onto her lap and clutched it.

"I just got those results back, and I'm clear."

Latishia placed her hand over her heart and took deep breaths. Gina looked down and rubbed her forehead.

Kat still paced. "Sorry to be so angry, but he didn't wear a condom and risked infecting you. There're antibiotic-resistant strains of syphilis out there." She stopped long enough to remove her glasses and run her hand over her face. "On top of that, Phoenix can't take penicillin, which would be the first round of defense." She put her glasses back on. "That was so irresponsible. He understands all too well about disease transmission because of his job. Now he may have infected who knows how many other women? What was he thinking?"

I knew why Kat was so angry. Her senior year she was gang-raped during a college fraternity party, she'd had to take antibiotics because one of the scumbag fraternity boys gave her gonorrhea. Jack was the result of that rape. The Divas made sure Kat finished school and helped her throughout the pregnancy. This incident was part of what cemented us together.

"He was reasoning with his dick," said Gina, as she tucked her feet under her skirt.

I held up the letter, which fluttered from the breeze of the twirling ceiling fan. "Latishia, you once said Todd had balls the size of BBs. You over-estimated their size. He has Nano balls." I shook my head with disgust. "'Don't tell mom,' I mean, really?"

"I think Joyce should know what's going on, but I know you don't want to hurt her," said Gina.

"I'm beginning to wonder if men are worth the trouble." I sank back in my recliner. "I've dated three men so far, Mr. Cheapskate, Mr. Stalker, and Mr. Yellowstone — none of them have worked out."

Calmer now, Kat sat lotus style beside Gina on the couch. She looked at me, her brows drawn together. "I know about Mr. Cheapskate, but you lost me with the other two."

I recounted the peculiar date with Kent and his unsettling appearance at Lowe Mill on Saturday night.

"Whoa, that's freaky. How did he know you were there?" Latishia untucked her feet and sat straight. She wiggled her pink-painted toes into my oriental carpet.

"After the movie Friday night, Kent asked me what I was doing on Saturday. I mentioned that I was attending an event at Lowe Mill."

Kat pulled off her glasses again, rubbed one eye and blinked. "Okay, that makes sense, but what's with Mr. Yellowstone?" She held the spectacles up to inspect them, wiped them with her blouse and replaced them.

"That's Nathan. I sense all this suppressed anger seething below the surface, waiting to spew forth like a geyser at Yellowstone National Park. If you'd seen him Saturday night, y'all would understand. It was like he wanted Kent to take a swing in that parking lot so that he could tear into him. He even admitted as much. Then later while we were discussing the incident, I asked him why he was so angry all the time. He got pissed off, took his bread, and left."

"I've had a run of bad luck, too," admitted Kat. "It seems like all the good ones are married. The guys coming out of divorces aren't worth dating, and the rest seem to be hiding from me. When I worked at the hospital, doctors wanting a quickie hit on me on all the time. I'm not the "sex in a supply closet" kind of woman. Now I'm working for

Dr. Howard and most of his patient's push walkers. I'm not looking for a quickie. I'm looking for a potential mate and a father for Jack."

I folded Todd's letter and shoved it back in the envelope. It would serve as a reminder that he was good riddance. "How can four dynamic women like us have such difficulty finding a decent guy to date?"

Over the years I'd heard single women in my therapy office complain about the trauma of dating and the dearth of good men. Until now, I'd thought they were exaggerating the situation.

Gina ran her hand through her curls and sighed. They sprang back to their former state like springs. "All the men I've dated seem to be smooth talkers who morph into total assholes."

Buffy, who was lounging next to Latishia, shook herself and jumped down. She padded toward the kitchen. I heard the flip, flop of the dog door.

"I know your problem, Gina." I stretched and yawned. I'd had a hard time falling asleep last night. My trepidation over last night's events had circled my mind like a flock of buzzards until the wee hours.

Gina looked my way. "Yeah?"

"You're dating lawyers. Isn't being an asshole a requirement for the job? You excluded, of course."

Chapter 46: Brent

As a psychologist, I've had many single men express much angst over the ritual of dating. One of the often-asked questions is, "After you have the lady's phone number, how long should you wait before you call?"

I always replied, "When you're ready to do so."

I'm not sure how long Brent waited to call because to be truthful, I was busy. When he did call, he asked me to a Contra dance a week away. Having never experienced Contra dancing, I was curious and agreed to go.

A day or two before our first date, Brent called again and asked if I wanted to go to a Zydeco weekend in early October.

"Let me get this straight. Are you asking me to a weekend event two months away? We haven't had our first date yet."

"The reservations are limited. They try to encourage gender matching so everyone has a potential dance partner. The reservations need to be made early," said Brent.

"What are the sleeping arrangements?" I tapped my pen against the desk.

"It's at a summer camp, so there are bunkhouses. I'm camping in my tent, and you're welcome to share it."

I liked camping, but I didn't know this guy that well. With a dismissive tone, I said, "We haven't had our first date yet, so I'm not sharing your tent."

Disappointment tinged his tone, but Brent agreed to reserve a space for me in an all-girls bunkhouse. Having visions of summer camp, I imagined lumpy beds, snoring roommates, and scampering lizards. A shiver crawled across my scalp and down my spine when I thought about the spiders.

"Brent, by the time this Zydeco event occurs, we may not be speaking to each other — what then?"

Brent chuckled. "If that's the case, we won't go together, and you'll still have a reservation."

That sounds reasonable.

The next day I met the Divas at Starbucks. We crowded around our favorite table in the corner. I discussed the Zydeco weekend with them. They'd all taken a few lessons taught by the Zydeco Stompers, so they decided to attend, too.

"You don't want to stay in a bunkhouse; they're rustic," said Latishia, her lips pursed as she did her neck thing.

"I bet they're noisy, too," said Gina, shaking her head back and forth.

Kat rubbed her lower back. "The beds are probably uncomfortable, and I bet they're bunk beds."

Gina suggested we stay at a bed and breakfast or the State Park Lodge, located nearby. She pulled out her laptop and started a search for accommodations. All the bed and breakfast places within twenty miles were booked. I phoned the Lodge and to our surprise, they only had two rooms left. We booked them. Each room had two double beds. Gina and I would bunk together, and Kat and Latishia agreed to share the other.

"This is my first dance weekend event!" I tingled with anticipation as I rubbed my hands together.

Gina pulled up the event website, and the Divas signed up for the event.

"There's a costume party planned for the second night," said Gina. "It's a pirate theme!"

"Great! You know how much I love costumes," I said.

The Divas and I brainstormed our ideas to become swashbuckling pirates.

Chapter 47: The First Date

Since I'd had some time to observe Brent beforehand, I allowed him to pick me up at my office. He arrived on time, which won big points with me. After some discussion, we decided to dine at Logan's.

I'm not a lady who asks for a small salad and pushes it around with my fork. However, I don't eat a huge portion, either. Once seated in the booth, I considered the menu. My mother had taught me to be mindful of the gentleman's budget. I could hear her in my head: *"Phoenix, choose one of the three least expensive entrees or order what the gentleman orders."* I'd eaten here before and knew the portion sizes were daunting.

I looked at Brent over the top of my menu. "Would you consider splitting a meal? All their entrees are huge."

From the smile on Brent's face, I knew I'd scored an *atta-girl* point with him.

"That's a sensible idea." His face glowed.

The entrée came and was more than enough food for both of us. I took the spare plate provided, portioned off a third, and gave Brent the rest.

"So what made you go back to college?" I asked while placing butter in my part of the steaming baked sweet potato.

"I worked for a local company, and got caught in a big layoff. I enjoyed the time off for a month or two while I worked on my house and yard. The job market was lean at the time, so I decided the time was right to get a Masters in Computer Science."

"What company?"

He told me, and I wasn't surprised. The company had a reputation of acquiring contracts and losing them, which caused massive layoffs.

"I needed a job that was flexible, so I accepted a position as assistant to a professor at the University of Alabama here in Huntsville."

His attention was on cutting his steak, which we'd both agreed to order cooked medium. A lock of his dark hair fell over his forehead. I wanted to reach over and run my hand through it, to feel the texture, to smell the scent of his shampoo. *What is it with hair and me?*

He looked up, and I jerked.

"Is your food all right?" He arched a brow.

"Great." I smiled and reached for my fork and knife.

Thirty minutes later, we declined dessert and Brent paid the bill. Logan's was located within a mile of the church gym used for the Contra dances. We parked and followed the signs that directed us to a door at the back of the church, strolling hand-in-hand. We walked into the gym and Brent paid for the dance at a nearby table. He brought back a self-stick nametag that said, "Phoenix." I peeled off the backing and plastered it over my heart.

I soon learned Contra dancing is similar to square dancing; however, it's danced in lines, not squares. I observed couples moving up and down the line, dancing with multiple people.

"A Contra dance is a colorful sight," I said.

"You could say the dancers tend to gravitate toward unique attire," said Brent, slipping an arm around my waist.

There were combinations of clothes at this dance that would make a New York fashion designer consider suicide. The ladies wore vibrant skirts that flared during turns, and the men wore shorts or jeans. I wore jeans, a tee shirt, and my flashing tennis shoes. *If we come back, I'll wear a skirt.*

We held hands, waiting for the next set to begin. I was turning to sit in one of the metal chairs that lined two walls when I saw a man stride in the door wearing a skirt. Not a kilt, a skirt. At least I thought it was a man.

"Is that a guy wearing that light blue skirt?" I was trying not to stare.

Brent peered over my head. "That's a guy, or it's a really hairy woman." The music began, and Brent took me in his arms to the call, "Swing your partner."

The other unusual aspect of Contra dancing is the disparity of the ages of the participants. I danced with a septuagenarian as we moved up the line and Brent danced with a child. While this dance experience was out of the ordinary for me, it was upbeat.

Contra dancing done well is fun. When I made a mistake, it was a hoot. I missed quite a few calls, so we often laughed our way to the next pattern. When I got lost, the more experienced dancers were kind enough to herd me to the next position.

Smiling, Brent whispered in my ear a tidbit of sage Contra wisdom, "Better never, than late."

We left the dance tired, sweaty and laughing. Brent drove me back to my office, where he kissed me good night in his car. I looked into his eyes, ran my hands through his hair, and kissed him again. I loved the silky texture of his brown locks. He was warm and solid.

I wasn't sure about my feelings for Brent, but he passed the kissing test with a five-star rating.

"I'd love to see you again sometime," Brent murmured in my ear.

"You will, at the Zydeco event in October."

He chuckled. "I want to see you before then."

He had a nice laugh and an easy sense of humor. My commitment phobia meter still hovered around an eight on a one-to-ten scale, and I was as skittish as a kitten surrounded by coyotes. Despite this, I agreed to another date.

It was a fun and safe first date, which for me was just what I needed. The divorce had left me feeling as if someone had emptied a colossal injection of a numbing agent into the emotional center of my brain.

Chapter 48: The Tests

We all evaluate our dates for flaws, with specific attention focused on what went wrong in our previous relationships. I didn't want to make the same mistakes. After my experiences with Kent and Nathan, I was a bit more cautious with Brent.

Being a scientific-minded guy, Brent seemed to approach this evaluation process in a different fashion than I did.

I allowed our dates to progress in a natural way, while I observed Brent and his behavior. I knew I had the ultimate test napping at my home — my four-legged child, Buffy.

It made sense to me that with degrees in physics and electrical engineering, Brent preferred the scientific approach. That didn't mean I enjoyed being his current research subject.

Once, while we sat at a table waiting for our pizza at the Mellow Mushroom, he asked, "How do you place the forks, knives, and spoons in the dishwasher?" He tilted his head to the side as he waited for my answer.

I couldn't believe he was asking me about my dishwasher practices at a time like this.

"Brent, what exactly are you asking?" I could barely concentrate due to my growling stomach. The spicy smells of sauce, pepperoni, and cheese bombarded my senses.

"Face up or face down?" He gestured up and down with the palm of his hand.

I sighed. "I place all the utensils, but sharp knives face up." I gulped some sweet tea, hoping that settled the issue. *Good grief. It's just eating utensils!*

"I place *everything* face up, so it's exposed to the spray and more thoroughly cleaned." Brent crossed his arms and raised his chin as if this were so doggone important.

"I agree, face up is ideal; however, safety must be a primary concern. That's why I place sharp pointy objects down. I watched my friend Gina get stabbed by a knife that pointed up, while she was trying to unload her mother's dishwasher. It's better to rewash a knife than to make a trip to the emergency room."

Drawing his brows together, Brent considered my answer. I imagined the wheels of logic turning in his brain. If his bouncing leg was any indication, his neurons were firing at lightning speed. The leg bouncing reminded me of Todd.

"You're right, that's the best way."

I had a keen awareness of Brent's propensity for gathering data. I guess his scientific mind needed it. What did it matter to me? I had no plans to remarry. Let him gather his data.

Brent finagled different approaches to try to see my home. I assumed he wanted to gauge my level of neatness and organization. The harder he pushed, the more I resisted.

Before our third date, he smiled with child-like anticipation. "I can pick you up at home. There's no need to drive into your office on a Saturday night."

"No problem for me to drive in, I can feed my turtle, Betty Joe." I grinned as I watched his shoulders slump.

He experienced much initial angst since I blocked all efforts for him to complete this observation of my living environment. I suspected he feared I was hiding something.

Brent finally passed my safety inspection, or maybe I felt he'd suffered enough. I invited him to my home for a Sunday lunch of roast beef cooked with potatoes and carrots, along with a salad.

When Brent walked through the door, I watched to see how Buffy would greet him. She circled him with her tail twitching, executing her "pet me" routine. Dropping to one knee, Brent scratched whatever part came available, as Buffy pranced around him. I saw a delighted grin cross his face.

Buffy could read people better than Freud. Bursting with intelligence and doggie wisdom, she sniffed Brent while he sweet-talked her.

"Hi there, girl. My, aren't you pretty," he crooned.

Buffy was a beauty. Her fluffy fur was white with amber highlights, and her ears were so long she sometimes dipped them in her water bowl while drinking. Her bobbed tail twitched with excitement as Brent loved on her. I found it interesting that she fawned over Brent and met Nathan with raised hackles.

"Her ears are soft, like velvet." Brent stood and sniffed the air that was laden with the aroma of roast. "I don't know what you're cooking, but it smells fabulous." He craned his neck, looking around my home before he hugged me. "Your house is *very* nice."

I gave him the grand tour, watching his every move. When he entered my bedroom, his gaze roamed up to my trey ceiling.

Stepping closer, he said, "That's cool, did you paint this?"

"Yes, I wanted to wake to blue skies every morning, no matter what the weather."

He noticed that the majority of the paintings were my watercolors and oils. He examined each one, and gave a nod of approval or offered an insightful comment. "You're a talented lady," he said at last.

I served lunch at my breakfast nook table because it was cozier than my long dining table. The burgundy tablecloth and fresh flowers in a small vase made the occasion appear a bit more romantic.

Brent scooped meat and loads of potatoes and carrots onto his plate. He attempted to cut the roast beef, but it fell apart. Forking some into his mouth, he chewed and closed his eyes.

"Mmmm, this is good." The corners of his mouth tilted up. "It's so moist and tender." He reached for his glass and downed some sweet iced tea before he speared a chunk of potato. A captivated expression filled his face as he savored the flavors.

From his positive response, I surmised that I'd passed two tests at once: my home passed inspection, and I was a good cook.

"Where'd you get your dog?" Brent chugged down half a glass of tea.

I rose, pulled the small pitcher of tea from the fridge, and placed it on the table.

"A friend of mine is a vet. I asked him what breed of small dog he felt would be best for me. He had a cocker spaniel puppy he'd bought for a guy who helped him with a flat tire. The man planned for the pup to be a Christmas present for his kids but died of a heart attack right after Thanksgiving. The wife didn't want the dog, so he asked me if I wanted her."

"That's an interesting way to acquire a dog. Sad about the guy dying."

I dabbed at the corner of my mouth with my burgundy cloth napkin. "It was sad, but I took one look at Buffy and I knew she was mine."

"She's a beauty, and her fur is so soft," said Brent. He helped himself to seconds of everything while I refreshed his glass of tea.

I thought, *Did he eat today?* I'd barely touched my meal, and he was on round two.

Brent shoveled in the final bite on his plate and wiped his mouth.

I picked up my plate and took it to the sink. Brent followed my example. I stood on my tiptoes and hoisted a Tupperware cake carrier half-full of chocolate chip pecan cookies from the top of the fridge. After handing the container to Brent, I grabbed the two dessert plates I'd left on the counter. Back at the table, Brent wrested open the lid, and the smell of fresh-baked cookies filled the room. A rapt expression spread like soft butter on warm toast across his face.

"My favorite," he said, placing three cookies on his plate. He passed the container to me. "Want one?"

Choosing a cookie, I continued the story.

"Buffy's an excellent judge of character. She seems to like you."

Brent stuffed the last bite of a cookie into his mouth and swallowed. "I like her, too." He eyed the container. Gaze shifting to me, he raised a brow.

I smiled and handed him the container.

"I have a friend who bought a pot-bellied pig for a pet," said Brent, as he reached for another cookie. "It would beg at the table and squeal when you ignored it. Then it would scrape its hoof down your shin." He snatched two more cookies.

"Ouch." I cringed at the thought. I noticed some crumbs stuck around one corner of his mouth.

"It hurt. That pig scraped my shin once. Sam had to give it away to someone who had a farm. I noticed your dog doesn't beg at the table."

I couldn't take my eyes off the crumbs. Reaching down, I brought my napkin up and wiped my mouth as a hint. Brent continued to munch, a contented expression on his face as his eyes glazed over. Perhaps it was a rush of serotonin from the chocolate chips.

"She's trained not to beg and is never given table scraps." Buffy was snoring under the table, her muzzle resting on my foot.

The crumbs taunted me. I couldn't take my eyes off them. I cleared my throat.

Brent stopped chewing and focused on my face.

I pointed at the corner of my mouth.

His eyes widened, as revelation appeared to snap in his brain. He wiped the corner of his mouth with his napkin–the wrong one.

I pointed to the other side of my mouth.

Wiping with enthusiasm, he stopped and raised both brows.

"You've got it."

Brent smiled and nodded. "Buffy, you're almost as sweet as your momma's cookies." He reached down and stroked her head, while he gave me a wink.

Brent pushed away from the table, stood and toted the cookies to the kitchen counter. We talked some more while he helped me wash the dishes.

We settled on the couch to talk. Buffy slept with her head on one of Brent's knees. Brent passed the four-legged kid test with flying colors.

Chapter 49: Nathan Meets the Divas

Nathan phoned and apologized for his abrupt departure on our last date, and I apologized for analyzing him. To make it up to him, I asked him to accompany me to a barbecue that Latishia's parents were having on Saturday. In truth, I wanted to see if the Divas picked up on any unsavory vibes.

We drove over the Tennessee River in Decatur with the top down on his ruby-red Sebring convertible. I piled my hair under a Crimson Tide cap and donned sunglasses to protect my eyes from the sun and the wind.

"Which Diva is Latishia?" Nathan braked for a red light.

I turned toward him and smiled. He too, wore a Roll Tide cap to protect his bald pate, not from the wind, but the sun. "She's the loan officer. Her dad, Willy, is a genius with a grill. They have ribs. I can't wait."

"Remind me of the other ladies' names."

I pointed. "Turn right here. Gina's an attorney, and her date is some guy from Sicily who's visiting her family. I suspect her mom's trying to set her up with a nice Italian Catholic guy. I'm not sure how much English he speaks."

Nathan turned on his signal and turned left as I directed. "Is she divorced?"

Crepe myrtles were ablaze with vibrant pinks, reds, and fuchsias, creating a show of color. Begonias, a staple of Southern landscapes, were bunched in large mounds of color in the flower beds of many of the houses we passed.

In awe of the spectacle, I hesitated before answering. "Nope. Never married and no kids."

"Isn't that almost a sacrilege in an Italian Catholic family?" While waiting at a red light, Nathan glanced my way and pulled off his cap. He ran his free hand over his head before snugging the cap back down.

"She considers herself to be the black sheep. To make it worse, she's a divorce attorney."

Nathan chuckled as he braked at a stop sign. "She really is a rogue black sheep."

White crepe myrtle blossoms drifted like snow on the light breeze dancing in whirlwinds on the pavement. I had the urge to open the door, run into the street and twirl among the blossoms with my arms held wide.

I cleared my throat before I continued. "Kat's a nurse, and she's invited an EMT she met at work."

"Who's Latishia bringing?" After braking at another stop sign, Nathan reached over and moved a strand of hair out of my face.

I adjusted my sunglasses. "Believe it or not, a blind date that her dad, Willy set up."

"This sounds like it could be interesting."

I laughed. "It could be a hoot or a complete disaster. Turn into that drive with the orange and blue balloons on the mailbox. Care to guess what college team Willy supports?"

The 1950s house was covered with Miami stone on the front, and a green siding down the sides and back. A dark green metal awning with a white stripe along the edge shaded the porch and matched the paint on the concrete porch and stairs. White wrought iron railings surrounded the porch and extended down both sides of the stairs like welcoming arms. A variety of annuals bloomed in the beds.

Nathan parked in the drive and opened the car door for me, before reaching into the back to retrieve the cooler.

I shaded my eyes with my hand. "They'll be in the back yard, so we'll go on back."

I could hear Dante and Jack yelling to each other. We entered through the wooden gate on the left side of the house. The boys were tossing a football across the long yard, which offered plenty of room to cavort.

"The boy holding the football is Dante. He's Latishia's son. The other kid is Jack, and he's Kat's."

Nathan nodded as he craned his neck to take in the situation. I watched for his response. In a way, this event was a test. I'd never mentioned the ethnicity of the Divas and wanted to see how he responded. If he couldn't accept them — he was toast.

"Willy!" Flinging my arms wide, I walked over to the towering man who wore a "King of the Grill" apron and gave him a big hug. "This is my friend, Nathan."

They shook hands as they eyed each other's ball caps.

"I should've known you'd bring another Alabama fan. Girl, when you gonna wise up and start dating an Auburn man?"

I giggled. This banter was a running commentary. Todd was an Alabama fan, and Willy never approved.

"Don't you be giving me a hard time, now. Just remember who won the National Championship."

Willy crossed his arms and frowned. "Do you have to keep reminding me?"

"The important thing is whether you're cooking enough ribs?" I lifted the lid and peeked into the grill. Heat and a luscious aroma blasted me, and made me drool like a teething infant.

"Phoenix, I cooked enough ribs to feed the Alabama and Auburn football teams. Did you bring enough potato salad?" He cocked a brow.

"She made a huge bowl, and it looks delicious." Nathan held up the cooler. "And it weighs a ton."

Willy grinned. "You ever had her potato salad?"

Nathan shifted the cooler from one hand to the other. "No. She brought some to an event once, but it was all gone by the time I got there."

"Well, you're in for a treat. Wait until you taste my wife's turnip greens, fresh from the garden."

Reaching for the cooler, I said, "I'll leave you guys to the grilling. I'm taking this potato salad inside. We don't need any food poisoning because it got hot."

Once I was in the back door, I set the cooler on the breakfast table and walked into the long galley-style commercial kitchen.

"There's my girl!" Mama Snide pulled me into her arms and gave me her signature sway to the left and right, while she squeezed the air from my lungs. She hugged from the depth of her soul and always smelled of baby powder and whatever she was cooking. Mama Snide, a genius soul food cook, ran a catering company from her kitchen.

I inhaled to replace my depleted oxygen and asked, "Do you have room for the potato salad in your fridge?"

She flitted one hand to dismiss my question. "There's always room in my fridge."

Indeed, there was open space in her commercial walk-in fridge. I lifted the heavy bowl and slid it onto a shelf. Shivering, I left and closed the door. I replaced the lid on the cooler and turned as Latishia grabbed me by the arm and pulled me into the living room, out of hearing range of her mother.

She leaned close and whispered. "You've got to help me if this guy turns out to be a dud."

"What am I supposed to do, kidnap you?"

"Oh, Lordy, this will ruin the whole event for me if he's a freak." Latishia grabbed me by the arm again, pulled me into a bedroom, and closed the door. She yanked on the chain until the ceiling fan produced hurricane force winds and pulled her shirt off over her head. She stood arms out, her brassiere cradling watermelon-sized breasts that would drive most men wild. I'm a D cup, but Latishia made me look prepubescent by comparison.

"Hot flash?"

She nodded. "I'm so nervous, I've had to pee three times in the last hour."

"Too much information," I said. "Just be yourself and an excellent hostess. Everything will work out in the end, maybe."

"What if I don't want to go out with him? What do I do then?"

I shook my head. "Tell him he's a great guy, but he's not your type. Suggest that y'all can be friends."

Latishia pulled on her shirt. "What if I don't want to be friends?"

I sighed. "How old are you? This isn't high school, you know."

"This situation is different. Daddy set it up, and I don't want to hurt his feelings."

I patted her arm. "Willy only wants you to be happy. He'll understand if love sparks don't generate between the two of you."

We emerged from the bedroom with Latishia fully dressed, and left the house to enter the shaded back yard.

Willy declared in a booming voice, "Here she is now."

Latishia froze in place at the top of the stairs. I peeked around her to see what was happening. Everyone standing under the blooming mimosa tree turned to look at us.

I took the opportunity to survey the situation. Closest to the steps stood petite Kat, with her exotic Asian looks, and her guy, an EMT who was a tall, well-built guy with a head full of surfer-boy blond hair. *What a dichotomy,* I thought.

Gina's date was four inches taller than her and handsome in a dark, Italian way. I looked past Nathan and spotted Latishia's date standing next to her daddy. He looked like a black Jack Sprat. Even dressed in a tee shirt and jeans, he looked like a bow-tie intellectual.

I whispered, "At least he's not a gangster-wanna-be wearing ten pounds of gold with a diamond in his tooth and a rap sheet a mile-long.

"You know Daddy wouldn't set me up with anyone like that."

Willy presented Latishia with an upward sweep of his large hand. "Jerome, I want you to meet my little princess. Latishia, this is Jerome, the computer genius that saved your momma's system when it got that nasty virus."

I bit my lip and slid a sideways glance at Latishia. She gripped my arm and yanked me beside her. I wiggled free of her grip and propelled her forward to meet her prince. I saw her shoulders straighten, which caused her bosom to rise to its full glory.

Jerome's gaze locked on target. His eyes glazed over and a goofy smile spread across his face.

She descended the stairs like a queen at a formal ball, and I followed in her wake. When she reached Jerome, she extended her hand. Jerome took it and his grin widened. They stood there for a while eying each other. The silence stretched like high-priced elastic.

"Hi," I stepped forward to shake his hand. "I'm Phoenix, and this is my date, Nathan."

The awkward moment passed, and there was a flurry of introductions. Gina's escort was Antonio, but he preferred Tony, and Kat's was Derrick.

Everyone grabbed a beer, wine or soda, and socialized until Willy declared the ribs to be perfect. The men gathered around the three picnic tables, which Mama Snide covered with red-checked tablecloths. They lifted them, and placed them end-to-end. Willy plopped a humongous platter of ribs on the center table and covered them with aluminum foil.

I elbowed Nathan and whispered, "Save me a seat near the ribs."

I followed the other Divas into the kitchen, where Mama Snide deposited large containers of potato salad, coleslaw, baked beans, corn on the cob, and turnip greens into our waiting hands. We transported the goodies to the tables. Mama Snide was the last to come, with a platter of sliced ripe tomatoes.

Willy rushed to her side. "Let me take that heavy plate, Honeybun."

The one thing I've always loved most about the Snide's is the way they express their love for each other.

I loaded my plate with ribs and a dab of this and that.

I took one bite of the ribs and nearly swooned. "Oh, my, Willy, these are too good. If you give up the mechanic business, you should open a barbecue restaurant." I licked the sauce from my finger.

The table became quiet as each of us dug deep into our mounds of food. Everyone came up for air on occasion to compliment one dish or another.

I weigh once a week, but it wasn't going to be tomorrow.

Mama Snide grinned and winked. "I hope y'all saved room for dessert."

Everyone groaned and rubbed their bellies.

Jerome sat straight and smiled. "What's for dessert?"

With a twinkle in her eye, Mama Snide said, "Pecan pie, chocolate cake, and homemade buttermilk and pineapple ice cream."

I could tell she approved of Jerome by the way she smiled at him.

"I've died and gone to culinary heaven," I moaned. "My three favorite desserts!"

I was definitely not weighing tomorrow.

"You men play with these young'uns, and us ladies will put the food away." Mama Snide gave her husband a playful wink. "Willy, will you start the ice cream for me?"

"I sure will, honeybun."

As the Divas gathered the platters and bowls of food, Dante and Jack grabbed the disposable plates and dumped them in the garbage can. After I had placed my empty potato salad bowl on the counter, I walked back out to gather the flatware.

Nathan, Tony, and Derrick were tossing the football with the boys and throwing Alabama, and Auburn taunts at each other. Jerome helped Willy start the ice cream freezer.

When I walked back inside, Mama Snide glanced over at me. "Phoenix, put all those utensils in that small side of the sink that's full of hot sudsy water. They need to soak."

Like a pro, Gina slapped plastic wrap over the leftovers. Latishia arranged them inside the fridge. Kat rinsed items and placed them into a strainer until Mama Snide could load them into one of her two dishwashers. I swooshed the silverware to loosen the debris. Within fifteen minutes, we had the dishwashers running and the kitchen ready for a health department inspection.

Delighted to have that task behind us, we sauntered outside and flopped our backsides into lawn chairs. Sheltered from the sun by a giant oak and an understory dogwood, we sipped strong iced tea, sweet enough to make my teeth ache, and watched the men play touch football. The guys were unaware that we existed at that moment, so we were free to have a chat. We sat in a conversational circle, ready to gossip.

Mama Snide took a deep gulp of tea and held the sweating glass against the side of her face. "Latishia, what do you think of Jerome?"

Latishia craned to look around me just as Jerome got hit square in the chest with the football and fumbled it.

She shook her head. "He doesn't seem very athletic."

"True," said Kat, "but he has sexy brains. Did you hear him talking earlier?"

Latishia crossed her arms. Her lower lip began to pooch forward into a pout. "It's not his brains I want to see naked."

"Latishia!" Mama Snide tried to look stern, but she giggled instead.

We all laughed. I was feeling drowsy from the humidity and too much food. The heady smell of honeysuckle from the neighbor's yard was intoxicating.

"Hey, in my opinion, his computer skills more than makeup for his scrawny biceps." Gina sipped her tea as she watched the guys.

Leaning over, Latishia gave him another gander. "Maybe."

"What's the story on Tony?" I asked Gina. "He's quite attractive and speaks excellent English."

"It's a conspiracy between our mothers. He just finished his degree in microbiology. His mother's worried he wouldn't marry and have bambinos to pass on the family name."

"Grandchildren are important," said Mama Snide.

Gina leaned forward and swept a glance around to make sure none of the guys were within hearing range. "What his mother doesn't know is there's a real reason for her to be concerned."

"Why is that? Does he have a medical condition? He looks pretty healthy to me," said Kat.

"He's gay." Gina sat back and watched our faces.

All five of our heads turned like synchronized robots to stare at Tony. He leaped into the air, caught a pass and sprinted like a gazelle for a touchdown. Wiping the sweat from his brow with his forearm, he yanked his shirt over his head, exposing well-developed pecs and six-pack abs.

There was a collective sigh from the Divas.

"It's just not fair," I said, shaking my head.

"Total waste," said Latishia.

Mama Snide looked sad. "I'll pray for his mama. Unless he adopts, there'll be no grandchildren."

"Tell us about Nathan." Gina lowered her sunglasses and looked at me with one of her "tell all" looks. "I was surprised to hear you were bringing him. I thought y'all stopped dating when he got mad, took his bread, and went home."

"It's like Kat said, the man has sexy brains. He's a considerate person from what I've seen, except there's this underlying something." I waved my hand to shoo away a fly. The little varmint flew away and came back to dive-bomb me.

"What does that mean?" Mama Snide was fanning herself with a cardboard fan attached to an oversized Popsicle stick. The fan advertised a funeral home.

"He seems angry or irritated at times, and he gets this sneer on his face when someone does something that he doesn't think was intelligent," I said. "To me, it feels like he thinks he's superior."

Kat tucked her hair behind one ear. "Has he done it to you?" Now the fly buzzed around her.

"No, but if he does it to other people, he's capable of doing it to me. And then there's his head."

"What's wrong with his head? I don't see nothing wrong with his head?" Mama Snide craned her neck to inspect Nathan.

"Underneath that cap, there's no hair. Maybe all those high-powered neurons burned it off." I picked up my chair and shifted it over a foot to get back in the shade of the dogwood tree. My movement attracted the fly.

"Phoenix has always had a thing for a thick head of hair. It cranks her Prius." Gina laughed at her joke.

"Great, my date is a toothpick, Phoenix's date is as bald as a bowling ball, and Gina's Italian stallion is gorgeous but gay," said Latishia. "That leaves you, Kat. Tell us about your surfer boy."

"Derrick's an EMT with the Huntsville Fire Department. I met him when I worked in the emergency room at the hospital. I hadn't seen him since I began working for Dr. Howard."

Mama Snide dabbed at her face with a tissue, shoved it into the pocket of her skirt, and started fanning again.

"Two weeks ago someone fainted at the dentist's office in our building," said Kat. "When I left for lunch, the ambulance crew was rolling this huge guy out of the building. Derrick and I saw each other in the parking lot and talked for a few minutes. He asked for my number. We've been talking some, so I decided to ask him to this feast, so y'all can vet him."

"He's hot." Latishia rolled her eyes and fanned herself.

"Latishia! Girl, I don't know what I'm gonna do with you." Mama Snide gave her *the look,* the one I've seen freeze Willy in his tracks. It had the same effect on Latishia.

"Girls, you need to pick wisely when it comes to a mate. The wrong man can make your life a septic tank, but the right one can make it sweet as sorghum syrup." Mama Snide pointed her fan at Latishia. "You need to look past a gentleman's physical appearance down deep to the good stuff."

"But, Mama," Latishia whined, bottom lip protruding again, "shouldn't there be at least some form of physical attraction? I don't want to marry a man that makes me want to gag."

"I didn't say he had to be ugly as Hades, but sexual chemistry can get you into *big* trouble, and it doesn't last. Better to look for good character in a man who cherishes you, and who can make you laugh." Mama Snide nodded like she was adding a period to her advice. "If you're lucky, you'll find one like your daddy who's good looking, too."

Latishia once told me that Mama Snide was pregnant when her boyfriend beat her so badly she spent two days in the hospital. It was touch and go, but Mama Snide didn't lose the pregnancy. She broke up with Latishia's biological father as soon as she got out of the hospital.

Willy met Mama Snide when Latishia was a month old. Mama took her car to his shop to have the water pump replaced. He refused to charge her and asked her to a movie. Six months later, they married. Willy hired an attorney to assist in terminating the birth father's parental rights, and he adopted Latishia.

Aware that it had become quiet, we turned to see the flushed faces of our guys as they headed our way.

Willy tossed the football in my direction, and I caught it. "What've you ladies been talking about over here, while we've been running around impressing y'all with our might and muscle?"

Mama Snide giggled like a teen. "Why we've been talking about y'all, and that's all I have to say about the subject."

"Woman, I'm hot and hungry, and the ice cream should be ready by now." Willy pulled his wife to her feet and kissed her.

"Willy, behave yourself!" She pushed him back with her palms.

We pulled ourselves from our comfortable seats and followed Mama Snide into the house like imprinted ducklings, to retrieve the desserts and think over her advice.

Chapter 50: Time for a Break

It started as a lark. We were sitting at a round table at the local meat and three in the Five Points area, enjoying breakfast on a Saturday. We were tucked away into a back corner. I had my back to the wall because I hate when a waitress ambushes me by reaching over my shoulder to top off my coffee after I've doctored it to perfection. Gina was to my right, Latishia to my left and Kat occupied what I considered to be the prime ambush seat since her back was to the room. It didn't matter because she was drinking hot tea.

Gina stretched and yawned. "I need a break. We should go to Florida, hit the beach and get a tan."

Latishia spread jam on her third biscuit and cut a sideways glance at Gina. Latishia loves biscuits the way I love popcorn. "I don't need a tan, and if you get much darker people are going to think we're sisters."

"Oh, come on, Latishia, think of the relaxing sound of the waves, the beautiful sunsets on the water, drinks with little umbrellas, and *the men*." Gina's gaze fixed on Latishia.

The biscuit paused in front of Latishia's mouth. "Did you say, men?"

Kat tucked her inky black hair behind one ear. "That sounds good to me. It's been years since I've had an adult-centered vacation that doesn't involve superheroes and roller coasters."

"Same here," said Latishia. She held up her cup to signal for a refill.

"I like roller coasters," I said.

All three of them looked at me as if I was a lunatic.

"I throw up on roller coasters," Gina said. "The last time I was forced to get on one of those in Georgia, I tossed my cookies." Gina shook her head. "No roller coasters."

Latishia wrinkled her nose. "Too much information." She pushed her cup to the edge of the table when the waitress arrived with the coffee.

I placed my hand over my cup and shook my head at the waitress when she aimed the pot in my direction. "Getting time off is my problem. I'm booked two weeks ahead, and I would need to find a clinician to cover emergency calls for me."

Gina looked around the table. "I suggest the third week of September. The kids will be in school, it's off-season rates, and the weather will still be warm enough." She nodded when the waitress poised the pot over her cup.

We all fell silent. I tried to think of who would cover my emergencies. I was sure my next-door neighbor would watch Buffy, since their dog, Ratsy, was best doggie buddies with mine.

Gina doctored her coffee with cream and sugar. "Margie, in the townhouse next to me, will feed Jasmine and Oscar. She loves my Siamese. I have a month to clear my caseload and give the judges notice." She tasted it, winced, and added another sugar.

"My parents will watch Jack, and I'm sure Dr. Howard can call in his retired nurse for a week. She's still licensed and told him she would fill in for vacations." Kat poured another cup of tea from a small silver pot into her mug.

Latishia dusted crumbs from her hands. "My momma will watch Dante. I just need to clear it with my boss at the bank."

Without another word, all four of us reached for our smart phones to check the dates.

Chapter 51: Florida Here We Come

After assessing each of our vehicles, the Divas decided to take Kat's minivan on the trip to Florida. If it could carry her parents, grandparents, and son, it could carry four Divas and our luggage. We all agreed to limit our luggage to one suitcase, a cosmetic case, and a pillow if desired. Since Latishia lived in Decatur, she was the last to be picked up for the journey south.

We had all complied with the luggage agreement — except Latishia. When we pulled up and tooted the horn, she came out of the house hauling two flamingo-pink suitcases down her sidewalk. Dante trailed behind her, carrying a cosmetic case and a pillow. Behind him, her mother waddled with a gait that warned of a future hip replacement.

Latishia was the spitting image of her mother; only her mother's coarse gray hair was pulled back into a bun. Willy was probably at work since Friday was a big car repair day.

Kat blocked the sidewalk, her hands on her hips. "How many suitcases are you bringing?"

Latishia failed to meet Kat's gaze. "Just these two little ole cases."

"Why do you need two?" Kat widened her stance. "We agreed to one large suitcase apiece."

Latishia pointed at the bag to her left. "That one's for my clothes and the other one is for my shoes."

Kat shook her head and sighed, just as she always does before she gives in.

Latishia jutted her chin forward. "A lady has to have the right shoes to wear with each outfit." She crossed her arms as best she could over her ample bosom.

Gina and I piled out of the van to greet her mother. Mama Snide gathered me into an embrace, giving me her little sway to the left and right before releasing me.

She held me out at arm's length. "Phoenix, girl, you're skin and bones. You need to come stay with me for a week or so, and I'll put some meat on your bones."

Gina was behind me, waiting her turn. "Momma Snide, this is the way guys like their women nowadays, so Phoenix is in fashion."

"What's wrong with men? Don't they know they need something to hang onto besides bones?" Momma Snide encased Gina. "Now sweetie, you have some padding on those ribs like a woman ought to have."

Gina shot me a smug grin and sashayed to the back of the red minivan to help Latishia load her bags.

"How many pairs of shoes do you own?" she grunted, as she lifted the pink luggage into the back of the van.

"Fifty-two." Dante grinned as he backed out of Latishia's swatting range.

"Boy, have you been in my closet countin' my shoes again?" Latishia shot him a threatening glare, guaranteed to singe further information from his tongue.

"That girl of mine does love her shoes," chuckled Momma Snide. "She's gonna have to build an addition to the house for her shoes and clothes." She shook her head. "When I was a girl growing up on the farm, we were lucky to get one pair of shoes a year."

Latishia wrapped Dante's skinny form into a hug that made him look like a hotdog in a bun.

"You obey your Maw Maw you hear?"

"Yes, Mama."

"Shotgun!" Latishia raced to the front passenger door. She could move remarkably fast for a woman in platform heels.

Knowing there would be no chance of ousting her from her chosen seat, Gina and I crawled into the back, me behind Kat and Gina behind Latishia.

As we pulled away to begin our journey, I could hear Latishia sniffling in the front. "I already miss my baby."

I saw her pull a tissue from her purse to dab her eyes.

Gina rolled her eyes. "You're not going to do that the whole way to Florida, are you?"

"You don't understand because you're not a mother." Latishia honked into a Kleenex.

Gina crossed her arms. "I don't hear Kat carrying on, and she's a mother."

"That's because I did all my crying before I picked y'all up," said Kat, eyes fixed on the road.

"Well, we're off like a herd of turtles," I said, trying to get off the subject of motherhood. "Who knows what adventures lie ahead?"

"To adventure," we all chorused before Latishia reached for another tissue.

Chapter 52: On the Road

The trip to Florida took longer than anticipated. There appears to be a direct correlation between menopause and an increase in the number of tinkle breaks. Seven-hour trips also offer ample opportunities for discussion.

Gina nudged me. "Have you heard anything from Todd?"

"Nope, but I hear things about him almost every time I go to Decatur for my art lesson. Mary Kate Smithers is in my class and lives in his neighborhood. Todd started attending her church several months after the divorce. According to her, he's still spreading rumors that I asked for the divorce. Oh, and I got a call from my busybody ex-next-door neighbor, Ruth."

Latishia turned in her seat to look at me in the back seat. "The religious zealot? What did she say?"

"Frank, the neighbor across the street who shot at Todd, has filed for divorce and moved out of the house. According to Ruth, his 'fornicating wife' Deloris is so afraid of him that she moved in with her sister in Tennessee. The house is empty and for sale." I shifted in my seat and adjusted my seatbelt, which felt like it was digging into my collarbone.

Kat glanced at me in the rearview mirror. "I bet Todd was a nervous wreck, knowing that his lover's husband was living across the street and looking for an opportunity to shoot at him again."

"He's lucky Frank was such an awful shot. Ruth told me he fired five times and nary a one hit Todd." I nudged Gina. "Has Bird asked you about the Wesson oil and birdseed payback?"

"You mean Bird Shit," said Latishia.

I chuckled as I reached down, slipped off my sandals, and wiggled my toes. I was admiring my nail polish that matched the pink suitcases in the back when Latishia started giggling. Soon we all were laughing.

"There's nothing like sneaking around behind a titty bar in the middle of the night, dispensing Diva justice," said Latishia.

"I've seen the asshole twice since then. Mr. Bird turns his head and pretends he doesn't see me." Gina shrugged as if it didn't matter, but her face clouded over like a thunderstorm ready to break loose.

"How do you feel when you see him?" I asked. I knew Gina's veins pulsed with passionate Sicilian blood, so I was curious.

"I have this compulsion to punch him in the face and kick him in the nuts, but that would be unprofessional." A sneaky grin oozed across her face "So instead, I took the top off my grande caramel macchiato, tripped by accident, and spilled the entire contents all over the front of his Brooks Brothers suit, starched white shirt, and Jerry Garcia tie. It's a shame he was on his way to court."

Kat glanced back at us in the rearview mirror. "What'd he do?"

"He said the 'F' word, right there in the doorway of the courtroom in front of his client, who was a little old lady. She admonished him for his language and told him it was an accident. He looked so pissed" Gina grinned. "I thought his eyes would pop out of his head. Of course, he couldn't tell his client why he was so mad."

"That's awful." I laughed along with the other Divas. "Did you go to confession?"

"Of course I did." She crossed herself for good measure. "I confessed on Saturday afternoon. Father 'O'Reilly directed me to say one Our Father and two Hail Mary's. That's enough about my adventures. What about Jerome, Latishia?"

"He is the sweetest guy, but there's just no sparks. Shoot, it's hard to imagine hot sex with a man you're afraid you might break or squash. We decided to be friends."

The vision of Latishia, naked, straddling Jerome's skinny frame, kicked off my giggle box. Her boobs alone could smother him. The laughter spread around the minivan like a contagion.

After I wiped my eyes and could breathe again, I asked Kat, "What about Derrick?"

I saw her smile in the rearview mirror. "We still see each other and the sex is fabulous, but our schedules are incompatible. He's caught the night shift and I work days, so we snatch a few hours together when we can. He's trying to get on days, but it may be awhile, because he doesn't have as much seniority as some of the other guys."

"That's too bad." Latishia started squirming in her seat. "I've got to pee."

"Again?" said Gina, rolling her eyes.

Kat shook her head, turned on her blinker, and pulled off at the next exit.

Chapter 53: Florida at Last

We'd chosen to stay at the Southern Breeze Hotel. One of Latishia's clients owned it and gave us an additional discount from the off-season rate.

“Jason told me it’s a six-story hotel that contains ninety-nine rooms and is painted coral with turquoise accents and doors,” said Latishia.

“That should make it easy to spot from the road,” said Kat.

“The decor is supposed to be retro, old Florida.”

When we arrived at the Southern Breeze Hotel, we were all ready to stretch our limbs. Stiff from sitting so long, we shuffled like little old women toward the lobby. We stopped to admire the three green, ceramic sea turtles placed in the mosaic tile in front of the doors.

Latishia was the first through the door. The rest of us ran into her when she came to a sudden, immovable stop in front of us. Peering around her, we all inhaled at once. The description Latishia gave us did little to prepare us for what we saw. A riot of color assaulted our vision.

“Wow!” Latishia moved further into the room.

“Wow, indeed!” My head swiveled from left to right.

Shaped like a T, we stood at the cross section of the lobby with the long end in front of us. To the left was an area of small, round coral tables surrounded by wrought iron chairs with matching coral cushions. To the right was the set-up for the complimentary breakfast. The interesting part was the lobby itself.

“These are gorgeous!” Gina rushed toward the glass shelves in front of the plate glass window directly ahead of us. The shelves held an astounding array of art glass vases that must have been worth a fortune.

The window looked over a dune to the Gulf of Mexico. Relentless waves washed tons of water ashore. The sun highlighted the foaming crests. A dark blue at the horizon, the water shifted in shade to a lighter blue, and then to light emerald green, before it crept across the sand.

“Lordy, I’m glad my Dante’s not here. That child is all knees and elbows right now. I’d be buying a broken vase for sure, maybe two or three.” Latishia walked to her right, toward an accent table nestled against the wall. “Ooh, look at these cute coral-shaped lamps. I’d love to know where they bought them.” She reached out a tentative finger to touch the closest one.

To the left, a turquoise leather sofa and two chairs sat atop a multicolored striped rug. Behind the sofa, an array of white plates with colored polka dots flanked a glassed and framed tapestry of the state of Florida.

"Oh my gosh, look at this adorable curved couch," said Kat.

The upholstery was coral, with white sea turtles. Kat, a turtle fan like me, sat down and ran her hand over the fabric.

I found myself drawn to the front of an Art Deco black-and-glass display case, which was stylishly wider at the top than the bottom. A giant clamshell sat on top. Inside the case was a beautiful assortment of collector-quality shells. I love seashells, and I'd brought my blue bucket to collect any shells I might spot on the beach.

A perky lady in her twenties greeted us in a lilting Jamaican accent. "I'm Dasia, welcome to the Southern Breeze."

She checked us in with speedy efficiency, informed us that our rooms came with a fridge and a microwave, and handed us our key cards. We all had fifth-floor rooms with balconies facing the Gulf. After Gina, Kat, and I had hauled our luggage onto the elevator, Kat and Gina grinned as they watched Latishia labor in our direction with her extra luggage. There was no way her bags would fit in the remaining space.

Kat yelled, "Meet us in the lobby in a swimsuit in twenty minutes."

Then she reached out and poked the button to our floor, and we watched the door close on a huffing Latishia.

"Was that mean?" Kat asked after the elevator began to rise.

Gina crossed her arms and lifted her chin. "She broke the suitcase rule."

"If you didn't wait because Latishia and all her luggage wouldn't fit inside the elevator, it wasn't cruel. If you closed the door to punish her for bringing too much luggage, it was mean and y'all need to get over it." I eyeballed them, but they refused to look at me, instead choosing to stare at the shiny surface of the elevator door.

The elevator dinged and we rolled our luggage to our appointed rooms. Mine was the closest to the elevator, Kat's was next, and then came Gina's room. Poor Latishia had the longest walk, bless her heart.

After I had unpacked, I changed into a coral one-piece swimsuit with a flouncy attached skirt. I decided to try to counteract the calories I was destined to eat by racing down the stairs.

I arrived in the lobby as Latishia walked off the elevator.

She was decked out in a bright Hawaiian floral print one-piece with a fuchsia pink wrap tied around her hips. A wide-brimmed white hat that had a matching fuchsia scarf tied around it covered her braids.

I was a bit surprised by the bright colors. I'd never seen Latishia wear fuchsia, but she did color-coordinate with the lobby.

"Latishia, I'd always envisioned you in a sexy leopard-print bathing suit," I said.

"I brought one. Maybe I'll wear it tomorrow."

That led me to wonder, *How many swimsuits did she bring?*

Dressed in black one-piece suits, Gina and Kat stood talking near the water dispenser. "Let's do it, ladies." Gina led the way.

We ventured onto the patio, which contained a rectangular pool surrounded by turquoise lounge chairs.

Kat had pulled on oversized prescription sunglasses before she peered around. "What? No hot tub?"

"I was looking forward to a good long soak," I admitted.

"You can't have everything for the discount we got." Latishia gestured at the chairs. "They do love turquoise around here."

Let's go!" Gina raced over the wooden boardwalk that protected the sea grass-dotted dunes and hit the sand at a full run. She threw her arms in the air and executed a series of ballet leaps as she headed toward the water.

I hurtled with much less grace behind her. Kat leaped with the grace of a gazelle in imitation of Gina. It was apparent who had ballet lessons as a child and who didn't. Latishia trudged through the loose sand, puffing away behind us.

We squealed with delight as the chilly waves splashed us.

"Damn, I know where I'm coming the next time a hot flash tries to barbecue me on the spot." Latishia grinned, leaned over, and splashed us, which precipitated a splash battle.

“Stop! How old are y’all? Ten?” yelled Kat as she tried to keep her sunglasses dry.

I filled my little blue bucket with water, crept up behind Gina and dumped it on her head, to the delight of everyone but Gina. She screeched, hair plastered to her head like a wet poodle, and chased me down the beach, cursing in Italian.

Latishia and Kat cackled when Gina caught me. She wrestled my blue bucket away from me and bent to fill it with water.

I raced back toward our friends. The muscles in my legs were burning from the effort. By the time I reached them and hid behind Kat, I had a stitch in my side.

Miscalculating my evasive maneuver, Gina flung the water. It hit Kat, square in the face.

The horrified look on Gina’s face said it all.

Kat reached up, took off her dripping sunglasses, and held them at arm’s length.

Latishia’s mouth gaped open. “Uh, oh.”

Still struggling to breathe, I walked from behind Kat. Unlike Gina, Kat’s dripping hair made her look like a drowned Yorkie.

Gina’s eyes were wide with apprehension. “Oh, Kat! I — I’m so sorry.” She giggled. Her hand flew to her mouth trying to hold it in. “No, really….” She giggled again.

Kat was giving her a thin-lipped, “this isn’t funny” look. But it was. Latishia started chuckling, which tickled me into laughter. I couldn’t help it. I saw the corner of Kat’s mouth twitch a couple of times before she broke into laughter, too.

We all laughed so hard; we had to sit down in the sand. An older couple holding hands walked past us, staring as if we’d just escaped an insane asylum and missed our afternoon dose of medication.

After we had settled down, we traipsed down the beach, me stopping to pick up shells along the way.

“What’re you going to do with all those shells?” asked Kat.

“Decorate with them and use them in craft projects.” I listened to the satisfying *chink* as another shell fell into my bucket.

A beautiful sunset was in the making. The sun played hide-and-seek behind purple clouds tinged with red, casting "This is God" rays onto the undulating ocean.

"How can anyone look at that and not believe in God," said Latishia, with fervor.

"Or Buddha," said Kat.

"Where do y'all want to eat tonight?" Latishia planted her hands on her hips, looking determined to discuss our dinner options.

"A friend of mine said the Bay Steamer was the place to go." Gina reached down, snagged a shell, and dropped it into my bucket.

After murmurs of agreement, we all stopped and watched the sun go to bed.

Chapter 54: Swizzled

The Bay Steamer looked more elegant than most of the places in the area. The exterior looked classy with a coastal Mediterranean motif. Inside, thousands of tiny lights covered the ceiling, making it seem magical.

We sat in a long wooden booth, Kat and Gina on one side and Latishia and I on the other, and mused over the menu.

"Wow, look at this steamer bucket for four. It has everything — crab legs, mussels, shrimp, new potatoes, and corn on the cob." Gina pointed at the option.

"If it has crab legs, I'm in," I said.

"Me too." Kat picked up the wine list.

"Good, it's decided," said Latishia.

Kyle, our waiter, took our order while we admired his youth, vigor and great tanned legs. I looked anemic next to him, one of the disadvantages of being a redhead.

"You ladies may want to stay close to home tonight," he told us. "There's a wicked storm brewing in the Gulf, and it's due to hit around eight. The weather forecaster is predicting tornado warnings as a possibility."

"Damn," said Gina. "We just left Huntsville, Alabama, the tornado capital of the South."

"No worries, it'll be clear tomorrow and the rest of the week." He grinned and winked.

"If we don't get blown away first," mumbled Latishia.

Kat handed Kyle her menu and in her usual calm manner said, "What will be, will be."

Our waiter deposited a metal pail that brimmed with food. The only conversation was "mmm's" and "ahh's" as we worked our way though the seafood and created a mountain of napkins. When we finished, it looked like a group of toddlers had been eating at the table.

"Dessert, ladies?" Kyle asked. "We have fresh key lime pie."

"I can't move." Latishia rubbed her stomach and groaned as she slid further down the seat.

The rest of us shook our heads. I wanted the pie, but I didn't have anywhere to put it at that moment. If I could sit for thirty minutes or walk on the beach first, I could manage it.

I could hear the whistling wind as it rustled the palm trees outside.

"What next?" asked Gina, as she tore open a packet that contained a wet wipe.

I stretched and dug through my purse in search of a credit card. "I suggest we take Kyle's advice and go back to the hotel."

We settled the tab and raced to Kat's van while the clouds spit rain at us. Back at the hotel, we struggled against the rising wind after we exited the vehicle. Sand was blowing across the parking lot, and the palm trees were rattling. Latishia's braids whipped around in the wind like Medusa's snakes. Once inside, we all took a deep breath.

I looked around. Kat and Gina looked like they'd walked through a hurricane. I didn't dare venture a guess about the state of my hair.

Latishia flipped her braids over her shoulder. "Where is that bar, aren't they supposed to have live entertainment?" She gave us a saucy grin. "Remember, ladies, what happens in Florida stays in Florida."

Gina tried to finger-comb her unruly curls. "What's gotten into your little ole Southern Baptist soul?"

"Let's just say I've got a little 'sand in my soul.' " Latishia cocked a hip and rested a fist on it.

"You've read too many of those billboards on the way down here," I said.

Kat was wiping the rain off her glasses. "Let's meet in the lobby in fifteen minutes."

I rode the elevator to avoid the deluge of rain that was pounding the stairs. I raced to my room, brushed my teeth and tried to run a brush through the tangle of my wind-blown hair.

After we had gathered in the lobby, we wandered down the hallway and stood in a half-circle outside the turquoise upholstered door of the Swizzler. The porthole-shaped window in the door had a martini etched on the glass.

Latishia shook her head. "Yep, they sure do like turquoise around here."

"That door looks like a tufted piece of furniture. How did they do that?" asked Kat, as she reached out to touch it.

"To me, it looks like someone took off the back of a vinyl booth at a diner, cut a hole for the window and hung it as a door," said Gina.

"I like it," said Latishia.

"Let's go, ladies." I squared my shoulders and pushed through that door into a narrow rectangular cocktail lounge.

The bar was to the right. It was a tight squeeze to move past the patrons seated there. The left wall was a colorful tropical mural complete with palm trees, monkeys, hula girls and a guy sleeping in a hammock. Halfway down the room the bar curled toward the wall, and the space opened to accommodate small tables.

"Wild," said Kat, turning in a circle to take it all in.

"Welcome to the Swizzler Martini Bar, ladies. I'm Don, your friendly bartender." He winked and smiled, as he eyed Kat. Her rotation gave him a 360-degree view of her in her floral sundress. If his grin was any indication, he seemed to appreciate the view.

Kat turned in his direction and her gaze locked with his. I could see the smitten expression and twinkle in her eyes as she gave a seductive "come hither" smile. Don was just her type, tall and slender, with a head full of salt-and-pepper hair.

I rested my hand on the padded turquoise edge of the bar and looked around. Each chair was made of black wrought iron and turquoise upholstery, designed to look from the back like a martini glass with an olive. The tables, in shades of pink and charcoal, were shaped like kidney beans and were surrounded by lower versions of the martini glass chairs.

"Is there any entertainment in here tonight?" asked Latishia.

"He should be here in…," Don looked at his watch, "ten minutes."

"Look at these." I pointed to five framed displays of swizzle sticks.

The Divas crowded around, each pointing out her favorites.

"Here's one from the Tropicana in Las Vegas," said Latishia. "I've always wanted to check out 'Sin City.'"

Gina gave Latishia an incredulous look. "You're Southern Baptist. What're you going to do in Vegas?"

"Um, missionary work?" Latishia twirled one of her braids. "That is, right after I see the Elvis museum."

"Good grief, could we not discuss Elvis? Todd *loves* Elvis." I dropped my forehead to the padded bar edge and thumped it a few times.

"No kidding?" Kat shook her head. "You want to see the Elvis museum?"

"There's one from the Copacabana, in New York." I pointed. I'd use any diversion to get the subject off of the "King of Rock and Roll."

"Ooh, there's one from The Poodle Room, Fontainebleau," said Gina, peering over my shoulder at the pink swizzle stick that depicted a poodle.

"Here's one of ours." Don reached across the bar and presented a swizzle stick to Kat.

Kat accepted it. "Oh, it looks like a monkey."

"Turn it around," said Don. "The back looks like Mickey Mouse."

We all stood squinting at the swizzle stick pinched between her delicate fingers.

"And this is our signature piece." Don pointed at the back wall behind the bar where a black wrought-iron martini-glass-shaped device rested on the counter. It held all the martini glasses from their stems.

"Where are you guys from?" Don's gaze focused on Kat's exotic face.

Gina climbed onto one of the delicate barstools. "Huntsville, Alabama."

"Alabama or Auburn fans?" Don finished topping off a beer and handed it to a guy further down the bar.

"Roll, Tide, Roll!" Gina, Kat, and I pumped our fists in the air. Alabama had won another National Championship, so we Crimson Tide fans were entitled to a year to celebrate and brag.

"We'll get along just fine." Don grinned and winked again at Kat.

Kat looked down at the swizzle stick she was twirling in her fingers and blushed. She glided onto the barstool and perched with the grace of a ballet dancer.

Latishia, on the other hand, wasn't faring well. Every time she attempted to hoist her bootie onto the stool, it would swivel and dump her. It was a small moving target for a voluptuous woman. Latishia was beginning to lose patience.

I noticed a giant of a man whose broad shoulders filled the doorway of the bar. He smiled and watched as Latishia once again tried to mount that finicky stool. He strode forward. "Excuse me, ma'am."

She turned to face a broad chest covered by a light blue shirt. I watched her work her way up past the buttons to a face that looked hewn from dark granite. The man's caramel eyes twinkled with amusement.

"Aaron Jones, ma'am. May I assist you?" He smiled down at Latishia's upturned face.

Our chatter stopped as all the Divas' eyes focused on the gallant gentleman.

"Porca troia!" Gina's mouth hung open as she eyed the guy with obvious appreciation.

"Why yes," Latishia answered. "This stool is shifting around like a broncing stud…; I mean horse."

Freudian slip, I thought. I could tell by his manner and posture he probably spent some time in the military. My guess would be Air Force since Eglin Air Force Base was nearby.

Without pause, he placed both large hands around Latishia's waist, bent his knees, and with one fluid motion lifted her like a feather and placed her on the round cushion.

Latishia giggled like a girl and looked up at him from under her lashes. "Have a seat, Aaron. I don't know if you're a hero or not, but you're certainly mine."

"It'd be my pleasure, ma'am." Aaron slid onto the seat next to hers.

"Latishia Snide." She held out her hand. He engulfed it in his and gave her a mischievous grin.

"This is Phoenix, Kat, and Gina." She waved her free hand in our direction without taking her eyes off his face.

"Nice to meet you, ladies." He nodded in our direction.

"That's two down," whispered Gina. "There's only the two of us to keep each other company."

"Where do you live, Latishia?" Aaron asked.

"Huntsville."

"Alabama or Texas? Please say Alabama."

"Why?"

Aaron rested his forearm on the bar as he flashed white teeth. "My company is transferring me to Huntsville, Alabama, in a couple of weeks, and I don't know a soul there."

Latishia reached over and patted his large hand. "You do now."

I scooted onto a chair and leaned forward as I rested my hands on the rim of the bar. "Hey Don, what's the specialty drink here?"

"Martinis. We have a whole list of flavors, but chocolate martinis are our signature drink."

All the Divas' heads turned in his direction. If there was one thing we could all agree on, it was chocolate.

"Chocolate!" Gina's eyes sparkled, anticipation clear in her voice.

"I want one of those. I'll treat this round, ladies." I sniffed the air. "Do I smell popcorn?"

"Yep." Don tilted his head toward the turquoise door. "It smells like my manager got the machine set up. Help yourself."

A popcornaholic, I followed my nose to the hallway outside the door of the Swizzler to a freestanding machine. I could see why they set it up here, since the bar didn't have an ounce of free space. The butter smell made my mouth water.

I jumped when Gina walked up behind me and touched me on the shoulder.

"Geez, don't sneak up on me like that."

"I wasn't sneaking, you were in a popcorn trance," said Gina.

"Gina, this is the first time I've been in a bar as a single woman in twenty years. It feels sorta weird."

Gina laughed. "You mean eons, right?"

I hip bumped her. "I'm not that ancient. You'd best keep in mind we're the same age."

"Do you miss being married?"

I nodded. "Parts of it. I have to admit I haven't had this much fun in years."

We watched as fluffy corn broiled over the top of the popper and into the pile below. I opened the glass door and grabbed the shaker of butter salt sitting on a nearby table. Shaking it over the popped corn, I returned the salt to the table. After shoveling the popcorn into bags with a scoop, I handed them one by one to Gina, who delivered them inside to the Divas and Aaron.

Back in the bar, I settled on my stool and savored the flavors of butter and salt as I crunched into the warm popcorn. I rolled my eyes toward heaven.

"If you think that's good, taste this." Don placed a martini glass rimmed with dark chocolate in front of me. A tiny red plastic monkey swung by one paw from the edge of the glass.

I swirled the swizzle stick, took a sip and closed my eyes to savor the melody of flavors.

"This is my new favorite drink," I said and took another sip. The contrast of the chocolate martini and salty popcorn was decadent.

"Mine too," said Gina, a true chocolate lover.

"It's good, but a bit too sweet for me." Kat tweaked her blue monkey and smiled as she watched it swing on the edge of the glass.

More people came into the bar, and the volume of the conversations rose.

A crack of lightning flashed through the glass door on the other end of the lounge. Seconds later a foundation-shaking rumble of thunder followed. All heads turned toward the solid glass door, the only barrier between us and the horizontal slashes of rain beating the concrete pool deck.

Dasia stuck her head in the bar from the hallway. "Hey, everyone, we're under a tornado warning. I need all of you to come to our shelter area."

Latishia slid off her chair, pulled her long shirt down over her butt, and grabbed her martini. "I'm taking my drink. I may need to calm my nerves."

We all grabbed our drinks and followed Dasia to a long hallway off the lobby.

"This is it?" Gina looked around. "There's no place to sit." She handed me her drink, put her back to the wall and slid like an eel to the floor. After she adjusted her position and crossed her ankles, she reached for her drink. I handed her my glass, too. Following her example, I dropped with less grace into a cross-legged position beside her and retrieved my chocolate martini. Kat shrugged. Still holding her glass, she melted to the floor and adjusted her stance to a full lotus.

"Show off," said Latishia, grinning. "I'm not sitting on the floor. I'll get my pants dirty, and I'd never make it back up."

Kat looked at her from the floor. "If you'd come to my yoga classes, you could get up and down without a problem."

"If I came to your yoga class, I wouldn't be able to walk for a week."

Aaron plopped down a chair next to Latishia. "Your chair awaits you, my lady."

Latishia turned in surprise. "You're such a sweetie," she crooned, as she flashed him a radiant smile.

"Aim to please, Ma'am." Aaron sat on the floor beside her, resting his back against the wall, with one knee propped up and his wrist draped over it. He exuded testosterone in waves. I was happy that Latishia had found a man who appreciated her style. I prayed he didn't turn out to be a closet creep.

The hallway became crowded as people came down from their rooms. Discussions bounced off the walls, and the air soon became warm and stuffy.

An hour later, the weather threat was over. We had no damage but there were reports of possible touchdowns in Pensacola, thirty minutes up the beach.

After agreeing on a time to meet for breakfast, Gina and I decided to go to bed. Kat and Latishia ambled back into the Swizzler.

When I arrived at my fifth-floor room, I found a white bath towel stretched across the front of my door. It was soaking wet. I could feel the rain pelting my back as I stood there trying to open the door.

"I'm getting drenched," Gina yelled.

"Me, too!" I pushed into my room and slammed the door shut. Remembering the towel, I knelt, opened the door, snaked my hand outside and grabbed it, pulling it toward me as I closed the door. Sighing with frustration, I stood up and turned around to face my balcony door. *I wonder if that one is leaking as well.*

I walked past my king-sized bed and saw a puddle spreading under the door. The rain beat against it like a hundred gnomes demanding entrance. I retraced my steps past the bed, turned right into the bathroom, and grabbed two white bath towels. My plan was to open the door, place a towel in front of it, close the door, and place another one on the inside to soak up the water from the carpet.

That was the plan.

I opened the door and bent to place the first towel, but the wind and rain drove me back. I fought my way back to the door, eyes squinting against the blowing rain, and laid out the towel. Now soaked to my undies, I slammed the door, locked it, and set the safety bar.

The door flew open and caught on the safety bar. Wham! *What in the world! I locked that sucker.*

Bam! I crammed it shut and relocked it.

It flew open again. Wham!

Angry, I heaved it closed again. Bam! Leaning my entire weight on the door, I heard the click that announced the latch had finally caught.

Soaked to the skin, my chest heaved from the exertion. The phone rang, and I sloshed over to answer it. I glanced in the mirror as I picked up the handset. I looked like Buffy after a bath.

It was Gina.

"Phe, what are you doing over there? Why are you slamming all the doors?"

I explained the situation.

"Wait, let me check my balcony door." There was a long pause. "Merda, I need to put down some towels."

The dial tone buzzed in my ear.

I peeled off my wet clothes and stood shivering to adjust the water for a shower when the door banging began next door. I climbed in the shower and laughed as I trembled under the steamy hot water.

Chapter 55: Blown Away

The next morning, I opened the balcony door and stepped over two soggy wet towels. I bent and pulled them onto the balcony and then leaned over the rail to see the sunrise to my left. *Gorgeous!* Orange and yellow stained the clouds and the waves pounded the shore.

I raced inside and snatched my camera to take photos. The wind was so strong that I had to place the strap over my head to assure it wouldn't be blown out of my hands as I leaned over the balcony rail for a shot.

Ready for coffee, I dressed and bounced down the stairs. Not many people were in the breakfast area. I perused the options and decided on waffles. I poured batter into a small cup, filled the waffle maker and flipped it over. While it cooked, I helped myself to crisp bacon and scrambled eggs. I set them on a table for four, filled a coffee mug and doctored it with cream. By then, the waffle machine binged. I flipped it over, opened the lid and speared my waffle with a fork. After I grabbed a packet of syrup, I picked up the waffle and coffee.

I was sitting at the table, dumping a stevia tablet into my coffee, when Gina appeared. She wore white shorts that showed off her tan legs and a shirt with a giant pink flamingo on the front. She looked cute, except for her hair. Her wavy curls looked like they'd doubled in size overnight.

I was enjoying my breakfast when she plopped down opposite me with a cup of coffee and a plate with four slices of bacon.

"Is that all you're eating?" I cocked a brow.

"I'm waiting on my waffle." *Bing*. "Oh, that's it. I'll be back."

Gina returned to her seat and sliced her waffle into precise squares with her knife.

"What happened to your hair?"

Gina grimaced. "The water is so soft down here it took me forever to wash the shampoo out. Then I decided to take the stairs. By the time the wind and the salt air got hold of me, it expanded out of my control. I'll pull it up in a scrunchy when I get back to the room. Any sign of Kat or Latishia?"

"Nope. We agreed to meet in thirty minutes. We'll see if they show up. I suspect they had a late night."

Gina and I were on our second cup of java when Kat stepped off the elevator. She looked like she was sleepwalking her way to breakfast. She tracked straight to the hot water dispenser, plopped a tea bag in her cup and then turned to scan the room. I gave a little wave and smiled. She nodded, and her hand flew to her forehead as she walked in our direction. She slid on the seat to my right and groaned.

"Hangover?" Gina grinned and swallowed some coffee.

"That and I stayed up until three. I'm not used to drinking more than two glasses of wine. Staying up late never affected me this way in my twenties."

"Your twenties are long gone." I frowned as I pulled a fatty section off of a slice of my bacon and looked up at her. "Don didn't take advantage of you, did he?"

Since Kat's gang rape in college, I've been a bit of a mother hen.

She shook her head no, looked like she instantly regretted it, and dropped her forehead down on her crossed arms. "He was a perfect gentleman. Did you know he's a retired detective?"

"Yeah? What kind?" I finished my coffee. I was debating the pros and cons of a third cup in my mind.

"Homicide."

"I'll be right back, don't say anything until I get back. Gina, you want another cup?"

"Sure, leaded."

To rationalize my coffee consumption, I filled mine with decaf. I returned and set down the cups. "Tell all."

Kat pushed herself up and rubbed her temples. "He worked in Chicago and retired on disability after fifteen years. He took a bullet. He seemed fine, but not for active duty. He always wanted to live where it was warmer, so he moved down here and took the job as a part-time bartender at the Swizzler."

Gina chewed and swallowed her last bite of waffle. "How does being a cop qualify him to be a bartender?"

"He paid his way through college by tending bar." Kat took off her glasses, laid them on the table, and rubbed the bridge of her nose before she took a sip of hot tea.

"Did you two hook up?" Latishia was standing beside the table with her hand on her hip.

We all jumped. I never heard her walk up.

Kat rubbed her eyes and yawned. "How long have you been there?"

"About the time you said he took a bullet. Now answer my question." She gave Kat *the look* she usually reserved for Dante when he was naughty.

Kat put her glasses back on. "We made out a little, but that was it." She smiled. "That man can kiss!"

"What about you, missy?" I gave her my patented "tell the truth" look.

Latishia's complexion darkened. She reached up and twirled a braid.

"You and Aaron did it, didn't you?" I laughed.

"Well, he is a fine hunk of a man." She flashed a naughty grin. "We have a date tonight."

Gina glared at Latishia. "After what happened to me, do you think it's safe to go traipsing off with a guy you barely know?"

"You don't understand; it's a group date. Don has tonight off, and he agreed to come with Kat. Aaron even has a couple of guys in mind for you and Phoenix."

"What!" Gina and I said at the same time.

"I don't know." I pushed back my chair. "I don't like mystery dates."

Gina's curls were bouncing as she shook her head.

"Oh, come on. Please!" Latishia looked like a two-year-old begging for candy in the checkout line. "Pretty please with sugar on top." She held her hands together as if praying.

I rolled my eyes and looked over at Gina, who shrugged her shoulders.

"All right," I said with reluctance.

Grinning, Latishia turned and with swaying hips headed to the breakfast bar. While she was busy reading the directions on the waffle maker, we all leaned in close to discuss the situation.

I placed my forearms on the table. "Kat, what happened last night?"

"Those two talked and laughed until the bar closed. I stayed while Don closed down. I guess they left and went to her room."

"She looks like a woman in love, with an after-sex glow." Gina leaned back in her chair to eye Latishia, who was pouring coffee. "One thing for sure, she doesn't have to worry about breaking Aaron, like she did Jerome."

"Oh, my!" A lady to our right pointed at the large flat-screened television attached to the wall.

It showed flattened houses and ripped up trees — the destruction of someone's life savings.

"Where is that?" I strained to hear the report over the clamor of conversations.

Aaron appeared at our table. "It's in Pensacola. A tornado hit there last night."

"Aaron, do you still have today off?" Latishia hurried over with coffee in one hand and a waffle in the other.

"Sorry, Dumpling. I'm a volunteer firefighter. I was called in to help with the mess over in Pensacola. I'll be free by five. I can meet all of y'all in the lobby at 7:00."

"You be careful, you hear?" Latishia put down her waffle and coffee and rose on her toes so Aaron could wrap his arms around her. He kissed her with unexpected tenderness for a man his size.

The rest of us exchanged meaningful looks.

Aaron waved goodbye and strode out the front door of the hotel. Latishia planted her plump rear end on our table's last empty chair and tore into her waffle like she'd run a marathon.

"Dumpling? Did he just call you Dumpling?" I asked, with an incredulous tone.

Latishia shrugged as she soaked her waffle with syrup. "He said I was as tasty and lovable as a dumpling."

"Too much information," I said, holding up my hand.

Kat rubbed her temples. She took a swig of tea, sat straighter and fixed her gaze on Latishia. "How can you be this perky? You stayed up as late as I did last night."

Latishia paused, fork midway to her mouth. With a look of disdain, she said, "I didn't try every type of martini on the drink menu."

"I didn't either."

"Excuse me, almost every one of them. Besides, I exercised off all my drinks and then slept like a baby."

Gina leaned forward and grinned. "I bet he's hung like a horse."

My mouth flew open. "Gina!" I promptly closed it, thinking about that Great Dane at the Concerts in the Park.

Gina leaned closer and lowered her voice. "A man that size can't have a teeny tiny wanger. Am I right, Latishia?"

Latishia's face darkened, and she looked down at her plate and grinned. "Let's just say he's a mighty man."

"How long?" If Gina leaned over anymore, she would be lying on the table.

Latishia cocked a brow as she frowned at Gina. "Lordy, girl, I didn't pull out a measuring tape."

Kat yawned, covering her mouth, and shook, as if trying to wake up. "Why not, you packed everything else."

"Ladies, we need to respect Latishia's privacy. Besides, she didn't ask the measurements of any of our dates," I said, sending a scathing glance in Kat's direction.

"You and I didn't have dates," said Gina.

Kat rubbed her forehead. "Please ignore me this morning. I'm the hung-over bitch hag from the South."

"I'm sorry too, but inquiring minds and all that." Gina sat back in her chair and stretched. "I'm ready to walk on the beach."

"Me too." I pushed back my chair and stood.

Latishia pushed away her empty plate. "I'm game."

Kat lifted her head from her folded arms and glared at us. "Okay, but I'm not going far."

We left the lobby and stepped out onto the concrete deck of the pool. The fence surrounding it and the sand dunes beyond blocked the wind that was still blowing in from the east. I closed my eyes and faced the sun. The warmth felt good.

I followed the Divas over the boardwalk and onto the sand. It seemed a good bit windier on the boardwalk. We left our sandals near the steps and headed for the beach.

Latishia was the first to run toward the water. Her braids flew out behind her like flying snakes. Gina did little ballet leaps as her hair went wild, whipping this way and that.

I stepped past the shield of the dunes, and the wind hit me, causing me to stagger under its force. The blowing sand felt like a thousand bee stings. I grabbed my sunglasses and held them in place.

I turned my back to the gale and yelled, "Kat, go back!" The wind tore the words from my lips.

Kat stumbled out to join us and turned into the wind. She only weighed 98 pounds with her pockets full of change. Struggling to regain her equilibrium, she threw her arms wide for balance. The wind filled her nylon jacket, lifted her up off her feet and knocked her flat on her back.

"Holy shit!" Gina waded through the deep sand trying to get back to the boardwalk.

I beat her to Kat's prostrate form. I yelled, "Latishia," but again, the wind ripped the words from my mouth. In desperation I whistled, the whistle my dad taught me and used when he wanted me to stop playing and come in the house. I saw Latishia turn and trudge through the sand in our direction.

"What happened?" Latishia was breathing in great heaving breaths.

"The wind caught Kat's jacket, picked her up and dropped her on her back," I said, trying to shield Kat from the wind and stay on my feet at the same time. At 120 pounds, I felt the gust shoving at me with bully hands.

"Haven't I told you that someday a big wind would blow you skinny folks away? See, if you were a substantial woman like me, you wouldn't be having this trouble." Latishia reached down and pulled Kat to her feet.

We locked our arms together and formed a wind barrier around Kat until we were behind the dunes.

Huffing from our exertions, we grabbed our sandals and ran over the boardwalk into the pool area sheltered by the dunes.

"My gosh, what speed are those wind gusts?" Kat pulled her jacket close around her and shivered.

I pulled my phone out of my pocket and brought up my weather app. "Thirty mph winds with 40 mph gusts."

Kat leaned over and ruffled her hair to get the sand out. "Well, now I know what those idiots feel like on the weather channel. You know, the ones who stand out in hurricane force winds and tell us not to do it, because it's not safe."

"Good grief, I have sand in my ears, my eyebrows, and my hair," I said.

Gina shook her curls back and forth, trying to rid herself of sand. "I suggest we hang out at the pool, and then go eat lunch and hit this little gift shop I've heard about before we shower and change for dinner."

"As long as I can nap and you wake me to turn over in thirty minutes," said Kat.

Latishia crossed her arms. "Girl, you're not a turkey we have to baste. You need to set the timer on your phone."

We returned to our rooms to change into swimsuits. I ducked into the shower to wash off the grit first. Once back at the pool area, we lined up our turquoise loungers to face the sun, set the timers on our phones and proceeded to roast our hides. Thirty minutes later, a cacophony of alarms trilled. We roused ourselves, reset our alarms and turned over. When our time was up, Latishia looked the same, Kat and Gina had the beginnings of a golden tan, and I was a pale pink, despite sunscreen. Since the ginger shade of my hair was between strawberry blonde and classic red, I would never sport a dark tan like Gina.

We agreed to meet back at the lobby and headed to our rooms once more.

Back in my room, I showered and succeeded in getting the sweat and the last of the sand out of my hair. I changed into a skort with a matching golf shirt. I was so famished; I felt I could eat an entire grouper. Sun does that to me.

* * * *

When I arrived in the lobby, the rest of the Divas were standing in a group around a pudgy lady with beautiful long brown hair.

"Here she is," said Gina. "This is Donna, the manager. She said The Original Crab Trap is better than the one on the beach. She gave Latishia the directions to get there."

"Sounds good to me." I introduced myself to Donna and shook her hand.

"I used to work in Huntsville at the Doubletree near Martin Road. I decided to move down here in January. A fresh start and all."

"She recommended we go to Pandora's Steak House on Wednesday night because they have a special on their prime rib." Latishia had one hand planted on an ample hip. By the dreamy expression on her face, I could tell she could almost taste it.

"You don't want to miss that prime rib. It's delicious, with a loaded potato and a salad, and the price is right. I may try to get there myself, depending on how things go around here." Donna looked over at the reception desk and frowned.

Gina nodded. "I'll be ready for a break from seafood by then."

"Me too," Kat agreed. "Do we know where the guys are taking us tonight?"

Latishia started twirling her braids again. "It's a secret. Aaron won't tell me. I tried to wheedle it out of him."

"Thanks for the information, Donna, hope to catch you later." Kat waved and walked toward the exit.

We trailed behind Kat, who stopped when she stepped out to the covered drop-off area. Gusts of wind were rattling the palm trees.

Kat pushed her glasses up the bridge of her nose as she watched the palm trees bend. "Maybe I should get downwind of Latishia."

Latishia laughed. "I'm coming." She moved Gina and me to the side the way Moses parted the Red Sea, took Kat by the arm, and trooped toward the parking lot. Gina and I linked arms and fought the wind together as we made our way to the minivan.

Once inside, Kat had to run the windshield wipers to remove the sand. "Jeez, I hope I have some paint left on this van by the time I get home."

"I loaded the directions to the restaurant into my phone before you joined us in the lobby." Latishia tapped on her phone and Siri gave us step-by-step directions. Fifteen minutes and one bridge later, we were there.

I squinted out the window as we pulled into the parking lot. "It doesn't look like much."

"All the good local places look like that. They leave the fancy places for the tourists." Latishia leaned over to look through the driver's window. "This is the place. Donna said it was near a harbor and has a deck that overlooks the water."

Kat parked close to the building and killed the engine. "Y'all can sit outside in this wicked wind, but I don't want to be blown over the railing."

Gina laughed. "I see it now in my mind's eye. We'd need to attach an anchor to you."

"Laugh away, Gina, but you weren't doing a flying nun imitation." Kat dropped the ignition key into her purse.

"Keep it up, and you'll have to convert from Buddhism to Catholicism," I said, laughing.

"Too much guilt," said Kat, shaking her head.

Gina opened the sliding door and jumped out. "Yeah, that's true, but there's always confession."

I crawled out behind her.

Kat held on to Latishia the whole way until we were on the porch of the Crab Trap. Inside there were two rooms, each with a bar and the outdoor deck Donna described. We sat at a tall table, perched on high chairs next to a window that overlooked the deck, water, and moored boats.

"The best of both worlds." Kat gestured toward the view. "A great view of the water and our food won't be blown off our plates."

The bar was to our right, and Gina eyed it as she fingered the drink menu. In the end, she ordered iced tea like the rest of us. The service was efficient and friendly. We were sipping our tea and nibbling on our lunches within fifteen minutes, which was good since I was feeling a tad puckish, a word I picked up on my trip to London before Dad was diagnosed with cancer. We finished our grouper po'boys and sat back.

Gina wiped her hands on a fresh paper napkin. "I'm fueled for shopping."

"Me too, are we going to that banana place?" asked Latishia. She stretched her arms behind her head, causing her girls to rise to their full glory. A passing male waiter, distracted by the magnificent sight, tripped on the leg of a chair and dumped his tray of drinks on the patrons seated at a nearby table.

Yowling and cursing, the three men jumped to their feet and backed away from the table.

"Did I cause that?" Latishia wore a wicked grin.

Gina and Kat turned to see what had happened.

"Cause what?" asked Gina. "What are you talking about?"

The three guys stood dripping as the waiter handed each of them a white bar towel, all the while apologizing.

Gina turned back around and answered Latishia's question. "Banana Bart's. It's across the bridge in Destin."

"Time to leave," I said. I scooted off my stool and nudged Latishia. "Those are deadly weapons, try to keep them under control in the future."

We piled into the minivan. The rest of us attempted to tame our wind-whipped hair while Latishia found the address and tapped it into her phone.

"'Head 'em up and move 'em out,' " I said, waving an imaginary lasso over my head.

Gina rolled her eyes. "You've been watching those old reruns of Rawhide, haven't you?" She was digging in her purse looking for something.

"Give me a break. Clint Eastwood looked good, way back then."

"I'll admit, he was hot when he was younger." Gina pulled a scrunchy from the purse and pulled her hair back to tame it.

En route, we passed through a section of the National Seashore and an area owned by Eglin Air Force Base. Sand dunes covered with natural grasses and trees were on both sides of the four-lane road. The Intracoastal Waterway was to our left and the Gulf of Mexico on our right. Wind buffeted the van, and sand blew across the road like a silica blizzard.

"I'm having difficulty keeping my van in the lane," Kat said. "Is it supposed to be this windy tomorrow?" I glanced at the rearview mirror and could see her brows furrowed in concentration.

Gina reached forward and patted her shoulder. "I checked the ten-day forecast this morning. It's sunny with three mph winds tomorrow. The winds are supposed to reduce to ten mph by tonight, so you'll be safe."

We drove over a long, tall bridge and were in Destin.

"Wow!" Latishia leaned forward in the passenger seat. "Daddy and Mama came down here when I was little, so he could deep-sea fish. There was hardly anything in Destin. I can't believe this."

I pointed to the left. "There's McGuire's Irish Pub. I bet that's an interesting place."

Ten minutes later Latishia warned Kat, "Slow down. It's on the right up ahead. There it is, see the sign?"

The gift shop was located in an old house painted in primary colors. The siding was yellow, with red trim around the windows that spanned the front. The rest of the trim was royal blue, and the doors were bright green. We pulled into a graveled drive and parked in the back. The shop backed up against an inlet and had a dock. We piled out of the van.

"It certainly looks unique," said Kat.

Once inside, we all looked around. I felt my eyes widen. I wasn't sure how the owner crammed this much merchandise into this old house.

"Welcome to Banana Bart's," chimed a melodious female voice with a distinct British accent. We turned in unison to our left. A brunette, middle-aged woman stood behind a counter by the door. She reminded me of an elementary school teacher, though I couldn't pinpoint what gave me that impression.

"Thank you," I said, as Gina and I cruised by the jewelry. Latishia and Kat disappeared into a room full of pirate things. I suspected they were looking for gifts for Dante and Jack. We spent over an hour combing that place for treasures. After I had walked around once, I did it again, because the merchandise was too dense to see in one sweep.

"I love this place." Latishia handed me a stack of cards. "Look at these pirate playing cards I found for Dante. He likes to play rummy with his granddaddy."

"Those are cute." I read the information on the outside of the box, which claimed to provide a mini history lesson on each pirate.

"I'm getting this pirate board game for Jack. The whole family can play." Kat held it so we could see the top that depicted swash-buckling pirates.

"Now that's cool. I would buy that for a kid if I had one." Gina sighed. "If I buy something for one niece or nephew, I have to buy for all six."

"Not if you buy a board game for each household," said Latishia.

Gina tapped her chin with her finger for a moment and then took off for the pirate room. She came back with three different pirate games and a grin on her face. "This way when my nieces and nephews visit each other, they have a different game to play. Good idea, Latishia."

I chose a ceramic mermaid that caught my eye. She was about a foot long and was lying on her tummy, with her arms folded to hold her upper body upright at the waist. She wore a crown of orange coral with two clownfish nestled inside the branches. One long golden braid cascaded over a shoulder and the other down her back. The bra and the scale-covered lower section of her body were shades of dark blue, with orange stripes along her tail fin.

Latishia looked over my shoulder. "Oh look, she has a slut tattoo of a fish on the small of her back, and she's all puckered up waiting to be kissed."

My back stiffen. "Where do you come up with these things? My mermaid is not a slut."

"Hey," Latishia held up her hands, "it's not me, that's what the kids nowadays call tattoos in that area."

Gina joined us. "She's a candle holder. You can put a votive candle in the tailfin that's sticking up."

Latishia grinned and pointed at my mermaid. "It's an Auburn mermaid, see the blue and orange."

She knew that would set me off. I glared at her. "It's *not* an Auburn anything."

"Now ladies," said Kat. She reached over and took her, examining the ceramic sculpture. "Her face is so delicate. I like her. If you don't buy her, I will."

I reached out and grabbed *my* mermaid. "Too bad, she's mine."

We paid for our purchases. The clerk wrapped them with care, and then boxed and bagged our goodies.

"I noticed your accent," I said, as I reached for my package. "I was in London two years ago for a week in the spring."

"I'm from Castle Combe. It's a quaint little town. If you go back to England, go visit the castle there."

I nodded my thanks. "I hope to go back someday."

Pleased with our treasures, we piled into the van and headed back to the hotel.

Latishia sniggered and glanced over her shoulder. "You sure you don't want me to take that Auburn mermaid off your hands?"

I crossed my arms. "She's *not* an Auburn mermaid!" I shook my head with disgust. "I swear you're as bad as your Auburn-loving daddy. Need I remind you that you graduated from the University of Alabama?"

"That's only because I received a scholarship to attend that school."

"You're not fooling me one bit. You loved the Alabama campus." I leaned forward and pointed between the seats. "Turn up ahead into The Donut Hole."

Kat slowed the van and turned on the blinker.

Latishia turned to look at me. "You got a doughnut craving?"

"No, but on our way to the gift shop, I noticed a sign advertising fresh homemade key lime pie," I said.

We parked in the shade of a tree and disembarked for a culinary adventure. Once inside, we all slid into a shining wooden booth, polished by people's backsides. A perky blonde, wearing a nametag that proclaimed she was Julia, welcomed us.

"Is your key lime pie good?" I could almost taste it by the mere thought.

"Yes ma'am, it's sinful."

I closed the menu and handed it to her. "Julia, I want a slice, as well as coffee with cream."

The rest of the Divas also ordered a slice. Within minutes, fresh coffee and tea for Kat arrived. I took a sip to cleanse my palate as Julia placed the pie in front of me. It looked good. I cut a bite with my fork, which sliced with ease through the creamy layer, and crunched through the graham cracker crust.

"Looks fresh," I said and tasted it. The filling was creamy with the perfect combination of sweet and tangy. The crust was perfection, crunchy and tasty with a hint of cinnamon.

"How do you get the crust this crunchy?" I asked Julia, who was pouring a refill on our coffee.

"We put chopped pecans in the crust. Did you taste the cinnamon?"

"Yes, it enhances the overall flavor. I love the differences in the textures of the crust and filling."

"I hate to say it," said Latishia with a shake of her head, "but it's better than Mama's. Don't you dare tell her I said so, you hear?"

"It's the best I've ever eaten. Outstanding idea, Phoenix." Kat winked at me and took another bite.

Gina scraped the plate to extract every morsel. "My mouth wants another slice, but my spreading backside says stop."

Kat sipped her tea and yawned. "I don't know about y'all, but I need a nap."

Latishia dabbed at her mouth with a napkin. "I'm running low on sleep, too. We want to be all fresh and gorgeous for our guys tonight."

Gina and I exchanged glances when Latishia said "our guys."

"We're on a holiday, and siestas are allowed on vacations," I agreed.

We settled our bills, piled back in the van, and headed to the hotel for a snooze to regain our strength for tonight.

Chapter 56: Mystery Dates

Aaron told Latishia the guys would meet us inside the Swizzler. I wasn't so keen on the idea. Drinking on an empty stomach was a sure-fire way for me to become tipsy, and this didn't seem wise before a mystery date.

My phone rang, so I excused myself to escape the rising din in the bar. Pushing through the rear exit door, I walked out to the concrete patio of the pool area and parked my backside on one of the turquoise chaise lounges. The number looked familiar.

Brent Power's cheerful salutation was followed with, "Are you having fun? I can hear the ocean in the background."

"So far, yes. Although I'm happy those tornados missed us." I found myself smiling. The mystery dates were forgotten. Of all the men I'd dated so far, Brent was the one who made me laugh and feel tingly.

"I had my eye on that storm system. I was relieved when I heard it missed Fort Walton."

Did Brent's voice hold a note of concern? The idea of him being concerned about my safety somehow raised my cheer level by two points.

The door from the hotel flew open. A group of children spilled out and beelined to the pool.

"We were sequestered in a hallway for an hour during a tornado warning. Other than that, it was driving rain and high winds." I recounted Kat's "flying nun" incident earlier in the day, and we shared a laugh.

"When do you get home? I've missed you."

"Saturday afternoon." I placed my hand over my free ear. The kids in the pool had decided to start a splash battle, punctuated by high-pitched squeals.

"Would you consider having dinner with me Sunday night?"

"I'd love it." I pumped my fist and grinned, my eyes glued the whole time to the antics of the frolicking children.

"Great, I'll call you Sunday, and we'll finalize the plans."

I looked over to find Latishia craning her head out the door of the bar, waving for me to come.

"Gotta go. The Divas are ready to go eat."

"Be careful, okay?"

There's that concerned tone again. "Will do."

I strolled toward Latishia, who sported a grin usually reserved for when she found the perfect shoes to match an outfit.

"Wait till you see *your* date." She grabbed my arm and pulled me inside.

I blinked as she towed me toward the bar, blinded by the shadowed interior.

Aaron stood at attention. "Phoenix, I'd like to introduce you to Colonel Brian Holcomb. Colonel, this is Dr. Phoenix O'Leary from Huntsville, Alabama." Aaron looked back and forth between us, bouncing on the balls of his feet like a kid waiting for an "attaboy."

I grabbed Latishia's arm and squeezed as I stared at the sexy colonel. At six feet, he was tan and lean with mischievous green eyes. His well-groomed dark hair showed a splash of gray at the temples. I felt a welcome tingle down south in Dixie. Maybe my emotional Novocain was wearing off. I certainly hoped so.

This mystery date isn't going to be so bad after all. There was definite chemistry.

Unsure of how to address him, I said, "Hello, um, Colonel?" I extended my hand and gave him my most charming smile.

“You’re not under my command, so please call me Brian.” His broad grin produced dimples. He took my hand and didn’t release it.

“Since you’re not one of my patients, please call me Phoenix.”

I’m a sucker for dimples. My stomach somersaulted while my heart tap-danced in my chest. I felt an irresistible desire to run my fingers through Brian’s hair. To stop myself, I jammed my free hand into the pocket of my sundress.

“May I buy you a drink?” Brian released my hand and gestured toward the bar.

“No, I’d prefer to wait until I have some food in my system.” I tried to pinpoint his accent. Not Southern, but he’d been in the South long enough to smooth the sharp edges of his speech.

“Wise decision, my dear. I’m hungry myself. Aaron, let’s get some chow.”

Gina walked over, pulling a handsome blond man by the hand. “Phoenix, let me introduce my date, Captain Christopher Jones.”

“Call me Chris.” He gave me a friendly wave with his left hand. Gina had possession of his right, and it didn’t look as if she planned to surrender it anytime soon. She arched one brow at me and grinned. I knew that look; Gina was pleased with her date.

Aaron stood to the side, a smile creasing the angular planes of his face. The ladies and gentlemen all seemed happy with their matches. I wondered if Aaron should leave his current position and start a matchmaking service.

Kat finished her glass of wine. No martinis tonight, I noticed. Don’s beer glass was empty.

“Follow me.” Aaron gestured toward the door. We followed him out in single file until we reached the hallway, where we grouped in pairs. Brian offered me his arm, so I slipped my hand into the crook while observing his chiseled face under lowered lashes. He had sharp cheekbones with a strong jaw. Everything about him oozed authority and commanded respect.

Aaron led us to a van that looked large enough to seat all eight of us. After unlocking the doors, he helped Latishia into the passenger seat and ran around to the front of the vehicle to claim the driver’s seat. Brian offered me his hand, and I climbed inside. I decided to crawl to the back seat. He joined me, his thigh warm against mine. My stomach fluttered as I placed my hand over it, wondering if I would be able to eat.

"Where are we dining?" I asked. The other couples were squeezing their way to their seats.

"McGuire's Irish Pub," yelled Aaron from the front.

"We saw that place on the way to Banana Bart's," said Gina, as she wrestled with her seatbelt. Chris reached across her to buckle it.

Brian shifted in his seat and draped his arm over my shoulders. "McGuire's motto is "feasting, imbibery, and debauchery." His grin was wide, exposing straight white teeth. "It's a well-loved establishment by locals and tourists alike."

"It's more than just a restaurant," said Don, as he turned to face us. "It's also a micro brewery. They have Pale Ale, Irish Red, Porter, Irish Stout and for wussies like you, Phoenix, root beer."

"I'm glad you said root beer, I was getting worried." I wiped my brow as if relieved. Everyone laughed.

"How do you know so much about the beer at McGuire's?" asked Brian, as he leaned forward, resting his forearms on the back of the seat in front of us.

Kat looked over her shoulder at us. "Don's the part-time bartender at the Swizzler."

Don leaned over and kissed Kat's temple. "Let's just say I was checking out the competition."

The trip past the undeveloped dunes felt different at night. Dark and spooky, the road had a deserted feel to it. When we reached the high bridge, the lights of Destin boggled the senses like a Southern Vegas. The Divas had thought the exterior of McGuire's was unique during the day, but at night it looked like a leprechaun had performed Irish magic. Kelly green lights lined the entire roofline.

"Wow!" said Latishia.

"Wait until you see the inside," said Don.

Aaron found a spot in the narrow parking area. After several ins and outs to straighten the large van, he had it tucked neatly in the space. In a courtly manner, Brian assisted me from the van. He enveloped my hand in his and led me in the correct direction.

We all squeezed in the door past a group of people who seemed unaware that they were blocking an entrance. This behavior has always been one of my pet peeves, along with seniors stopping in doorways with their walkers, and people breaking in line.

"What's all that hanging down from the ceiling?" Latishia looked up, frowning. "It kinda looks nasty from a distance."

Aaron placed his arm around her shoulder and pulled her closer. "It's autographed dollar bills, Dumpling."

Kat, Gina and I exchanged glances when we heard the "Dumpling" pet name again. Kat shook her head while Gina performed her patented eye roll. She perfected the move during adolescence, and I'm surprised one of her parents didn't slap that expression off her face before she reached adulthood. I covered my mouth to hold in a giggle.

"How many dollars do you think are up there?" I looked at Brian.

"Don't know." He shrugged his shoulders. "A lot."

A nearby waiter heard my question and walked over.

"The legend is McGuire ran the bar and Molly served the drinks. When she received her first tip she pinned it to the wall behind the bar. Their friends liked the idea, so they started signing dollar bills and attached them to the walls and ceiling. It's now a tradition." He paused briefly to watch the group of folks blocking the door leave. "To answer your question, it's estimated there are over a million dollars tacked to these walls and ceilings. The owner has an accounting firm come in and count them every year."

"I hope they have those bills insured. What if there was a fire?" Gina asked as she walked closer to view some of the signatures.

"Oh yeah, they're — ."

"What about theft?" interrupted Brian.

Mr. Information leaned closer and lowered his voice. "We had an employee pull a bunch of bills down once. He was arrested."

"How'd they catch him?" Latishia moved closer to hear the answer.

"The signatures on the bills made it easy to spot the stolen ones. He took them to a local bank and tried to cash them in for larger bills."

"Dumb fuck," bellowed Brian.

Surprised and embarrassed by his outburst, I moved away a step or two.

Mr. Information frowned at Brian. "If you'll follow me, I can seat you now because we have a table open for eight."

Brian chose a chair and pulled it out for me, and then took the seat to my left at the head of the table. Aaron sat at the other end with Latishia to his right. Don and Kat were to my right, and Gina and Chris sat across the table from me.

Don picked up his menu and said, "Ladies, just so that you know, this isn't the original location. This Destin location has only been open since 1996."

Latishia opened her menu. "Good, if they've been open that long, they should know how to cook."

I skipped past the bar food on the menu and perused the Irish dishes. "I know what I'm having, the Irish lamb stew with a root beer."

Brian guffawed. "You don't want a root beer, do you?"

"Yes, I do."

Our waiter arrived and introduced himself. "I'm Hank, and I'm willing to do almost anything for a good tip." He grinned, looked at me and asked, "Can I take your drink order, ma'am?"

As I opened my mouth to order, Brian said, "Give us two Irish Stouts." He gestured to include me.

I felt my jaw drop.

"I'd prefer a root beer instead — ."

Brian interrupted, "Bring her a Stout." He issued the request as an order to a low ranking soldier.

My temper blazed like a bonfire threatening to singe a million dollars of autographed bills.

"*If* you insist on ordering that beer for me, you better be ready to drink it, because I won't." I turned and smiled up at Hank, but my tone was titanium. "Please bring me a root beer."

"Yes, ma'am." Wise to the situation, he turned and busied himself with the rest of the drink orders. The Divas looked at me with worried expressions.

It was pretty clear to me that Brian anticipated having his way. *He better wise up in a hurry because I'm not a private under his command.*

A short time later, Hank returned with our drink orders. He placed a root beer served in a frosted mug in front of me. *Just the way I like it.*

"What would you like for dinner tonight, ma'am?"

Again, Brian spoke before I could. "The lady will have lamb stew, and I'll have a ribeye, rare, with another Irish Stout." He closed his menu with authority. Then he reached over, slipped mine from my grasp and handed them both to Hank.

I felt my back stiffen as I locked gazes with Gina. *It's a good thing I didn't change my mind about the entrée.*

Both of Gina's brows shot up. On occasion, a man has ordered for me in an expensive restaurant, but he has always asked my permission first.

Gina ordered corned beef and cabbage, Kat decided on fish and chips, and Latishia selected Irish steak and mushroom pie. The rest of the guys ordered steak or seafood entrees.

After Hank had left, Kat leaned over to ask Brian, "Aren't you concerned about eating your steak raw?"

"Why would that concern me?" Brian's voice assumed an authoritative tone.

"Raw meat can carry Salmonella, E. coli, Shigella, Staphylococcus and Listeria bacteria," said Kat.

"Never had a problem before." He moved his hand as if he shooed a fly. "What are you, a doctor or something?"

"Nurse."

The conversation lulled.

I sipped my root beer, which was delicious and reminded me of the root beer floats I had as a child.

Brian drank from his mug of Irish Stout and wiped the foam from his lips with the back of his hand. "Now that's a beer. You should try it, Phoenix."

"I don't like beer, never have."

"How do you know if you don't try it?"

I shrugged my shoulders and reached for his mug. I sipped a mouthful, scrunched my face and wished I had a polite way to spit it out. I choked it down. "Yuck!" I grabbed my root beer and drank several gulps, trying to cleanse my palate of the vile brew.

Brian drew himself up to full stature. "I can't believe you don't like that beer. It's good."

Don came to my defense. "That's a stout brew. Most folks who don't like beer can't tolerate a stout."

I could have hugged him.

Brian harrumphed. I glanced down the table. Latishia was giving my date a squinty-eyed glare. I heard Gina mumble something in Italian — not a good sign.

The food arrived, breaking the tension. My Irish stew was full of lamb, onions, potatoes, and other tasty veggies. I tasted the steaming concoction and sighed. It was a delicious all-in-one meal.

I glanced over at Brian in time to see him slice open his steak. Blood oozed from the meat and filled the plate. I turned away, covered my mouth with my napkin and closed my eyes while my stomach settled. The sight of that bloody steak didn't sit well after I had to swallow that yucky beer.

Brian poked me with his elbow. "Would you like to try my steak?"

"No thanks, Brian, I like mine cooked medium." I avoided the sight of the massacre on his plate. I wasn't sure why it bothered me so much. I'm not usually sensitive to gory things.

Brian gave me a haughty look. "Don't be such a wuss."

Gina scowled at Brian. "È stronzo."

I knew the translation was "you asshole."

Aaron was looking concerned at the other end of the table, his gaze bouncing between his boss and me. *I'm not going to let this jerk ruin dinner for everyone.* I decided to ignore Brian and enjoyed my delicious meal.

Forty minutes later, everyone decided to forego dessert.

"Anyone up for a little dancing?" asked Aaron.

"You know I am," said Latishia, gazing up at him with flirty eyes. If she flitted those lashes any faster, she'd make herself dizzy.

The gentlemen paid the tabs while we Divas beelined for the ladies' room.

Latishia scooted into the handicapped accessible stall and closed the door. "What do you think of your guys?" she asked, her voice drifting from the stall.

"I think Chris is fascinating. He's traveled all over Europe," said Gina, who was reapplying her lipstick. "Including Italy."

I removed my travel toothbrush from my purse, loaded it from my tiny tube of toothpaste, and soon looked like I was foaming at the mouth.

"I don't know about Phoenix's date," said Kat. "I thought maybe Brian was old-fashioned when he ordered for her, but that whole thing about the rare steak and the beer has me wondering."

Gina blotted her lipstick. "I didn't like that either. He seems bossy and controlling to me."

I spit out the toothpaste in the basin, rinsed my mouth and dried my toothbrush with a paper towel. After dumping it in my purse, I grabbed my lipstick.

Latishia came out of the stall and shuffled toward the sink, still adjusting her clothes. "Phoenix, if you don't feel comfortable with this guy, we'll call the rest of the night off."

I looked at everyone's reflections in the mirror. They were all nodding in agreement.

"That's sweet, but I don't want to ruin everyone's fun just because my date has a massive case of commanditis. I'll be fine. But if I'm not —"

"Say the word," said Latishia. "Let's have a code word or signal."

Gina rolled her eyes again. Kat looked pensive.

"Headache," I said. "If any of us has a sudden headache, that's it. Agreed?" I looked at each of the Divas. They all nodded agreement.

When we exited, Brian boomed, "Here they are. We were afraid you ladies crawled out the window and escaped." He took my hand. "Phoenix, I owe you an apology."

"Oh?" I took an involuntary step back.

"What makes people interesting are their differences. You don't have to like what I like. I haven't dated much since my divorce, so I'm a bit rusty."

I pasted on my most gracious smile. "Apology accepted. Let's go dance." I appreciated the apology, but it was pretty clear to me that Brian liked to have things go his way. *He needs to keep in mind that I'm* not *under his command.*

Chapter 57: The Day After

Late the night before, the Divas had all agreed to eat breakfast at Another Broken Egg, off Highway 98, in Fort Walton. We wanted to sleep late, and the free breakfast ended at nine. As planned, we met at ten in the hotel lobby.

Latishia had Aaron in tow, both grinning like kids.

Gina clung to Chris's hand with that satisfied look that I knew oh so well. By the expression on Chris's face, he was the luckiest guy in town.

Don had his arm slung over Kat's shoulders. They both seemed so comfortable with each other, like a nut and bolt.

I was alone.

We all piled into the van and in a jiffy arrived at the restaurant. Warm paprika-colored walls welcomed us when we entered. With great efficiency, the staff pulled tables together to seat us all. As the odd woman out, I sat at the end of the table, with Latishia to my right and Aaron on my left.

"I wanted to apologize for Colonel Holcomb's behavior last night. He got drunk, and, well...." Aaron's gaze dropped to the table.

"Aaron, the sins of the colonel aren't passed on to you. It wasn't your fault," I said.

The waitress took our drink orders. When the coffee arrived, the ceramic mugs were a welcome sight. I had a slight headache.

Don ran both hands through his hair and sighed in frustration. "Like I told Kat last night, I wasn't quite sure what to do. When the four of you went to the ladies' room at McGuire's, I told that asshole he was acting like a total jerk, and if he didn't cool it, you'd go back to the hotel."

"So that's why he apologized." I sat back in my chair. "I wondered what brought on that great insight."

Don gave me a wry smile. "Phoenix, I know you're capable of handling yourself, but I swear, the cop in me wanted to cuff him and haul him off to jail."

"I wanted to punch him out," said Gina. "Sorry, Aaron, I know he's your boss, but the man is a complete ass."

"Not much longer," said Aaron. "I move to Huntsville a week after y'all leave here."

Chris leaned back in his chair and crossed his arms. "Well, I'm still stuck with the guy until I get orders."

I dropped two stevia tablets into my coffee. "Colonel Bossy Pants was sure he would bunny hop into my bed last night." I added cream. "I'll admit, I thought he was hot, at least at first."

"Me too." Gina plopped her mug on the table, sloshing some coffee over the edge. "I just knew he was a good match by the way y'all looked at each other."

"Then the twerp opened his raw-meat-eating mouth and managed to offend *everyone*." Latishia patted Aaron's hand across the table. "Sorry, Honey Bear."

"Honey Bear?" I looked over at Aaron. "You're what, six-five?"

His face darkened. "Yep."

Gina giggled. I looked her way in time to see Chris nudge her with his elbow. Kat sat back in her chair with her hand covering her mouth. Don examined a painting of a rooster on the wall across from him with keen interest.

I stirred my coffee. “Anyway, my initial physical attraction waned as Colonel Bossy Pants tried to ply me with drinks, order me around like a private, and paw me on the dance floor.” I sipped my coffee, grimaced, and added another cream. “Strong coffee.”

“What happened that set him off?” asked Kat.

“I saw it all.” Gina waved her spoon to get our attention. “Phoenix lifted his wandering hand off her ass during a slow dance. He went berserk. Next thing I knew, he was cursing like a tattooed biker. I thought he was going to hit her.”

“Me too,” I said. “I was ready to kick him in his military-issued jock strap. Oh, and don’t forget, he called me a ‘frigid bitch.’ ” I tried my coffee again. “Yuck.” I added more stevia and stirred, wondering what brand of coffee they used.

“Again, I’m so sorry, Phoenix,” Aaron’s shoulders hunched as he looked down at the cup encased in his large hands.

I gave him a playful punch on the shoulder. “You’re responsible for your behavior and no one else’s. I can see why he’s divorced, though. Enough about Colonel Bossy Pants, I’m ready to try the Cinnamon French Toast.”

As we ate breakfast, I watched my friends smile and flirt with their guys. Deep down I was happy for them, but I was also jealous. I wondered how my world could be so stable for so many years and then crumble apart within a matter of months.

After breakfast, we all decided to go back to the hotel and hang out on the beach.

Chapter 58: When You Stop Looking

After a day on the beach, my nose was pink, and I needed a break from group activities with the Divas. If I had to watch my friends smooch with their newfound love interests one more time, I might barf out all the green jealousy filling my gut. *I wonder if they felt this way when things were all lovey-dovey between Todd and me?*

I told the Divas to enjoy their dates without me. They protested at first, concerned about leaving me alone.

Latishia planted her fists on her hips. "What are you gonna do all by your lonesome?" Her patriotic bathing suit cover-up flapped in the breeze, making her look like a flag at half-mast.

"I have a murder mystery I'm *dying* to read." I chuckled, but no one else joined me. "Did you get it, *dying?"*

They all stood there, their gazes drilling into me. I shrugged, turned and walked over the walkway, and parked my backside on one of the turquoise lounge chairs by the pool.

"Come on, Phe, we'll worry about you." Gina plopped down on the chair beside me and laid her head on my shoulder.

"No, you won't. After a few 'Poor Phoenix' remarks, Chris will have your undivided attention, as it should be." I made shooing motions with my hands. "We'll do girls' night out tomorrow when the guys have to be elsewhere."

"Maybe Phoenix needs some time to herself, ladies." Kat gave each of them a measured look. "Call us if you need us for any reason." She reached into her beach bag and tossed me some keys, which I caught midair. "Here are the keys to the minivan."

That decided, they finally left me to fend for myself.

I grunted as I rose from the chaise lounge. *Good grief, when did I start grunting when I stand up? I'm not that old — am I?*

To prove that I was still a vital woman, I walked up the five flights of stairs to my room and arrived only a tad winded. I felt better about myself. After a warm shower, I dressed, applied makeup and styled my hair. *Just because I'm alone doesn't mean I have to look like a reject.*

Donning some strappy sandals and a sundress that showed off my minimal tan, I headed for the elevator. No way was I going to tromp down the stairs in those heels. Strolling past the Swizzler, I traipsed to the lobby.

Once there, I snuggled down in a comfortable chair, parked my feet on the ottoman and began to read. Soon I was engrossed in the mystery. The protagonist, Charlie Stone, was in a high-speed car chase pursuing a serial killer when I felt that itchy uncomfortable feeling I get when someone's staring at me.

I saw a man's polished loafers near my chair. I ignored him and kept reading.

He cleared his throat. I looked up. And up.

"Is this chair taken?" The tall man gestured toward the seat on the other side of a shared end table.

"Well, yes."

His shoulders drooped a bit.

"I believe it has your name on it somewhere." I smiled. *He's attractive.*

He chuckled. "Love a woman with a sense of humor. Mike Janson." He gave a little bow and lowered all six-plus feet of him into the chair. "And your name?"

"Phoenix."

"Were you named after the town in Arizona or the bird?"

"Bird."

Quiet returned, and I sank back into the racing plot. The tension in the scene continued to build as the killer approached a roadblock.

"What're you reading?"

I sighed and lowered my book to look at him.

Mike flashed sparkling white teeth that I was sure made his dentist proud. *Damn, he has dimples and all that thick brown hair.* I took an instant to center myself and said, " 'Deadly Compulsion,' it's a thriller."

"Is it interesting?"

"Yep."

Visions of Colonel Bossy Pants groping me danced across my mind. I crossed my leg away from Mike and refocused on the story.

"What's the book about?"

I lowered the book again, sighed, and gave him my "get lost look." When he failed to take the hint, I asked, "Do I know you?" I coated the words with barbs.

He grinned as if amused, stretched his long legs out in front of him and crossed his ankles. "Not yet."

I shook my head and tried to read. I couldn't concentrate. I felt the prickle of his stare. *Good grief, Phoenix, he has other things to do than gawk at you.* I glanced over to prove my point. He was, indeed, staring at me.

"Why are you watching me?" Irritation bled into my words.

"You're a beautiful woman."

I rolled my eyes and raised my book to eye level.

"I'll be damned. You really don't know that you're beautiful."

I ignored him and reread the same page three times.

"That book must be *interesting*."

I turned to face him. His grin widened to display his dimples to maximum advantage. My lower regions tingled. *Why am I such a sucker for dimples?*

A guy I dated in college discovered my middle name is Dixie. He'd sing, "*I wish I was in Dixie,*" every time he tried to invade my panties. The song now played in my head. It struck me as weird that I should remember that song now.

"Is that book so interesting that you wouldn't consider having dinner with me tonight?"

"I don't know." I cocked a brow. "How fascinating are you?" I looked him up and down. He wore khaki pants with a blue dress shirt open at the collar. The sleeves were turned up to reveal sexy tanned forearms.

He coughed out a laugh. "Apparently not as intriguing as you."

"What makes you think I'd go eat dinner with you?"

"I'm a nice guy, you're a lovely lady, and we both need to eat." He shrugged as if it made logical sense.

I'm not sure what happened to my good sense or my rules about dating. Pheromones invaded my lady parts and all the blood left my brain. Before I thought it through, I was sitting in Mike's rental car en route to Floyd's Shrimp House, singing *Dixie* in my mind.

Carnal urges are a dominate force.

Floyd's boasted a large white sign with red lettering that declared, *All you can eat popcorn shrimp $9.99.* Giant red neon shrimp stood on each side of the sign. Statues of pelicans rested on the roofline where the stairs led to a porch.

A waiter led us to prime seats on the deck overlooking the Gulf. Mike pulled out my chair, and I thanked him. After several minutes of indecision, I settled on a menu item.

"Know what you want?" He peered at me over his menu.

"I'm thinking about boiled shrimp. You?"

"Fried oysters." He pumped his brows in a comical way and gave me a sexy wicked grin.

Way down south in…, chimed in my head.

A bronzed, perky waitress popped over to our table. She looked like she was still in high school. "Hey y'all, what would you like to drink?"

One of my Mom's favorite clichés dinged in my head: "In for a penny, in for a pound." I had a feeling I was going to be in for more than a pound. It had been way too long since I'd quenched my carnal lusts. *I might just need a drink to loosen my panties*. "Margarita, please."

"Make that two." Mike turned his blue eyes in my direction. "Here on business?" He unwrapped his flatware and placed them in a neat row to his right.

"Pleasure."

"Alone?"

"No, I'm here with three friends."

Mike jumped from his seat, leaned across the table and deflected a soccer ball that almost whacked me on the side of the head. I never saw it coming.

I sat there stiff as steel, unsure if it was safe to move.

"Sorry, lady," some boys yelled from the beach below.

"Just some kids kicking around a soccer ball. The youngest one lost control of his kick."

We both looked up as Ms. Perky delivered our drinks with an unsteady hand.

"Y'all ready to order?" She shifted from foot to foot, order pad at the ready.

Mike made a palm-up hand signal in my direction, indicating I should order first. I let go of my pent-up breath. *I'm more traumatized by Colonel Bossy Pants than I realized.* "The boiled shrimp, please, with fries and steamed veggies."

Our waitress bounded away toward the kitchen to place our orders, her blonde ponytail swishing from side to side.

"Wanna bet she's a cheerleader?" Mike winked and raised his drink to his lips to take a sip.

"No way will I take that bet. I've already named her 'Ms. Perky' in my mind."

He paused and cocked his head. "Funny, I thought I was the only one who gave people pet names. Where do you live?"

"Huntsville, Alabama. You?"

"I work for NASA. Just moved to Huntsville from Houston."

"Hmmm, small world." I eased my overfull margarita closer before picking it up to take a sip. "What's your job at NASA?"

"Physicist and electrical engineer. You?"

"Psychologist."

His eyes briefly widened as he placed his drink on the table. I waited for the usual responses of, "So does that mean you're analyzing me," or "Let me tell you about this problem I have." He said neither.

"So you're traveling with friends?" He cocked a brow that seemed to ask, "Where are they now?"

"Yes, they're out on dates." I reached for my napkin-wrapped flatware and began to unroll it.

"What happened to your guy, if you don't mind me asking?"

"He didn't seem to think we were a good match." I slid the flatware to the table and laid the napkin in my lap.

"Oh?" He placed his forearms on the table and clasped his hands in front of him, giving me his full attention.

"He spent the entire blind date last night trying to boss me, and then he attempted to grope me on the dance floor of a local club. Let's just say I wasn't tolerant of that behavior."

My eyes strayed to his muscular forearms. His fingers were long and his nails well kept.

He sat back in his chair, frowning. "That's no way to treat a lady."

Ready to change the subject from Colonel Bossy Pants, I said, "Anyway, my friends and I came down to get away and have some fun on the beach."

"Have y'all been friends long?" He leaned an elbow on the table and placed his chin in his hand.

"I've been friends with Gina since grade school, but we became friends with Latishia and Kat while we were attending the University of Alabama." I wiped salt from my mouth with the napkin.

Mike lifted his glass in a toast. "Roll Tide."

I smiled. "I knew there was something I liked about you. Did you attend Alabama, or are you just a fan?"

"I'm an alumnus."

His attention strayed to the beach soccer game. I followed his gaze and tensed. Those kids were moving closer to us.

One of the taller boys kicked the ball toward the ocean. Soon they were all in pursuit, kicking up sand as they ran. I realized I was holding my breath and exhaled my relief.

Mike was staring at me with a quirky smile.

Feeling his attraction to me, I started blathering. "Latishia, bless her heart, is an Auburn fan, but she received a scholarship to Alabama.

Her dad is a die-hard Auburn guy, so it nearly killed him to have his baby girl go to the *enemy school*."

Mike chuckled. "I bet it did."

"Here's your food, y'all," said Ms. Perky, in a singsong voice.

Mike's fried oysters piled next to a steaming hot baked potato and asparagus looked delicious. The sight of my boiled shrimp, fries, and steamed veggies triggered a Pavlovian reaction, causing me to salivate as my stomach growled.

"Sounds like your stomach thinks you've been neglectful." Mike stabbed an oyster and ate it.

I sniffed and rolled my eyes heavenward. The food smelled delicious. I placed my napkin back in my lap and began peeling shrimp. Dunking one in the cocktail sauce, I bit it off close to the tail and chewed. "Mmmm."

"Good?" Mike looked up.

"Oh yeah, I'd forgotten how good boiled shrimp is when it's fresh."

I crunched into a crispy hushpuppy and chewed while I peeled another shrimp. I swiped it through the sauce and ate it.

My throat felt scratchy. I cleared it and drank some of my drink. I waved to Ms. Perky and croaked, "Water."

"Phoenix! Are you okay? Your face looks blotchy."

I felt like my throat was swelling. I clutched it with both hands.

"Are you choking? Do you have food stuck in your throat?" Mike was out of his chair with his hand on my arm.

I shook my head no and gasped, "Can't...breathe."

Mike's voice boomed across the room, "Is there a doctor in the restaurant? This lady can't breathe."

Two burly guys wearing gray uniform shirts sat two tables over from us. They jumped to their feet. A chair banged to the floor.

"We're paramedics," said the blond one. He reached me first, looked at my plate and asked, "Ma'am, are you allergic to shellfish?"

I shrugged.

"Do you feel like your throat is closing?" asked the dark-haired paramedic.

I nodded yes.

The blond guy told his partner, "Go get the case. She's beginning to look like a grouper. See her lips."

I thought, *Grouper? What's wrong with my lips?*

Within minutes he was back. He dropped the case on the floor with a bam.

I jumped. I was beginning to feel woozy and panicked. *Oh my God, am I going to die looking like a grouper?*

While the blond guy yanked my dress up, exposing my thigh for all to see, his partner plunged a yellow tube-like thing with an orange tip into my thigh. It contained a needle that hurt, and I yelped.

The dark-haired paramedic looked me in the eye. "It's an auto-injector Epi-Pen. You should be feeling better soon. The waitress phoned for an ambulance, and it's on the way."

My throat began to loosen, and my breathing improved. But now my heart began to race, pounding against my chest wall like it wanted to escape. I took one hand from my throat and clutched at my chest while struggling to breathe. Mike was kneeling behind my chair, rubbing my shoulders and crooning reassuring words in my ear.

The sirens were earsplitting. I pulled my hands from my throat and chest to cover my ears. After a final *whoop, whoop*, the sirens died.

When the gurney arrived, Mike stood and shouldered the paramedics out of the way. He picked me up in his arms and placed me on the gurney. My hands flew to pull the hem of my sundress down while I clamped my legs together. *Good grief, I'm about to die with grouper lips and I'm worried about flashing my undies?*

Mike leaned over, kissed me on the forehead, and said, "I knew you'd be an interesting date. I'll follow the ambulance to the hospital."

Chapter 59: Ambulance Rock and Roll

Before I knew what was happening, I was strapped to the gurney and in the ambulance. The ambulance took off with sirens blaring. I could hear *Old Time Rock and Roll* from the radio in the front competing with the sirens.

Everything in that ambulance jiggled and rattled. With every turn, I was grateful I was strapped to the gurney. I slid forward when the ambulance came to an abrupt stop, and felt it begin to back up accompanied by loud beeps.

When it came to a complete stop, the back doors opened. I was pulled out and rolled through the emergency ambulance entrance into a tiny room. A nurse came in and took my vitals.

"Your blood pressure is a tad high. Does it tend to run high?" She pulled off the cuff.

"No, it usually runs low, but I'm scared half to death, and they shot me up with an Epi Pen," I said.

She ran a thermometer over my forehead. "That would explain it. Be back in a jiff to start your IV."

When the nurse returned, she inserted my IV like a real pro. I hardly felt the stick. After securing the IV in place, she said, "The doctor will be in to see you soon." She covered my bare legs with a warm, white blanket and left. Moments later, Mike raced in the door, eyes wide with what looked like panic. "Are you all right?"

"So far." My tongue felt thick. "Do I still look like a grouper?"

I'd no sooner asked the question when my stomach gave a massive lurch. I turned and barfed over the side of the bed. Mike dodged sideways toward the foot of the bed to make sure I missed his shoes and pants. I wanted to snap my fingers and disappear in a poof.

He held his nose and in a nasal tone said, “This is the most exciting date I’ve ever had.”

“You don’t get out much, do you?” I put my hand on my forehead while I tried to control my queasy stomach.

A doctor in dark blue scrubs raced past Mike into my minuscule room. He stepped in the vomit and skidded feet first halfway under my bed.

Just let me die now, Lord, so I don’t have to face the humiliation.

I pulled myself up and peered over the sidebars on my bed into the startled brown eyes of the doctor.

“I’m so sorry. Are you hurt?” I asked.

I could hear Mike chuckling.

The doctor put down a hand to push to a sitting position. He placed it in a chunky section of my stomach contents. Raising it, he scrunched his nose as he watched the mess drip off his hand.

Mike’s subtle chuckle had advanced to a guffaw.

A nurse came in the room, followed Mike’s gaze to the floor and gasped. With eyes as big as Frisbees, she picked her way with care to the doctor’s side and assisted him to his feet.

The frowning doctor wiped his hand on his scrubs. “Call housekeeping to clean up this mess and move her to another room.”

He looked back at me. “I’ll be back.” He started out the door, stopped, and turned toward the nurse. “Oh, and get her a vomiting pan.”

“Do you think you can walk to the room next door?” the nurse asked.

I nodded and slid out of bed onto the clean side of the floor. Once we were in the next room, Mike handed me my purse.

“I thought you might need this.” He grinned. “This will make quite a story to tell our grandchildren someday.”

Startled by the remark, I narrowed my eyes. “I don’t have children.”

“I have one daughter, Rachel. She and my son-in-law, Mark, told me she was pregnant before I left for this trip.”

"Then you can tell *your* grandchildren about the crazy date you had with a woman you met in Florida."

He cocked his head and winked. "We'll see."

Twenty minutes later the doctor walked back in the room with clean scrubs and damp hair. "Now tell me, have you ever had a reaction like this before?"

"No. I was eating boiled shrimp, and then I couldn't breathe. I don't understand. I had shellfish when I first arrived on Saturday. Nothing happened." Then I remembered I felt a little itchy when I went to bed that night, but there was no rash the next morning.

"There were two paramedics at the restaurant that saved my life. They told me I had grouper lips."

The doctor's gaze drifted to my mouth. He tried his best to maintain his composure, but the corners of his mouth kept twitching up. He stood in front of a computer terminal, did some typing and read the screen.

He shoved the terminal toward the wall. "Mr. and Mrs. O'Leary —"

My gaze shot to Mike. His grin widened, maximizing his dimples.

"Dr. O'Leary. I'm not married," I corrected, frowning at Mike.

"You've developed an allergic reaction to shrimp. I suggest you avoid all shellfish to be on the safe side. I'll write you a prescription for antihistamines and a corticosteroid." He turned to face Mike. "Can you take her to a pharmacy to get her prescriptions filled?"

"Yes, I'll take care of that."

The doctor smiled down at me. "You were lucky, just fish lips and a little facial swelling. If you had hives, you'd be miserable. I'm going to order a cortisone shot before you leave, so don't begin taking the cortisone pills until tomorrow. Start the antihistamine tonight before you go to bed. If you get worse, come back." He nodded and left.

Next to arrive was a fresh-faced young lady with a clipboard full of forms who wanted my driver's license and insurance card. Thirty minutes later, I surrendered my credit card for my co-pay and in return received a shot, two prescriptions, and paperwork.

I excused myself to go to the ladies' room. My primary purpose was to find a mirror. One look and I nearly peed my pants, which in an instant changed my priority.

When I emerged from the stall, I looked in the mirror again. My lips looked as though an inexperienced plastic surgeon had gone crazy with lip fillers. My skin was splotchy, and my hair needed combing. The only two good things I could say were that I was alive and I didn't vomit on my new sundress.

I pulled my toothbrush and paste out of my purse to freshen my mouth, which tasted awful. I brushed my hair, powdered my face, and decided to forego the lipstick. The lips didn't need any further embellishment. I left the ladies' room and walked toward Mike.

He grinned and ran his hand through his hair. "You're a hell of a date, Fish Lips."

For some reason, the way he said it was both endearing and hilarious. We laughed as he took my hand and led me to his car.

We managed to calm our laughter to intermittent giggles by the time we pulled into the drive-thru of a CVS Pharmacy. We did fine as long as we didn't look at each other. While we waited, he touched my lips with his index finger and asked, "Does it hurt?"

I shook my head.

He leaned over and kissed me with such tenderness. It was the most sensual kiss I'd ever experienced. As he pinged a ten on my kissing meter, the Dixie area of my body tingled. I was hoping for a repeat performance, but the pharmacy clerk slid open the window.

"Your prescriptions are ready."

Chapter 60: Explanations

Mike pulled into a parking space at the hotel, leaned over and kissed me again.

"You have a strange idea of sexy," I said after the kiss ended.

He chuckled as he released his seatbelt. "It must be the fish lips. They're driving me to kiss you."

He opened my door, helped me out of the car and kissed me again.

With a teasing tone, I asked, "Does this mean that when the swelling goes down, it's over between us?"

He laughed. We walked inside, hand in hand.

I heard Latishia's voice boom across the lobby. "Sweet Baby Jesus, there she is now."

The Divas rushed forward to surround me, while Aaron, Don, and Chris hung back and eyed Mike.

"Thank goodness you're alive. We've been calling your room and cell phone." Gina wrapped me in her arms. After a quick squeeze, she held me at arm's length. "Mio Dio, what's wrong with your lips?"

Mike started chuckling. Three pairs of narrowed Diva eyes swiveled in his direction. The sight wiped the smile right off his face.

Latishia stepped forward with her fists on her hips and her giant bosom heaving. "Who the hell are you, and what did you do to our Phoenix?"

Mike looked down at Latishia, raised his hands in a gesture of surrender and took a step back. "Honest, I didn't do anything to her."

Before he could say another word, Kat squeezed past Latishia and shooed Gina aside. She took my face in her hands and examined it. "Have you seen a doctor?"

I nodded and gestured toward Mike. As best as I could with swollen lips, I said, "This is Mike Janson, my date for the evening. During dinner, I had an allergic reaction to shrimp. Mike and two paramedics saved my life. Mike followed me to the hospital, took me to the pharmacy and brought me back. He's my hero." I grabbed his arm with both hands and squeezed.

Gina said, "We had shrimp the other night and you didn't react this way."

"We can develop an allergic reaction to anything at anytime," Kat said.

"Let's sit down. My feet hurt and I want to hear the whole story." Latishia grimaced as she looked at her three-inch heeled sandals that matched her coral blouse.

"If you wore sensible shoes, your feet wouldn't hurt." Kat's tone echoed pure reason.

Latishia snorted. "If shoes were supposed to be sensible, why would they come in so many styles and colors?" She flipped her braids over her shoulder and took mincing steps toward the seating area.

Kat took me by the arm and guided me toward the furniture in the lobby. She turned to Don. "Would you get her some water, please?"

"Sure." Don changed directions and trekked toward the hotel's complimentary water dispenser.

Kat led me to the turquoise sofa and helped me sit. I grabbed Mike's hand and pulled him down to sit to my left. Kat was on my right; her fingers cool on my wrist as she checked my pulse. The rest of the group arranged themselves facing me.

Don returned with his eyes focused on the plastic tumbler of water he was carrying. He didn't see Aaron's foot and tripped.

Icy water splashed my face and trickled between my breasts.

"Oh!" I jumped up, pulled the front of my dress out and looked down.

I heard a combined intake of breaths. After I wiped my eyes with both hands and blinked, I saw the Divas and their dates staring at me with shocked expressions.

"Phoenix, I'm so sorry!" Don's face turned crimson.

I looked over at Mike, who was wiping water off his blue shirt. He looked back at me. I could feel droplets dripping from my hair onto my bare shoulders and the swells of my breasts. We both broke into gut-wrenching laughter.

The desk clerk showed up with fluffy white towels. Mike, Kat, and I toweled off while Mike and I did our best to suppress our giggles.

"Now that everyone's dry," Latishia shot Don a glare, "let's hear this story."

Mike told the story in incredible detail. His audience now included the desk clerk. Everyone oohed and ahhed in all the right places. When he came to the part about the ER doc sliding flat on his back under my hospital bed, most of our listeners scrunched their noses, but not Kat. I thought she would fall off the sofa, she laughed so hard.

"You made it back to the hotel safe despite everything, and then Don splashes you with water," said Aaron, his massive shoulders heaving up and down with his roaring laughter.

Don, who was still standing, glared down at Aaron. "Well, if you hadn't left your big size thirteen shoes in the way, I wouldn't have tripped."

"Fourteen," said Aaron.

Don crossed his arms and frowned. "What?"

"Fourteen. Man, you didn't have a chance in hell of missing these clodhoppers of mine."

Don's shoulders relaxed, and a slow grin spread across his face.

I rocked forward to stand. Mike shot to his feet and helped steady me.

"It's been an eventful night," I said. "I'm going to bed. I'll see you ladies tomorrow."

All the Divas hugged me. Latishia squeezed me so hard; I was sure my lips inflated another two inches.

I took Mike's hand. "Walk me to my room?"

He winked. "I'd thought you'd never ask."

Between the winking, the dimples and the kisses, I would have to watch my heart around this guy, *if* I ever saw him again. In the elevator, I asked, "When do you go home?"

"Early tomorrow morning. I have a meeting the next day about the outcome of this trip. Otherwise, I'd take a few days vacation and stay until you left."

After Mike and I exited the elevator, we walked to my room. I would have protruded my lower lip in a pout about Mike's leaving, but how could he tell with my lips so swollen? I looked at my feet. "I'm sorry I ruined our date."

Hooking his index finger under my chin, he lifted my face and kissed me again.

"None of it was your fault, but it made for a hell of an evening, my Darling Fish Lips."

He wrapped me in his arms and kissed me until my head spun, while the lyrics of Dixie chimed in my brain.

Chapter 61: Girls Only

The next morning I woke feeling drugged from the antihistamines. I looked around to orient myself. It was hard for me to believe that last night ever happened.

I slipped my feet into my moccasins and padded into the bathroom. My bladder felt like it might burst any second.

I looked in the mirror. Most of the swelling and blotches were gone. All that remained of my grouper lips were a slight kissable fullness. Thoughts of kissing brought Mike to mind and sent a tingle to my southern regions.

I showered, dressed, put on makeup and dried my hair. After looking so deplorable when Mike left me last night, I was determined to appear human today. *Perhaps I'll see him at breakfast.*

I was about to leave when I noticed the note under my door. I opened the envelope and pulled out the single sheet of folded paper. In tiny neat penmanship Mike had written:

My Darling Fish Lips,

You're the most interesting and intriguing woman I've ever met. I must know more.

Mike

I missed him. Darn! My heart sank. *Don't be silly. You barely know the man.* I folded the letter, reinserted it into the envelope and placed it in my suitcase for safe keeping.

When I went downstairs, I found the Divas grouped around one of the larger tables in the lobby, eating. I grabbed some coffee, chose a cheese Danish, and joined them.

Kat scrutinized me and smiled. "You look much better today."

I smiled back. "I feel better."

"I can't believe you, girl." Latishia gestured with a slice of crisp bacon. "We leave you on your own for one night, and you have the adventure of your life."

We all laughed.

"Where's what's-his-name? You know, your hero guy?" Gina sat holding her coffee, elbows on the table.

"Gone. Mike had to be in Huntsville by this afternoon." I slid into the empty chair and set my Danish on the table.

"Just like that," Latishia snapped her fingers, "and he's gone? No goodbye?"

"He told me goodbye last night. I did find a note slipped under my door this morning."

Gina leaned closer and put down her cup. "What did it say?"

I told them.

Gina reared back. "My Darling Fish Lips! You've got to be kidding."

"I think it's cute." Latishia popped her last bite of bacon into her mouth.

"This from a woman whose guy calls her 'Dumpling,' " countered Gina.

"Now ladies, play nice. What do we want to do today?" Kat checked her watch and removed her teabag.

"Snorkeling?" Gina sat straight, looking at us like a little kid who just heard the words, chocolate chip cookies.

Kat shook her head. "I don't feel comfortable doing that after Phoenix's allergy attack. She's still a little puffy and on medications."

Gina shrank into her seat like a deflated balloon.

"I know, a dolphin cruise!" I looked at them for a response while I tore my Danish in half.

Everyone liked the idea. Gina shot from her seat like someone lit a firecracker in her thong. She came back waving pamphlets. Grinning like she found pirates' treasure, she plopped them onto the center of the table.

Latishia picked one and examined it. Her eyes widened. "This is for an airboat ride to look for gators. I've always wanted to ride an airboat."

"Me too," I said.

Kat frowned. "Which one, dolphins or gators?"

"Both," said Gina. "We can do the early dolphin cruise. The airboat ride doesn't leave until dusk. We can have our dolphins and our gators, too."

So it was decided, but first, we'd have fun on the beach.

Chapter 62: Dolphins

We bought the tickets for our dolphin cruise and stood on the dock trying to decide which boat was ours. The wind combed my hair as I thought about the trip. *I'm going to look for dolphins. If I were still married to Todd I wouldn't be here. He gets motion sick in a tub of water.* The Divas boarded a boat with about twenty other people. Gina had insisted on the package that served wine. After glancing around, I began to have my doubts. It appeared to me that some of the passengers had a head start on the festivities and were already staggering.

I decided to chill and have fun. It would be okay as long as no one fell overboard or upchucked his or her complimentary wine inside the boat.

The minute the captain cleared the no wake zone; he kicked it into high gear and almost dumped half of the standing passengers on their backsides. Then he cranked the music up to "deaf by the end of the cruise" level, which was painful to me.

I fumbled in my belt purse for the drummer's earplugs I always carried, made by the hearing aid specialist on the first floor of my building. Once the plugs were in place, I felt my shoulders relax.

I braced myself against the railing and took photos with my Cybershot camera of the seagulls pacing the boat. The crew handed out bread for the passengers to toss to the gulls, and it was apparent our feathered friends knew the routine. Clutching several slices, Latishia bulldozed her way between the guy to my left and me.

"Come here, baby bird. Come to Aunt Latishia."

I looked at her and laughed. While she crooned sweet nothings to the birds, I snapped photos as fast as I could. I knew some would be bad, but with shots like this, I knew it was a numbers game.

"Shit!"

I lowered my camera and looked at Latishia. "What?"

"Crap. You know, caca. That bird pooped on me, and after I fed him some of that tasty bread. How's that for gratitude?" Latishia frowned, crammed her last piece of bread into my hand, and left. I heard her behind me asking for the location of the ladies' room.

Gina squeezed in next to me. "What put a hornet in Latishia's braids?"

I laughed. "An ungrateful bird did the deed on her."

"Ahh, merda." Gina nodded her understanding.

I'd heard Gina use that word before; it was the Italian version of poop. I handed her the bread. "I suggest you throw it as far as you can and don't entice them to come close like Latishia did."

The bread ran out, and the gulls gave up the chase.

After thirty minutes with no dolphin sightings, I was beginning to believe this would be a mere ear-splitting, rock-and-roll boat ride, instead of a dolphin cruise. To my surprise, the captain bellowed, "Dolphins portside."

Unknown to me, I was standing on the port side of the boat. I could feel people's bodies pressing against me, pushing me against the railing as they tried to see. Unable to breathe under the onslaught, I clicked away, trying to track the pod's progress.

There were five adults and one baby in the pod. The sun glinted on their dorsal fins when they rose. Everyone oohed when they heard the woosh sound from the dolphins' blowholes.

After the dolphins had swum past us, the crowd moved as one to the back of the boat to follow their progress.

Gina gave me a wild-eyed look. "I thought they were going to squeeze the pee right out of me. I've got to find the head."

She disappeared, and Kat moved to stand beside me. "What's with Gina?"

"Bladder crisis."

"Serves her right. She sweet-talked two different crew members out of extra wine."

"Really?" I gave Kat an incredulous look. "I gave her my glass because I didn't like it. No wonder she has to go so bad."

Kat thumbed over her shoulder. "Latishia's on the other side of the boat, telling folks she was shit on by a demon seagull with beady red eyes."

"I can't wait to hear how she jacks that story around to tell poor Aaron."

I heard, "Woohoo!"

Kat and I followed the gazes of the people standing near us. Some long, lanky guy clad only in purple swim trunks stood on top of the roof of the boat. While holding onto a pole, he wiggled and gyrated like a male stripper.

Kat pushed up her glasses. "Isn't that one of the crew members?"

"Yep. I'm certain the captain will make him get down." I shaded my eyes with my hand and looked at the captain. He was gyrating, too.

He shoved the throttle forward to increase the speed, and to my amazement, cranked the music up louder.

I heard Gina yell, “Take it off, big boy.” I whipped my head in the direction of her voice. There she was, waving dollar bills in an upraised hand.

I looked at Kat. “Tell me I’m not seeing this.”

Kat pointed. I followed the direction she pointed and to my astonishment, our Southern Baptist, Latishia, was dirty dancing with some big ole boy I’d never seen before. She was grinding her ample backside in the vicinity of his crotch.

“Is she drunk?” I asked.

Kat shrugged. “We best go get them before they get arrested for something indecent. You get Latishia. I’ll get Gina.”

I had to push and shove my way to the other side of the boat to reach Latishia. Once there, I reached for her arm. “Come on, Latishia, it’s time to go.”

“Get lost, bitch.” The big guy planted his palm on my chest and pushed. I landed on one of the seats.

Latishia saw him manhandle me. Her eyes narrowed as she swung her bejeweled canvas shoe and buried it deep in the guy’s crotch. He dropped to the deck and curled up like a roly poly bug. His high-pitched wail of pain went mostly unnoticed, thanks to the blaring music and the fact that most of the crowd had shifted to the other side of the boat, to look at some pelicans sitting on poles.

Gina and Kat saw the incident. They rushed over and escorted Latishia and me to the front of the boat so that we could disembark first. The music came to an abrupt stop, and the captain shifted to idle speed. The party was over.

The boat nudged the dock. A crewmember tied it to the cleats and lowered the plank. I glanced over my shoulder and saw the big guy rise to his knees and focus his beady eyes on us.

“He’s getting up,” I said, terror making my bladder spasm. *Don’t pee. Don’t pee. Don’t pee,* I chanted in my head.

Latishia, Gina, and Kat swiveled their heads in unison toward the threat.

He gained his feet and swayed. We ran like we had the force of a Saturn V rocket propelling us.

"Come back here, you cunts!"

We made it to the minivan and climbed inside. Kat peeled out of the parking lot and lost us in the traffic.

Chapter 63: The Great Escape

I held on and prayed we wouldn't have a traffic accident. Kat had a woman-possessed gleam in her eyes as she swerved in and out of lanes as much as the traffic allowed. She eventually veered onto a less congested road that paralleled the Gulf and slowed to a reasonable speed.

My bladder was screaming; *I've got to go!* I knew one laugh, cough, or sneeze would mean disaster. "Find a restroom," I said, gripping the back of Kat's seat. "Now!"

"Me too," said Gina.

Kat sped past a restaurant almost hidden between two towering condos. Screeching to a halt, Kat threw the gearshift into reverse, backed up, and pulled into a parking lot. The establishment was painted bright orange with turquoise trim and named The Back Porch. In the front, there was a wood totem pole of blue marlin fish, and several palm trees dotted the landscape.

We crawled out of the minivan. I did a fast mincing walk, trying to avoid jostling my cranky bladder. *Hold on,* I begged, as I walked up a ramp through a covered dogtrot between the restaurant and a gift shop. I approached the hostess and with a pleading tone, said, "We need a table for four, but first, I need a restroom."

She pointed at a door to her left.

I pushed through the rough-hewn door, praying in my mind, *God, please let a stall be empty.* Seeing an open door, I exercised every ounce of willpower to get my shorts down before it was too late.

When I exited the ladies' room, I found Kat and Latishia waiting near the hostess stand. "Where's Gina?"

"In the restroom," said Latishia as she examined a menu.

"I didn't see her."

"There's two," said the hostess.

When Gina came walking our way, she was trailing a long strand of toilet paper that had stuck to the bottom of her shoe. I laughed, but then checked my shoe. *Phew! No paper hitchhiker.*

I could tell Kat was peeved by the way she was eyeing Gina, with her arms crossed and her foot tapping. Latishia and Gina's antics on that dolphin cruise had resulted in a few bruises for me and could have caused more trouble.

Neither Kat nor Latishia mentioned the toilet paper. I suspected Latishia never noticed it because her nose was still stuck in the menu. Kat smirked as she eyed the paper that followed like a devoted puppy. *Yep, Kat's angry.*

Despite my aching hip, I felt guilty, so I opened my mouth to tell her.

The hostess beat me to it. "Ma'am, do you know you're trailing toilet paper?"

Gina froze mid stride. She looked down and frowned as she tried to dislodge it from her shoe with a scrape of the heel. After glancing around to see if anyone was looking, she bent and snatched the offensive tissue. Crumpling it, Gina placed it in the startled hostess's hand as if she was giving the young woman a tip.

The young lady looked quite appalled. She scrunched her face into a "yuck" expression and walked off, holding the ball of tissue like it was feces.

The Divas settled around a wood table positioned perpendicular to a rail that separated us from the beach. I sat next to the rail, with Kat to my right. Gina and Latishia, the "bad girls," sat across from us. The scene reminded me of my date with Mike. Remembering my shellfish allergy, I decided to play it safe and order fish.

After the waiter took our drink orders and left, Gina banged her fist down on the table, making the salt and peppershaker jump. "Heavens to Betsy, Latishia, what did you think you were doing with that redneck on the dolphin cruise?"

Latishia's lower lip protruded. "I was just doing a little bootie dancing."

"Well, I've got bruises because of your bootie dancing." I rubbed my hip to emphasize my point.

"Lord have mercy, don't get your curlers in a wad. I took care of it." Latishia crossed her arms and jutted her jaw. "I kicked that guy's balls into his mouth. He might have to spit them out to reattach them."

"Maybe so, but he was getting up and looking for us while we ran down the gangplank," I said.

Latishia waved away a fly that buzzed her iced tea. "He was still all bent over and holding his family jewels. It wasn't like he could run in that condition."

"Nonetheless, it was irresponsible," said Gina.

Both Kat and I snapped our gazes on Gina like a pair of laser beams.

Kat said, "This from a woman who drank four glasses of wine and yelled 'Take it all off,' while you waved dollar bills in the air. That was a dolphin cruise, not a strip joint."

Gina pasted a contrite look on her face. I suspected she would be going to confession after we returned home.

Kat was frowning, causing a furrow in her brow. "I'm serious. We need to reel it in a little. I don't want to get arrested down here. We're professional women."

I looked at Latishia and Gina. "What do you plan to tell the guys?"

Latishia's eyes bulged with alarm. "I don't plan to tell Aaron anything. He's not my fiancé or husband, and y'all better not be telling him nothing."

“That’s right,” said Gina. “What happens at the beach stays at the beach.” Both of them nodded their heads in a united front as if that was the final word on the matter.

Our waiter came, and that was the end of the discussion.

I enjoyed my flounder; except for the concerned glances Kat kept sneaking in my direction. She made me feel paranoid, so I escaped to the ladies’ room again to make sure I didn’t have grouper lips. After reassuring myself that my lips were normal, I checked my shoes for toilet paper and made it back in time for key lime pie and coffee.

Full and happy, we waddled back to the minivan. Latishia keyed in the address for the airboat rides into her phone before we left the parking lot. Siri gave us step-by-step directions, but it seemed like it was taking a long time to get there.

When we arrived, the place was near a large concrete bridge that crossed the water.

Gina scooted forward to between the seats and peered through the windshield. “Sure doesn’t look like much.”

Kat shivered. “It looks snaky to me. Y’all see any snakes?” She opened the door to peer at the ground.

Gina screamed and pointed. “There’s one!”

Kat yanked her foot back in and slammed the door.

Gina collapsed into giggles in the back seat.

“That’s not funny!” Kat turned with a scowl and tried to swat Gina. She missed, shook her head, and glanced in the rearview mirror at me.

It took us ten minutes to cajole Kat out of the minivan. She made me inspect the area from the van all the way to the entrance to the building for slithering snakes.

A display of fake creatures greeted us when we approached the entrance. A five-foot alligator stood like a human, mouth open to reveal fierce teeth and jaws. Behind the alligator stood life-size statues of a pelican, a blue heron, and a white egret. Thank goodness, there were no snakes on display.

Two airboats bobbed at a nearby dock as the setting sun painted the bridge’s concrete pillars gold.

While we waited to purchase our tickets, a group of passengers lined up ready to board one of the airboats. The two pilots climbed on board and settled into the high seats in front of the enormous fan. The passengers trundled aboard, took their seats and put on protective hearing devices.

Latishia pointed, her voice excited and squeaky like a kid's. "Look, they're starting it up."

The wind and noise were tremendous. I watched in wonder, as the boat seemed to slide over the water. A great spray of water followed behind the craft.

Gina stood on tiptoes for a better view of the departing airboat. "That looks like loads of fun."

We waited on the dock for our pilots. The boat we were to board was painted pale sea-foam green, but the three vinyl bench seats and captain's chairs were a bright lime green. Each bench seat could hold six people.

I pointed at my camera. "I want to sit on the front row, so I have the best view for photos."

Kat shuddered. "I want to sit in the middle, so the snakes and gators can nibble on you first."

Our captain sauntered down the dock. Tanned a dark mahogany, he wore knee length khaki shorts and a neon green "wife-beater" tee shirt. The kid who was the copilot didn't look old enough to drive a car, maybe fourteen.

Kat nudged me and whispered. "He looks to be the same age as Jack. I'm not feeling confident about this. What if the captain has a heart attack?"

Latishia patted Kat's back. "You'll do CPR and save him."

The evening was pleasant and the water was smooth with barely a ripple. The sunset that painted the clouds maroon, orange and purple reflected on the water like a giant mirror. Pine trees and tall grasses lined the white sandy shores, offering the perfect place for an alligator to hide and wait.

"Everyone put on your ear protection," said the captain, before he slipped on his own.

While there was still light, the captain took his ten passengers for a thirty-minute joy ride. He skimmed across the water as he rounded islands of tall grass. I squealed like a little girl as the captain ran close enough to the reeds to make the boat tilt. He straightened the boat and shot across the water like an arrow. I felt like I was flying on the water. Kat gripped the seat and closed her eyes when it was too much for her.

When the sky darkened, the captain slowed to a crawl and told us we could remove our sound protection. His assistant took a high-powered light and shone it along the banks. A full moon reflected off the water, providing ambient light.

Latishia, who was sitting behind me, poked my shoulder. “What’s he doing that for?”

The captain heard the question. “You find gators at night by the gold reflection of their eyes.”

Within seconds, a golden orb seemed to float above the surface of the water. As we crept closer, we discovered a four-foot alligator. The gold eye had a red slit, like a cat’s.

“You may wonder if you’re safe on this boat?” The captain paused to let the question settle over us like dew. “Let’s just say, if that gator wanted on this boat, he could get up here.”

“Lord have mercy,” said Latishia.

I looked over my shoulder in time to see Gina, who was sitting next to her, cross herself.

Kat asked, “What about s-snakes?” She shifted closer to the center of the boat, crowding against a young girl with a ponytail.

“A buddy of mine had a water moccasin slither up on his boat once. So it can happen, but it’s unlikely.”

Latishia reached forward and rubbed circles on Kat’s back. “See, it’s unlikely.”

The boat was low on the water. I could imagine a gator crawling on board.

The eeriness of the dark combined with the nearness of the reeds and grasses made the whole experience seem like the buildup of a horror film before a giant reptile rears up to consume you.

The captain trolled to a different area where it was shallow. We watched as a spot-lighted ten-foot alligator swam along beside us. He was so close I could have reached down and touched him. I shot photos, praying at least one would be good.

We saw a total of six gators in the wild that night. I wondered how many were out there that we didn't see. I shivered, remembering a recent news story about a toddler killed by an alligator in Florida. The family was standing near a lake watching fireworks when the incident occurred. It would be easy to not see the danger at night unless you knew to look for those creepy glowing gold orbs.

The captain told us to put our ear protection on and sped along in the dark. I wondered, *How in the world can he see where he's going?*

Back at the dock, we filed off the boat. Each of the Divas had our photos taken in the captain's chair. Once on the patio, we were all allowed to hold a two-foot alligator. I was the first to step forward.

Years ago, I held a three-foot gator at Gator Land with a boa constrictor around my shoulders. I had the photo transferred to a tee shirt and gave it to Todd. He was in training that week and missed the entire experience.

I doubt that shirt fits him anymore, just like his wedding ring. The thought sank like a lead weight from my head to gut.

The little gator was solid muscle. Its skin was smooth and cool to the touch. I could see why people wanted to make boots out of alligator hide.

"Smile." Kat snapped my photo with my camera.

Gina posed with the baby alligator next, and then Latishia took a turn. Kat refused.

We were surprised. Kat was Zen-like about most everything she approached. I had no idea she had such an intense fear of reptiles.

"What if he bites me?" A shiver started at the top of Kat's head and shimmied its way down.

The older lady who played cashier and alligator wrangler didn't help matters. "Researchers say the force of a twelve-foot alligator's bite is about the same as the pressure of the weight of a small pick-up truck."

Kat backed up.

"Come on Kat, you know if you don't hold that little guy, you'll regret it later." Gina gave her a little push in the right direction.

Kat pushed her glasses up and crossed her arms.

Latishia said, "I don't want to hear you whine all the way home in the car about how sad you were that you didn't hold the baby alligator."

I put my arm around Kat. "The force she described was for an alligator that's bigger than the ones we saw tonight. This is just a baby. See that scrunchy around his snout?"

Kat nodded.

"That guy has little force to *open* his mouth. That's why he can't bite you unless the scrunchy is removed." Then I hit her with the kicker. "Don't you want to show Jack the photo of you holding the alligator? He'll think that's so cool."

Nothing propels a mom into action like her child. Kat stood tall with her chin held high and took possession of that alligator. The photo depicted a bug-eyed Kat, with a broad terrified smile, holding a baby gator with a blue scrunchy over his snout.

Chapter 64: The Last Day

The next morning we ate breakfast at what we'd come to think of as *our table.* The guys all managed to take off from work, so they could spend the entire day and night with us. As a psychologist and the only Diva without a male companion, I studied my friends and their beaus.

Latishia prattled to Aaron, "We'll spend the whole day at the Space and Rocket Center. I can't wait until you taste my daddy's ribs. Ask Phoenix if he makes the best ribs."

I raised my right hand and placed my left over my heart. "Willy is the King of Ribs, and Mama Snide is the Queen of Soul Food."

Latishia beamed, and Aaron grinned down at her. They were fast becoming *a couple*. It was clear they both had plans for a relationship that would continue in Huntsville. From conversations with Latishia, I knew Mama Snide and Willy were hot to meet the man that seemed to be their daughter's hero.

I was happy for Latishia. She and Dante's father Andre had been married only two years when he was killed in the crossfire during a convenience store robbery. I'm sure he had no idea that Latishia's hankering for a cold drink would be the death of him. A mere infant at the time, Dante never knew his father. Willy had stepped up as a male role model, just as he had for Latishia.

I shifted my attention to Kat, who was sitting beside Don without saying a word. Poor Kat. Instead of anticipation, I saw grief in her eyes.

From our private conversations, I knew Don had won Kat's heart, which wasn't an easy task. He seemed to be taken with her too.

She'd told me on the elevator last night, "I know Don's where he wants to be, and I want to be with him, but my life is in Huntsville with my family. I don't know what I'm going to do. The multigenerational bonds of a Chinese-American family are strong."

Kat was close to her parents and her Nai Nai, and I knew she wanted Jack to be centered in both the old and the new ways.

She kept sneaking peeks at Don as if she was trying to imprint every nuance of his face and gestures into her memory. It was painful to observe, like watching a loved-one say goodbye before death.

Chris said something in a low voice to Gina, and she laughed. Unlike Kat, she didn't appear to be in distress. She was enjoying Chris while she had him.

Thanks to the many years we've been friends, I could tell from her remarks that she'd placed Chris in the *guy* category. Anytime she wasn't serious about someone and was just enjoying the man's company, she called him by his first name, with *guy* attached almost like the last name.

Gina had been making statements all week. "That Chris guy is cute," and "That Chris guy is so funny." Chris had yet to make it past the *guy* phase.

I wondered if that might change, should he be assigned to Huntsville like Aaron. It was hard to tell with Gina. She'd always guarded her independence with fierce determination. I think her father's domination over her mother has scarred her in some way.

Then there was me. Since Todd jettisoned me from our twenty-year marriage, I've managed to attract a frugal retired engineer, a stalker, a bald guy with a sexy brain, a nice guy who's cute, a bossy colonel, and Mike, the guy who helped save my life. *Is single life supposed to be this complicated?*

It was a great day, even if I was the spare tire of the group. We went to a water park and pretended we were in our teens again. We laughed, squealed and splashed our way down every water slide. There were a few times I thought my heart would stop, but it kept on ticking.

Before dinner, we played miniature golf. The guys were in awe of Kat, who did her Zen thing at every hole. She had close to a perfect score.

Latishia was a different story.

"There's something wrong with this hole. The ball doesn't want to go in."

"Dumpling, if you'll let me show you —"

Latishia cut Aaron off. "It's not me. It must be the ball. Kat, let me have your magic ball. It must be rounder than mine."

Rounder? I exchanged glances with Kat. She shrugged and handed Latishia her neon yellow ball. There were two couples behind us waiting to play the hole.

Latishia sank the ball on the seventh stroke, on a par two hole. "Humph, something's wrong with this ball, too."

I watched Aaron turn his back and walk away to keep her from seeing him laugh. I knew he was laughing because his shoulders hitched up and down.

Better get used to it, I thought. Aaron would never have a dull moment with Latishia, and he would never be better loved.

When we added our scores at the end of the course, Kat finished below par. Latishia had the highest score and had sampled everyone's ball, searching for the roundest one that would give her a hole-in-one.

We decided to separate before dinner, so each couple could have a last romantic evening together before we left in the morning. I promised not to eat seafood so I wouldn't land in the hospital again.

We'd had a large lunch, so I wasn't all that hungry. When Kat tossed me the keys to the minivan, I knew where I wanted to go.

I drove to The Donut Hole, where I ordered a cup of decaf coffee and a slice of the best key lime pie I've ever eaten. I doctored my coffee with cream and sugar and took a sip as the waitress placed a large slice of pale green perfection in front of me.

The tangy scent tickled my nose. I took a bite, closed my eyes and chewed. I was alone again, but I didn't mind. I was where I wanted to be, in key lime pie heaven.

Chapter 65: Goodbyes

I've never been skilled at goodbyes. The other Divas weren't any better. I loaded my luggage into the van and walked out to the beach to say my farewell to the ocean. I couldn't stand watching my misty-eyed friends cling to their guys like they were emotional life rafts. It caused me to relive those last hours with my dad. My mind returned to that day.

The smell of impending death. The feel of his emaciated body through his blue-striped pajamas. Dad's raspy final breaths as he died. The black hearse driving away. Tears rolled down my cheeks.

Standing there watching the waves roll in reminded me that life is like the ocean — always moving and changing. It was time to let go of my Dad, release his spirit, and only confine his memory. He could no longer be my emotional buoy. That's why he named me Phoenix. It was time to rise from the ashes of my torched former life.

When I came back to the van, things hadn't improved.

Latishia was the most vocal and dramatic in her grief. I knew by the look on her face that she was deep-fried in love with Aaron and feared that something might happen to keep him from coming to Huntsville as planned.

Aaron kept reassuring her while he loaded her two large suitcases and cosmetic case.

"Dumpling, calm down. I'll be there in a week. Remember, you promised to find me an apartment in Madison near the Redstone Arsenal."

Kat was the one that worried me. Though her misery wasn't dramatic like Latishia's, in her it was palpable. Kat's loss seemed to ooze from her pores, silent but visible.

It was evident by his furrowed brow that Don understood the depth of her feelings, but didn't quite know how to ease either of their misery. When she hugged Don for the final time, it was like she was trying to absorb his very essence.

To my surprise, even Gina cried while hugging Chris.

Kat handed me her keys and squeezed my hand. "Please drive."

I drove away with my friends' faces pressed to the glass while they waved, but I didn't look back at the men we left behind.

Kat, who was sitting behind me, broke into sobs as I crossed the first bridge over the Intracoastal Waterway. Latishia boohooed in the seat next to me, and I even heard a sniffle from Gina. For the first ten miles of the trip, the tissue box passed back and forth from the front to the back of the van.

Gina gained control of her emotions first. "I'm going to miss Chris. He seemed to understand my need for independence and didn't want to squash me in a box."

Surprised, I glanced over my shoulder. That was the first time she hadn't tacked, "guy" after his name. "Maybe Chris will be stationed at Redstone someday. Can't hurt to stay in touch."

"Ladies, I'm in love. I don't think I can live without that giant hunk of a man." Latishia sniffed and wiped her nose with a tissue.

"Oh, I don't think you need to worry." I laughed. "He's smitten."

Latishia shifted in her seat to better see me. "Do you think so?"

"Oh, yeah, I'm sure. Your parents are going to love him. That only leaves Dante. I hope they don't have a battle of the testosterone."

"I'll talk to Dante when I get home."

"Kat, are you all right back there?" I glanced at her in the rearview mirror.

"No." Her voice sounded hollow.

Latishia shifted to look over her shoulder into the back seat. "You're in love, too, aren't you?"

I glanced in the mirror and saw Kat nod.

"Does he love you?" asked Gina.

"He says he does."

Sounding impatient, Gina asked, "Then what's the problem?"

There was a prolonged silence before Kat answered. "Logistics. Don's retired, I'm sure he doesn't want to raise Jack."

"Whoa! Did you ask him, or are you assuming this?" I glanced in the mirror and saw her frown.

"I guess I assumed that, but I can't leave my family. Huntsville's my home, and Jack's friends are there. He's just started at Grissom, and he already loves the marching band. He's playing the trumpet this year."

Latishia pointed out, "Fort Walton Beach isn't Don's home."

"True, but it's where he's always wanted to live."

"Do the two of you plan to stay in touch?" Latishia asked.

"Yes, but long-distance relationships don't work out. Then, there are my parents. They want me to marry a traditional Chinese man."

"What's your problem with Chinese men?" asked Gina. "I've never quite understood your reaction to them. I always assumed it was a rebellious thing when we were younger."

"They're control freaks with little dicks." Kat removed her glasses and wiped her eyes with a tissue.

We all burst out laughing. I laughed so hard; I swerved and had to get back in my lane.

I said, “I’ve met some nice Chinese men and most of them didn’t seem controlling. I can’t speak to the size of their um —”

“Ding dongs,” supplied Latishia. “Speaking of urinary devices, can we make a pit stop?”

I glanced over at her. She grinned, which emphasized the puffiness of her tear-stained, round face.

I announced, “I need some java,” as I pulled over at a Hardee’s in the first town we encountered.

Gina picked up the driving, so I slid into the back seat next to Kat. I reached over and squeezed her hand. She gave me a wan smile. Pulling her glasses from her puffy face, she used her shirt to clean the wet lenses.

Entwining my fingers in my long hair, I pulled it up and held it off my sweaty neck. I sighed. “It’s hard to believe a vacation that started with so much fun can end with so much heartache.”

“Amen,” Latishia sang out like she was in church. “‘It’s better to have loved and lost, than to never have loved at all,’ or something like that. Who said that, anyway?”

Gina glanced over at Latishia. “Alfred Lord Tennyson. When did you get all fancy pants on me and start waxing poetic by quoting Tennyson?”

Latishia heaved a sigh. “I guess when you fall in love, it does strange things to you.”

Gina spared a quick glance over her shoulder at me. “I feel bad about you, Phoenix.”

“Me?” I leaned forward to hear better.

“Yeah, you. Latishia meets the love of her life, and Aaron’s coming to join her in Huntsville.”

“Hallelujah!” said Latishia.

“I meet Chris and have a wonderful time. Who knows, we may hook up in the future.” Gina’s gaze stayed glued to the road.

“Praise, Jesus,” yelled Latishia. The rest of us jumped.

“Jeez, Latishia, this isn’t a tent revival, you know,” grumbled Kat.

“Sorry, forgot you’re a Buddhist and not a normal religion like the rest of us.”

Gina and I both sucked in air. I turned to look at Kat who sat stiff as uncooked lasagna noodles.

She pushed her glasses up before she spoke. “Latishia, I realize in the Bible belt of the South, Buddhism may not seem *normal* to you. In many parts of the world, Buddhism is the primary religion, and Christianity is considered *abnormal.* Believe it or not, there are approximately 530 million Buddhists in the world.”

“That’s a lot.” Latishia squirmed in her seat. “I’m sorry, Kat. I didn’t mean to say Buddhists aren’t normal. Your family is the only ones I know. You know I love you like a sister. Please don’t be mad at me.”

Kat inclined her head, “I love your Southern Baptist soul, too.”

The tension escaped from the interior of the van like air from a tire with a nail in it, a little at a time.

Gina turned on the blinker and merged onto Interstate 65 to head north. “Anyway, what I was trying to say is poor Phoenix got hooked up with Colonel…, what did you call him?”

“Colonel Bossy Pants,” I said.

“Then she meets what’s-his-name —”

“Mike Janson,” I interjected.

Kat piped up and said, “Bless her heart, then she had an allergic reaction and got grouper lips.”

“Don’t forget,” said Latishia. “She’s the only one of us who didn’t get laid.”

I rolled my eyes. *They’re making me sound so pathetic.*

With withering sarcasm, I said, “Y’all are doing wonders for my self-esteem.”

“What do you mean?” Latishia asked.

“My vacation was enjoyable. So there were a few blips on the scale to perfection. Stop making my adventures seem so pitiful, just because it wasn’t like yours. I wasn’t looking to find a man, and have been working to free myself from one. I do believe I’ve succeeded.” The moment the words left my mouth; I knew they were true.

The Divas were silent for a moment. Then Gina said, "Hear, hear."

After we had made it through Montgomery, Kat took over the driving. I moved into my normal seat behind the driver, and Gina sat to my right. Kat turned on the radio, and before I knew it, the music lulled me into sleep.

I jerked awake to an earsplitting combination of snores, snorts, snuffles and whistles. Kat yelled, "Latishia, wake up."

I heard a wheeze and a snuffle, and the snoring started in earnest once again.

Gina covered her mouth and yawned. "That sounds like a cross between a hog and a chainsaw. Is she all right?"

Kat reached over and shoved Latishia. "Wake up!"

"Wha…, where are we? What's wrong?"

I giggled. "Your snoring was about to vibrate the van off the road."

"Heck, I thought we were having an earthquake in the middle of a tornado," said Gina.

Latishia wiggled to an upright position. "I don't snore."

The rest of us yelled, "Yes, you do."

Kat added, "You need to take this seriously, Latishia. Sleep apnea is a killer, and it can cause you to feel tired all the time."

"And make you gain weight," I added.

Latishia crossed her arms. "I don't have that sleep whatever you said. I. Don't. Snore."

Gina and I looked at each other and shook our heads. I knew this wasn't the end of the matter, but it was the end for this day.

When we passed the Priceville exit, I knew our hometowns were close.

Latishia yawned. "I can't wait to see Dante and show him his new pirate game."

Gina stretched. "I can't wait to unpack my suitcase and take a long hot bath in my, oh so deep tub."

"When I get home, I'm going to sleep slap dab in the middle of *my* king-sized bed," I said with a determined tone. "No more clinging to one side like the other one still belongs to Todd. The entire bed is mine."

"You go, girl," Latishia said.

Clouds formed in rolling bands to the west and the winds that preceded the incoming storm buffeted the van. Kat offered no comment as she slowed to drive over the large bridge that crossed the Tennessee River.

I watched those threatening clouds with a sense of peace. For the first time since I heard those fateful words, "I want a divorce," I was grateful that Todd had ended our marriage. I was free to make decisions without having to argue my position, and to do as I damn well pleased. With a satisfied sigh, I thought, *Maybe single life won't be so bad after all.*

THE END